THE LAW OF LOVE

Also in the River of Freedom Series by Tim Stafford

The Stamp of Glory

Sisters

THE LAW OF LOVE

A Novel of the Prohibition Movement

Tim Stafford

THOMAS NELSON PUBLISHERS®
Nashville

Published in association with the literary agency of Alive Communications, Inc., 7680 Goddard Street, Suite 200, Colorado Springs, CO 80920.

Note to Readers: Many of the characters in this novel are based on (and named after) real historical persons who were crucial in the Prohibition movement. Most of the events described are, similarly, real and are told with as much historical accuracy as possible.

Scripture quotations are from the KING JAMES VERSION of the Bible.

Published in Nashville, Tennessee, by Thomas Nelson, Inc.

Library of Congress Cataloging-in-Publication Data

Stafford, Tim
    The law of love : a novel of prohibition / by Tim Stafford
      p. cm. — (The river of freedom series)
    ISBN 1-7852-6908-8 (tradepaper)
    1. United States—History—1901–1953—Fiction. 2. Prohibition—Fiction.
I. Title.

PS3569.T25 L39 2001
813'.54—dc21   00-052726
                                                     CIP

Printed in the United States of America
1 2 3 4 5 6 QWD 05 04 03 02 01

Contents

Book IV: Love Is Not Proud

Book I
Dreams Made Visible

Chapter 1
1910: Everett

The woman stood in line, holding Christ Our King Lutheran Church's thick crockery plate to her chest, both arms crossed over its cream-colored disk as though it were protective armor. Marion Nichols, known as M. K., thought that she had a remarkably beautiful face: pale, narrow, and still, framed by heavy, arching eyebrows and thick, dark hair. A little girl stood beside her, one hand hooked into her mother's skirts.

Nichols was not a Lutheran—there were few Lutherans in his upbringing at Hillsboro, Ohio—but had come to the church dinner at the behest of his editor at the *Daily Argus*. Mr. Henry Golis wanted to know if there were any church people who would vote against the dry referendum. The ordinance was on the ballot in just ten days, as were similar measures in many other Washington towns since the legislature last year had passed a framework for townships to vote themselves dry.

Golis thought that some of the Lutherans would be unenthusiastic about going without beer, and the newspaper could get a man-bites-dog kind of story. (In general, church people voted dry.) He had left it up to Nichols to find the Lutherans. Nichols had seen a notice for this church dinner, had paid his quarter, and got a plate piled with boned chicken and long, flat noodles swimming in a gray sauce.

M. K. was a friendly sort, young and unattached, who did not mind a

Saturday afternoon gabbing with Lutherans. He was too new in town to know anyone, and he liked to be active. He liked to talk, and the Lutherans would do as well as anybody to fill up some hours. Among the drab and stodgy Lutheran families, however, he did not expect to see such a beautiful woman. He did not look to see such a woman anywhere in a mill town like Everett.

She stood out like some Norwegian saint, he thought, her eyes fixed on invisible angels in that steamy, noisy room, with Lutherans chatting and shuffling, crowded together for the sake of food and friendship, refugees from the dreary blue mist that rose out of Puget Sound and dripped off the eaves of the little wooden boxes they called homes. The woman was unhearing of the noise and impervious to distraction; her narrow face looked serene and luminous as a gray moon sinking into the waters.

The little girl next to her was tiny, barely of school age, delicate-boned and dressed up perfectly in blue with a wide pink ribbon. She held out her plate along the food table while her mother piled it up. Nichols was not particularly conscious of how much food a little girl could eat, but he thought it unusual for such a small girl to take such a large amount on her plate.

He expected to see them join family or friends at one of the long, gleaming tables. Instead, the mother stood with one hand touching her daughter, making sure of where she was, while her eyes scanned the room. Then she led the way to the end of a table nearest the door, where a clutch of burlap sacks lay strewn over the wooden floor for wiping wet feet, and the spring-loaded door slammed open and shut regularly, letting in cold, damp air. The mother and daughter sat apart from anyone else, across from each other at the very end of the table.

Nichols often made up stories about people in his head, people he saw on the train or at his boardinghouse. Everett was an unromantic mill town, but he managed to imagine adventures for those small and hardened men he saw in the drugstore, handing over money with hands that lacked fingers and thumbs. Now he began to imagine a story for this mother and her daughter. There might have been scandal; perhaps the church had shunned them.

It is just as easy to interview beautiful women as ugly ones, Nichols told himself, and he got up to walk over to the pair. "Excuse me, is anybody sitting here?" he asked, before taking a seat next to the little girl.

The woman was not talking to her daughter, Nichols had noticed; she ate steadily and mechanically. The little girl had a head full of hair like her mother's, a shock of dark waves. She looked up at him curiously but then attended to her plate. She had already made a significant dent in the mound of food.

"I don't think I know you," he said to the woman. "M. K. Nichols." He stuck out his hand, and the woman shook it solemnly, but she did not volunteer her own name.

"I'm from the *Daily Argus*," he said. "I'm supposed to find out what Lutherans think about the election."

She barely looked at him. "I can't vote."

He would not have been surprised to hear a strong accent, for he had noted a Sunday service in Norwegian advertised on the notice board as he came into the church. But her voice was rich, clear, and uninflected American.

"If the suffrage bill passes, you will," he said. "But I want to hear your thoughts on the local option bill."

"Why don't you talk to a man?"

"They say that women are the real force against liquor."

Her eyes strayed over him for a moment before returning to her plate. "I don't have an opinion," she said.

Ordinarily in a town this size the very mention of a newspaper was enough to get people talking. The wealthy mill owners might have no time for a reporter, but ordinary people you met at church suppers wanted to give their opinions. They might complain ceaselessly about the newspapers and their inaccuracies, but let a reporter appear and they would sing like a canary. It was one reason M. K. liked being a reporter—people talked to him.

"That's a pretty little girl you've got there," he said. The girl looked up at him with a pensive expression, as though she had stored up far too much sadness for the five or six years she looked to be. "What's your name, sugar?" he asked. The girl just looked at him, however, as tight-lipped as her mother.

Nichols laughed. He had a high-pitched laugh, full of hilarity, almost a cackle. "Well, I like a quiet meal," he said. "I digest better if I don't talk." He glanced at the mother and thought he saw a glimmer of a smile, but if he did, it was gone before it passed halfway over her lips.

"You really don't want to talk?" he asked with a grin.

"No," the woman said, though not unkindly. They ate in silence until he had cleaned his plate, and then he said good afternoon. He went around interviewing others for their views on the dry bill and was relieved when they acted like normal people, telling him more than he wanted to know.

He kept an eye on the woman enough to see that no one else approached her—not one single soul. He saw that she and her daughter got seconds, filling up their plates again. While Nichols was interviewing an older man with a pink wart on his nose and nearly as much Norwegian as English in his vocabulary, they must have left. He looked up to see that they had disappeared.

She was so obviously out of his sphere, married, with a child, carrying a full weary load of responsibilities. He wanted nothing but to be free, to wander through his dreams unattached, far from Oberlin piety, far from the strings of his family. Nonetheless he was interested, as a young man is always interested in a beautiful woman, but more: he was curious how she came to be a stranger at a Lutheran church dinner. He thought he could put it in one of his stories.

———————

Nichols walked through the drizzle down to the newspaper office, located on the second story above a saloon on Hewitt Avenue. He had enough material for a piece. Golis would want more, but Golis had wanted church people and Nichols did not know where to find any more on a Saturday afternoon. Certainly not in the saloons, where he would usually go to get a sampling of public opinion.

M. K. unlocked the door at the head of the stairs, lit a lamp, and fussed with the wick, then sat down at his desk to write the story. Nobody was at the office. He looked down the row of desks, crowded together and thrown over with papers. Typewriters perched on desk-tops like gigantic spiders. He did not particularly like the hurried pace and sardonic humor of the place when it was busy, as it would be in a few hours, but he liked it even less when it was empty, lonely, and dark like this.

Nichols enjoyed company. His ease with people made him a decent reporter, even though he lost patience with detail and Golis sometimes had to haul him in and grill him to straighten out a tangle of facts. Yet the office, even when full of people, was not a convivial place for Nichols. Something in the work made newspaper men keep up a facade of world-weariness, and Nichols was just the opposite: sincere and hopeful. He liked to write plays and stories, but where was the money in that? Nichols worked at the *Argus* because so far he had not found another way to make a living.

He was glad to be in the West. At college he had found himself increasingly ill at ease with the crusading mentality that made Oberlin a center of Christian activism. He didn't want to be so good. He had discovered Shelley, and then (though the school disapproved) Byron. He liked to write long stories about the Indian wars, and he dreamed of adventures, but where did that find a place in the Oberlin idealism? After his graduation in June, he had wanted to get as far away as possible. By chance Henry Golis, an Oberlin graduate, had written to the school to find a reporter. M. K. had never before written for a newspaper, and he had only the vaguest idea where Everett was, but the novelty had been all to the good. Before he reached Seattle he had known, just from the unending forests and the low, drizzly weather, that he was in another country.

Most people did not see Everett as nearly so filled with possibility. It was a dank mill town on a peninsula formed where the Snohomish River swings north to enter the Puget Sound. Along the Sound, at Port Gardner Bay, the wood industries had made a snarl of smokestacks, piers, railroad tracks, and warehouses. Hewitt Avenue cut across the middle of the peninsula, the center of town with its dry-goods stores, saloons, and boardinghouses. North and south of Hewitt the mill workers had their little wood houses set on postage stamp–sized lots, with a sprinkling of grocery stores and churches. Beyond, always, were the deep spruce and cedar forests, an impenetrable blue-green horizon. But Everett was a town ruled by the whistles of the mills, a town that showed little curiosity about life beyond its surrounding waters and forests, except for the price of lumber.

Nichols had gone over his notes and begun to write a lead to his story about Lutherans when he realized that he did not want to do it now. He did not want to do it ever, but particularly he did not want to do it now in this lonely, dark, and cold room above a saloon. The rain had picked up and was peppering the windows. He could come back later when somebody was around. Maybe Golis would even tell him to find more Lutherans and finish it tomorrow. On Sunday he ought to be able to find plenty of Lutherans.

When he stepped out into the dark afternoon, however, he had nowhere particular to go. The rain had fallen off to a mere drizzle again, almost a fog that hung just above the tops of the brick buildings. Under the circumstances, not being a drinker, he saw only one destination that presented itself. He would go to the movies.

Until he left Oberlin, he had seen movies only occasionally and furtively because such entertainments were considered morally questionable. In Everett M. K. had made up for lost time. He found the movies utterly engrossing.

Andersen's was nearest, so he cut through an alley and up the hill to it. Only two o'clock in the afternoon, and already the darkness was coming on in a bleary mist. He passed a few hurrying pedestrians, but they barely looked at him when he smiled and said hello, as he always did. Andersen's was in a narrow brick building that had been a haberdashery. Nichols paid his nickel and stumbled in halfway through a reel on Samoa. The high-class educational films with their palm trees and native dances were not his favorites, and they were for few people in Everett, but what could the nickelodeons do? They were at the mercy of the exchanges. According to what Nichols read, the moving-picture companies couldn't make enough films to keep up with the interest, so every strip of film that could roll through a projector got played and replayed.

After Samoa ended in a sunset, the pianist played "Daisy Mae" while the projectionist put on song slides. Andersen's did not have a singer, and Nichols could not hear a single voice in the room singing along. He looked around in the darkness to see how many customers were present. It looked to be not more than twenty. Where was everybody? On a Monday or a Tuesday attendance was sparse, but Saturday?

The next reel was more to his taste: a domestic drama in which some crooks broke down a door in a mansion and threatened everybody with guns before a policeman heard cries for help and came on the run. The thieves tried to escape, there was a terrific shooting battle, and the chief of the crooks was killed by one of his own men. Just before he shot his boss, the man looked him straight in the eye and said, "Here's for what you did to my cousin, Bill." It was as real as if Nichols had seen it all himself. No, more real because he could see the thieves shout at their captives inside the house and the next moment see the police coming. In the nickelodeons you could see things in one afternoon that you might not see in a lifetime.

After that they had a newsreel about Barney Oldfield and the land speed record he had set in Florida, and then another song. The slides were good, printing the words as though they emerged from the unfolding petals of a rose. Since no one was singing, however, Nichols got up to go. He didn't want to see the first part of the Samoa reel.

He decided to walk up to the Nassau Street Cinema, which was just behind the Stag Saloon. In fact, you could enter through the saloon. The sign on the street said they had a reel from Biograph, and that was good news. Biograph made the best movies. He asked the ticket taker if they had many people, and she shook her head.

"Where is everybody?" Nichols asked. "I was just down at Andersen's, and the place was empty."

"I guess they are all waiting to hear Mr. Sunday," she said. "That's where I'm going as soon as I get off." She had a stubby nose and straw-blond hair streaked with brown. Nichols usually spoke to her—he came here almost daily—but he did not know her name.

The great evangelist Billy Sunday had come to town to campaign for the dry law. A committee of church people had built him on the edge of town a tabernacle big enough to hold three thousand people. It was the greatest thing that had ever happened in Everett, to have such a famous man. Nichols thought he might be the only person in town who had heard Sunday before. He had preached at the Congregational Church several times while M. K. was at Oberlin.

The Biograph was really good. The story, called *Shattered Dreams,* told about a young man who quarrels with his father over his desire to become an actor and gets thrown out on the streets to fend for himself. It was the sort of thing you knew happened to people sometimes, some-where. You might have heard of such a thing, but the movie brought you right into the middle, as though you were in the same room. The whole screen filled up with the mother's face, so close you could actually see the tears. You might live on the planet for fifty years and never have to look at a mother so heartbroken.

Nichols found it painfully disturbing, almost indecent, to look straight into the soul of the woman. In real life you would look away, back away, excuse yourself, especially since you did not know the woman. In real life she would never let anyone see her broken heart, most certainly not strangers.

Nichols liked the action pictures, but lately he had found himself drawn into these new Biograph reels. They had good action, and the human emotions were ravishing. In a small Ohio town like the one he had grown up in, people did not wear their emotions on their sleeves. You might speculate on what they felt, but you never really could know. In these movies, when you looked into the face of a mother whose son had left forever, you could hardly escape knowing. It made you feel in a way that was uncomfortable but also unforgettable.

The other reel was an Indian drama, the sort of film that Nichols ordinarily liked, but this was an old print full of holes, and his mind was so full of the Biograph he could not enjoy it. Still he watched the whole thing, followed by a newsreel about Halley's Comet, which was disappointing because they did not show the comet. Probably it was too dark to make a movie of it, bright as it had been.

When he left, Nichols leaned on the counter and told the blond ticket taker that he had liked the Biograph.

"They're always the best, aren't they? We had another one yesterday."

"I saw it," he said. "Don't you remember I came in after work? This one is even better."

He did not know what to do after that. The rain had stopped altogether, but the clouds had sunk low, shapeless, dull, cold, and heavy. It was an ugly afternoon. He was so used to the wood smoke from the mills he usually did not notice the smell, but this afternoon the low clouds seemed to force it down on top of him, and the bitter, cutting smoke rasped his throat. The newspaper office would be empty for at least another hour, probably until after supper. The *Argus* was an afternoon paper except on Sunday. They put out the Sunday paper on Saturday night. He was usually there until midnight.

These were the only times when he missed Oberlin. There, between clubs and the debating society, he had always been with people, had always been active. A mill town offered very little that was comparable. Most people stayed wrapped up in their church or family. M. K. considered going to another movie. Then he remembered that the Rialto had a play. People said that before the nickelodeons, traveling companies had come to Everett three or four days of the week. Business must have fallen off because they were lucky to see one play a week now, and he often missed it. Sometimes he had to cover a night meeting, and lots of times he just forgot. The movies were always on, you could go any time you wanted, they changed every day—and they were better. The movies showed you real life, with trains and horses and mountains and battle scenes, whereas a play could show only what happened in somebody's living room.

He liked plays, nonetheless, and so walked down the hill to the Rialto. It was a real theater, not just a store that somebody had converted to show movies. He arrived in time for the matinee. The posters announced *The Bride of Paris,* which sounded almost far enough away from Everett to satisfy him.

He sat down near the front at five minutes until four and was still waiting at a quarter after the hour. Were they hoping somebody else would buy a ticket? Hardly anybody had come. Nichols turned around and counted: eleven people, including himself. He wondered whether he could write some kind of short piece about the lack of an audience. It must be Billy Sunday.

Finally the curtain opened, revealing a maiden in mourning: a long black dress, a swooping black hat, and a veil. She spoke of her grief in a French accent—at least, Nichols supposed it was a French accent. Then she lifted her veil and took her hat off, placing it on a table. When she turned around, Nichols saw that she was the same woman he had encountered at the Lutheran church dinner.

She looked different—probably she was made up, he realized—but the still, pale, narrow face was unmistakable. He never took his eyes off her through the whole play. Could she see him? Could she recognize him as the man who had tried to talk to her at the church? Nichols did not know what actors could see; he had never been in a play to know whether the illusion of a one-way window was some kind of perceptual reality for the actors.

He got a further surprise when the little girl came on. He might not have recognized her. She was dressed in rags, a street urchin whom the widow first spurned as a beggar, then gradually recognized as a child with grief as deep as her own. In the last scene of the play, the child ran to her adopted mother dressed in an elaborate silk gown with a long train. It made a thrilling finale. Nichols applauded until his hands hurt, even though it seemed odd to do so with so few in the audience. They barely outnumbered the cast.

How is it that a face can penetrate us, that its eyes can burrow deep into the texture of memory? Sometimes a film actress had burned an image onto Nichols's mind, remaining like the blind spot after you look at the sun. But never had such an image crossed over into life.

In the play the woman's name was Marie Paul. M. K. knew that was not the woman's real name, but the mournful character of the play, with her drooping despair, had merged with the sad-eyed abstracted woman in the Lutheran hall, the one he had compared in his thoughts to a saint seeing angels beyond the noise of life. He did not know what the woman's real name might be, but he thought of it as Marie Paul. Although he knew she was not a widow from Paris, he could not help supposing that at least she had lived in that city and that her daughter must be rescued somehow from heaps of lost children on the cruel old continent.

He sat for some time in the empty theater pondering this, and then went out to the ticket window. Forget about Golis and his beer-drinking Lutherans; Nichols would make up an excuse. He wanted to see the play again. The signboard said the evening show—for one night only!—was at eight o'clock, but there was no one in the window. Nichols rapped on the glass; no one came. The other customers had long gone, and the street was deserted. He could see tiny beads of moisture swirling in the glow of a streetlight.

He went back through the glass doors into the empty, poorly lit theater lobby. From somewhere deep in the building he heard voices arguing, but he could not make out what they said. Then a door burst open from the auditorium, and a tall, heavy man in a thick gray suit emerged, looking angry. He stopped when he saw Nichols. "What do you want?" he demanded.

"I want a ticket for the show," Nichols said. "It's a great show. I just saw the matinee."

"There won't be another show. Everybody's gone to see Billy Sunday." The man snapped out his answers impatiently.

"Will they do it tomorrow? No, Monday?"

"They won't do it at all. Their producer skipped."

The man seemed to suddenly realize that he had nothing against M. K. He took a breath and spoke more slowly. "The producer ran out of money, so he skipped town this morning. I told the actors they could have anything they got today, but as you saw, they didn't get much. The whole tour has been like that, I guess."

"He left them? So what happens?" Nichols said. "Do they go on without him?"

"Nah. They don't have anywhere to go or any money to get there. They'll go home if they can get the price of a train ticket."

Nichols pursed his lips in a silent whistle. "Stranded then. The woman—what's her name?"

"Which woman? Oh, you mean her." A smile flickered over his lips. "I don't know her name. Mister, these are theater people." He looked at his watch. "You can go talk to them if you want. They're backstage."

The woman recognized him right away and told the others in her calm, uninflected voice that she had met him earlier in the day and he worked for the newspaper. The actors glanced at each other, unmistakably conveying an understanding. Nichols's first thought was that maybe they had something to hide.

He plunged right in nonetheless, offering to help them by writing a story. It would make an interesting piece, he told them, about a New York theater troupe with outstanding talents, stranded in Everett because of Billy Sunday. Perhaps some kind person, someone who loved the theater, would read it and help them. Nichols kept coming back to the idea until one of the actors explained the problem to him: "Mr. Nichols, it's a nice offer you're making, but now that the tour has folded it's not going to do us any good to have people know that we are actors. It's more likely to bring us trouble."

"Trouble with who?" Nichols asked.

The woman—he still had not learned her real name—spoke up so sharply she seemed to be challenging him. "With our boardinghouse, for one thing."

There were eight troupe members, counting the little girl—five men, two women, and the child. They explained that in a place like Everett, people would come out to see a play, but they would certainly not invite actors to dinner or let their children play with the little girl. Often a boardinghouse would refuse them a room for the night if the owner knew who they were. Vagrancy laws stood against them if they were out of work, as they now were. The little girl could be taken away under child-labor statutes. They didn't want publicity for themselves. Theater people were used to sliding quietly into town, putting on their play, and leaving on the train that night.

Given that, they treated Nichols with surprising equanimity, letting him stay backstage while they packed up their costumes and removed their makeup. In fact, they seemed to accept their situation with astonishing composure. Nobody was in a temper.

They told M. K. their different plans when he asked: some would take the train that night, off to Seattle or San Francisco or Chicago where they had friends and hoped to find some kind of work. Some had to wire relatives for money, which meant they would stay until they got an answer. One of the young men wanted to know whether there were jobs in the mills; he thought he might stay in Everett and try to save up some money.

All the time that Nichols talked, he could barely keep himself from staring at the woman. She, out of all of them, was least communicative.

The women were sharing a room in a boardinghouse a block off Hewitt. When they left the theater, burdened with suitcases, Nichols followed. He walked alongside, carrying one of the cases and listening in on their conversation, wondering how he could get the woman with the little girl to talk with him.

As they approached the boardinghouse, she suddenly turned toward him and asked whether he knew where she could look for work.

"You're planning to stay in Everett?" he asked.

She gave an almost invisible shrug.

"I might have an idea or two," he said. "I'll ask around."

Then because he was the kind to plunge ahead, he went on, "Do you have plans for dinner?"

"I plan to be with my daughter," she said.

"Well, of course," he said. "Of course, I'm inviting you both. Can you eat? It looked like you ate pretty healthily at the church."

For the first time he saw a smile on her face. It was a sleepy expression, focused inward, as though she were amused at something he could not see. "Sure, we'll eat," she said. "We eat whenever we can."

He had to wait for them outside the boardinghouse. The landlady came out and asked him what he wanted, and then every few minutes she poked out her head to stare at him. Nichols supposed that a boardinghouse had to guard its reputation jealously. He sat in a straight-back chair on the porch, looking out into the drizzle and thinking about his excitement. She was not a college girl, but a woman, an actress from New York. He wondered how old she was. There had been no mention of a husband in her plans, and she did not wear a ring. She looked to be as young as he, but age is hard to judge.

When she came out, he stood and said, "You never told me your name."

"Darla Brazile. This is my daughter, Linda."

As they walked, he kept rehearsing that name, Darla. Darla Brazile. She really could be a widow from Paris with such a name and with such a face.

Everett did not offer much choice in places to eat. It was a smoke-stack town, and saloons served most of the public food with their free lunches. Of course, you could not take a woman and a child into such places, even if you cared to. Nichols did not care to; he was not a drinker. He had left a lot behind in Ohio, but not his dry upbringing. Other than the saloons there was Kip's and there was Chaney's, and not much to choose between them. Nichols favored Kip's. It was raining again, and he had no umbrella, so they had an uncomfortable time dodging along the street from one porch or overhang to another. When they got there, they found it was closed and everything dark. He could not read the sign in the window until he lit a match; it read, "Gone to hear Billy."

"Who is Billy?" the woman asked.

"Billy Sunday," he said.

"Sounds like a cowboy act," she said. "What's he do?"

"He's only the most famous preacher in America," he said. "At one time he was a pretty good ballplayer in Chicago, but he gave it up for the pulpit. He's here for a week, preaching against liquor. They built him a tabernacle all his own, out on the edge of town. He's the reason your play isn't playing."

"Somebody said that, but I didn't understand it. It's tough playing across the street from Jesus. Is that what you mean?"

"I guess so, especially right now. These dry laws are on the ballot next week all over the state. It's the forces of righteousness against the powers of darkness. That probably keeps people from going to a play, particularly one about a widow in Paris. They don't want anybody to think they're siding with darkness."

"That's my luck," she said. "If we did a musical, they'd be having a convention for deaf people."

They went over to Chaney's, and fortunately it was open, bright and warm. There were places at the counter, but Nichols steered to a booth; he wanted to look at this woman.

She had put a scarf over her head to shield her hair from the rain. She took it off now. Her hair had expanded into a thick, glistening mop, which she shook out and then pulled back from her face with her hands. She had a small mouth, her lips compacted into a slight pout. Her eyebrows were heavy and dark, perfect half-moons. He could not help himself; he stared. She looked at him with easy composure, as though to ask whether he had ever looked at a woman before. Her daughter snuggled next to her, very quiet and keeping to herself.

"Tell me more about this Billy," Darla said when they had ordered. Nichols began to tell her what he could. He liked to spin a story, and she made a good audience, listening closely, making occasional wise remarks. She was funny in an offhand way that depends on a certain tone. She didn't say anything that would sound funny if you repeated it, but they were little remarks that dug between your ribs.

Her daughter, Linda, took a slice of bread, which she ate carefully and methodically, first all the way around the crust, then the middle of the slice in little bites. She paid no evident attention to their adult conversation.

They had ordered a bowl of fried chicken, which came with fried potatoes and creamed corn, and when it arrived, they ate hungrily. Nichols went from his experiences with Billy Sunday to describing his Ohio upbringing, while Brazile listened with a musing half smile on her mouth. She had very dark eyes that seemed not to reflect light at all but to swallow up everything like the pool at the bottom of a quarry. M. K. felt himself so excited, he told himself to slow down, to be easy, because he kept wanting to speed up and take off like a runaway horse.

"But you know all this," he said to her. "Hillsboro is probably the exact same as a thousand towns in the Midwest."

"No," she said, "I've played in a thousand towns, but I've never lived in one."

"Lucky you," he said and did his best to make his background sound interesting. Really, it was very ordinary. His father taught German and English at the high school. He was an impractical man who befriended the few German immigrants in Hillsboro in order to speak with them in the romantic language of castles and forests. His father cherished everything German, which created incipient conflict with Nichols's mother because her great love was the Woman's Christian Temperance Union. The Germans were beer drinkers and always a potential source of evil for his mother. She often told about the Woman's Crusade that, when she was a young girl, had started in his hometown.

"What is the Woman's Crusade?" Brazile asked.

"You've never heard of that, either? Oh, I forgot . . . you're an actress. It's famous in my little world. The women in Hillsboro started praying against the liquor traffic. They marched out of the church right into the saloons to start a prayer meeting. If the owner wouldn't let them in the door, they would kneel on the sidewalk outside, even in the mud and the snow. They would sing hymns and pray and beg the saloon owner to find an honest living. A lot of the saloon owners gave up after days of that—they couldn't stand up to the ladies. My mother told me about it constantly when I was a boy. I'm sure they were the greatest days of her life. She says they closed thousands of saloons and convinced hundreds and hundreds of drugstores to stop selling alcohol. The crusade spread all over the country, and then they made it into the WCTU. You've heard of that, I assume."

"Yes, I've heard of that. So you grew up in a dry home."

"Oh, bone dry. If somebody in Hillsboro drank, he would probably get mentioned at the Wednesday prayer meeting. Then I went to college at Oberlin with no idea it was the headquarters for the Anti-Saloon League. That's who is behind this dry campaign, you know. It started back at Oberlin."

"So I take it you don't care for Billy," Brazile said.

He had been talking on and on in an animated way. He felt very happy. "Oh, he's all right. If you've never seen him, you ought to go. He puts on quite a fight with the devil. Every night he challenges him to a brawl."

"Hmmm. My devil's a big one. I could use some help with him."

When she had put Linda to bed, Darla Brazile came out on the boardinghouse porch and sat with Nichols. She had been in one traveling company or another since she was ten, she said when he asked. Linda had been doing it since she was two. "Sometimes," Brazile said sardonically, "they want her, so they take me. She's become quite a little actress."

Darla's parents were dead, she said. At least, her mother was. She did not know her father's whereabouts. She had a sister in New Jersey. Then she stopped talking and looked so closely at Nichols, it unnerved him. He felt as though she were peeling his skin back with her eyes. "You want to know about Linda's father," she said.

"It's none of my business," he said, blushing.

"Maximilian Brazile," she said. "A handsome man from Argentina. He is not part of my life anymore. Brazile plays the clarinet. That's about as steady a life as acting. He would come, go, come, go. I couldn't count on him."

"When did you last see him?"

"When Linda was two. He would still come around. I told him I didn't need to see him anymore."

"You're divorced then?" he said with a catch of his breath. He had never known anyone who was divorced.

She looked him over again with that same examining look. "Divorced? I don't know whether I should call it that since we weren't officially married."

At the age of twenty-one, a newspaper reporter, Nichols thought of himself as quite worldly, but in reality he had spent his entire life around decent Christians in small towns. He wanted to ask other questions, but he lacked the daring.

"On Monday," she said, "what do you think I can do about a job in this town?"

"I'll ask my boss," he said. "And I'll come and see you as soon as I can."

Saying good-bye, he put out his hand. She squeezed it gently and then, to his surprise, pulled him toward her. She tipped her head to the side, kissing him, a gentle touch of lips before she pulled away.

He tried to kiss her again, but she smiled and shook her head. "Don't be a bad boy," she said.

Chapter 2
1910: To the Rescue

Monday morning Golis wanted to know where the Lutheran story had gone. Nichols sat right down at his desk and pounded it out. He made reference to the dearth of customers at the movies on Saturday night, but when he quoted from his notes of the Lutheran church dinner, it only increased his itchiness to be out of the office. His scribbled notes—pages frizzled from the rain, penciled doodlings he had made when somebody was droning on—pulled him directly back into that moist, noisy room where he had met Darla.

He called her that in his mind now—Darla. Learning about her past might have scared him, but really it intrigued him, lured him. Obviously, he told himself, she was respectable. Look at the way she dressed. She was a cultivated woman with nothing loose about her. But she had lived in the city. She had never heard of Billy Sunday.

The editor looked at him quizzically when he asked about a job for a young mother. "What's up?" he asked. Nichols told Golis about the troupe.

"I don't think we need any hard-luck stories this week," Golis said, taking his interest in a strictly professional way. "We've got to cover the election. I want you to go hear Sunday tonight. Get to him and find out what he thinks about Everett. Ask him whether there are any decent men on the other side, or are they all rum-soaked devils? I'm not interested in whether he makes nice. Ask him about Clarence Darrow. You know he's coming this week for the wets. Ask him whether he thinks Darrow is really for the little man. Ask him would he like to meet Darrow if we set it up. Sunday is staying at the Eugene Hotel, on Grand."

Nichols asked again about a job for Darla. Golis looked at him intently. "Not just a story, is it? Did you say she's a mother? She ought to get home to her kids."

"Her daughter is here with her. Remember? I told you she was in the acting company too."

Golis looked as though he felt almost sorry for him. "And you want to help."

"Yes, if I can."

"I don't think this is much of a town for her. There are just two classes of female in Everett, and the first get married and stay that way."

M. K. understood that Golis was impugning her morals, but he ignored it. "She just needs some money to get by for a while."

"Then give her the money. Now don't forget to ask about Darrow. I think that's a good angle. Ask Sunday whether he would have lunch with Mr. Darrow if we arranged it."

Nichols went up the hill with a bounce in his step. He would give her the money. He had enough to carry her through for a bit. Try as he might to think of a job for her, he drew a blank. Everett was a mill town and a man's town. If she could type or do figures, she might find something in a mill office, but she had said she couldn't do such things. Somehow the idea of giving her the money cheered him up.

He ran into her a block from her boardinghouse. She was coming down the hill while he went up, wearing a dark blue silk dress with tiny yellow dots, a simple dress that subtly emphasized her shape. He had not really noticed the rest of her, he had been so preoccupied with her face. He saw that she had a willowy, sinuous form, distinctly womanly.

"There you are," he said. "I was coming to see you. Where's Linda?"

"I put her in school."

He was surprised. "You really are planning to stay in Everett."

"Not necessarily," she said. "I try to get her into a class whenever we stay in one place for any length of time. She's anxious to learn, poor child."

It had rained hard earlier in the morning, and now ragged gray shapes were racing across the sky. The wind was tearing at their hats. "Can I buy you a cup of coffee?" Nichols asked. "I have some ideas for you."

They went into a drugstore and sat at the counter. Nichols stared ahead at a calendar decorating the wall. It was easier to talk about money without looking into her face. "One thing is," he said, "I'm supposed to go to hear Billy Sunday tonight for the *Argus,* and I wondered if you wanted to go with me. You know, you said that you might want to hear him. Linda could come too."

He found it difficult to read her feelings, she was so matter-of-fact in her answer, even when she said yes. He promised that she would find Sunday quite a show. He had seen him once when he leaped up on the pulpit—straight up, in one quick motion—to stand on top, brandishing his fists and challenging the devil to a bare-hands fight. This he described enthusiastically, his eyes flashing.

The way Brazile looked at him made him wonder whether she was laughing at him. "So what else?" she asked. "You said you had some ideas."

"I haven't been able to think of a job," he said. "I asked around. But I was thinking. I can help you along while you're stuck. I'd like to." He waited nervously, feeling proud for his generosity.

"That's very kind of you," she said, "but no thanks."

"But why not? I'd like to."

"My mother raised me never to accept money from strange men," she said. She parted her lips in a smile, almost a silent laugh. And although he tried to talk her into it, she would not budge. She just shook him off.

"I plan to look for work," she said. "I have a few ideas of my own."

Darla went straight down the hill to the Nassau Street Cinema. Having done just about every kind of popular entertainment known to man, she was perfectly willing to sing for one of the nickelodeons if that would pay the bills. She had seen the Nassau on the way to the restaurant the night before.

She might have asked Nichols the best places to try, but she preferred to keep a certain independence. He was a nice fellow, and he was certainly good-looking, but he seemed a little too eager to help. Men who are eager to help usually want something back.

She had been in a difficult position many times before, and she had always found a way ahead. Only two fixed considerations constrained her: she would take care of Linda, and she would stay in theater. To be a professional actress was all she had ever wanted for herself.

Acting meant, almost automatically, that you got in difficult positions from time to time. The jobs never lasted. You couldn't settle down like ordinary people, which made it difficult to take care of a child. However, she had chosen the life, and she would follow it. Other people gave it up for security, but that she had no intention of doing.

The blond ticket seller at the Nassau wanted to know what she needed when she asked to see the manager. "I'm a singer," Darla said. "I want to talk to him about a job."

"He doesn't have singers. He has a piano player."

"What he has and what he wants are two different things. It wouldn't hurt him to talk to me, do you think? He can just say no."

The blond with brown streaks in her hair reluctantly let her in, and she found the man in the projection room. It was a small and messy room, poorly lit, with film cans stacked up in the corner and old bills and notices thrown around. The manager was a short man with a pencil mustache. He wore a dirty little plaid hat perched on top of his head. Squinting at her in the dim light, he said, "I don't have a singer, miss. And you know, business is terrible."

"I know that," she said. "That's why you need a singer. Something to draw them in."

"I've got no money," he said. "Business is terrible."

"It'll pick up after the election is over," she said. "They always come back. And you ought to have something the other nickel palaces don't have. A singer."

"How do I know you can sing?"

"Let me sing after this reel. You won't have any doubts."

He said okay. She thought she had him then, even though they had not discussed money. *Get the job first, and then we'll talk money,* she thought. She went out into the dark room and found the piano player. He was just a kid who probably should be in school, about six feet tall and in need of a few solid meals. He told her the numbers, acting as cool as a veteran.

When the slides came on, she began to sing the words. She had a contralto voice, warm and unpretentious. It would not do for opera, but common audiences always liked her singing. She liked it herself. Even in the darkened theater—and having no certainty whether there were ten people or a hundred listening—she enjoyed the sound of her voice, projecting warmth and feeling outward. She always missed performing. When she got back on the stage and began to perform after an absence, it never failed; she was excited and yet comforted because she was in a world where nothing could impede her, nothing could interfere. She might never be a star on Broadway, but she was a professional actress, and no one could take away this pleasure.

As she had expected, the manager put up no argument, except about money. He said he could give her only two dollars a day. "Maybe more when the customers come back."

"That's very nice of you, and I need the money," Darla said. "But the boardinghouse costs that much for me and my daughter. We have to live, you know."

"You didn't say you had a daughter," he said and raised it to $2.50.

"When the customers come back, I want three dollars," she said and took the job. She thought about Mr. Nichols and their plans to go to see Billy Sunday, but decided there was nothing she could do to get news to him that she had found work.

———

M. K. arrived at her boardinghouse, a square, two-story blue frame house with a little fenced yard facing the street and a long swing on the front porch. Linda was on the swing, dressed immaculately in the same blue dress he had first seen her in, with a short black coat. Her little legs swung loosely in front of her, eight inches above the porch deck.

"Mother isn't back," she said. "I'd like to go if I can. She said I could go."

"Of course you can," he said and reached out a hand to pat her shoulder. She reached up and took his hand in hers, interlacing her fingers. The gesture affected him. For a moment he found himself unable to speak. He had not realized that he missed his younger siblings.

"You think we should wait for your mother?"

"No, she said not to wait."

He was surprised at himself, taking to a little girl so fondly. Maybe it was a result of being with Billy Sunday that afternoon. He had gone up to Sunday's hotel room and found the man stretched out on the bed, ready to talk. He liked Sunday much better than he had expected. The man was a good-hearted, transparent, friendly fellow, lacking much education but extremely affable. They had hit it off.

Unfortunately Sunday said he was too busy to have lunch with Clarence Darrow. When Nichols asked his opinion of Darrow, Sunday had darkened and said that he didn't see how Mr. Darrow could claim to be for the little man and yet support the saloons. "Liquor is the little man's worst enemy," Sunday said. "I think I know something about that." Nichols thought he could use that quote. The *Argus* had taken a stand against the dry law, but Golis was trying to be evenhanded in case the drys won.

That night they had quite a crowd at the tabernacle—a large shingled roof set on fir pillars, with bleacher seats so fresh from the sawmill you could get sap all over you if you were not careful. Linda held his hand through much of the service. She was a grave little child. She did not wiggle.

Sunday did not jump up on the pulpit, but he did stand up and challenge the devil to a wrestling match, holding a heavy chair over his head, threatening the devil and waving the chair like a matchstick. Later, when he made his appeal for commitment, he told them to slide home to heaven while he himself flew across the stage, slid into the choir, and popped up to his feet as though he were spring-loaded, shouting, "*Safe in the arms of Jesus!*" The crowd roared and applauded.

He did it in such a winsome way that it was impossible to take offense. He had a touch of the raffish country-boy ballplayer, but you could never question his sincerity. He wasn't dumb, either. The crowd began the evening sober and quiet, but he had them laughing and cheering by the end.

Afterward, when they were walking home, Linda wanted to know what it meant when Mr. Sunday invited every man down front to shake his hand and say that he would live his life all out for Christ. "Why did they want to shake his hand?" she said.

"He's quite a famous man," Nichols told her. "A lot of people would like to say that they have shaken the hand of Billy Sunday."

"They did that with Mr. Brannigan when I was in his play in New York. He never invited them to come down for it, though. They would wait outside in the back."

"Well, this was different," Nichols said. "Mr. Sunday wanted everybody to shake his hand to show that he would really devote himself to Christ. It wasn't *just* to shake the hand of a famous man."

———————

Nichols went to hear Darla at the movies every day. He could not see her while she sang because the room was dark and her form a shadow. But he could listen and imagine her standing before him. He could close his eyes and see her face, her waves of dark hair. He never sang along with her, no matter how popular the song, but merely listened. Her voice was lovely, deep, and alluring, reminding him somehow of his mother's singing when he was a boy. The nickelodeon was mostly empty all week as they came up to the election, so for the most part Darla sang solo.

It ought to have been a great week for a reporter. He got a terrific story when it came out that a well-dressed couple from out of town were making the rounds of the business community, wanting to buy real estate. When they had their pens out and ready to sign the contract, they would inquire as to the seller's dry sympathies, and when they learned he was a wet, they would walk out in a temper. They did the same thing half a dozen times. That story sold some papers. Clarence Darrow came to town to speak for the wets (who called themselves the Taxpayers Association), the second famous man to visit Everett in a week. Every night there were street brawls in and around the saloons, not to mention prayer meetings and door-to-door canvassing, along with all kinds of charges that this owner or that owner was threatening to fire his men if they didn't vote by his lights. Nichols could walk up and down Hewitt and get a story anytime.

Businessmen charged that the city would be ruined without the saloons to pay taxes, and of course, the preachers countercharged that the city was ruined if drunkenness continued as its operating principle. Those saloon taxes went for police to arrest the drunks, the drys said, and jailers to keep drunkards in jail and the welfare department to support their starving children. The city could give up saloon taxes and still save money if they eliminated drunkenness. It was easy to get a quote from one side and then go and get a better one from the other.

The politics might have fascinated Nichols at another time, but now he could think only about Darla Brazile. Whenever he could, he got over to the Nassau. She would sit with him while the reels were playing. By Wednesday he had gotten her to hold his hand. When she finished at nine o'clock, he would buy her dinner and walk her home.

Even though she was singing at the movies, she had a professional actor's disdain for them. Even vaudeville had more subtlety, she said. Nichols argued with her, and it gave them something to talk about over dinner. They discussed the day's reels and the acting they saw.

She came out with actors' and producers' names, with plays and venues that were completely unfamiliar to him. He acted as if he knew some of it, to keep from being a complete know-nothing. He liked hearing about the world of theater. Sometimes they talked about the election, and he told her the inside scoop on whatever story he had written that day. Darla listened with equanimity. She seemed to prefer listening to talking. Neither one of them said anything about what went on between them. She let him kiss her good night, sweet, soft kisses that put the gentlest pressure on his lips, like sipping at a soap bubble. He felt her shape against his chest momentarily.

When M. K. took Darla home after supper, she always said good-bye outside the house and went into her room quietly and alone, because Linda was asleep. The landlady was watching anyway. The relationship of mother and daughter was a subject of curiosity to M. K., and he watched and listened carefully to see how it operated. Linda seemed to be such a grown-up child, and Darla treated her as such, almost as an equal. She seemed to think of her daughter constantly, as though an invisible mental ring went between them.

Three or four afternoons Nichols stopped by the house, just to see Linda. She came home from school and changed her clothes, then played quietly with her doll, making no effort to go out or to find friends. Darla had arranged for the landlady to check on her and to feed her supper. Twice M. K. took her out for ice cream, and she held his hand. She had already grown very comfortable with him. Darla seemed to appreciate his willingness to stop in and see her.

It all happened very quickly, as things do when two people are thrown together in a strange town. Darla liked his artlessness, his midwestern straightforward and unsophisticated character. He thought of himself as running away from his small-town past, but by the standards of her experience, he was very safe. That he was enthralled with her she liked—who would not?—but what enabled her to relax into him was the thought that she could see right through him. He was a simple man, she thought, and a kind one, and not only trusting but also reliable. She had known a lot of people who were not reliable. He was kind to her daughter, too, and not only when Darla was there. If anything he did won her over, it was going to buy Linda an ice-cream cone while she was singing.

He liked her for very different qualities—for her delectable strangeness. No one he had known before lived a life remotely like hers. Then, of course, she was extremely beautiful. He had memorized her face. He could see it through the smoky, noisy air of the newsroom as he pounded out a story, or through the shady mist coming off the Sound as he walked up the hill to his boardinghouse.

On the Sunday before the election, the drys lined up all the Sunday school children, hundreds of them, to march through the downtown streets. They had a banner at the front of the parade, A LITTLE CHILD SHALL LEAD THEM. The wets lined up on the sidewalks, watching warily but not jeering. When Nichols saw this, he thought that contrary to Golis's predictions, the drys would win. Even a mill town has a hard time voting against its own children.

The drys did win by a narrow margin. At the same time women won the vote at the state level—the first victory for woman suffrage in many years. There was a great deal to write about, especially these twin victories for reform. Most municipalities in the state had gone dry. Now that women could vote, you could be sure they would stay dry.

After they put the paper to bed on Wednesday morning, Nichols felt so worn out that he went to his room and fell asleep. He had a south window that directed the full rays of the sun onto his bed, so he awoke in the afternoon hot and dazzled. For the first time in weeks blue sky had swept over the Sound. He felt cranky and inexplicably sad. He was unable to pass into dreams again; his thoughts circled slowly above his body like buzzards waiting on an injured animal.

Finally he forced himself to stagger to the sink and splash water into his face. After he scrubbed himself with a cloth, he felt more human, so he splashed more cold water and did it again. *Why am I sad?* he wondered. *Perhaps because the election is over.* Life in Everett would once again descend into the humdrum.

A breeze blew outside, and he felt invigorated by the chilly air beating on his face as he walked to the Nassau. Tonight he and Darla should do something special. He deserved that, considering all the words he had pounded out in the last few days, and considering how he had deprived himself of her company.

He found her in the projection room where there was barely room for the projectionist. She was talking in low tones to the manager, the man with a pencil mustache. Nichols stood for a while looking around at the stacks of film cans, the old movie posters tacked to the wall. Then he backed out and found a seat in the audience.

He could not even take his usual seat, for they had the biggest crowd in weeks. When Darla came out to sing, the patrons sang along, so he could not hear her clearly. Afterward she came and sat by him, and he slipped his hand over hers. The film was another Indian drama, so chopped and compressed that he could not follow the story. The crowd cheered loudly for the fighting sequences, but he thought they would have shouted for anything that moved quickly across the screen, maybe even a housefly.

"Can you get off early?" he whispered in Darla's ear. She shook her head.

"Are you sure? You haven't had a day off."

"This is the biggest crowd we've seen since I started. I need to work." She took her singing seriously. He had seen that.

He told her he would be back and then walked out into the brilliant sunshine. The sun was near to setting, throwing long shadows across the street. From certain streets he could see the light glinting off the water, and beyond, on the horizon, the storybook peaks of the Olympics, ordinarily invisible through the gray slime they called weather in Everett. Nichols walked briskly across the peninsula to the Snohomish River and its muddy flats. It was a long walk, but he wanted to go fast and hard, to use up his frustration. He asked himself what made him so unhappy. Of course Darla could not take off early. He did not own her.

As though to make up for the afternoon, Darla was unusually animated at dinner that night. She joined him in critiquing the Indian reel. She said that the people making movies knew nothing about drama at all. "They just stick a camera up and take pictures of people jumping around, and when they have shot a few thousand feet of film, they say that's a reel."

Nichols asked her whether she had ever considered working for the moving pictures, and she made a face. "I'm an actress," she said.

"And what are the people in the movies?"

She looked at him coolly, pausing before she answered. "Actors down on their luck."

"And aren't you?"

"Not that far."

Absentmindedly she put her hand out to take his. He held it gently, as silken and soft as a piece of fabric. Then she took it away, firmly, suddenly, as though she had remembered propriety. "Let's go," she said.

The streets seemed darker than usual because the sky was inky with pinholes of bright, cold light. They stopped at a dark corner to kiss, at first two mouths gently pecking at each other, and then, in a clench, exploring. Nichols could feel her two small hands firmly in his back. He had never kissed like this. He had no experience but only a sudden and unpremeditated urge to go deeper, never to stop.

But they did stop. Darla pulled away and rested her head against his shoulder. Nichols felt himself trembling slightly and was embarrassed. Surely she felt it too.

"Do you love me?" she said, almost as a sigh.

"Yes, of course."

"Like you've never loved anyone?"

"Like I've never loved anyone." It was true.

"Hold me tighter," she said, and they began to kiss again. He felt her hands against his back, moving, pulling, and he thrust his own hands inside her coat to hold her closer. He could feel the warm pliable flesh through her dress. All this was new.

Darla broke away again, and they leaned against each other, panting. "I wasn't planning on this," she said.

"Of course not," he said.

"I mean all of it."

He was confused, not understanding to what "all" she referred.

"If we go to your room, will anybody see us?" she asked. With reeling horror and amazement he understood "all." She wanted to be with him.

They walked there wordlessly, locked together arm in arm, their hips grinding together. He felt that he could look down on himself, like a guardian angel watching helplessly as his charge walks deliberately toward destruction. What was he doing? Why was he doing it? He knew that he would not stop, though, no matter what the punishment. His good Christian upbringing had fallen completely off him, like a garment in tatters that has seen its seams disappear. He was so used to its protection that now he felt naked, afraid. He was not at all sure this was a good thing that he did. Yet he would not stop walking.

They paused across the street from his boardinghouse. There was a single bare bulb on the porch, and inside the door a single staring light on the stairs. Nothing seemed to move. Nobody seemed to be home.

"You go and see whether the coast is clear," Darla said. "Then wave to me to come on."

Chapter 3
1911: Los Angeles

It was his first time to be with a woman, and afterward he was overwhelmed with the sheer enormity of what he had done. His body seemed to have turned inside out, and his soul seemed to surge inside him like a pounding sea. M. K. had entered that amazing fleshly world where quite commonly clocks stop ticking and thoughts narrow to physical urgency, where morals become only an afterthought. Sheer bodily pleasure would have left no space for regret or retraction if he had not fallen in love.

This is not to say he had no guilt or misgivings. Everything in his upbringing and his education condemned what he had done. It is one thing to reject the morals that you learned in Sunday school and quite another to open that locked door. Still, he might easily have expelled the guilt like a lungful of bad air, except that he could not bear to think of Darla misused. He feared that he had profaned her and that others would as well. That is a different sort of guilt from the fear that comes because commandments are broken.

On the morning after that first night, he said to her with genuine, if ambivalent, grief that he was sorry. She looked at him in a way that made him feel like a very young boy. Darla had been making her way in the world for a long time, and she had never had the luxury of second-guessing herself.

She gave him no reason for contrition. He *had* no strong reason, except that he loved her. The idea of her as a loose, lost woman, a beauty used and abandoned, all the clichés of a woman scorned that he had heard all his life but had never paid the slightest attention to, now seemed as sharp and true as the color green. He felt he had added to her troubles, had contributed another loss to her vulnerable life. He wanted to prize her, to lavish attention on her, to protect her, and to court her, yet all those courteous instincts broke apart like so much wet newspaper when he felt the sexual instincts rise. When he left her after they spent a second and a third and a fourth time together, he felt as sunk as a well on a dark night, as vacant as a cupboard in an abandoned house.

He asked her to marry him. She said no at first. She even laughed at him. He knew it was the only way out for him, however. They could not go on the way they were, he had not the remotest power to repent, and if she left him, he thought he would surely die. The only way ahead was to be with her forever.

Darla thought it was merely guilt prompting him, which was why she laughed. She had far too much respect for herself to get appropriated into his quest for salvation. Nevertheless, she listened to him closely—she was a careful listener—and understood after a time that he had other motives. Yes, he was guilt stricken, but he also feared for her. She was taken aback. Nobody had ever wanted to protect her, certainly not Brazile. She was not sure she liked it at first, but the idea grew on her. Besides, she did like him. She admired his handsome face and head, his jaunty way of walking and moving, his cheerful and voluble conversation. He made her comfortable, and she wanted him to stay.

So they were married in a city hall ceremony with Henry Golis as their witness and her daughter, Linda, as their flower girl. They had no honeymoon. Darla had to sing at the Nassau that same night. The landlady made them show her the marriage license before she let M. K. move in. It was not the kind of marriage that M. K. had anticipated for himself—if he anticipated anything at all. Yet it provided him with everything he wanted. He had Darla and also the comfort of knowing that he was to provide for and protect her.

———————

Two months later they arrived in Los Angeles. Darla could see no future singing for nickelodeons in a mill town, while M. K. had concluded that news reporting at the *Argus* was not for him. Not even Henry Golis could give them any reason to stay in Everett, so they said good-bye to him and a few others and took the train south. Darla thought she might get work in the movies, having heard from her sister that some of the New York companies were filming for the winter in California. Watching the pictures every day at the Nassau had caused Darla to moderate her thoughts on acting in films.

They liked Los Angeles from the moment they arrived. It cheered M. K. immensely to see blue skies in January and the bright desert sun tracing long bars of shadow from rows of palm trees along the broad streets. They especially liked the tall palms, which seemed impossible and ridiculous.

Los Angeles was a small city of 300,000, splayed out loosely over sloping terrain under high gray mountains, reminding M. K. of a village that has multiplied and spread but not grown up. The buildings seemed incidental to the landscape. It was a friendly, easygoing place where nobody knew you or where you had come from. M. K. always greeted everybody he passed on the street, and he found that people in Los Angeles smiled and greeted him back, as though it were normal to do so.

On the very first day they found a one-bedroom apartment built Spanish-style on a courtyard. The garden had two large orange trees covered with fruit, and a gaudy bird-of-paradise plant grew directly outside their doorway. When they had paid the rent, they were down to just five dollars, but M. K. couldn't worry about the low funds. Something about the place made him happy, almost giddily so. "We could just eat the oranges," he said.

Darla left the apartment early next morning, all dressed up to look for work. M. K. took Linda to school where she was received without much ceremony, as though they took in new students often. When the principal asked for her name, to write it down, M. K. said she was Linda Nichols. He did not think twice until Linda darted a surprised look at him and then smiled angelically. He decided not to correct himself. If she was happy as Nichols, they would call her Nichols.

After he left her, M. K. began walking, exploring. He traveled randomly, looking through neighborhoods, assessing shops, noting prices. He supposed he would get another job at a newspaper, but for the present he was glad to take the morning off. Several times he got into conversations, once with an elderly man watering his lawn (in January!), once with a policeman (who wore a very odd, old-fashioned tunic for a uniform, with a high, round hat). When he got tired of walking, M. K. went back to the apartment and placed a chair in the doorway so he could look into the garden. He wanted to sit and listen to the birds.

"Did you like your teacher?" he asked Linda when he met her after school.

"Yes," she said with the sober concentration he was learning to love. "They were nice."

"Who is 'they'?"

"The girls in my class. I like it here. I want to stay." She looked up at him as if to appeal for his mercy, a look of melancholy and vulnerability.

M. K. remembered that Darla had moved constantly during most of

Linda's life. "There's no reason not to stay," he said. "Let's tell your mother she doesn't need to go on the road anymore."

"But she has to do her work. She has to."

"Maybe something will work out here," he said.

Darla came home well after dark, carrying a bag of groceries. "Looks like somebody got a job," M. K. said. He was very glad to see her.

"Five dollars a day," she said. Her still, dark eyes seemed happy, full of satisfaction. "I think they would take you, too, if you want to give it a try."

She said her timing had been perfect. Fifty Biograph people had arrived from New York just a few days before, and they were setting up on a vacant lot on Pico Street. One of the girls knew Darla from a play they had done in New York, so they took her on.

"Biograph," M. K. said, tasting the word on his tongue. It seemed that everything turned up in their favor. "The same Biograph that we like? And you really got on?"

"Yes," she said, downplaying the marvel. Today they had shot a reel about a woman who was robbed and hit on the head, losing all her memory. Darla had been hired for a bit part, a next-door neighbor. "It wasn't so bad," Darla said as she took the food from the paper bag and put it into the cupboard. "They pay the same five dollars to anybody who acts, no matter what the part. You might have a leading role one day and then work a bit part the next, but you get paid. And you can go home at night to your family. Mr. Griffith is the man in charge, and I think I like him. I want you to come and meet him."

Linda held Darla's skirt with one hand, following her mother's movement. Darla looked down at her and smiled, asking about school. Linda ignored the question for something more urgent. "Will you have to go on the road, Mother?"

Darla leaned over and kissed her on the top of her head. "No, honey. No more traveling, at least for now."

The next day they walked Linda to school—she was very solemn about it, holding them both by the hand—and then caught a yellow trolley to the Biograph lot. It had a board fence running around it, but they walked through the gate without a challenge.

All morning M. K. had anticipated seeing the wondrous place. He did not know what he would find, but he knew it would be marvelous. Here within a plain wooden fence were made the movies that he so adored.

There was nothing much to see inside the fence, however. A large wooden platform, cluttered with guy wires and furniture, took up much of the lot. On one side stood a large, graying shed. In front of it was a long rack made of iron pipe, crammed with clothing for costumes. They heard a loud voice shouting instructions. When they walked nearer, toward a collection of people on the platform, they saw a pretty young woman in a red satin dress, seated in a living room set—a cluster of furniture and a wallpapered wall, all in the open air. The woman was talking on the telephone and registering different emotions as the voice shouted them at her. "You're shocked. Show surprise. You can hardly believe it. Now you're growing fearful. Something terrible has happened." Then the voice yelled, "Cut!" and the actress got up and stood aimlessly, while the voice kept talking.

"That's Mr. Griffith," Darla said, and she led M. K. over and introduced them. Griffith was a large man with a meaty head crowned by a wide-brimmed hat. His eyes were hooded, which gave his face a sinister expression. M. K. thought he looked like the model for a Roman emperor.

Griffith shook hands and asked whether M. K. had any acting experience. M. K. said no, he was a writer.

"What kind of writer?" Griffith asked, and when M.K. said a news reporter, he compressed his heavy lips in disappointment. "We need some scripts," he said. "They don't require any great turn of phrase, but we need good stories to film. Can't you write something like that?"

"Sure," M. K. said. "Tell me what kind of stories you want."

Griffith said, "Anything, as long as we can make pictures of it. Bring me something as soon as you can."

Griffith didn't seem to need a script, however. He ran the entire production out of his head. Nor did he stop for a meal. M. K. watched for some time while he held a sandwich in one hand, carrying on directing the movie. Then he set the sandwich down on a table and forgot to pick it up again.

Darla made short, critical comments about the acting. After a time M. K. stopped hearing much of what she said. He was fascinated by the filming process. A story had been disassembled into scenes and would apparently be assembled again. He wished for a paper and pencil to write down the scenes as he saw them, just so he could understand how the pieces fit the puzzle.

He left Darla at the lot in the afternoon. Griffith had told her to wait for another bit part, but M. K. thought he should meet Linda at school. Anyway, Griffith's request for a script had captured his imagination. "I want to see whether I can write something," he said to Darla.

What made Biograph movies better was simple, they found out: it was Griffith. Griffith had brought the camera in close so you could see the actor's emotions. He had figured out how to crosscut between different scenes to make the action suspenseful. And he knew how to choose the best actors and get the best work from them. The members of the company talked about Griffith as though he were a wizard and a god. The bosses, far off in New York, were a nuisance. They cared only about profits and did not appreciate Griffith's genius. They made life miserable for him, trying to cut expenses and claiming to be losing money on him. How could that be, with the millions of Americans going to see Biograph pictures every week?

M. K. realized that he actually knew many of the faces he saw on the Pico Street set, though they looked oddly different in life, like bent copies of their filmed selves. He would meet somebody and gradually put the face together with one he had seen on the screen—perhaps a pirate or a train engineer in the movie, but now an ordinary human being.

Mr. Griffith had a taste for the scenery all around Los Angeles, and he got it into his movies whenever he could. At least once a week Darla got up at four o'clock to take the red trolley out of town. They would begin filming at first light by the sea in Santa Monica or at one of the spreading, wild mountain areas that Los Angelenos called parks. M. K. could not go with her—somebody had to get Linda off to school—but when he went to the movies now, he often recognized where a scene had been filmed. Biograph wasn't alone; lots of companies were filming in Los Angeles.

Griffith was always the center of attention, always teaching impromptu courses on acting, offering bits of wisdom, jingling the coins in his pocket, urging them to study the world and imitate it in their art. The company filmed from first light until sunset, and then moved into the old wooden shed for rehearsals of the next day's picture. They were often up late. Yet nobody wanted to miss a rehearsal because that was when Mr. Griffith had his whole mind entirely on the actors.

The very first week Darla rehearsed the part of a young girl pleading to her father on behalf of a ne'er-do-well brother. She was to run between her brother and father, interrupting their quarrel, and then beg her father to relent from his furious anger.

"Darla, my dear," Griffith said after they had tried it the first time, "you look like an actress playing a part. You must become this young girl. You must move as she would move. You must feel as she would feel. Become her. Don't just act like her. Now try it again."

She did not really understand what he meant. Nevertheless, she tried the scene again. Twenty or more people were present because even those who didn't have roles came to the rehearsals to watch Griffith.

He rubbed his scalp while looking off into a corner of the room. "Darla," he said finally, "how does this girl walk? Show me how she walks."

Darla walked.

"But she is afraid that her father and her brother will destroy each other, isn't that right? Is that how a girl would walk if she felt that the very foundation of her world was about to break apart?"

Darla said nothing. She was embarrassed in front of all the company, who kept absolute silence. She, who was a professional.

"Why don't you study the world?" Griffith had turned away from her and seemed to be addressing the whole troupe. "Have you never watched to see how people look at funerals? I am sure you have been to funerals. Don't you see how the people move when they have lost a loved one?"

Griffith turned back to Darla. "Darla, let's try it again. This time, think not just of your brother and father, but act as one who can feel the tremors from the earth beneath her feet. If you must do it on all fours, then do it on all fours!"

Griffith shouted as she moved, "The earth is shaking! The earth is shaking!" And then, as she implored her father, Griffith said, "You are sinking! You cannot stand!" Darla felt her knees give way with emotion. She slid down, leaning against the father, and ended up crouched on her knees. "Let me see your face," Griffith said. "Show me how you feel."

Then he clapped his hands three times loudly. "Now we are beginning to act. We are beginning to live. Let us do it again."

When they did it once again, however, he put his hat on his head and took it off again, rubbed his hand over his thinning hair, then sat down on a stool and seemed to ponder their fate. Finally he looked up, as though he had just realized that anyone was watching him. A big grin broke over his heavy features. With surprising dash he skipped to Darla, put his arms around her, and began to dance a sort of polka. "Dance, let's dance!" he shouted. After he had done a few steps with Darla in his arms, he let her go. "That's enough," he said and clapped his hands again. "Enough rehearsal. Let's all go home."

Darla told M. K. about it when she arrived home that night. The way she started out, M. K. thought she was exulting in the triumph, but as she went on, her tone shifted in a way that he did not understand. He thought the soft curves of her face seemed to change substance to something stiff and unyielding. Her voice also sank to a lower register, and she ended her description by picking up a pan off the stove and smashing it down on a glass vase that sat on the kitchen table. Without a word she reduced the vase to tiny shards, methodically pulverizing it to dust.

"What was that for?" M. K. asked when she finished. He was utterly confused.

"Stupid fool," she whispered.

He did not know whether she meant him or herself or someone else. "Who's stupid?" he asked.

"Griffith!" she shouted. She went into the living room, sat down, and stared. M. K. cleaned up the glass. Then he realized that he had not seen Linda around. When he looked in the bedroom, he found her on the bed, reading a book. She said she was fine.

That was the only real outburst, but it told something about what

Darla felt. She had considered acting in the movies the sort of thing an actress might take on to pay the rent. But she found more than enough to challenge her. They made a movie every day, or sometimes one in the morning and another in the afternoon. Biograph had half a dozen girls who wanted the best roles, and Griffith never let them know who would win the prize until the last minute. Darla began to crave those roles not only because of the prestige they brought in the company, but also because she wanted to please Griffith. Even when she didn't understand what he wanted, his authority, his charismatic intensity, kept her giving every ounce of energy to him.

When Darla was tense about an upcoming role, M. K. would wake in the night to find her gone from the bed. Sometimes he would overhear her mumbling to herself out in the kitchen, rehearsing her part. Darla claimed that the movies did have words, only that you could not hear them.

On the second Saturday after their arrival they brought Linda along to watch the filming since she was off school. She seemed to be as interested as they were, standing very still, with a melancholy expression in her eyes, as the actors did their work before Mr. Griffith.

"Is that your little girl?" Griffith asked Darla when they came to a break. He got down on his haunches to talk to Linda, asking her what she liked to do and what grade she was in. He was watching her all the time, studying how the light affected her face. He straightened up slowly and looked intently at Darla through his large, hooded eyes.

"We need a little girl," he said. "Would you let her act with us?"

From that day on, Griffith treated them like his particular friends. He lived all alone in the Alexandria Hotel, and he loved to drop in on them at their apartment, always with flowers for Darla and a gift for Linda. His friendship made no apparent difference when it came to making the movies, however. Then he did not seem to favor Darla at all, and sometimes she thought he treated her very unfairly. When he was not moviemaking, he treated the whole family with grand generosity.

One Sunday he came and got them in a big car, and they drove to the inn at the top of Lookout Mountain. A graded dirt road wound up Laurel Canyon until they emerged on the top of the bareheaded hills with a view to snow-covered peaks in the east and all the way to the ocean at Santa Monica. They had lunch at the inn, overlooking the magnificent array. Griffith offered it up to them as if he had carried it to them on a tray.

"Mr. Nichols," Griffith said over coffee, "you see all this splendor. Do you think you can make a motion picture out of all this? You cannot. One spectacular shot you can make, but not a motion picture. To make a motion picture, you need to go down into those valleys, into the lives of those individuals who are invisible from these heights. You must get close enough to see their petty miseries. You must look into their eyes to see their little dreams. None of them matters to the mountains. None of them is even visible from these heights. But that is where you find a motion picture. Mr. Nichols, you want to write me a script, and I am anxious that you should write a script that I can use. You must get closer to your subject!"

M. K. had given Griffith several scripts, none of which he had wanted. Griffith spoke gravely, jingling the money in his pocket. "Mr. Nichols, you can start with the person who is nearest to you. Do you know who that person is, Mr. Nichols? It is yourself. Study yourself. Write about your own petty miseries, your own dreams."

For the time being, M. K. had forgotten the idea of getting a job. Darla's earnings, plus Linda's occasional payment, bought what they needed to live. M. K. was determined to write for the movies. He set up a card table in the front room where he wrote longhand drafts with a fountain pen. Later, when his scribbles and cross-outs had become unreadable, he would pull out his Royal and type up a clean copy. Darla was happy enough with the arrangement. She wanted him to succeed with Griffith, she understood the need for scripts, and anyway, someone should take care of Linda before and after school. Darla did not care too much about money either. It did not seem too important in a place where oranges grew in people's gardens.

For a time Griffith's advice made M. K. less productive. He would write and slash, write and fuss, write and tear up everything. He was not an introspective character. He liked stories precisely because they helped him to escape himself. Writing about himself was very trying.

Eventually he set out to write his biography in the third person, an exercise that he hoped would release his own nature to him. When he wrote about himself that way, surprising memories surfaced. He would have said that his upbringing had been ordinary, but the remembrances soon began to glow with strong colors and even sometimes to hum with particular music. He could see himself as a young boy, see himself as a character in a movie. He remembered the characters his father brought home. He remembered the pride his father always showed, telling him that his great-grandfather had been a famous abolitionist, Thomas Nichols, who had rescued runaway slaves in Alabama and taken them to New York.

Halfway along in his autobiography, M. K. had an epiphany and abandoned the project in order to prepare a script about a young man who leaves home due to his rich older brother's scorn. He saw the whole thing clear in his mind and worked hard at it all day until Linda came home. He greeted her triumphantly. He had just written the final scene.

Linda was in the third grade, although she was so tiny and delicate she looked younger. Even at the end of a school day she looked perfect and prim with that same watchful serenity her mother had. She was happy going to school, she told him—otherwise he might not have known. Whenever she arrived home, he dropped his work to make her a sandwich—butter and sugar was her favorite—and to talk to her. She liked to come home and draw pictures, sitting with him at the table as he wrote. M. K. was surprised that she had not made any friends to play with, but she assured him that the girls at school were nice to her.

He read her what he had written. She listened very patiently, giving no sign of her reaction. When he finished, she smiled with an expression that seemed almost patronizing. "Isn't there a good ending?" she asked.

"I don't know how to end it," he said. He had the son leaving on the train, and his mother weeping as she watched him go.

"It should have a good ending," she said. "A happy one."

That, he discovered, is one trouble with writing about yourself. It is hard to make the endings. He worked on it until suppertime, opened a can of stew and heated it up, then sat with Linda while she ate. M. K. usually waited to eat with Darla when she came home.

"What do you think would make my ending happy?" he asked Linda. She had been reading a schoolbook while he worked.

"I wish his brother would catch up with him and make him come back home."

"Why would the brother do that, though?"

"Maybe if the little brother had done something great, and he just discovered it."

He had the thing redone before Darla came home. The younger brother was a dreamer who wrote plays, and his older brother a successful businessman who scorned his brother's aspirations. The young man sent off his plays to theatrical agents and had them all rejected, one after another. His poor widowed mother was beside herself to stop her boys from their mutual enmity. The older brother even took away the younger man's girl and married her. Finally the younger left town, beaten down, while his brother threw barbs at his back.

Almost before he was gone, the postman brought an envelope. The mother opened it; it was a check for a large sum of money, payable for the latest play the younger brother had written. The mother showed the check to the older brother, begging him to catch up with his brother and give him the check. The older brother got into his car, racing alongside the train, finally catching it at a remote crossing. But the brake on his car failed, the car rolled onto the track ahead of the train, and the car was destroyed, killing the brother. At the scene, the horrified younger brother found his brother dead. The last scene showed the check, blowing across a field and out of sight.

Darla smiled. "I'll take it to Mr. Griffith tomorrow morning," she said. "I think he'll like this one."

———————————

Griffith did take the script. The movie was called *The Prodigal Son,* even though M. K. pointed out its differences from the biblical story. M. K. went to watch on the day they filmed it. In the morning they did all the home shots. Most of the afternoon was occupied with the train and auto wreck. Griffith had obtained a car that someone had run off a cliff on the coast. With that and a similar, intact car, along with a locomotive rented from the Southern Pacific, Griffith made numerous shots. There was no actual accident to film; Griffith said that they could trick the audience into thinking that they had seen the collision.

It was not exactly the way that M. K. had imagined it. The actors whom Griffith chose bore no resemblance to the faces he had seen in his mind's eye, and their movements seemed faster than could possibly be real to his way of thinking. But Griffith seemed satisfied, and once the filming was over, M. K. went home to dream of the silver images that would flash onto a screen. He had done it; he had made his dreams visible.

M. K. worked on new scripts every morning except when they had a part for a little girl. Then he went with Linda to the lot. He and Linda spent every afternoon together, and he read all his stories to her. Soon he was telling not merely his own memories, but the stories his mother had told again and again. M. K. was surprised that Linda found them so interesting.

When Darla's rehearsals did not go late, the three of them went for evening walks all over the city. Sometimes they took a trolley to a part of Los Angeles they had never seen, just to explore. It was always pleasant to be outdoors. Every day seemed perfect in the serene, dry environment, so warm in the afternoon and cool at night. They liked looking at the beautiful houses going up on the hillsides. They went to movies, too—newer movie palaces, luxurious theaters that charged ten cents and sometimes included vaudeville acts.

On Sundays they always took an excursion, often to Santa Monica, because they loved the ocean and it was easy to get there on the trolley. They had enough money to afford extra pleasures now, such as a fish dinner at Salazar's, a ramshackle Portuguese place overlooking the beach. On the trolley home Linda would fall asleep, and Darla and M. K. would lean on each other and talk of their plans and hopes. The movies, they felt, were carrying them in a great wave.

Chapter 4
1911: Iowa Picnic

Strangely enough, happiness made Darla anxious because it was so unfamiliar. She had been born Eunice Riley in Philadelphia, and Riley had disappeared when she was a baby. Consequently her mother raised her with what money she earned cleaning law offices, which was not much. Eunice had four older sisters, who began working before their ages reached two figures, and, of course, Eunice had been expected to do the same. Instead she had run away to a theater company, which took her in because they needed a child actor. She had been acting ever since.

When she was fifteen, too tall anymore to play a child, and too angular and boylike to play a grown woman, Brazile had entered her life. He was a musician who attached himself to the company, taking bit parts, making up playbills, doing whatever. Brazile was resourceful and playful, and he had loved her in his way. He had changed her name to Darla because, he said, the name read better in a playbill. He had also given her Linda, for which she was grateful. By the time she was eighteen, however, she had grown serious and womanly about her future. She saw that he wandered off repeatedly, that he would never make a father or a husband, that he could not be relied on. That was when she decided to refuse him the next time he came back.

She had learned to be on her own, to look around her for the next move, holding no expectations except that she had better be ready for anything that might come because it surely would. That was how she had married M. K. It had not happened within the same mental structure that M. K. knew, wherein a young person reached one long-anticipated and permanent decision that shaped everything to follow. No, she had merely seen it as the next move. If you had asked her whether it was a permanent commitment, she would have said yes because that was how you talked about marriage. But she really didn't have that kind of idea in her mental vocabulary.

Now their life seemed to move ahead as smoothly as a deep ocean swell. She was more used to the excitement of smashing onto rocks or narrowly avoiding them. The predictability and the safety made her nervous. She was accustomed to, and she liked, the drama of narrow escapes.

She could not have explained any of this uneasiness, but she felt it. She also felt that Linda was growing closer to M. K. than to her, and that they had lost the intimacy they had when traveling together. Of course, she was happy that the two of them got on so well together—she could not have tolerated it if they had not. Her natural sense of loneliness increased, though, as she felt, fairly or not, that her daughter had lined up with her husband.

None of this did she express to M. K.; she hardly understood what she was feeling. It simply made her restless and uneasy. Besides, she was preoccupied with making movies. That took her mental attention completely. It was beginning to look like the greatest break of her life, that she had ended up with Biograph and Griffith. It was neither easy nor secure, however, because Griffith would not let it be that way. He liked his actors on edge, and he kept them that way.

In June Mr. Griffith heard about the Iowa Picnic and announced the company would take the day off. He found the idea delicious and wonderfully ironic: that thousands of Iowans transplanted to this bizarre land of flowering trees should gather annually to celebrate the nostalgia of cornfields. The picnic had been held for more years than anyone could remember, and by now all kinds of people attended, not just those with roots in Iowa. As far as Griffith was concerned, that made it only more absurd.

The whole company planned to meet at the park. Darla got up early and, showing a surprising domestic industry, fried chicken and made potato salad. They bought fresh blackberries and cream at a store down the street. Linda was very excited. She had never been on a picnic, and she evidently thought it was something like a county fair. She kept asking, "Will there be singers? Will there be rides? Will there be prizes?"

They had quite a time getting on a trolley. The first three were so full, they did not stop, and to find space on the fourth, they had to worm their way to the back. Apparently the Iowa Picnic attracted more of a crowd than they had realized. By the time they got to the park the grounds were crawling with picnickers, so thick they could hardly find room to set out their blanket. They realized it would not be so easy to meet the others from Biograph. Linda, who always had to eat on schedule or she became weak and irritable, and who had suffered in the hot and crowded car, looked pale from hunger. They stretched out their blanket next to a bloodred oleander and ate while marveling at the parade of neatly dressed people.

"California is amazing," M. K. observed. "Just when you think you understand it, something completely surprises you."

He was happy to laze in the sun and watch the crowds, but Darla, when she finished eating, could not sit still. She didn't really like the dazed bucolic atmosphere. "Why don't we go find Mr. Griffith?" she asked.

M. K. made a countersuggestion, that they play pinochle, but Darla felt too fidgety. "I want to walk around," she said. "Come on, Linda, let's leave this old turtle."

"I want to stay with Daddy," Linda said. She had already stretched herself out on the blanket with one arm folded under her head.

Darla had not heard her call him Daddy before. At that precise moment she did not like it. "All right," Darla said, "you two can both be turtles. I'm going to look around."

"We're not going to be turtles," M. K. said. "We're going to play pinochle. Right, Linda?"

Linda said yes, and the satisfied way she said it annoyed Darla further. She left them and walked across the wide field, scattered with picnics, toward a grove of feathery trees. She glided right through a croquet game, around a mass of young people who were singing to a guitar, and into the shade. There she paused for a moment.

Something must be wrong with me, she thought. *Am I not happy that my husband is such a good man? That I have found a father for Linda? I should be happy.*

On the other side of the grove was a road where many people had parked their carriages. In fact, the road typified modern times. On the far side people had parked Fords and other cars in the field; and on this side, fancy and plain horse-driven vehicles were jammed up together. Some of the horses had been tied up in the shade of the trees; others stood switching their tails in the sunshine.

Beyond the roadway Darla could see a glade where more picnickers had spread their blankets. She walked that way and found, once she had crossed the road, that she was among a better set of people. Funny, how even at a picnic the different types found each other. Naturally M. K. had located the scruffier set. Here, one group had brought flutes and were pouring champagne. She caught a scent of the wine, sharp and golden. At one time in New York she and Brazile had drunk champagne regularly. Darla had a weakness for wine. She rarely got it—she could not afford it—but she liked it very much.

The spreading lawn stretched out thick with bright-colored blankets and figures dressed in white. About halfway across, Darla found one of the Biograph groups, several actors and set people. They hardly noticed her when she came up, they were laughing so. They had a bottle of brandy open, and somebody poured her a glass. The bright, clean scent cut into her sinuses. When she sipped, the medicinal vapors filled her mouth and hurt her throat. She had not had brandy in months. She drank down her glass.

Darla was pleased that M. K. did not drink, partly because it took the temptation away from her. In the theater somebody always had a flask or a bottle, and every company had a drunk or two. Even women drank in the world of the theater, though most of the time they did it on the sly. Darla had never liked being surreptitious in anything, so she didn't hide. She knew it wasn't good for her, however. She liked it a little too well. It could interfere with her work. Once, only once, she had been tossed out of a company because she drank too often.

Ordinarily men paid attention to Darla, but this group seemed oblivious. She stood next to them, holding her glass with two hands, wishing to be offered more. They were trading stories and laughing, and nobody noticed her. She thought they were a little drunk, the way they acted. Feeling slightly miserable, she tried to strike a pose, sure that somebody in the group would find her attractive. No one did. Finally she put down her glass and left them.

She considered going back to her family, but then realized that she was angry with them. M. K. and Linda seemed just a little too smug, a little too satisfied with themselves. Darla felt her mean streak coming out. She wanted to smash something.

At the top of a little rise she found Griffith, surrounded by a cluster of a dozen or more of the company. He, at least, noticed her, getting to his feet—he was seated on a portable camp stool—and extending his hand. "Mrs. Nichols, where have you been? And where is your husband? And Linda?"

"They are playing pinochle and couldn't be bothered," she said.

"I wish you would go and get them," Griffith said. "I want to talk to M. K. about a script. We need his mind to be writing good scripts!"

He began to tell the little circle what a fine writer M. K. was. Griffith had written plays himself before he became a director, and since he had coached M. K., and M. K. had followed his advice to write a successful script, he was naturally pleased. He loved to teach, and M. K. was proving a good student.

Today, Darla did not like hearing her husband praised. While Griffith was talking she looked around at what was left of the picnic. There were green olives in a dish and part of a cold ham with a knife stuck in it. A loaf of bread had been cut awkwardly, shredded as though with a dull blade. There was an open bottle of red wine. Darla felt a sudden and strong urge for that wine. She found a clean glass in a hamper and poured it full. The wine tasted strong and acidic with a rough, burning edge. In her frame of mind that was fine.

Nobody seemed to mind her. Griffith had gone off on acting, speechifying to his protégés that they must study life every minute. Even at this picnic, especially at this picnic, they must be learning. See the little gestures, he said, the mannerisms of eating and talking. Learn to imitate life in all its marvelous splendor!

She finished the wine and poured another glass. It tasted vile, but she made herself drink it. Then she felt it heavy on her stomach. You shouldn't drink wine after brandy, she knew. What was the saw? Wine on whiskey, mighty risky; whiskey on wine, mighty fine.

Since she was ignored, Darla thought she would go back to M. K. When she began walking, her feet felt strange and disconnected from her. The wine had made her a little light-headed, she realized. She wandered back through the field, finding it tricky to maneuver between the picnics, and feeling that other people, walking by her, threatened to undo her balance by rushing at her.

Without planning to, she happened on the other Biograph picnic again. The young men had gone off, leaving their food and their bottle of brandy. She stopped and studied the clutter. A glass was on its side in the grass next to the blanket. She thought it must be hers, though she could not remember putting it down. Picking it up and examining it, she got the bottle and poured the glass full. "So pretty," she said, swirling the amber liquid, and then she drank it down. Immediately she poured it full again, simply opening her mouth and emptying the glass down her throat. She tried to pour another glass, but the bottle was empty.

Immediately she wanted to sit down. Halfway to the ground, she understood that she had tipped off balance and slowly, helplessly, tumbled onto her face. Then, although she was quite conscious, she could not get up. She wanted to be sick, but she could not do that, either. She heard a loud roaring in her ears. It was a familiar noise. "I'm drunk," she said to herself.

Chapter 5
1912: Troubled Dreams

After the Iowa Picnic, M. K. found it necessary to be vigilant. Most of the time Darla's temptations with alcohol lay in the background, with both of them happy to pretend they had forgotten the problem. Then another incident would happen, and their lives would be upset again. When there was a money problem at Biograph or a movie Griffith considered particularly important, he became more demanding, more grandiloquent, more Griffith. It all made Darla fretful, and those were the times she required more watching. She drank when she worried. She kept her feelings hidden under that serene surface, and you would never guess she had to work very hard to keep her control. She said, incredibly, that the drink made her feel more in control.

M. K. had not quite forgiven himself for letting her go off that day at the Iowa Picnic. While he had been lying on the grass without a care, Darla had been falling into harm. M. K. had not forgotten the woeful, withdrawn look that appeared on Linda's face when they located her mother, who lay on the grass barely able to pronounce words. He would have done anything to prevent that scene.

Other people at Biograph seemed to find Darla's problem unremarkable. They certainly were not overly committed to helping him be vigilant. But then, he had to remind himself, they did not love her as he did.

He tried to talk to her, to use an argument to ferret out the cause of her inexplicable behavior. That was no use. She agreed with him and could even summon tears of remorse. Then she did it again. She agreed that the stuff was poison and yet hid her habit from him.

He tried to use sharper words and harder questions, striking her, as it were, with his resolution. She merely drew back. He could feel her shrink away, not timidly, but with a hard withdrawal that seemed to him like a rebuke.

Sometimes she accused him of moralizing, of making their lives into a melodrama. "Anybody would be a drunk," she told him once, "if she had to live with you." The thought occurred to him that he was reacting just like his mother with her hysterical fear of alcohol. But he had no desire to hold a prayer meeting. What he felt had nothing to do with morality or religion. It was a scientific fact that alcohol was a poison. He could not abide to see his wife, Linda's mother, harm herself.

At another time, maybe the day after accusing him, she begged for him to help her. He did not know how to help her, especially when she lied. There was no other way to describe it: she lied.

Words did nothing, so he watched her. He tried to intercept the poison. How else could he help her, who said one thing but did another? He went with her as often as he could, doing his writing in the evenings so that he could accompany her to the lot and escort her home at night. She felt it, of course—knew that he was watching her—and told him that she was not a child and did not like it.

"Then prove it by not drinking," he retorted. He got very angry, which shocked her. M. K. was ordinarily a friendly and mild man, but when something upset him, he could be outrageous.

Once he came home to find her lying on the sofa, having vomited on herself. He tried to keep Linda from seeing it. It was terrible to watch Linda's face pull back into a mask of misery.

He had not stopped loving her. If anything, he felt the love more strongly, like a sweet, thick syrup. He felt confused and punch-drunk, like a deep sleeper who has awakened to a fire and cannot separate his dreams from the realities flaming over him.

Roy Overholt appeared one morning while they filmed in Chatsworth Park. He was a tall, sandy-haired young man who wore faded work clothes and dusty boots. He looked to be a farmer or a ranch hand, except that working men didn't usually show much interest in moviemaking. Usually only kids stayed around for long when they were on location, but Overholt spent several hours of the morning standing next to M. K., watching Darla and her little homesteading family being confronted by a fierce Indian band.

"I'm in oil," Overholt said when M. K. grew curious enough to introduce himself. "Union Oil. We have a couple of wells going in up there." He gestured vaguely into the hills.

"You're not a roughneck, are you?" M. K. had recently heard the term and liked the sound of it.

Overholt smiled. "No, I'm a geologist."

It turned out that Overholt had worked all over California, following the oil strikes. "Yeah," he said, "it's an interesting life. A lot of lousy camps and tough guys, but when you hit it . . . The biggest party you've ever seen is nothing to it. Except what a mess! The stuff sticks to everything. A gusher would be a first-rate disaster if the junk wasn't worth a fortune." He smiled. "I can't see why nobody has made a movie about that. Your company ought to. Especially a gusher." He spoke with a deeply satisfied enthusiasm for the chaos.

M. K. had sold four scripts to Biograph, and one to the Kalem Film

Manufacturing Company. He felt he was getting a knack for it, but he was running out of ideas from his past, so the man's notion interested him. He asked questions about the oil business and then wrote down Overholt's address. He liked him—liked his relaxed, masculine attitude and his enthusiasm for the movies. Overholt appeared to have seen practically every Biograph picture.

Overholt was right—nobody had made a movie about oil, even though you saw the business everywhere you went in California. M. K. wondered whether there was a single spot in LA where, if you climbed up on a roof, you would fail to see an oil well. He could imagine it in a picture: the gawky rigs, the dirty men, the atmosphere of happy disaster as thick, black oil sprayed and gushed up from the ground. They could make it like a Western, only set in the industrial age.

He had trouble writing it, though. He didn't know how the business worked, and even though this had nothing to do with the plot—he concocted a story about a poor boy wanting to marry but shunned by the girl's money-hungry father—it bothered him. He felt that the basic story was all right, but the background needed realism. M. K. left a note at Overholt's hotel inviting him to the apartment.

Overholt appeared two days later on a cool, rainy night, dripping water all over the floor from a yellow slicker he wore. He had walked, he said, even though it was more than a mile from where he lived. "I like it when it rains," he said. "I like sucking in that fine wet air."

He stood taller than M. K. remembered, perhaps half a foot taller than M. K. himself. His hair was wild from being under the hood of his slicker. He was a formidable physical specimen.

"Well, who is this?" Overholt asked loudly, smiling at Linda. She was reading in her chair, her feet dangling above the floor. She stared with watchful anticipation while M. K. introduced her. "Are you in the movies like your mother?" Overholt asked. "You look just like her."

Linda didn't answer. "Yes," M. K. said for her. "She's been in several Biograph films."

"Biograph is the best."

M. K. offered to make a cup of coffee while Overholt read the script. "Call me Roy," Overholt said. "I'd love a pot of coffee." He threw himself down on the sofa, splaying his legs outward, then took the script M. K. offered and let out a deep sigh as he began to read.

When M. K. returned from the kitchen, he found Overholt staring into space. He took his cup absentmindedly, then put it down on the table, stood up solemnly, and extended his right hand. "So," he said slowly as he shook M. K.'s hand, "you're a writer. A real writer."

"Sure," M. K. said. "That and a nickel will buy you a cup of coffee."

"This is fabulous. You've got it right, brother. I don't know how you did it."

M. K.'s face broke into a grin. "You think it's good?"

Soon they were discussing the kinds of shots a director might use. Overholt turned over a page of the script and began sketching on the back. He had a free, quick hand to draw the kind of equipment drillers would use to cap a gusher. They went through the script page by page, their conversation wandering off the subject in various directions. Overholt was funny; he threw out sardonic asides that made M. K. cackle hilariously. Meanwhile Linda stayed right where she was, reading her book, hardly seeming to notice them.

It got on toward nine. M. K. suggested another pot of coffee, but Overholt said he had better go.

"I'm sorry you can't meet my wife," M. K. said. It was the first he'd realized she was late. He had forgotten all about her. At the same moment it struck him how happy he was to be able to talk and laugh and dream with another man. It was the first time in a very long time, he felt.

"Yes, I was looking forward to it. I feel like I know her, seeing her on the screen, you know."

"I know," M. K. replied. "I found it so strange when we first joined Biograph. All these vaguely familiar faces walking by, I thought I was at a family reunion."

As they stood up to say good-bye, M. K. heard the screen door open. "Oh, good," he said, "that must be her now."

They waited for her to come in, but heard only vague scratchings and shufflings against the door. Then a set of keys clattered to the concrete, and they heard a muffled sigh of despair. M. K. walked over and opened the door. Darla was bent over, picking up her keys, and when she stood, her face looked askew, as though she tried to hold it in a proper expression but had forgotten how. She had a strange, panicky look in her eyes.

"Mommy!" Linda shouted and ran to throw her arms around her legs. Darla leaned over to embrace her, but she saw Overholt and quickly straightened up. M. K. wished that he could sink into the floor and disappear. He had no doubt that Darla had been drinking. His disappointment was stronger because of how free and delighted he had felt with Overholt.

M. K. managed to introduce Overholt as the man who had given him the idea for his script.

"Gusher," Darla said.

"Excuse me, Mrs. Nichols?" Overholt said.

"Gusher. That's the name of the movie M. K. is writing, isn't it?" Darla seemed to rush her words, trying to act friendly but unable to obscure the fact that something was amiss. "I think he told me it's all about some fellas that strike it rich. Let's not be formal. Call me Darla. Have you struck it rich in the oil business?"

"Not if you mean money. I'm just a geologist."

"What else could I mean besides money?" she said with a little shriek, meaning to be funny.

She was trying very hard to be natural, M. K. could see. It was like a bicycle going forward with a wobbly wheel. He knew it could not last, but he was surprised that it went at all.

Then suddenly, without even excusing herself, Darla wrenched free from Linda and scuttled, not very gracefully, toward the bedroom. "I don't feel well," she said as she disappeared.

"I had better go," Overholt said after a short silence.

"Wait just a moment, please," M. K. said. "I'll walk with you. Let me check on her first."

The room was dark, and he saw her only as a dark lump on the bed. "Are you all right?" he asked.

"Does it matter?" she asked. "What does it matter? Go on with your friend."

"It matters to me," he hissed.

He left her and went back into the living room. Overholt had put his slicker on, and he appeared to be making some pleasantry to Linda. She had gotten back into her chair and taken up her book.

"My wife isn't feeling well," M. K. said.

"I'm sorry. She didn't look well."

"Let me walk you to the corner. Is it still raining?"

"I think it stopped."

A wet wind had picked up, and the cool air felt good in his face. M. K. did not know what he could say, but he wanted to soothe the situation. His mind was seething with embarrassment. They walked together out of the apartment garden and onto the street. "If you want to catch a trolley, you go up there three blocks," M. K. said, pointing.

"I think I want to walk. I'm not in a hurry." Overholt stopped. "You better get back to your family."

"There's no hurry," M. K. said.

Overholt heard the hint of bitterness and hesitated. "If your wife is sick, she'll want you."

"Oh, she doesn't want me. I'm the last person she wants right now." This came out of him impetuously, angrily. He felt that he was coming undone in front of this man.

"I might as well tell you the truth. The only sickness my wife feels comes out of a bottle."

A long silence reigned—at least it seemed long to M. K.

Suddenly, as if on impulse, Overholt grabbed his own coat lapel and pulled it out from his slicker for M. K. to see. They were under a streetlight. "Can you see that?" he asked. "I always wear this pin. Can you see it?"

"What is it? A boat?" The little silver pin glistened in the soft gloom.

"Yes, it's a boat. I get it for being part of the Fishermen's Club. Do you know what that is?"

"No. I don't think I've heard of it."

"The Fishermen are a group of men who have taken a pledge to be fishers of men. That means we're trying to pull others into the boat."

"What kind of boat do you mean?"

"Jesus' boat. You know, when Jesus called His disciples, He told them He wanted them to be fishers of men." Overholt paused for a moment. "I want to help you any way I can. That's the meaning of that pin. I've been pulled out of the water, and now I want to do the same for others."

Deep, sagging disappointment struck M. K. He did not want to hear about Jesus. He wanted to minimize the whole affair and get away as soon as he could. "I don't see how you can help," he said. "She gets into the bottle. It's not very often. Just once in a while. Nothing we can't handle."

"I could tell you some wonderful things I've seen," Overholt said. "Men's lives get changed around. Women's too. I never went far astray, but I was lost nonetheless. Jesus turned around my whole life and set me on a new direction."

"Yes," M. K. said in growing vexation. "I'm sure. Well, good night. I hope we can see you again."

Returning to the apartment, M. K. felt his irritation curdle. It was his mother's old creed: give it all to God. Who would have thought that a man like Overholt would come out with that?

Linda had gone back to her book. When he went to her side, she turned her cheek toward him, receiving his kiss in a sweet and elegant way. She was so delicate. "It's a bit late, tiger," he said gently. "You should be getting ready for bed."

"Can't I finish this chapter?" she asked.

"How much longer?"

She thumbed the book. "Three more pages."

"All right. But don't cheat me. Don't start another one."

M. K. went into the bedroom and sat on the bed, rubbing Darla's back. "I'm sorry," she said after substantial time had passed.

"Sorry for what?"

"Sorry that I ruined your evening."

That answer, being so trivial and maudlin, angered him. "I don't care about the evening. Why can't you see it? Darla, you're becoming a drunk!" He made a wild gesture with his arm, not seeing the lamp in the dark, and accidentally swept it off the table and onto the floor. Kerosene was everywhere and shards of glass scattered. They cleaned it up together. At least she was well enough to do that. Linda came in and they sent her sternly off to bed.

"Marion," Darla said when they finished, and she had wearily climbed back into bed without even undressing. She used his name only rarely, when she wanted his full attention. When he was a boy, he had hated to be called Marion, but he did not mind hearing it from her.

"Marion, I have some news. I haven't had a drop. Are you ready? I think I am pregnant."

For perhaps a full minute he listened to the sound of his breathing. How many emotions rushed through him: joy, foolish embarrassment for his assumptions, and relief that all was well. "Really?" he said. "Darla, really pregnant? A baby?"

"Yes," she said. "Are you happy?"

Darla did not know whether she was happy or not. She knew very well that a baby would change her life. She had been young when Linda was born, and then her work had been something she took for granted, for she had fallen into it so easily and so young. She had no thought that becoming a mother might close other doors for her. Now, though, she could not help seeing that, at the very least, she would be unable to work for some time after the baby came. After that she would be older and, perhaps to Griffith, would seem older.

M. K. listened to her worries, but he found it hard to take them seriously. He felt excited by the impending birth, and he wished his wife shared his hopefulness. This merely showed, Darla said, that he didn't care about her acting the way that she did. And he could not refute her.

Darla got just one decent role after her pregnancy began to show, in a movie made from a script M. K. wrote with her in mind. The film was a comedy in which a pregnant woman tries to spy on her husband, whom she suspects of drinking, but she accidentally makes herself conspicuous by clumsily kicking over milk bottles, tripping over a stool, and allowing her bulging profile to be seen through the doorway. This fit with Darla's sense of how ridiculous she was as a pregnant woman. In fact, the script was inspired by her complaining. She felt as graceful as a cow, she said.

During the last month, she was so uncomfortable, and the chances of a role so slight, that she stayed home. They found it difficult, both of them occupying their small apartment all day, M. K. trying to write while Darla chafed over her discomfort and her boredom. M. K. joked that his labor pains were worse than hers, but she did not laugh.

At least they had no battles over her drinking. Darla said it made her sick to think of the stuff. When M. K. told Roy Overholt this news on their way to a nickelodeon one night, Overholt stopped in the street and shook hands. He said it was a miracle, an answer to his prayers. M. K. doubted that, but he was glad that she had quit.

The baby came in November, a perfect, small baby boy whom they named David, after M. K.'s father. (Unacknowledged but just as true, he was named also for David Wark Griffith.) It happened in a small, private hospital where Mr. Griffith had insisted Darla go: a quiet, sunny place with ten or twelve beds and a garden. Griffith sent a huge bouquet of flowers, the largest the nurses had ever seen.

The labor was short, as is often the case with second children, but it seemed to M. K. that it lasted forever. He was confined to a waiting room, from which he could hear cries occasionally and distantly, and sometimes footsteps in the hospital corridor, footsteps that were sometimes so rapid he thought someone was almost running. No one told him what went on, and the cries and the footsteps would die away and leave only silence and fearful mystery. He imagined terrible things. He had her dead half a dozen times, but then the silence would swallow that up too.

Finally the doctor appeared, calm and well-tanned, smoking a cigarette, and congratulated him on having a son. M. K. was speechless with joy and relief. When the nurse finally let him walk down to his wife's room, at least an hour later, Darla was sitting up with David in her arms. She was embarrassed to be seen with her hair greasy and plastered every direction, but M. K. didn't see that. He saw that her tight and lifeless skin had been smoothed and relaxed, given color, made vital again. He was overwhelmed by a sense of astonished well-being. All his fears fell away. He found himself unable to speak.

He had studied Darla's face for any sign of injury because his fears had been all for her. Now he leaned forward, looking closely at the baby she held. "Should he be so yellow?" he asked.

"Dr. Adams says he will pink up," she said. "In a few days."

"Can I hold him?"

She held out the baby carefully, as though handling a nest of wild bird's eggs, and M. K. took the tiny figure into his hands. The density of the body was astounding: the warm, limp weight in his hands, so precious and defenseless he did not know how to handle it, so he merely held it cupped in his two hands like an offering. He remembered seeing his father hold his brother Warner.

"Hold him in your arms," Darla said. "Like this." She made the sign of cradling, and M. K. drew David cautiously in to him.

"It was worth it," he said to Darla. "It was worth all you went through, don't you think?" This came as a revelation to him. He had known that having babies made up part of the normal progress of a man and a woman on earth, but he was just discovering why.

"Yes, it was worth it," she said and reached for the baby to take him back. The moment David was out of his arms M. K. wanted him again; he felt a hunger pang to hold that shape.

A week later they carried him home on the trolley. Linda had come, too, her first chance to see her new baby brother. When they reached the apartment, Darla carried David in, talking to him all the way like a little girl playing dolls. "This is your new house, David. You see the pretty garden? This is our garden. Now we go inside. In we go. Do you see your bed?" It was so unlike her; she was so unsentimental. M. K. and Linda followed behind carrying Darla's suitcase and a bag of baby bottles and diapers and other paraphernalia they had already acquired at the hospital. When Darla put David down in his new bed, he cried only a few moments and then snuggled down to sleep. All three of them stood over him, looking down like museumgoers peering into a glass case.

Then Darla led them quietly out of the bedroom. She asked them to sit on the sofa. "I want to tell you something," she said, and then hesitated because her voice had caught. She was ordinarily serene, but overwhelming emotions had arisen. "I don't like to be overly dramatic, but I have been thinking. I'm not going to drink anymore. And not just because I've lost a taste for the stuff. This little boy is such a gift to me. Just as you are, Linda, every bit as much, but I have been very stupid, and suddenly it has come to me. I see it now." She stopped again and swallowed. "I can't waste it. I want to say this so you will hold me to it. No booze."

M. K. went to kiss her, but she was too overcome with emotion even to respond. She hung her head on his shoulder and let him squeeze her.

"Don't you want to say something to your mother?" M. K. asked Linda, who had not moved from her seat on the sofa.

"No," she said lightly.

"Aren't you happy to hear what she said?"

"Yes," Linda said. "But I want to wait and see how she does."

M. K. could only stare at her. She seemed utterly sure of herself, grown up at nine years old. "You want to wait and see how she does?" M. K. asked.

"Yes."

Chapter 6
1913: The Possibilities of Change

You could never quite tell what Griffith was thinking, what game of chess he played. One Monday in the spring of the new year, he began to refer to a script he called *The Sweetheart's Banquet*. He did not even say when the filming would begin. He told Darla in front of the whole company, however, that the script had three wonderful female parts. Everyone assumed that Mabel Normand and Lillian Gish would get two of them, but did he mean that Darla was to be given the third? She was just back to work after six months at home. There were other contenders, and Griffith made no promises or indications. Yet why, otherwise, would he tell her about the female parts?

Darla did not find it easy to leave David. She often thought of him and actually felt his warm, dense form, his firm mouth—or felt the physical absence of them—in the hours when she waited to do her bit parts. She had become a stranger at Biograph. Over the six months of her absence the company had made well over a hundred movies. People had come and gone; procedures and equipment had changed; the world had gone on. She felt, and was treated, as a newcomer. With no familiar slot to fall into, she rattled and flopped like a loose part. And then to wonder whether she would get a major part, and whether Griffith was toying with her, and for what purpose, made her extremely anxious.

On Wednesday they filmed a comedy about a family with too many children. It was a hot day, which contributed to Darla's mood. Darla disliked heat. In the middle of a spring morning Los Angeles might feel cool as mint, but if you were out in the sun in the afternoon, a baking heat flared into your face from every surface. She had only a small part in a street scene, but had to wait most of the day to be called. The bright heat glared all around as she waited under an awning. Bored and irritable, anxious about her career, she began to think about a drink.

She could not take alcohol as seriously as M. K. did. She knew it was bad for her, but alcohol was available more or less constantly in the theater, and she was used to it. Most people handled it. Even the drunks sometimes managed surprisingly well. She knew it bothered M. K. profoundly, and she remembered her pledge to him, but for her it was no great affair. Sometimes she felt that she needed the stuff—like now. The desire could obliterate everything else.

George Brubaker, who ran the film lab, kept a flask in the darkroom. She strolled back to his office, housed in a back corner of the large, old shed. *Everything at Biograph seems temporary and improvised,* she thought. The old shed had reefs of miscellaneous items strewn around— costumes, hooks, coils of wire, boxes of nails, furniture. It might have been a farm shed. *Someday I will get tired of this life,* Darla said to herself, but immediately added, *Not yet.*

"Hello, George," she said and sat down. Brubaker was sitting at a cluttered table writing purchase orders. He was a stubby man with enormous shoulders and a shaggy mustache. The office reeked of chemicals. He was not a particularly friendly man, but he liked to talk about his work.

He was not long in pulling his flask out of a drawer and offering her a drink. "It's hot today," he said. "You need to keep your strength up."

She almost told him no. He had already pulled a glass out of the drawer, however, and he quickly poured a finger into it and held it toward her. The scent seemed to jump across the room to her.

Two good drinks and she felt more relaxed. They talked about how Biograph had changed, about some of the new people. It was stuffy in the crowded little office, and Darla began to bead with sweat, but strangely enough she felt a pleasure in it after she loosened up. The smell of the liquor mingled with the perfume of the darkroom chemicals, to her not an unpleasant combination.

"Are you getting a part today?" Brubaker asked. He spoke in a Dutch accent, though he must have been an American for twenty years. At first Darla thought he referred to *The Sweetheart's Banquet* because that was on her mind. Then she realized that he meant today's film about the large family.

"I have a bit part," she said. "In fact, I had better go. It wouldn't do to be missing when Mr. Griffith calls. Thanks for the drink."

She walked out of Brubaker's office into the glare. It was the first drop she had taken since David was born. She felt more relaxed because of it but, at the same time, more anxious. She suddenly thought of her pledge—it had for a time escaped her mind. It was too late to regret now, however.

On the set they had a mock-up kitchen with a stove and about eight small children. The idea was that Mrs. O'Shaunessy tried to keep her disorderly children from going near the hot stove and burning themselves. Griffith was yelling directions, the children were swarming in and out of the camera's view, those who were meant to cry because they had touched the stove weren't demonstrating pain to Griffith's satisfaction, the supposedly exuberant children looked dull and lifeless, and two little girls with blond hair, twins evidently, had sat down on some wooden steps and begun to sob vigorously.

Griffith thought that the proper way for children to show exuberance was to skip. He could not be convinced that children did not naturally skip any more than they naturally played Hamlet. He grew more and more insistent, yelling loudly that the children must be happy and skip. He threw his hands in the air and demonstrated. The children stared at him. Darla watched the chaotic scene as though she were in a daze until Griffith saw her and turned on her. "Darla Nichols, will you please help me instead of staring like a milk cow in her stall!"

Burning with embarrassment, she stared for just a second longer and then went to the little twins and tried to quiet them.

One twin wanted to crawl into her lap, while the other sought to escape. One would stop crying, and the other would run off. Then the second would be crying when she caught her, and the first would catch the impulse and both would wail. Darla wanted to slap them, but restrained herself. Eventually she was able to get them quiet and inject them back into the scene.

The sun was poking her eyeballs, and a little green stalk of headache was beginning to grow on top of her skull. Another drink would calm her nerves, but she had drunk enough. She felt too torpid already. She felt played out, absolutely limp.

And yet the smell of the liquor, that bright, clean, cutting medicine, flashed through her senses. It would smooth off the top of the headache, making it possible for her to endure this afternoon. *If I only had one drink*, she thought, *it would not be too much, and after I have satisfied that little craving, the temptation will leave me alone.*

What if M. K. came? She had already had two drinks, and he would know it at once. *He watches so carefully, always suspicious. Nothing else seems to matter to him*, she thought.

On the other hand, two drinks or three, there was not much difference. If he showed up, M. K. would be angry with her regardless. And surely he would not come to the set, with David to care for. She was not sure she could endure these crying children as she was.

She took pride in the fact that drink never interfered with her work. She did not think Griffith even knew that she ever took any alcohol. An extra drink, if it kept her calm, could only help.

It would not hurt to see whether Brubaker was still in his office. She went quietly through the prop room. The air was heavy inside the shed, hot and still, like an attic on a summer afternoon, but she was glad to escape the shrieking glare. Nobody answered her knock. She tried the doorknob and found the little office open. She thought she would just sit down and wait until Brubaker returned. It was a good place to rest her head.

The bright, clean medicinal scent came into her mind so keenly that she salivated. If Brubaker were here, he would surely offer her a drink. Her glass was where she had left it, on his table. She picked it up, inspected it, lifted it to dribble one drop down the side and into her mouth. That was a good taste, so faint it was barely detectable, but good.

Then without even an inner argument she began pulling open Brubaker's drawers, looking for the pint. She found it, about three-quarters full, and poured herself a glass. Then she stuffed the bottle back into the drawer. Surreptitiously she drank, sipping because she wanted to enjoy it, yet anxious enough about someone finding her that she kept sipping steadily until it was all gone.

It was not something to be proud of, taking liquor on the sly, but she doubted Brubaker would mind, even if he were to notice. And how would he notice? Had he marked the bottle? Surely not. If he had wanted to hide the bottle, he could have easily enough. If he were here, he would offer her another drink.

Now, at least, the little attack was over. She could put drinking out of her mind. She had satisfied that craving, and she felt better too.

She would be able to handle those little blond dreadfuls. The stuff did relax her.

She sat in the stuffy office, waiting for Brubaker, feeling relaxed, and shortly it occurred to her. One more drink would be good. She had already had one—and she would need to explain what she had done when Brubaker came back. That would be the honest thing. She was no good at resisting anyway. She got out the bottle and poured herself another drink.

Then she lost track of time. She thought she was waiting for Brubaker, to explain that she had borrowed some of his whiskey, but he did not come. Perhaps she napped. Eventually she thought that she had been away long enough. She had better find out how the moviemaking was coming along.

When she emerged from the shed, she noticed that the light had changed. How long had she been gone? No matter, she could still see the cluster of children, with Griffith standing over them, near the camera. When she was still ten yards away, he spied her.

"Where have you been?" he asked quite loudly. "Where. Have. You. Been?" He glared. "We are trying to make a film, Mrs. Nichols. We cannot quite afford to wait on you."

She tried to answer him, to tell him that she had a headache and needed refuge from the sun, but she found that her tongue was mushy, and words would not come out right. He cut into her. "It's all right, Mrs. Nichols, we made the scene without you. You can go home now."

Of course, the news got back to M. K. since it was all over the lot. He did not talk to Darla at first—he could not, feeling that he did not trust his own reactions. If he began talking, he was afraid he would shout—or worse—and Darla had made it obvious that on this matter she considered him moralistic and officious. M. K. feared that she might slip away from him, like water between his fingers, if he made the wrong move. He felt that she no longer belonged to him, that she had drifted off out of his reach.

He tried to have it out with Brubaker, who was the suspected source of booze, but Brubaker wouldn't deal. He said in that harsh Dutch accent that what he did with his own habits was his own business. M. K. said it was his business what Brubaker did with his wife, but when Brubaker hinted about thieves and sneaks who took what did not belong to them, M. K. had no heart for it and backed off.

Whenever he tried to talk to Darla about her problem, it came out of his mouth as judgmental and stiff. He did not want to talk that way, but what other way did he have? She alternated between tearful repentance—which he always thought was false, just another way of eluding him—and angry, vengeful rebuff. Once when he tried to have a reasonable discussion, she deliberately opened the kitchen cabinet and began to smash all their dishes on the floor, one at a time. M. K. tried to stop her, and she took the whole stack of plates and threw them in his direction. Instinctively he tried to catch them, but they crashed to the ground. When she was angry, where did the tearful repentance go?

The only thing she seemed to consistently understand was that it was unprofessional to let drink interfere with her work. She was humiliated that Griffith had seen her drunk—humiliated and afraid. But she could not see, would not see, that the problem was much larger than that.

M. K. took charge of David during the day, he wasn't getting any writing done, and when evening came, he desperately wanted to go somewhere and do something. Many evenings he went out with Roy Overholt. Overholt had no family, so he was always ready to go. They usually went to the movies, always inviting Darla to go along. Sometimes she did, and then Linda and David came too. With Overholt along, they had no choice but to keep up a pleasant front, and that was all to the good. Apart from liquor they could be as happy together as ever.

But Darla often told M. K. to go without her since she needed to get up early the next day. The truth was that the two men had more fun when they were alone. Sometimes they went to two shows in a night, taking in as many as eight or ten reels, and then would walk in the warm night air for miles and talk about what they had seen. M. K. would get home past midnight and find Darla asleep.

Overholt was a very religious man, and he frequently invited M. K. to church meetings. Fortunately he was easily put off. M. K. did agree to go to church on Easter since that was a special day: brighter, more active than other church Sundays, a sort of spring pageant. If he were in charge of a church, it would be all Easter Sundays. Also, he wanted to give Overholt the satisfaction of hearing him say yes to at least one of his invitations.

Church had become torturous for M. K. during high school and college. He never felt better than on a Sunday morning when he was able to get up and think that he was his own man and did not have to go to church, not ever. Yet on this Easter he found that he enjoyed dressing up. Darla looked simply stunning in a blue-and-white dress with a wide straw hat. He enjoyed the impression they made going together. He liked feeling Darla's hands on his chest as she adjusted his tie.

Yet when Overholt asked them to go again, M. K. put him off. He had gone once, it had been fine, but that was enough.

He did go to the Fishermen's Club, only because Overholt pressed him so hard. "It's for men only," he said, "young fellows our age." That appealed to M. K. or at least made him curious. Overholt said it was not a church service, even though they met at the same Immanuel Presbyterian Church where he had taken them at Easter.

At the meeting M. K. found himself grimacing more than once as some neat young fellow in a suit gripped his hand with iron fingers. M. K. guessed there were about eighty in attendance who all seemed to know each other. A corps of cheerful middle-aged women served them a solid meal, and then the men cleared the tables themselves and crowded into a large classroom. Someone banged out a hymn on the piano, and they sang lustily. Halfway through, it occurred to M. K. that he might have been in one of the German beer halls his father's friends frequented, singing songs of the fatherland.

An older man with thinning gray hair and an easy manner got up and introduced himself as "Daddy" Horton. "This is the man I told you about," Overholt whispered. "The godliest man I know. He founded the club." Horton introduced their speaker, Dr. R. A. Torrey, as the new head of the Bible Institute of Los Angeles. Torrey was a large, solemn man who stood up to the podium with his front side puffed out like a penguin. He launched into them using a very strong tone, and at that point M. K. wished he had never agreed to come. He did not want to get browbeaten with religion.

He changed his mind about Torrey, however. Torrey's text came from Isaiah, the passage where Isaiah sees God in the temple. What struck M. K. was that Torrey did not plead with them to come to God, as though God were a simpering female. No, he warned them that they must justify themselves before a holy God. He did not beg them to come; he informed them as men they would be brought into the awesome presence.

M. K. found himself thinking of Darla and her problem. In Torrey's terminology, she had chosen darkness over light. She was cultivating sin, which the holy searching eyes of God must see and cleanse by fire. He wondered how Darla would respond to a message like this. Perhaps this was the warning that would get her attention. Perhaps a man like Torrey could reach her where M. K. could not.

At home after the meeting he tried to tell her how it all had struck him. "I thought of you, darling," he said shyly. "I wondered whether it would help you with the drinking."

"I don't think religion has got anything to do with it," she said with a look in her eye that warned him to lay off.

———————

Even though Darla begged him not to, M. K. went to talk to Griffith. "She's getting booze on the lot," he said. "Somebody in the company is helping her get it." He had followed Griffith home to his hotel, and they sat in the dim, deserted dining room with its heavy ruby tapestries. Griffith sat poking at his salad with his fork. His large, heavy face showed no trace of emotion.

"She won't tell you who this is, though?" Griffith asked.

"She says it is her fault and has nothing to do with anybody else."

"Don't you think she is right about that?"

"Not really. Yes, she is responsible for what she drinks. But when someone is very susceptible to temptation, other people matter. She doesn't want to drink. She's weak."

Griffith took a bite of salad, chewed it slowly with his powerful jaws, swallowed carefully, and then said, "I'm sorry to hear this. I admire Darla, as I hope you know already. She has considerable talent."

"Such a talent can be ruined by drink."

Griffith nodded thoughtfully and went unhurriedly back to his salad. Eventually he asked, "Why did you come to tell me about this? Especially since Darla asked you not to?"

"One word from you, and that will be the end of the supply."

"Do you mean for me to talk to the particular individual? I don't know who that would be."

"I thought if you talked to the whole company, there would be no need to identify anybody in particular."

"Suppose I did that and they paid me no attention. Suppose the liquor continued."

"I don't think it would. They look up to you like a god."

"Well, perhaps, but I am not an avenging god. I do not swoop down with my talons on anyone who disobeys my word. That is not how Biograph works."

"I'm not asking you to punish anyone. Just a word from you and the thing would come to a stop and quickly."

"You think so, do you? I think you underestimate the appetite of a theater company." Griffith paused, holding his fork poised in the air, his hooded eyes bearing down hard on M. K. "If I say it, as the boss of our little company, I must mean it. And that means I must be willing to punish it. I am sorry, Mr. Nichols, but I don't think I can help you. I would do anything I could for Darla, as well as for you and Linda and little David. But I cannot turn Biograph into some kind of army camp."

"Mr. Griffith, plenty of companies have rules against drinking."

"That may be so, but what do those companies make? Bolts? Steamships? Making movies is a different matter and requires a different kind of atmosphere."

M. K. had to walk all the way back home since the last streetcar had gone. It was a warm spring night with the perfume of flowers in the air—the sort of night when it is nearly impossible to imagine evil stalking the earth. M. K. had not anticipated Griffith's complete resistance. And now, thinking it over, M. K. could not account for it. What was Griffith's objection exactly? Did he fear some loss of his dignity? Was he leery of being taken for a killjoy? Was it possible that Griffith was something of a drinker himself?

A moon was rising out of the eastern sky, fat and yellow. Griffith would not change his mind. He never did, no matter how people talked to him. He was stubborn in the way that geniuses are.

Perhaps they should quit Biograph and leave LA. If Darla could get away from the people providing her with drink, she would be fine. Perhaps even in Ohio. But M. K. could not think of returning to Ohio. Surely they need not give up everything and flee. He would be embarrassed even to suggest it to Darla.

The answer must lie in her. She needed to give up the stuff. Of course, she had done that when David was born. With such sincerity of heart, she had pledged it!

———————

Darla heard M. K.'s key in the lock and felt her stomach tighten. She sat in their only upholstered chair, a square, upright green seat. M. K., who liked to sprawl, complained that the chair was uncomfortable, but Darla sat up straight, her back barely touching. She hated that M. K. had gone to see Mr. Griffith—hated because it humiliated her.

Her difference from M. K. was that she took things as they came, and he projected forward, so that a single cloud became a hurricane, and a particular event predicted a life. He thought too much.

M. K. came in looking sad and sober, but Darla was relieved to see him calm. He heaved a sigh and collapsed on the sofa. "I thought it out all the way home, Darla. I realized I can't stop your drinking. Griffith could, I think, but he won't do it."

Suddenly struck with tenderness for him, she got out of her chair to go and sit by him. "Am I really so bad?" she asked, curling against him.

"I didn't say you were bad, Darla."

"But you worry about me, don't you?"

"Yes, you and Linda and David. Our children, Darla. What kind of life will they have if their mother can't control her habits? Where can it lead?"

She said nothing but buried her head in his shoulder.

"I want you to think about this, Darla. You know and I know where the bottle leads. You've seen it and I've seen it."

"All right," she said. "I'm sorry."

"It's not enough to be sorry. You have to do something." Trying to contact her eyes with his, he lifted her chin.

"I try," she said, pulling away. "Marion, I do try. You don't give me any credit. There have been so many times I have said no. There are so many people who put temptation in my way. Give me credit for those times I say no."

"All right, full credit for the times you show some self-control, but, darling, that's not enough. Please, Darla, this is terribly important to me. And to you. And to our children."

"All right, Marion, I know it is important, but why do you nag me so much? I can't understand how you could humiliate me by going to Mr. Griffith. You are treating me like a child!"

"If you act like a child, what am I to do? Darla, I have tried everything I can to help you. And you promised. Right here on this very sofa, with nobody pressing you to do it, you told me and Linda that you would stop. That's the way it should be, Darla. You should realize how important this is and make the decision yourself. If you won't do that, should I just sit back? Well, I guess so because Griffith doesn't take it seriously and I guess you don't, either."

"You are so egotistical," Darla answered.

"Egotistical!" The word made him raise his voice. "Is it egotistical to care about you? How is it egotistical?"

"You have to have it just the way you want it," she said.

They made up in the morning, and for Darla the argument became just one more problem in the background of her life. The question of how Griffith would treat her was far more pressing, and she was relieved when he gave her a good part that week.

On the other hand, M. K. replayed the conversation, making quite a domestic drama out of it. He embellished every comment in his mind. He suspected that Darla believed he, not she, had caused the fight—that she was the victim of his unreasonable and demanding nature. It was very odd. Darla's life was crazy, and he showed the symptoms. He frothed at the mouth, he ranted, while she was calm and reasonable.

When M. K. brought it up with Overholt, looking for sympathy, Overholt surprised him by telling M. K. how to get his own life right rather than Darla's. Overholt took a stricter view of alcohol than even M. K., but for Overholt every issue was fundamentally simple: either you had Jesus or you didn't. He was quite sure that M. K. didn't. Darla didn't, either, but M. K. couldn't do her the least amount of good until he put himself right with God. It was just a waste of time to try to be good without the power of Jesus.

M. K. had heard his line of thought, albeit in a different form, all his life. Jesus, Jesus, Jesus had been the full text of his mother's philosophy. Fortunately for their friendship, Overholt didn't badger him or make emotional speeches. He had his point of view, but he didn't weep or moan about it. M. K. felt that so long as he let Overholt know exactly where he stood, he would not bring up Jesus too much.

One evening as they were walking home, Overholt asked M. K. whether he had ever asked Jesus into his heart.

"Look, Roy," M. K. said, feeling that he had reached the limit, "I went to Oberlin College. You could take every Holy Roller in Los Angeles and put them together, and one floor in one dormitory at

Oberlin could out-Jesus them in five minutes. I know all about Jesus. I live a decent life. Don't you think that's enough?"

Roy said it wasn't good enough. He said that if M. K. had given Jesus his life, he would be on fire for Jesus. He said that Jesus would wash away all his sins.

"Well, all right. What sins are we talking about?" That stopped him, but only temporarily.

Overholt wasn't hysterical the way his mother had been, but he persisted. A couple of times M. K. tried to pull out Darwin or science or contradictions in the Bible, but since he had been educated at Oberlin and not Ohio State, he did not have these laid down in his mind as familiar touchstones. That didn't take him far against Overholt's confidence, especially since Overholt was a geologist who probably knew more science and certainly more Bible than he did. M. K. could have found books to bolster his skepticism, but he didn't care that much.

M. K. maintained that he was a Christian, baptized, confirmed, educated. To ask for more seemed unfair, even fanatical. Overholt said that true religion was a matter of the heart and the spirit, that he was not called to judge M. K.'s religion but that anybody could see the moon and call it yellow.

"What do you want me to do?" M. K. asked one night as they circled the block, talking, after coming back from a Fishermen's meeting. "You've got me going to those meetings. What more do you want?"

"I don't care if you never go to another meeting," Overholt answered. "Going to a meeting won't forgive your sins. It won't keep you from hellfire. God is the only One who can do that."

"Who says He won't?"

"Who says He will? How do you know you're right with God?"

"Well, how do *you* know? How does anybody know for sure?"

"I know because I have the sure promise of God," Overholt said, "written down in God's own Word, the Bible. That's the only authority to put your weight on, M. K. It says there, 'If thou shalt confess with thy mouth the Lord Jesus, and shalt believe in thine heart that God hath raised him from the dead, thou shalt be saved.' Romans 10:9. That's my authority. The Bible says you must believe and confess your faith out loud. If you've done that, it's settled. Have you ever done that? Ever believed and confessed?"

Suddenly Overholt's voice seemed to come on M. K.'s ear as though from some distant reach. "The Bible also says, in Jesus' very words, 'Behold, I stand at the door, and knock: if any man hear my voice, and open the door, I will come in to him, and will sup with him, and he with me.' Revelation 3:20. Have you ever opened the door to Jesus?"

M. K. tried to think whether he had, in fact, ever put himself right with God in this way. Though the Bible verses rang familiar, he could not remember ever hearing the message. A vague sense hung over him that even with his religious upbringing he had perhaps never believed, perhaps never confessed. M. K. had stopped his forward progress down the sidewalk. He was thinking so hard that he forgot to move his feet.

"I don't know." He felt great turbulence of soul, feeling sorely unsure.

"You can know right now. It's a very easy thing to pray the sinner's prayer. We can do it right here and now, and you'll be cleansed and directed toward heaven from the moment when you do."

M. K.'s head felt absolutely stuffed with buzzing ideas. He did not know his own status before God, and he felt that there were many questions he needed to raise within himself. One idea, however, did not quite sink beneath the others. He must help Darla at all costs.

"Why not make your eternal destiny sure? You can know for sure where you are headed if you want to."

Surely Overholt was right. If he could be sure, why not be sure?

M. K.'s head felt as large as a house. He was thinking at a high speed, but the ideas just flashed past, and he could not stop them to examine them closely.

"It's not so difficult," Overholt said. "If you want to be sure of your relationship with Christ, you can do it in a few minutes. Don't you want to? Only pride keeps men from it."

M. K. reached out to the question like a lifeline. Did he want to? "Yes," he said. "Yes."

Overholt made him get down on his knees on the sidewalk. Overholt knelt facing him, placing his two hands on his shoulders. He told M. K. to bow his head and pray the words of the prayer after him. He led him, one phrase at a time, through what he called the sinner's prayer. It was a very simple set of requests with no confusing words: admitting his sinfulness and his need for Jesus as his Savior, and requesting that Jesus take hold of his life, forgive his sins, and give him eternal life.

"Jesus Christ, I pledge my life to You."

"Jesus Christ, I pledge my life to You."

"With Your help I will obey Your Word."

"With Your help I will obey Your Word."

"And follow You all the days of my life."

"And follow You all the days of my life."

"In the name of Jesus. Amen."

"In the name of Jesus. Amen."

Overholt stood up and pulled on M. K.'s hand to lift him. He threw his arms around him in an emphatic hug. "Now you know," he said with a triumphant flourish. "Now you know for sure that you are a child of God. No matter how you feel, you can be certain from this day on that Jesus has entered your heart because He always does just what He promises."

But M. K. did not feel that he knew it for sure. He felt no different, except more confused and disturbed than ever. He had said the words, but he was not certain of the state of his heart as he had said them.

When M. K. got back to the apartment, he found that Darla had gone to bed. He was, to tell the truth, relieved. He felt remarkably weary, as though he had shoveled sand all day. Overholt had reminded him that real faith involved "confessing with your mouth." He did not really want to tell Darla about the events of the night. He was glad to put that off until at least the morning. He was glad to escape into sleep.

Chapter 7
1913: Judith of Bethulia

M. K. sprawled in the middle of their bed, covers kicked into a tangle. The sun was streaming in the window, and he could hear not a sound from the front room. Ordinarily he did not lie in bed, but today it seemed that he could stretch out forever in these warm sheets, floating in time. M. K. felt deliciously lazy. Where could his family be?

The memory of last night came back to him. He remembered the prayer he had prayed, and the fatigue and frustration that had weighed on him when he went to bed. He did not feel any of that now.

Had he really knelt with Roy? On the sidewalk? Recalling it brought M. K. a surge of energy and excitement.

Quite suddenly the reason for his feelings dawned on him. He was— what had Overholt called it?—a new creature. Last night that had seemed as far off as the moon. This morning it seemed demonstrably true. He felt as though every molecule in his body had been exchanged.

He could not recall ever in his life *wanting* to pray, but in the night, while he slept, it had become as definable a want as hunger or thirst. M. K. wanted to pray.

He got out of bed and checked the front room. Nobody was there. Linda had long since gone to school. Darla had left a nice note telling him that she had taken David to Maria's. M. K. felt his heart fill up with love for

Darla, and for David, and for Linda. It came effortlessly, not that he *should* love them, but that he did. Still in his pajamas he knelt by the sofa and began to pray for Darla. The words came easily, tumbling out. He was full of compassion, full of love. He felt no more desire to shout at her.

How amazing! he thought. *How wonderful!*

Darla had noticed how peacefully her husband slept. Usually he got up with her, but today he was as still and soft as a lump of butter. She let him lie and took David to Maria's in the baby carriage. Maria lived only three blocks away, and her house was already bustling with Mexican brothers and sisters. They all seemed to light on David at once, treating him like a little god, hugging him, tickling him to make him laugh.

Darla took the trolley line to its end, from where Griffith had arranged cars to transport them to the set at Chatsworth Park. They were carried far out into the hills and dumped at a flat spot churning with dust and people in the pale early light.

Nothing she or anybody had seen in the movies prepared them for what was happening at Chatsworth Park. Griffith had erected an entire street for Bethulia, the Israelite city. The Assyrian army had a tent city of its own. There were scores of horses, and behind the tents, under some oak trees, what looked to be real chariots, eight of them. People said he would film a real battle.

For five years Griffith had been producing one-reel films on almost a daily basis, movies that the nickelodeons ground up like sausage. A few companies had begun to make multireel films, which they distributed first to vaudevilles or opera houses around the country, and then eventually rented to the nickel theaters when the prints were torn and burned and mended and scratched. Not Biograph, though. Features were expensive to make, and they required special treatment to sell. Nothing was easier or more profitable than one-reel films that the nickelodeons would take in almost unlimited quantities.

Griffith complained that he was forced to paint on a canvas the size of a postage stamp. He began to talk in hints about something far grander, a film he called *Judith*.

In the spring he had begun to call meetings with the men who built sets. In the evening rehearsals he occasionally tried on scenes. The story of *Judith* was epic and biblical, a Jewish woman who saves the nation of Israel by seducing Nebuchadnezzar's general and then beheading him in his sleep.

Now, finally, they were ready. Whether New York knew or understood was irrelevant. The location was crawling with unfamiliar faces, and those familiar persons whom Darla greeted seemed as lost as she was. Some asked her where they were to go and what they were to do.

She at least knew her role: Judith's maid. Griffith had created a subplot in which the maid disguised herself as a man and joined the army. She would fight bravely against the Assyrians in one of the early battles, though the Assyrians would win in a rout. Then she would return to her mistress, the beautiful but widowed Judith, and admit her duplicity. This was the mechanism by which Judith would be introduced into the story.

It was a good role, the first significant part Darla had been given since David was born, and certainly a plum in this amazing project. She wished for a script to study. Reading and rereading the Bible version (for Judith was part of the Catholic Bible), she had learned nothing helpful. There the maid showed no personality at all. Perhaps it would be up to her to invent the role.

Darla wandered the location, marveling at the work in progress, looking for Griffith. She came upon a handful of Biograph familiars sitting on a fallen log on a hillside above the set for Bethulia. Someone had seen Griffith, and he had said to wait there. A bottle was passed. Darla took a drink before she even thought what she was doing. Then it was too late, and the liquor was a warm glow in her stomach. When the bottle passed again, she took another slug.

She despised herself for being weak, but she also despised M. K.'s moral superiority. It made her hate to go home. He would look down on her and question her. His neck would go stiff and his speech ponderous as he showed his righteousness. Darla hated that.

Instead, to her surprise, he greeted her quietly and warmly. They ate stew together out of their large, white soup bowls while she told him about the day's filming. Griffith had eventually orchestrated a massive crowd scene among the army of the Assyrians. He had stood on a ladder and shouted through a megaphone. M. K. was extremely interested in her description of the logistics. Darla did not tell him about the waiting or the liquor, and he did not ask.

"What did *you* do today?" she finally asked.

He hesitated for a moment, as though trying to gather his thoughts. "I prayed," he said at last, "and I read the Bible." M. K. looked at her with a little idiot grin, and then he broke into an incredulous laugh. "Darla, the most amazing thing has happened to me. Last night when I was out with Roy, I prayed to commit my life to Christ. He had asked me why I shouldn't be certain about it. So I prayed with him. It was very simple and no mumbo jumbo, and at the time it didn't seem to do anything for me. I wasn't even sure it was real. But something wonderful has happened. This morning I woke up a completely changed man. Darla, I can't tell you how remarkable I feel. Have you ever known me to read the Bible before? I wasn't even sure we had a

Bible. But today I couldn't stop reading it. I didn't even know what was in there. Have you ever read it?"

She tried to be happy for him, but he made her quite uneasy. She had never understood why some people wanted to talk about God. It was like old people talking about their teeth.

M. K. got the Bible and wanted to read a passage to her. He tried to explain it, not noticing that her face was bland and unresponsive. *He's like a drunk,* she thought suddenly. *He's not aware of his surroundings.*

M. K. asked if she would like to pray with him. "Why don't you pray for us both?" she said. When he did, she noticed the very happy tone of his voice, almost like a kitten purring. While she listened her attitude changed. It had been a long time since she had seen him so cheerful, and a long time since he had talked to her so easily. He did not have the unpleasant saw blade edge that religious people often get, wanting you to agree with them or else they very quickly start rasping on you.

When he had finished praying, she leaned over and kissed him. "What made you do that?" he asked.

"I like seeing you so happy," she said. "You're very attractive."

He leaned over and kissed her. Midway through the kiss, he put his arms around her and pressed close against her. Her hands ran up and down his back. They sank down in the sofa together, pressed close.

Very early in the morning M. K. got up and made breakfast while Darla dressed. They ate porridge with just a single lamp between them on the table. They talked softly, in fact little at all, to avoid waking Linda.

M. K. walked her to the trolley. They were the only ones standing in the shadowy street, still lit by streetlights, though one team of horses clattered past on the pavement. M. K. had already examined his feelings and found the same dreamy peace, as soft as whipped cream. He expected that Darla must be feeling at least some of the same emotions he did, but really he did not find it easy to focus on her at all. He was caught up in his own bubble, which reflected only his own image back at him. He had a difficult time thinking any harm because such overwhelming joy rose up in himself.

He did notice, as they waited, that Darla was tapping her fingernails against her purse. This surprised him because he recognized it as something she did when she was agitated. In fact, he associated it with her problems with alcohol.

"Do you have a trying day ahead?" he asked.

"Griffith said he would film my war scenes," she said. "I don't know what he wants."

He recognized the tone. She could become very tense trying to please Griffith. "He'll tell you what he wants," he said. "Mr. Griffith will have thought of everything. He wouldn't give you this part if he weren't confident you can do it."

"Of course I can do it," she said. "I'm a professional."

The streetcar was rattling toward them. "Yes, you are," he said and kissed her on the cheek.

The rest of the day he spent almost idly, daydreaming. He had intended to work on a script, but he found himself happily distracted by his thoughts. Linda was at school, David at Maria's house again. M. K. thought that he ought to have kept David since he couldn't seem to get any work done. However, he was happy to be alone. Somehow, sometime, his mind would light on something he could write. He simply could not focus in his current state of mind. Once again he found himself reading the Bible, although today he also found himself laying the book down for long stretches of time to wonder at what had happened to him.

He had not even thought of Overholt, so it came as a surprise when he heard a knock at the door. Overholt's smooth, energetic face gave him a happy jolt, and he could barely get him in the door before he began telling him the news.

Overholt wanted to know every detail of M. K.'s transformation, and of Darla's response. He loved to hear that M. K. had been reading the Bible, and he wanted to know just what parts. The two of them walked over to Maria's house to get David, and at the apartment again they talked on while the baby guzzled his bottle. Linda came home and showed a picture she had made at school. Even she seemed to catch some of their excitement. There seemed so much to talk about. All the facts of M. K's life had been suddenly imbued with hope and color.

Overholt thought M. K. should write scripts based on the Bible. When M. K. described the sets Griffith had built for *Judith,* Overholt said anything was possible in film now, even the plagues of Egypt. They got out the Bible, and he showed M. K. stories he barely remembered from Sunday school, stories like Esther and Gideon.

The sun sank and they cooked meat loaf and ate together with Linda, talking and teasing her. After putting her to bed, they went outside and sat on the grass in the little apartment garden until it was late and Overholt thought he ought to go.

"Where do you suppose Darla is?" he asked.

"I don't know. They were going to film her part in the battle today. They must have been caught up in that."

On her way to Chatsworth Park, Darla thought a little of M. K.'s religion. Since he seemed happier and less meddling—since it did not interfere with her—she let it go rather quickly. She thought of *Judith*. The maid was so anonymous in the story, so lacking in personality, that she was almost a bit part. Yet Griffith had enlarged her part, giving it a heroic dimension, using it to bring the audience into the main story. Perhaps Griffith in his devious way had deliberately dangled it before her to see if she could steal the show. So Darla hoped.

Yet she was unsure whether Griffith even minded her. He liked her, yes; he had sent her flowers in the hospital. When his mind turned to business, however, when he looked for faces to light the screen, perhaps he did not think of her. She thought sometimes that he considered her a friend but not a first-rate talent. That kind of thought could make her anxious and angry.

At Chatsworth Park she found that, as yesterday, she had to wait. Again, as yesterday, she began to drink from a bottle she was offered. By the time Griffith called for her in midmorning, she felt more relaxed and focused.

In the opening scenes, as Griffith explained them, she was to over-hear plans for battle, then sneak out and dress herself in a soldier's uni-form, disguising her femininity. She would march with the army into battle.

Griffith called her over before the scene in which she would steal a soldier's uniform. He was wearing a wide-brimmed black hat with the entire crown cut out. Someone, perhaps Lillian Gish, his latest favorite, had told him that the sun would stimulate his hair to grow. He looked slightly bizarre with his black coat and tie and the misshapen hat.

"Darla," he said, "you are a beautiful girl, but you must remember in this scene your beauty is in the background. Of course, we see you are a woman, but you make yourself a warrior. Put your womanhood aside. You go into battle as a man. Remember, a warrior is what we want to see."

While they were filming, Griffith kept urging her toward greater expression. "More furtive, Darla. Haven't you ever seen a cat sneaking? Move like that. Think how a cat moves."

He did not seem pleased with her effort, however. In fact, he filmed her twice, which he very rarely would do. "Courage," he kept shouting at her as she seized the clothes and put them on. "Have you never seen a man who wants to fight? Courage!"

When they finished that scene, he said nothing to Darla, not a word of praise. It was early afternoon. Darla had not eaten, and she felt slightly faint. The sun was hot and the dust had stuck to her face, so she felt grit in her nose, in her eyes, and on her lips when she licked them. They would film the scene of battle next, but Griffith needed time to explain the movement of troops and line them up in position. Darla was placed in a square of soldiers who were then left in the sun for an hour. Somebody passed a bottle along, and Darla eagerly reached out and took a pull, then another. Courage! That was what he wanted. Well, they said that alcohol gave a person artificial courage.

Filming the battle was unlike any acting she had ever done. Darla never knew what she was to do or whether she did it poorly or well. They ran en masse one way. They ran back. They ran toward a contingent of Assyrians. They hacked with their wooden weapons. The chariots maneuvered among them. Sometimes the horses were urged into a gallop and the chariots bounced behind, almost comically. Then the operations ceased, and they stood in the heat for an hour or two.

Only once was Darla clear that she herself, individually, stood in the camera's eye. When the troops raced into battle, she was carefully positioned to be visible. They ran across the camera's view three times. Each time Griffith shouted at her, "You are a warrior, Mrs. Nichols!"

The men griped. They saw no sense in what they did. Most of them were not actors, but had come to earn a few dollars and to see what it was like to be in a movie. They complained of the heat; they said that the uniforms didn't fit and they scratched. Several flasks were circulating now. Whenever they had to charge, the men would compete to shout the most ridiculous slogans. One blond-headed man with a large stomach insisted on "Vote for Taft!" and soon there were factions shouting for Taft, Roosevelt, and Wilson.

This was all good-natured, even if uncomfortable and hot, but Darla found herself increasingly agitated. She felt that her career was vanishing as she ran back and forth—that nothing could come out of this heat and chaos, where she could not even know when the camera was on her. If she could only think, think clearly, how to seize the opportunity. She felt she needed to act, but her thoughts were sloppy and unfocused. Alcohol had blurred her, yet in her anxiety she took more. Half the troops were tipsy now. Some had begun to sing old Republican campaign songs.

In the midst of the army's rout, she was to climb into the back of a chariot and escape to her mistress. The way Griffith conceived it, the action was complicated. The army would run from the Assyrians, and three chariots would race after. In the confusion of battle Darla would climb into one of the chariots, throttle the driver, and take the reins herself, running away. The trouble was that the troops were half-drunk and did not listen, the horses were tired from being in harness all day, and Griffith was inexperienced at directing crowd scenes.

The first time they tried it, the action was so laborious that the horses barely reached a walk, then stopped and waited patiently while Darla ran across the scene and got into the chariot. Griffith shouted through his megaphone, "No, no, no. There must be dust and speed. The chariot must be impeded by the desperate army. Move, move, move!"

They did it again. This time the three chariots came down on the army at such breakneck speed that the men took one look at them and scattered. They thought they would be run down, as indeed they might have been. Darla held her ground, however, and as she saw the chariots coming, she conceived of something she might never have done if she were thinking clearly. She decided to leap into the chariot as it passed. That would make the scene great. That would show great courage.

Then she thought better of it. She thought the chariots moved too quickly. She feinted toward one, then pulled back, whirled and ran away, directly into the path of another. It happened so quickly, no one had time to call out, nor did the driver of the chariot have opportunity to slow the horses. Darla was run down.

Griffith was the first to get to her, but she was already unconscious. The horse must have kicked her in the head, they decided, for she had no mark on her except some ugly bruises on her arm and a small trickle of blood from her ear.

Book II
The Power to Do Good

Chapter 8
1914: Beginning Again

When M. K. thought of LA now, its dry, colorless climate repelled him. He didn't care whether he ever went back. The place and all its memories, good and bad, could be bagged up and discarded from his life. He had left all that; it was gone forever. The thought of palm trees made him sick.

Washington was mercifully different. Here, even with the sun out and the jewel-green shores of the Sound stunning his eyes, there was no warmth. The wind tore out of the west, pushing long strands of cloud and nicking up whitecaps on the water. It was hard weather, and somehow it seemed right to him, like a hermit's island pitched to his misery.

M. K. Nichols sat in the glassed-in cabin of the Everett ferry, reflecting on the difference that weather and place made in his mental state. Washington brought memories of Darla, too, but they were different memories, uncomplicated romantic memories of their first weeks together. He could venture those memories. They were the sort he had always thought one might carry from a beloved, gripping the heart but not with nails. That was simply because there had been no hint of alcohol in their lives when they were here.

Almost a year had gone by since Darla's death, and just now he was beginning to feel like a human being again, to have an interest in his surroundings. It was not that the pain had diminished very much. With no effort at all he could recapture her just as he had first seen her when they called him to Chatsworth Park. All the way there in Griffith's black car he had curled up within himself, afraid to ask how badly she was hurt. They had taken him to where she lay on her back in one of the Assyrian tents, splayed out in a careless sleeping posture like a rag thrown on the ground. He had known she was gone. Mere carcass she had seemed, like any dead thing, horse, dog, or cow, and when he thought of it now, he wanted to hurt someone, even himself.

No, the pain had not diminished much. The difference was that he thought of it less. Once Darla had filled the whole horizon, and now she had fallen far enough behind that her death had taken a smaller perspective, the way a distant high mountain may seem to be on a level with other, lesser mountains that stand nearby.

He made himself remove his mind's eye from Darla and focus on his company on the ferry. He was sitting on a bench across from George Conger, the man national headquarters of the Anti-Saloon League had sent to Seattle three years before to revive the state organization. Next to Conger but a little apart on the polished wooden bench sat Mark Matthews, the towering, skeletal pastor of the First Presbyterian Church of Seattle, the largest Presbyterian church in the world. Seated alongside M. K. was Evelyn Amble, a dimpled, talkative woman with a simple, wholesome, animated face. Evelyn came from a well-off timber family, had graduated recently from the University of Washington, and now gave many hours of her time at the Seattle ASL office.

"Mr. Conger tells me that you once lived in Everett," Evelyn said to M. K., and he nodded without looking at her. He felt that Evelyn was attracted to him, and he could not bear to even think of it.

"It's a curious town," Matthews said. "Perhaps you can explain it to me. First they voted to go dry, then two years later they went wet again. My friends tell me that it's full of Reds. They tell me that the most popular Saturday dance is given by the Karl Marx Club."

"It's a mill town," M. K. said, glad to talk and distract his mind from his memories. "That explains most of its peculiarities. Everybody's position is defined by the mills. Are you an owner? You belong here. Are you a worker? Then you're over here. The shopkeepers and the businessmen try to balance both sides."

"And who is for temperance?" Matthews asked.

"The churches primarily. Businessmen think temperance will hurt trade. Mill owners think their workers will go to Seattle to drink, and they'll have a harder time getting them back on Monday. And the workers are split between the ones who want to make Everett a decent place for their children and the ones who just want to be left alone to drink."

"What about the Reds?" Matthews asked.

"It depends on which ones. A lot of them voted dry in '10," M. K. said. "Of course, they don't feel very happy working on the same side as the churches. But they see the saloons as stealing from the workingman, keeping him from saving any money or having any backbone."

They docked in Gardner Bay at a dingy industrial wharf. The wind practically carried them uphill along Hewitt Avenue, past the saloons and the cheap hotels, and into the commercial district. *You don't have to think of her*, M. K. told himself. *She's not here.* He could not help it, however. Her memory was printed on the street. It was a happy memory, and he let it come. He remembered running into her right here in that polka-dot dress.

They met the local temperance leaders in an office above a grocery store. Three were ministers: a Presbyterian, a Methodist, and a Baptist. Another man owned the grocery store downstairs, and the fifth was a teacher. They all shook hands solemnly, wearing the same hangdog expression, unhappy and determined, and they told the same story when they sat down to talk. Everett had gone to the dogs since they repealed local option. The saloon owners had brought in prostitution and gambling, the town was full of drunkards and vagrants and unemployed people, and crime was out of control. The pastors said they got men coming to their churches every day asking for loans because they had drunk everything up.

"You're very fortunate, I can tell you, that you made it up Hewitt without being propositioned or robbed," the Baptist minister, Pastor Towns, said. He was a round-faced, pink-skinned little man with a hank of black hair lying down on his forehead.

A lot of the businessmen stood against doing anything to clean up the town, they said, because it would only send the loggers to Seattle on Sundays. "What they can't see is that the saloons are at the heart of all our troubles," Pastor Towns said. "A timber economy is going to go up and down. We can't help that. But what does a town do with those variables?"

George Conger cleared his throat. "You're describing why we need this state law," he said. "People won't have to fight this out in every municipality in the state. And we won't pit town against town anymore. Every place will live by the same laws.

"The thing to stress," Conger added, "is that it's a moderate measure. It doesn't make drinking illegal. It makes the liquor business illegal. A man can still import his own whiskey if he wants to, and he can drink it in his own home if his wife will let him. Measure Three doesn't outlaw any of that. What we're going to outlaw is one man making a living off his fellow human beings' weakness. You want to keep the emphasis there. Even people who drink will vote against the saloon."

"Mr. Conger, are you saying we're not taking a stand against drunkenness?" The question came in a waspish tone from Pastor Towns.

"I'm saying that we're hoping to win this election," Conger said dryly. "To do that, we must win the votes of the moderate factions. The saloon and the liquor traffic are their weak points. For the drunkard they may feel some sympathy."

That evening they met in a larger gathering at the Methodist church, about forty men including most of the city's pastors. Matthews preached a roaring sermon regarding "the snare of the fowler"—the pernicious trap of the saloon, which lured men in with the appearance of harmlessness, and never let them escape.

M. K. felt his heart pounding hard in his chest as he listened. Matthews was a fine, strong preacher who painted a lurid picture of the evils of the liquor business, the coldheartedness of those who lived by destroying others' lives, especially the poor men who bought whiskey instead of shoes for their little children. He quoted from the 139th Psalm: "'Do not I hate them, O LORD, that hate thee? And am not I grieved with those that rise up against thee? I hate them with perfect hatred: I count them mine enemies.'

"It is not enough," Matthews said while leaning his tall, bony frame forward over the rostrum. "I say it is *not* enough to worry about evil. It is not enough to complain about evil. It is not even enough to pray about evil. We have got to hate it. We can, if we will, eliminate the evils of drink from the state of Washington. Yes, it can be done. I am not talking about someday in the sweet by-and-by. I am talking about now and here! But to do that, we cannot be lukewarm. There is no place in heaven for you if you are a tepid reformer! Jesus Christ will spew you out of His mouth! You have got to hate the liquor trade."

Since coming to Seattle, M.K. had been attending Matthews's church. Already he felt an excited pride in the man's ministry. The building bustled with activity, Sunday school teachers adored his Linda and David—David literally ran to his class—and unfailingly every Sunday M. K. would hear Matthews preach and come away inspired. Sunday morning was the one time in M. K.'s week when he did not feel like an empty bucket.

Conger took the podium and, in a much more businesslike and sys-tematic tone, painstakingly explained how they were to divide up their territory by precincts, each one with a captain and ten canvassers. Their job between now and November was to develop this organization, to strengthen the convictions of those who already supported Measure Three, and to promote voter registration. He introduced M. K. as a man the ASL had brought from California, a professional writer who would coordinate and produce the written materials that were so crucial to bringing logical and factual arguments to bear. M. K. stood to be recog-nized, and at the sound of applause he felt his heart pounding hard again. Did he not hate the liquor interests? He knew that he did. His hatred was the only thing that gave meaning to his life now. That, and his children.

They took the interurban train back to Seattle, the schedule being more convenient than the ferry. Evelyn again shared a seat with M. K. and asked him all kinds of questions about himself. Word had reached her, as it always did, that he had written for the movies. A lot of church people disapproved of the movies, but nevertheless, they were mesmer-ized by his involvement. That was how M. K. had begun writing for the ASL. His fame as a writer for Biograph had been spread and exagger-ated in his church in Los Angeles.

Evelyn was a chatty sort, easy to talk with. Half an hour into the trip he realized that his enjoyment was more than the pleasure of conversa-tion. She was a woman. He caught himself looking at her this way— watching the glimmering of her lips in the dim light of the car. This recognition of his heart shocked him so that he broke off the conversa-tion, hardly answering her questions and staring morosely into the dark-ness outside.

He had sworn to himself that no one would ever replace Darla. He had dedicated himself to her memory, which was the very reason he had joined the ASL.

He remembered again that awful day when she had died, and his thoughts drifted to the funeral. Roy Overholt had helped arrange it at the Immanuel Presbyterian Church. Griffith had paid all the expenses and bought a huge mass of flowers, all white, to decorate the casket. Guilt, M. K. supposed. Guilt, as though white flowers could undo anything. Griffith had come to the graveside, too, and M. K. had shaken hands, but he could not bear to talk to the man. He had turned away when Griffith tried to say something. After the funeral, he knew he could not write for Griffith anymore. He found that he could not write for any of the movie companies. He could no longer bear going to the movies.

He and Griffith never spoke what was surely on both of their minds: that he had appealed to Griffith to cut off the booze, and he had refused. It might have been different. Darla might be alive today. M. K. hoped that Griffith had taken a good look at Darla in her casket. That perfect face, that gentleness and simplicity, turned to wax. He hoped Griffith had taken a good look at the children, Linda and David, as they walked into their mother's funeral.

The Fishermen's Club had rallied around him, though. They had brought meals. Somebody, probably Overholt, had paid his rent. Most of all they had visited him. Nobody from Biograph had visited, not even Griffith. The men from the Fishermen's Club came every day; they listened to him talk, talk, talk; they prayed with him. Only in their presence, and the presence of God with them, had M. K. felt any peace. Sometimes that peace had seemed almost visible, a sort of milky golden haze. He had clung to his new friends, especially Roy Overholt. Never had he felt so close to God, not even when he first came to Christ. He talked to God constantly when he was alone.

The bitterness of these memories clutched at him. He shook it off—literally shaking his head so that Evelyn asked him if he was all right.

"Oh, I'm just thinking about something," he said.

She had asked him why he came to Washington, and he had given her a vague platitude about the dry cause. He did not want to go into the past. He was not at all sure he could let anyone see how very thin were the membranes that held his guts inside. Nevertheless, the platitude was true to this extent: he had pledged to the memory of Darla that he would do all he could to protect others from the evil that had killed her.

"You weren't involved with the dry cause when you lived in Everett, were you?" Evelyn asked, looking at him with luminous, smiling brown eyes. "How did you come to be committed, Mr. Nichols?"

She must have sensed that something was hidden. He settled for a fraction of the truth. "After my wife died, I was writing for a magazine of the Bible Institute of Los Angeles, which is a new school connected to my church. They wanted me to write something on the temperance movement, so I went to the library and did some reading. I didn't realize until then how different the ASL is from the temperance my mother preached when I was a boy."

The library had a reading room with long oak tables and tall rectangular windows that let the afternoon sun sweep over the room. He had sat there for hours, hardly knowing the passage of time.

"And how do you describe that difference?" Evelyn asked, smiling and encouraging.

"My mother was always talking about the devil and sin and the power of prayer. That's fine for Christian people who are highly religious, but most people want facts and commonsense arguments. I'd say that the ASL is very rational, and it deals with scientific information. I like that the ASL works with everyone, Democrat or Republican, even with individuals who are not personally dry. It's a very modern organization, the ASL."

"Yes," Evelyn said. "I can feel the difference, but I could never have described it. You put that so well. And you sensed this just from reading publications?"

"Yes, and then I was invited to the ASL Jubilee celebration in Ohio. In December, last year."

"Oh, I heard about that."

"It was very stirring. Five thousand people were there. You could sense the momentum, the undeniable momentum. Wayne Wheeler welcomed us all by saying that presently ten states have localized and quarantined a great national evil, just as slavery was quarantined on the verge of the Civil War. The nation cannot exist indefinitely half dry and half wet, he said. You know, just like Lincoln said. That was when we committed to work for a national amendment."

"It's very exciting to think of that."

"I thought it would take years and years, but I'm beginning to change my mind. Who can say, the way the tide is running? A few years ago local option seemed quite an achievement, and now we're working for a state law. From the town, to the county, to the state, to the nation. I think we may live to see it."

"Especially now that women are getting the vote. They bring a more charitable disposition to the state, don't you think?" She had told him that she had worked in the WCTU campaign for the woman's vote in Washington. She thought prohibition was the next step.

M. K. did not answer. The mention of a womanly disposition reminded him of Darla, and his enthusiasm withered right before her.

M. K. got home in the dark, hurrying up the hill from where the streetcar left him. He had taken a house high on a narrow street. Below, the yellow lights of Seattle spread over an invisible floor. He ran up the brick stairs. As soon as he rattled the front door, he heard the drumming of David's feet on the wooden floor. Before M. K. got in the door, David flung his body against his legs. M. K. lifted him up by the armpits and tried to shush him, though his soft body jerked with sobs. Mrs. Stewart stood across the room with her hands folded in front of her, her face mixing disapproval and concern. Her hands clenched and relaxed and clenched again, holding each other back.

"Has he been this way all day?" M. K. asked.

"Oh, we've had some lovely times together," Mrs. Stewart said with a prim cheerfulness. "And Linda has been a perfect angel," she added.

Linda had appeared silently, also standing across the room. Looking at her always made M. K. sad, perhaps because her expression was naturally somber, perhaps also because she looked so much like her mother. M. K. extended one arm, and she came and slipped under it so he could hold her against him with one arm while gripping David in the other. He maneuvered toward the sofa and sat down, pulling Linda next to him.

"Has he been like this all day?" he asked Linda.

"He wouldn't eat. Mrs. Stewart tried everything and he just refused."

"David, are you hungry now? Do you want me to get you some food?"

David only sobbed, his little body jerking against M. K.'s chest like a caught fish.

"David, how can Daddy go and do his work if you won't help Mrs. Stewart? You have to mind her and your big sister too."

Mrs. Stewart still stood in the kitchen doorway with her hands crossed. She was a small, red-faced, redheaded woman whom Reverend Matthews had found for him. M. K. had told Matthews that unless he had a house and a housekeeper, he would be no good to the movement. Matthews had arranged everything.

Mrs. Stewart advanced and held out her arms for David. "Come now, David, your daddy is home. Why don't you let Mrs. Stewart fix you a bowl of chowder? Don't you like chowder?"

But David was inconsolable. He would not let go of his father, so

M. K. ended up telling Mrs. Stewart thank you, she could go, and taking both children into the kitchen to find some food.

David allowed his father to spoon chowder into him, but Linda, though she had a bowl in front of her, made no pretense of eating. M. K. looked at her, and she looked back unembarrassed, a deeply melancholy expression on her face.

"Was it terrible?" he asked. He felt that his own bright, windy day had fallen into shadow.

"Why can't you stay with us?" she asked him. "You used to stay at home."

"I have a different job now," he said. "I have to go to the office, and sometimes I will have to travel. That's why Mrs. Stewart is here. Don't you like her?"

He waited for an answer while putting another spoonful of chowder into David's mouth, but Linda merely stared ahead, that same sad, lost, concentrated expression on her face.

He repeated the question. Linda said, "She's all right. But I miss Mother." With that she fell into tears, and David, hearing her, also began crying again. M. K. ended up sleeping with both of them in his bed. In the early morning he rose quietly, dressed while they slept, and went off to the office leaving the two children still unconscious in the forgetfulness of sleep. Mrs. Stewart was already there, making a good, hot oatmeal breakfast.

The ASL office was a small, shabby space cluttered with mimeograph stencils and reams of cheap paper, stacks of newspapers and magazines from other ASL offices around the nation, and coffee cups. It had once been a house. M. K. had an office of his own at the head of a flight of steep stairs. The little room had been carved out of an attic and had a steeply pitched ceiling. M. K. paced a good deal when he was writing, and now whenever he stood and unconsciously began to pace, he met the obstruction of the ceiling within two steps. For the first few weeks, he found this constricting his writing, but eventually he got used to it.

People were constantly in and out of the office, from the merely curious who wanted to talk, to women like Evelyn Amble who came in to run the mimeograph or stuff mailings into their envelopes, to important political men like Reverend Mark Matthews or the mayor, George Coterill, who had been elected on a reform platform. M. K. edited the *Citizen*, the ASL's newspaper. He found that most of his ideas for coverage, and most of the news he reported, grew out of these unplanned conversations in the office.

M. K. mused sometimes on the difference between this and his job with the *Argus* when he had lived in Everett. He remembered how the *Argus* had been skeptical about everything, even what they favored in their editorials. The dry cause left no room for cynicism but on the contrary was earnest and sincere—and yet good-hearted and intelligent and hopeful.

He published reports on the effects of the anti-saloon laws that had been passed across America. Now that local option laws had spread almost everywhere among small towns and cities, now that Sunday closing laws and high license fees were being tried in many larger cities, and whole counties and states had banned the sale of alcohol, he could choose from a wide variety of sources. It was amazing to him that so many authorities from so many points of view found the results so positive. Health improved, children got better nutrition, crime declined, public drunkenness disappeared, and industrial accidents dried up when the liquor interests lost. No question, the world was a better place without booze, and it was an easy thing to prove it in the *Citizen*.

Despite these plain facts, all the Seattle papers opposed Measure Three. They had various objections—that drink was not the government's business, that the ban on saloons and alcohol sales involved a naked seizure of private property, that the law would prove unenforceable. M. K. took it upon himself to dispute their positions. He demolished each of their arguments in turn, citing the relevant editorials and naming the editorialists. He drew on the mass of publications from the national ASL and from the discussions he heard in the ASL office, but the shape of his editorials, and his careful and specific answers to each point the wets raised, was his own. He made an impact. Evelyn told him that people talked of his pieces wherever she went. She urged him to publish them all together in a pamphlet.

M. K.'s greatest innovation, though, had to do with photography. Each issue of the *Citizen* published a pair of photographs, one showing the sumptuous home of a brewery or saloon owner, the other the slum conditions around one of his saloons. M. K. bought a big news camera secondhand and learned how to take the photos. He liked tracking down the information, being very careful to get the facts correct so that when the outraged owner or his lawyer called, threatening a suit for slander, M. K. could simply suggest that he close his business if he did not like his ties to it exposed.

Candidates from both parties tried to win their support, which they never would have done, even just five years before. M. K. was privy to meetings where endorsements were weighed in a very sophisticated manner, politically speaking. In some cases the ASL would endorse an individual who was not personally temperance-minded or whose commitment to the cause was minimal. Politics dictated that the ASL back the candidate most likely to get elected and to vote correctly on important bills, regardless of his personal habits or opinions. The ASL could swing elections, so all kinds of politicians were willing to work with the group.

Politics were interesting, but M. K. found that the really interesting temperance story lay in the lives of millions of people like himself—people who knew the true cost of a drink and who hoped for a better country than had ever been thought possible. He thought politicians responded to deep currents of opinion among common people.

They might really be at the turning point where a modern, educated, industrialized society would put aside its sodden past. Centuries of drunkenness might truly come to an end. That was the dream that sometimes helped M. K. put aside his own affliction.

The house M. K. rented had a scruffy lawn and rangy hydrangeas lining a brick stairway. In the evening he always paused for a moment before climbing the front stairs, listening for the sound of crying and sometimes hearing it. He often worked later than he had intended. He did not find it easy to go home.

Mrs. Stewart gave him her views about David. "He cries all the time," she said. "If he doesn't get his way, he cries like a babe."

"But he is a baby," M. K. said. "Not yet two."

"That doesn't excuse such whimpering. If you can't teach him better, Mr. Nichols, he will grow up to be despised by everyone. He is old enough for some discipline. Don't think," and she shook her finger at David, who was clinging to M. K., "that you can cry like that when you get to school. The teacher won't have it."

Mrs. Stewart admired Linda tremendously: "I don't see how you can do so well by one child and have such a problem with another."

She would not cook his dinner. She complained when he came home late, obliging her to stay longer. Fortunately Evelyn Amble was willing to baby-sit on those nights when he had to attend a meeting.

The children liked her. Yet he had to pay her, and it seemed awkward to have her as a friend and as someone he paid. Of course, she did not want the money, but he felt obliged to give it. She was a sweet woman, easy to talk to, very ingratiating. M. K. feared she had something more than friendship on her mind. Not that she said anything to show it.

All other nights he had to cook and clean up and bathe David and put both children to bed. Sometimes he felt so weary he could barely stand by the sink to do the dishes, and he leaned his forehead on the cupboard overhead as he ran the plates through slippery, soapy water. Then he wondered how he could go on. He missed Darla so much. He occasionally woke in the middle of the night to find that he had fallen asleep on Linda's floor after he prayed with her as he put her into bed. Yet then when he went to bed, he often could not sleep. He lay awake thinking of things he did not want to think about and trying to pray, wishing that he could bring back that milky haze of peace he had experienced with his friends in Los Angeles.

In the late spring, on a windy, bright day when he had gone out to buy some groceries, he happened to pass by Spring's Theater in downtown Seattle. A sign advertised that *Judith of Bethulia* was showing. Yes, it was the Biograph film. The print, he had heard, had disappeared into Biograph's vaults after Griffith left the company. Now it had come out.

Before he could prevent it, a picture of Darla had formed in his mind: her perfect face, her unblinking eyes, her soft, dark hair. The memory struck him so forcefully that he wanted to cry out, his chest bursting. No, he did not want to see her again. No, he did not want to know how she had looked on the very day of her death. He did not want to have anything to do with it, ever again.

So he walked on. He had not gone fifty yards down the busy pavement, blind to the crowds and the weather and the newspaper vendors, when he slowed and stopped and then started back. He bought a ticket and went in.

He wanted just to see Darla and then to go. But he had come in somewhere in the middle. The scene he was watching showed Judith already with the Assyrian general, primping, seducing him, waggling her body, and lowering her eyes as she spoke to him. M. K. watched dully through the end and then stayed through a brief intermission and a short on circus clowns before the picture restarted.

He was confused. He could not place the first scene in the script as he remembered it. The film jumped into the action of battle, the rout of the Israelite army before the Assyrians. Immediately a scene came with Judith pledging to the elders that she would preserve them if they would delay their surrender. Finally Judith's maid came in, and it was not Darla, but someone else.

M. K. walked out into the dazzling sunlight, stunned and confused about his feelings. They had dropped Darla entirely from the movie. With a pair of scissors they had cut her out and gone on with the show. The excision struck him as an enormous crime. How could Griffith simply eliminate her with such a cold heart? M. K. would not see her again, even in the movies. Somehow this fact brought back the whole weight of his grief.

Chapter 9
1914: The Cost

"Here we are," Samson said, pulling on the brake of his Ford and turning off the engine, which rattled and choked before it died. "You remember the house, M. K.? We used to come here every birthday."

"I'd forgotten that," M. K. said. "Our birthday checkup. Why did we do that?"

"Dad," Samson said with a shake of his head. "He must have heard the idea from one of his Kraut friends."

Their father had passed away a year ago, so soon after Darla's death that M. K. had felt it only as a secondary blow, slamming into the same bruise but leaving no distinct mark. Here in Hillsboro, Ohio, he felt its meaning since the old family farm and orchard were gone, sold to strangers, and his mother lived with his brother now. Samson had made by far the greatest success of all the seven children, such that he could buy the doctor's house. He was a blond, bullet-headed, hardworking businessman six years older than M. K. They were half brothers. Samson had taken the Nichols name after his own father's death and his mother's remarriage.

His brother's house, looking so respectable and homely, eased the sense of dread in M. K.'s mind. For him it would always be Dr. Washington's house, a large brick structure on a corner lot with a huge, thick elm spreading equally over the lush green lawn and the rutted street.

A wide wraparound porch was littered with children's toys: a doll, a rope, a baseball glove, a bow, and four arrows. If he had to surrender his children, this was a comforting place to leave them, even if it was to his brother.

David ran immediately from the car and toward the porch. He clambered up the steps on all fours and took up the bow. Samson laughed. "There's a boy who knows what he wants," he said.

As they unloaded the suitcases, their mother shuffled out of the door, wearing a faded housedress. She stared at the car, as if not sure who was there. M. K. had not seen her since his college graduation. He had eagerly thought of her as he came, but now he hesitated. She seemed to have shrunk down, like a prune.

Seeing David holding the bow, she took it from him. "You do not need that," she said. "It is not yours."

"Oh, Mother, let him have it," Samson protested. She stared at him for a moment and then handed the bow back to David, who flopped down on his rear and put the string in his mouth. Samson laughed again. "He knows what he wants," he said. "Come on, let's get in. Linda, if you go around the back, you'll probably find your cousins."

The adults sat in the living room and carried on small talk. Arlene, Samson's wife, served coffee, even though it was a hot summer's day and the extra heat of the beverage made them bead with sweat. M. K. had written to his mother in June, asking whether she could take on the children, but he had not realized until now just how dependent she had become. Periodically she would chime in with a remark that apparently came from some other conversation. She had always been sharp, capable, overwhelming sometimes to a boy, but now she stared and seemed barely to follow. Clearly M. K. was putting his children into the care of his brother, not his mother.

Samson and M. K. had never been close, and Samson had bullied and scorned M. K. when they were children. Their quarrels harked back to a time when M. K. was only nine and Samson, fifteen, was already contracting a team he had bought with his own money for hauling. M. K. had been given a bill to take to a farmer. He claimed to have delivered it until the bill was found in his coat pocket where he had forgotten it. Samson had never let M. K. work for him again, and through all the years, they had never cleared the air. No doubt this was partly due to their different origins, Samson being one of five children of their mother and Harold Reynolds, and M. K. the first offspring of David Nichols. The two families had never perfectly merged.

"So you aren't making movies anymore," Samson said. Their mother fanned herself in the warm summer air, but the two men had their hands carefully placed on the arms of their chairs, as though strapped down. "I figured that was the perfect job for you."

"No, I've had it with the movies," M. K. said, deliberately wary of asking why the job had been perfect in his brother's estimation.

His brother told him anyway. "I figured making up stories, that would fit you."

"Why do you think I've moved on, then, Sam?"

"I don't know. You tell me."

"I'm not making up stories anymore, I can tell you that."

"You're working for the Anti-Saloon League. That's what Mother said."

"That's right, Sam. It's solid. Nothing made up in this."

Samson raised his eyebrows. "If you think you're going to get rid of the stuff, I can tell you it's just another one of your dreams, Marion." He had always used M. K.'s given name when he wanted to communicate his scorn. "The drunks will find a way to get booze. You know we have local option here, but do you think it has stopped the Crandalls from getting the stuff?" The Crandalls were known for their shiftlessness.

"Haven't they put the saloons out of business? I didn't think I saw any when we were coming through town."

"Sure, they put the licensed businesses away, and now the Crandalls make it up in their basement and don't pay any taxes at all. Do you consider that an improvement?"

"Actually I do. We aren't dreamers, Sam. We know that drinkers will drink, even if the law is against them, just the same as robbers will rob and murderers will murder. We aim to make it more difficult for them, though. If they have to do it secretly, if they can't sell it on Main Street, if they stand a chance of going to jail, a lot of them will give it up, and a lot of boys who might have been tempted won't ever get the chance. It works, Sam. You look at the statistics anywhere that's dry, and you'll see that they have a lot fewer social problems."

"When I was a girl," their mother began in the wearying, wheedling tone both brothers well remembered, "this town had so many saloons, a woman could not walk down the sidewalk for all the drunks. My mother would never let us girls go down Main Street on a Saturday. Then we started the Woman's Movement, and we prayed them closed. We literally prayed them closed. Marion, I wish that I saw more praying from your people. It is all very cold, the way they do it here."

Neither son wanted to hear their mother's remembrances, so they let Arlene bring more coffee and settled into discussing plans for the children. M. K. felt dread flooding over him again. They treated it like such a normal matter, but to him it was horrifying, like negotiating your own suicide. He could not manage David and Linda. He loved them more than his own life, but a man could not raise children. If anyone could, M. K. could—he had taken care of David as a baby even—but when you had to work, it was impossible. Roy Overholt had come to Seattle to visit, he had seen how it was, and he had urged M. K. to consider whether his family could help. That was why M. K. had written his mother.

He had not meant to turn them over to his brother. Now they were here, and what alternative did he have? He could not take them back—

he could not raise them. Mrs. Stewart was impossible. Why had he not focused enough to understand his mother's situation? She was an old woman.

"We have plenty of room for them," Arlene said. "They can share a room for now. As long as they can get along with their cousins, they'll be fine here."

"Thank you," M. K. said. "You're very generous."

"I'll want some money for their care," Samson said. "They do pay you in that organization, don't they?"

"Yes, they pay. How much do you think I should send you?"

"You need to start now. You brought a checkbook, I hope."

"I brought cash," M. K. said. "You tell me how much." He said it boldly, but he could not help feeling swept over by despair that his children were treated in a crass and financial way, and that he must be a part of it.

Two nights later M. K. was sleeping in Purley Baker's modest three-bedroom home in Westerville, Ohio, national headquarters of the Anti-Saloon League. For a very long time he lay on his back in the sagging single bed of the Bakers' spare bedroom, listening to their clock chime the hours and feeling intensely the absence of his children. At Samson's his son had thundered in and out, back and forth, through and around the house like a miniature buffalo. The contrast with David's straitened, indoor life in Seattle could not help making M. K. smile. It must be good for the boy to be in Hillsboro. Yet the emptiness M. K. felt was palpable, like a ghost presence beside him in the room.

That morning they had all eaten breakfast together. To M. K. it had felt like a prisoner's last meal, though the children had seemed oblivious to his departure. David's cousins had adopted him like a little pet, and

Linda seemed comfortable with her aunt Arlene, who certainly made much of her for her quiet ways and her beautiful face. M. K. for once had little to say. He had simply looked at the children, trying to memorize them.

Samson had stood up and said it was time to go if he wanted to make the train. M. K. had wanted no train station farewell; he preferred to say good-bye here and now. He ran his arms around David, feeling his plump, ripe body soften to him. He did not want to cry, to scare the children in any way, so he merely kissed Linda on the cheek, a sweet, soft, lingering kiss. Then he stood up and left, not looking back.

Already M. K. could feel the distance growing like darkness between him and his children. He probably would never know whether David had cried himself to sleep or Linda had become morose when she looked up from her play and realized his absence. He would not know their doings, their scrapes and sicknesses, their friendships and quarrels. Their lives had, for him, fallen off the edge of the earth. It seemed the cruelest fact of life to him, the densest of shadows adding on to his loss of Darla.

And why was he doing it? At the moment the dry cause felt flimsy, improbable, a weak excuse.

———————————

In the morning, still feeling the spin of the good-bye, M. K. had breakfast with the Bakers. Purley Baker was a man in his fifties with a small face and close-set eyes, his chin wrapped neatly in a goatee. The table setting was tidy and completely functional. They filled the bowls from a huge pot of oatmeal on the stove, and cream had been skimmed from the milk can to pour over it. None of the bowls matched, and his water glass had the thick rim of a jam jar.

Purley Baker was a very important man. For more than ten years he had been general superintendent of the ASL; before then he had headed the Ohio organization. Baker was an ordained Methodist pastor with only a grade school education, but Mark Matthews had told M. K. that he would not suffer fools. "Don't let that country preacher facade fool you. Purley Baker is a fighter."

Baker did seem like a simple, sweet soul. He had little to say, and he ate from his oatmeal almost daintily, half a spoon at a time dipped out of the bowl, slipped into his mouth, and savored. M. K. made polite compliments to Mrs. Baker and anxiously waited for her husband to initiate conversation.

"I want you to meet with Cherrington," Baker said at last, after taking the last bite of cereal. "You know that he heads up all our publications. I understand that's your line of work."

"Yes, sir."

"Are you an educated fellow?"

"Yes, sir. I graduated from Oberlin College."

"That's where Reverend Russell comes from, you know. He's the gentleman who started the ASL and talked me into joining it, even if I was a rough country pastor who could barely read and write."

Since Baker was smiling a thin, sardonic smile, M. K. smiled as well. He had met Russell last year at the Jubilee, but he did not feel he needed to say so.

"Well, publications are very important to our work," Baker said. "I hope you'll get on well with Cherrington."

For three quarters of an hour he grilled M. K. about the Washington election. They expected the vote to be close, and M. K. was not surprised to find it a matter of interest in Westerville. When Baker had all the information he wanted, he leaned back, clasped his hands together, and gave an appraisal from the perspective of the national organization.

"That's quite an important election there in the West, but don't be too surprised if we call you east in a year or so. The time for the states is passing. We are fighting for a national amendment now."

He glanced at M. K. for an instant, then focused his little eyes, pig's eyes, M. K. thought, on the breakfast table. "There's a ballot measure in California too. You came from there, didn't you, so you know all about it."

"Yes," M. K. said, "but the ASL didn't favor that vote. Mr. Gandier didn't think we could win, even with the women voting now. The Prohibition Party forced the vote on us."

Baker glanced at M. K., his mouth set in a little smile that M. K. did not understand. Later, when he thought of it, he took it to be astonishment that M. K. might think he did not know all about California.

"We like to win, Mr. Nichols. It's not that we're proud, not at all. But a loss is a bad thing because it gives our enemies encouragement. A victory makes us seem invincible, and our cause inevitable. That's very important, Mr. Nichols. It's not a matter of convincing them that wet is bad and dry is good because they already know that. Everybody who has walked past a saloon knows which side stands for good and which for evil. Sometimes we have to remind them, but that won't spell the difference between success and failure. What matters is what people consider possible. Just now we're starting to convince this country that it really could do without the liquor business, do without it entirely. Up until now they haven't accepted that as a possibility, no matter how much harm they see liquor do.

"You've seen the maps, I'm sure, the ones in which the dry areas are white and the wet are black?" M. K. nodded yes. The maps were in every ASL office. "We have made progress. The white has spread. But so long as we rely on local option, there will always remain some black spots on the map. At some point those remaining black spots will begin to fight back.

In fact, we're seeing that here in Ohio, right now. The brewers are putting out a bill giving municipalities the power to go wet even if their county is dry. They say it's a vote for local control, which is exactly the drum we beat when we got the local option passed. If the liquor men succeed, we will actually lose ground here in Ohio where this campaign first began.

"The national amendment can ride over them all. It will eliminate the entire liquor industry and leave them nothing to fight back with. They do it for money, Mr. Nichols, for money alone, and they do it with the profits they take from the needy. When we eliminate their sources of money, there won't be any fight left in them.

"Mr. Cherrington believes we can get the national amendment in five years, and he says that we must do it in five years because the census is coming in 1920 and we have so many foreigners pouring into the cities. Our political strength is going to be cut by a large factor. We need to do it before then."

This was news. "At the Jubilee," M. K. said, "they talked of twenty years, perhaps fifty years of gradual progress."

Baker smiled that same thin smile again. "Mr. Nichols, in a war there is hardly ever gradual progress. A close battle can become a rout before you turn your horse around." He paused, lifted his napkin, and patted his mouth with it. "You don't need to put that in your newspaper. We'll let the liquor interests think they have twenty years."

————

Baker walked with him under tall, leafy trees to headquarters, just two blocks away. Westerville was thirty minutes by street railroad from Columbus, but it had the classic small-town smug comfort that M. K. so hated in his college years.

He felt his spirits lifted by Baker's mention of the national amendment, and his suggestion that he would call M. K. east. It was important work. At any rate, it was cheering to think of working at such a speed. Perhaps in five years they would be finished, and he could reclaim his children.

Headquarters was a simple two-story brick house on State Street, wherein M. K. discovered a very familiar warren of desks, posters, papers, and offices. Every ASL office looked the same, the same cheap furniture and clutter and the same posters on the wall. The very map Baker had mentioned, showing the checkerboard of dry and wet regions in the United States, was prominently displayed in the entryway. Seated in a narrow hallway outside Baker's office were three district superintendents from the south of the state. Each one of them had a briefcase in his lap, and they stood up together, eager as dogs, when Baker came in. Baker shook hands gravely, introduced M. K., then pointed M. K. toward Cherrington's door.

When M. K. stepped into Cherrington's office, he met an immediate contrast. The blinds were drawn. Cherrington had a painting behind his desk and no posters. The books on the shelves had been arrayed in rows according to height. The room was uncluttered, sophisticated, modern, like nothing else in the ASL.

Cherrington himself was a heavyset man in his thirties with a fleshy face and dark, deep-set eyes. He made no attempt to be friendly. In a perfunctory way he asked a few questions about M. K.'s travel plans and then asked what he could do for him.

Tender as his feelings were that day, the slightest hint of hostility set M. K. adrift. His first reaction to Cherrington's unfriendliness was to doubt why he was there and to wish that he could flee. He kept his composure, though, and said that Baker had sent him in. "I'm here to learn anything I can," he said apologetically. "I'm new to this kind of writing."

When M. K. thought of it, it seemed odd that no one had ever spoken of Cherrington with particular fondness, for Cherrington had spent several years heading the Washington office, and most of the people in Seattle knew him. M. K. had looked forward to meeting him since Cherrington was a college man and a journalist.

He looks like a thug, M. K. thought, remembering the many Biograph films with snarling criminals in close-up. It was only a momentary glimmer of imagination while Cherrington scowled, but it helped him recover himself.

"I certainly don't know what to do with you," Cherrington said. "What do you want?"

"Could you show me the printing plant and explain the various divisions?" M. K. asked.

Next to headquarters was a large square building for the printing presses. The noise inside was hellish: a constant hammering from heavy industrial machines, while workmen poked at their spindles and shuffled stacks of paper into position. Crews of women picked pages off a stack and inserted them into a rotating collator; a bindery stamped and stapled newspapers and pamphlets. The smell of ink and newsprint crowded the air, and everywhere you looked were publications: towering stacks of newspapers, box upon box of booklets, magazines bound in bundles with twine. Cherrington shouted in M. K.'s ear when he asked questions, and M. K. did get a rudimentary idea of Cherrington's publication strategy. The main impression, however, was of a staggering volume. The national movement really must be substantial to use so many hundreds of thousands of publications.

When they stepped outside again, away from the thundering noise, M. K. asked whether it was the biggest printing press in the world. After a few seconds of frowning, Cherrington said, "No, not the biggest."

His hostility seemed to relent a little after that. They were producing literature in twenty different languages, he said, providing a weekly news sheet for small-town newspapers, and publishing about thirty different editions of the *American Issue* because each state organization had one tailor-made.

As they went back into the office, M. K. ventured to say that Purley Baker had mentioned that he might invite M. K. to work on the national campaign. Cherrington's face turned dark immediately. "See if you can win your little election in Seattle first," he said and turned away.

That last bit of malice stayed with M. K. all the way back to Seattle. Riding the train with nothing to do but think, he asked himself a dozen times whether he ought to quit this work. He thought of his brother's contempt and Cherrington's inexplicable animosity.

I drifted into the ASL, he thought. Yes, he had pledged, crazily perhaps, that he would make something of Darla's death, so it would not be in vain. But his association with Biograph really pulled him in as the churches heard of his testimony and wanted the glamour that came from his association with the movies. One contact had led to another until the ASL caught on to him. And what should he have done? Refused? He had been without a job.

Back in Seattle, the ASL office seemed stale and ugly to him. Everyone was busy; no one seemed to know where he had been. M. K. told George Conger about Cherrington's strange unfriendliness. Conger listened with his cold, ugly smile. "Cherrington might be somewhat vain."

"I don't see what . . ."

"People talk about you, you know. Coming from the moving-picture industry with a movie star wife. The two little children. Besides the work you've done."

M. K. was quiet because the mention of Darla always came crashing down on him.

"I suppose Mr. Cherrington is a little jealous of you," Conger said.

It struck M. K. as extremely peculiar that a leader of the national organization might be jealous. He remembered, though, that Cherrington had turned cold at the mention of Baker's interest in bringing him east. *A stupid reaction,* he thought. *Joining the ASL was like entering a monastery: one left all worldly hopes behind.* He could not really believe that a man in Cherrington's position would have any other idea.

Despite not quite believing in Conger's assessment, it helped M. K. to fall back into his work. The underlying suggestion that people talked of him and admired him restored his sense of doing something worthwhile.

Of course, he had more time now that the children were gone. He went in to the office before anyone else, and he was usually there until midnight. As the election drew steadily nearer, he had more meetings to attend, more events to publicize, and more pieces to write for the general press. Thousands would read and comment on his work. His words might swing the state. He sat in strategy meetings every day, emerging with lists of tasks that must be done quickly and well. That left little time to think of the children, which was all to the good.

The campaign brought him into frequent contact with Evelyn Amble. They traveled together to meetings, they ate together on the road, and in the office she was his most reliable help. Evelyn was utterly different from Darla, whose independence and beauty and singularity had struck him and everyone else. Evelyn was comfortable, agreeable, happy to be useful. She hardly got noticed, but she was a good friend and a faithful person. Her face was pleasant and easy to enjoy.

She looked at him and spoke to him with an attitude no one could misinterpret. To her credit, however, she never hinted at anything.

Sometimes he did think fleetingly that he might marry her and bring his children home. That thought, however, he put quickly away whenever it surfaced. He did not love her, and he did not want to try to love her. He thought she understood his feelings.

The campaign is enough, M. K. thought. It should satisfy them both that (as they and everyone in the ASL felt) an unthinkable shift of mood was in the making. They would eliminate the liquor business first from Washington, and then from the nation. M. K. thought that he felt this more personally than almost anyone else. For him it would be a redemption for suffering, proof that he had done something to make up for the terrible loss.

On election night M. K. and Evelyn worked at the headquarters with a dozen others. They trailed early, but as the night went on the tide began to turn, and they saw the dry votes creeping closer to a majority. Sometime after midnight, victory began to seem inevitable, and yet the totals teased them. For hour after hour the dry vote trailed by a few hundred. Then very early in the morning they went into the lead, and Evelyn, with a shriek, threw her arms around M. K. He hugged her and kissed her—innocently, to be sure, but both felt the electricity.

He walked home in bright early sunshine. The newspapers had it in the headlines: "State Goes Dry!" Mount Rainier was clearly visible to the southeast, and across the Sound the peaks of the Olympic Peninsula shone above a wreath of clouds. This was Seattle: a dreary, hard city surrounded by pristine wilderness. M. K. felt very tired and extremely elated.

The next day, when he came into the office, Evelyn was already there. The moment he saw her, her look warned him. She acted very formally and skittish, asking for a moment of his time. They headed up the stairs to his office without talking.

"I'll come to the point. I think we ought not to see each other anymore," she said.

"Evelyn! What do you mean? See each other?"

She ignored him and said that she would not come to the office anymore. He asked her why, acting all innocence.

Her face was a deep red. She took a deep breath. "I love you, Marion," she said. "It is not right for me to say it to you. The man should say it first. But I have waited and waited, and I think finally I have come to understand. You are still married. Darla passed away, but in your mind she is still alive. I can't come between you."

M. K. was caught speechless. He was stung by the realization that she suffered too. He should have been straight with her. He had done nothing to encourage her hopes, but he had done nothing to set them down, either. Perhaps, without meaning to, he had encouraged her.

He could not quite tell her the truth, not so bluntly. He could not say that he did not love her. He told her that she was melodramatic. He said he hoped that they could be friends. He valued her friendship, he said, which was true.

"It doesn't matter," she said. "I can't see you anymore. It's too difficult for me."

Underneath his protestations he felt a mixture of sadness and relief. She was right. Nobody and nothing could compete with Darla. In a sense, he had left his kids in Ohio because he wanted to live devoted to her.

Chapter 10
1917: Washington, D.C.

M. K. got his summons to Washington, D.C., from no less than Purley Baker, who wrote a simple note on plain white stationery asking M. K. to move to Washington as the ASL's information officer. M. K. stared at the paper, treasuring the streaks of ink, the scribbled signature. During the rest of the day, he left the letter in plain view on his desk, half hoping that someone would notice it. No one did, of course, and since Conger was out of town, M. K. felt obliged not to announce his plans to the office. In a way the pleasure was greater, however, knowing his call and carrying it like a secret jewel.

Baker did not mention who would pay him or how much. He did not say to whom he would answer. M. K. did not concern himself with that. He knew he would be cared for. That was how the ASL operated: like a family.

His work was easy to wrap up. They still had battles to fight in the state, but nothing to match the significance of what they had already done. Within a week M. K. had all his things in two suitcases—he hadn't accumulated possessions in Seattle—and was on the train. As the car pulled out into a gray, bleary rain and he said his good-byes to Seattle out the water-streaked window, M. K. wondered that not a single soul had come to see him off. The train squealed and coughed. It was a foolish and sentimental thought, but in the back of his mind he had thought perhaps Evelyn Amble would appear.

For months after the 1914 election, M. K. had gone into the office expecting that she would appear, that one day her sweet, dimpled smile would swim into view again, and their friendship would resume. She never did. She was as good as her word and stayed away. He expected, too, that he would hear news of her. That seemed inevitable, considering how many common circles they knew. A few times he overheard a conversation that he thought referred to her, but never did he hear anything definite. She seemed to have evaporated from his life.

He was a gregarious, friendly man, who laughed infectiously and had a light touch in conversation. He truly liked people, and people he met were drawn instinctively to his company. Yet he seemed to find himself increasingly solitary for reasons he could not grasp. Sundays were the worst since he did not go to work. Those hours dragged. He still enjoyed the Presbyterian church, hearing Mark Matthews preach, but without the children he seemed adrift as soon as the service ended.

The contrast between his friendliness and his lack of friends baffled him, but it was not really hard to understand. He was dreamy, easily distracted, more likely to react warmly to people he happened upon than to pursue an intentional agenda. He spent a great deal of time at his work, which required long hours in his office and frequent trips to the state capital in Olympia. He never applied his mind to the people around him, but took them as they were.

With his children it was different. He thought about them constantly, he wrote to them, and when he could afford it, he sent gifts. Each summer since moving to Ohio they had come out to Seattle on the train, and for two or three weeks his life was utterly changed. Not that their visits were easy. Linda and David were too far apart in age to be companions to each other, and they seemed as lonely and forlorn floating around in his house as he felt being there himself. David had been just two when M. K. took him back to Ohio, so when he was miserable or lonely or tired he cried for Aunt Arlene and did not go to his father for comfort at all.

Linda, on the other hand, was now in her teens and therefore missed her friends in Hillsboro. When M. K. tried to talk to her about her mother, she showed no interest at all. Throughout her visits, M. K. felt that she was champing to go home every minute.

A year is such a long time in the life of a child, and he missed all that happened to them between visits. Did his work make up for it? He asked himself that sometimes. Of course, it was not the ASL that kept him from his children; it was the fact that he could not raise them by himself. The work was part of the equation, though, because it was part of his whole life of sacrifice.

By now the mountain of Darla's life and death had receded far enough away that he seldom gazed at it; it did not fill the sky any longer. Nevertheless, by habit and conviction, he was tied to his work by her death because it had launched him into it, and it still comprised the core of his conviction. He might have been any missionary remembering that fiery moment of the soul when the millions of Chinese marching into hell caught his mind and his heart and he said, "Here am I, Lord, send me." He thought of himself that way, as a secular missionary. Though he would never have said it out loud, he felt that to make sacrifices as he did, outside the church, was cleaner, free from any taint of hypocrisy or religiosity.

Perhaps, too, he would live to see his calling fulfilled in a way that a church missionary never could. Events were rushing toward their fulfillment, he felt, because people could see that prohibition worked. Even such a staunchly wet paper as the *Seattle Times* had come around, admitting it had been dead wrong to oppose prohibition. The editor, Major

C. B. Blethen, surveyed the positive results in business, health, family life, and savings. He wished they had passed Prohibition years before, he wrote. "Yes, sir, we have found in Seattle that it is better to buy shoes than booze."

Nineteen states were dry now, double the number from just three years ago. In 1916, Michigan had voted itself dry, the first industrial state east of the Mississippi to do so. By 1917, the Washington legislature was ready to outlaw liquor shipments altogether and make the state bone dry.

Three years ago, the national amendment had seemed tantalizing but improbable. Today it seemed incredibly near. For M. K. to be called east could mean only one thing: Purley Baker believed that the day was at hand.

M. K. stopped in Hillsboro on his way east. He wanted to get to Washington, but just as much he wanted to see his children. To some extent, his two great ambitions went together: he held in the back of his mind the idea that if they passed the national amendment, somehow he could reunite his family.

Since M. K.'s last visit, Samson had built a garage behind the house for the Ford. The two men had a moment there as they got the suitcases out of the car. The air was brutally cold. "So what now?" Samson asked, pausing with a suitcase in his hand. "You're going to the capital, but to do what? Arlene and I were wondering if you had a real job there."

"I guess it's a real job if you consider the ASL real," M. K. said to his brother.

"Well, I admit you can pass the laws," Samson said. "I wouldn't be too sure about what happens after that, though. I don't believe you will be able to enforce those laws. They'll become a joke before we're done."

"They're not a joke in Seattle," M. K. said. "If Ohio ever passes a state law, you'll see. It's actually easier to make a statewide law work because you don't have those pockets of opposition. And when we pass the national amendment, it will be easier still. With the booze business shut down, who is going to agitate for it?"

"Is that why you're going to Washington? For a national law?" For the moment Samson did not seem hostile, but genuinely curious.

"Sure," M. K. said. "That's where the excitement is going to be for a while. Let's get in."

His children were in the living room by the stove, watching a game of checkers their cousins were playing. Linda got up and gave him a sober kiss. David seemed not to know what he was supposed to do. He recognized his father, but could not quite remember why. He cheered up when M. K. presented the baseball he had brought. Arlene did not allow him to take it outside, and he had to be told several times not to bounce it on the stairs.

The rest of the family went back to checkers, Arlene to her knitting, Samson to a good-natured chiding of his son Jonas, who was almost grown and nearly as big as his father. No one seemed to feel compelled to speak to M. K., once they got through a few questions about the weather in Seattle.

This is a family, he thought, watching them. *They are as comfortable together as limpets on a rock.* It was good that David and Linda could fit into it. It was a normal way to grow up, and he could never have provided it for them.

"Linda, why don't you sing for your father?" Arlene asked.

Linda looked up, and instantly M. K. thought of her mother. That stillness of face, that alertness and readiness. Arlene had written that she sang in the choir.

"Linda," Arlene continued, "please do. I'll play. Your father has never heard you sing, and you have such a pretty voice."

"What shall I sing?" she asked. It did not take very much pleading.

"Sing that new song about the garden. We all like that."

It was something he had never heard before, a haunting and melancholy tune about meeting Jesus in the garden, talking to Him, walking with Him. She sang it with a simple, soulful, low voice, letting the music carry her along rather than attempting to push it or to show off her voice. M. K. was astonished to see the self-possession she had as she stood by the piano, seemingly lost in the song.

The family was lost in it too. "Bravo," M. K. said when she sang the last note. "That was beautiful. Such a song. You remind me so much of your mother."

She pressed her lips together and blushed. "I don't like it when you say that, Daddy," she said. "Don't tell me I'm like my mother."

"But why not?" he asked in astonishment.

"She died of drink," Linda said. "Didn't she?"

"Linda, don't speak that way of your mother!" Arlene said.

"Why not? You do."

"I do not. I never even knew your mother. Never met her."

"But you say she was a drunkard."

M. K. interceded, though he felt as if someone had kicked him. "That's all right!" They looked at him as though surprised, as though he had no part in this argument. "Linda, your mother did have a weakness for drink. It's true. Nonetheless, she was a wonderful, beautiful . . ." He found he could not say another word.

Later on Arlene told him that she worried about the friends Linda had made at the high school. "I don't know why she likes them, Marion. She sings in the choir, and there are quite a few lovely girls her age in Christian Endeavor. Yet she wants to be friends with those other ones. I don't know why."

———————

M. K. arrived in Washington on a rainy Friday afternoon. He took a cab directly to the Bliss Building where the ASL had its headquarters just across from the Capitol grounds. He had never been in Washington before, and so he paused on the curb, trying to make out the Capitol rotunda through the dense thickets of bare branches. He knew what it would look like from the pictures in school textbooks, but to stand outside his new office and see the real thing—that was something else again.

The building had a seedy look, with a frayed carpet running up the stairs and long, ugly scratches on the mahogany paneling. M. K. rode the elevator to the third floor. A secretary hardly looked up. Her typewriter continued to clatter while she gave a tight smile. When he introduced himself, she stopped her hands and smiled more broadly. "Reverend Cannon is the only one who's here," she said. "But he's leaving for Virginia this minute."

As she spoke a tall, gray-haired, spectacled man appeared in the doorway, putting on his hat. M. K. had seen Cannon in meetings, but up close he seemed overwhelmingly austere, colorless, straight. "Come on, Gladys. Bring your book and I'll dictate on the way to the station," he said. Then he recognized M. K.'s presence. "You must be Mr. Nichols," he said. "Is that right? I am James Cannon. Come along too. I have to be at Union Station in ten minutes. We can talk on the way."

They clattered down the stairs, Cannon talking in a rapid-fire sequence. "We have reserved a room for you at Mrs. Slidell's boarding-house. It's only three blocks from the office, and it seemed convenient. Gladys can direct you. Let me give you a list of matters you'll want to attend to first. Gladys, perhaps you could note these down for Mr. Nichols."

Outside on the shining pavement they waved and caught a taxi. Once in the car, Cannon proceeded to throw out a carefully numbered list of assignments for M. K. They included writing press releases, letters to congressmen, and briefing papers for aides. "With your free time I recommend that you spend as much time at the Capitol as you can. The more familiar you are with the workings of Congress, the better. Mr. Wheeler can help you."

When the taxi reached the station, Cannon launched himself out the door without a word of good-bye. He carried only an umbrella and a light valise, and he walked briskly into the station.

"Is he always in such a hurry?" M. K. asked the secretary, who was going over the hieroglyphs in her notebook.

She gave a wry smile. "Always, Mr. Nichols. Sometimes I go on the train with him to the first or second stop, and then take the next train back. He is the hardest-working man I ever saw."

The secretary, Gladys Noonan, did not know just when Cannon would return, but she gathered that it might be weeks. "He is never in one place for long," she told M. K. on the ride back to the office. "He has a house in Virginia at the woman's college he runs, he has a house in North Carolina at Lake Junaluska, the Methodist conference grounds that he more or less runs, he keeps a cot in Richmond, and he is here much of the time. We never know where to find him." As a Methodist clergy, Cannon was not an employee of the ASL, but he ranked among its highest officers, especially now that the Democrats were in power in Washington. The Ohio leadership was entirely Republican, and only Cannon had links with high-ranking Democrats.

On Monday morning M. K. met Wayne Wheeler. M. K. had seen him before, too, but up close he seemed much smaller, almost flimsy. Wheeler was very short with big, spectacled eyes, a loose, slack-jawed grin, and ears that stuck out. His jacket looked as though it had been used as a pillow, and his tie was crooked. He greeted Nichols with a slap on the back, then invited him into his office, where neat stacks of paper took up every square inch of his desk. Wheeler sat down and put his feet on another chair. There was a poster prominently displayed behind his desk showing his picture and the slogan, "Wayne B. Wheeler, the Fighter, the Man Whom the Brewers Fear."

"I hear you met Cannon on Friday," Wheeler said. He had a strong, raspy voice. "That was a stroke of luck. Lightning strikes are more predictable than Cannon sightings." He gave another goofy grin. "Cannon is absolutely brilliant. He has ice in his veins, not blood. Between him and the Speaker of the House, we can pull Virginia any way we like. But he makes enemies, you know. He's not always charitable to those who disagree, and he has made a lot of enemies. My way is to make friends. And be there. Always be there."

M. K. liked Wheeler immediately. He was a farm boy and a graduate of Oberlin who had gotten his law degree going to night classes. Serving as legal counsel for the ASL, he had argued the Webb-Kenyon law before the Supreme Court. His victory, announced in January, had been a stunning defeat for the liquor powers and their fancy lawyers. Now dry states had the right to stop interstate shipments of alcohol, which meant they could effectively go dry, bone dry if they liked.

For all that, Wheeler seemed like a friendly farmhand dressed in his only suit for a day in the city. They talked about Washington, D.C. Wheeler relished hearing M. K. describe what he had seen over the weekend, the way any city dweller likes to hear his country cousin marvel over the big buildings in town.

"I'll tell you what really amazed me," M. K. said. "At the White House there were women picketing the president, demanding the vote. Maybe I'd read about that, but I don't remember. They were well-dressed, respectable-looking women literally carrying signs and banners criticizing Wilson. Have you seen this? They were right on the sidewalk outside the White House."

Wheeler chuckled with delight. "Oh, that's the Woman's Party," he said. "A bunch of radicals."

"Everywhere I've been, woman's rights and temperance go together," M. K. said. "Don't they here?"

"Oh, yes, oh, yes," Wheeler said. "Even those Woman's Party gals are with us if it comes to that. Goodness, they all know that liquor hurts the woman and her children. This Woman's Party business makes me wonder whether women understand how to do things in a man's world of politics, though. Is it something about women? You know about the Woman's Movement."

"I heard about it every day growing up. My mother was in it."

"That's not so much different from picketing the president if you think of it."

"Except that they were praying and singing hymns."

"For the saloon owners it probably didn't make much difference. And you remember Carrie Nation? She would go into saloons and bust them up. Smash mirrors and bottles and furniture. Aren't you old enough to remember that?"

"It was before my time. But I've heard of it. My mother didn't approve of Mrs. Nation."

"Are you that young? A lot of people forget that those saloons were operating outside the law, but the law wasn't being enforced. That's why they were afraid to arrest her. She was within her rights.

"Those gals made quite an impression, but they didn't get rid of the saloons." Wheeler leaned forward in his chair with a delighted smile on his lips. "Those aren't our tactics because they don't hurt the liquor powers. They slap the face of the liquor power, but we aim to hit the body. Did you ever box? You pound the body. The brewers and the whiskey manufacturers don't like it that somebody busts up their saloon, but they really hate it if you get into their kitchen, where they make the stuff. And do you know where that kitchen is?" Wheeler, entirely delighted with himself now, got out of his chair and walked over to the window.

"There," he said, pointing. "That's their kitchen. Come and look at it."

M. K. joined him at the window. The office had an unobstructed view of the Capitol. "We're in their kitchen," Wheeler said, "and they don't like it. They don't like it at all."

Wheeler turned his chair around and straddled it, gripping the back as though to keep himself from jumping up again. "Mr. Nichols, I know that Cannon gave you quite a list of things to do. I understand you're a talented young fellow, and no doubt he and Dinwiddie will have a lot of work for you. But I will tell you something. Come over and sit with me in the Senate gallery, and you'll learn about the kitchen. You take all the time you can to sit with me in the kitchen, and you'll find out how things truly work in this city. Come anytime you want. You're welcome." He gave a broad wink. "I can show you how we cook things up in the kitchen."

———————

On a February day, after M. K. had been in Washington a month, he was taking exactly this advice. Both Wheeler and Cannon were in the Senate gallery, listening to tedious debate on a post office appropriation. The Senate reminded M. K. of a hotel lobby on a Saturday morning: stale, sleepy. At first he had wondered how so important a man as Wheeler could spare so many hours to listen to such boring debate. After a week or two he began to understand that more went on than met the eye.

From the gallery Wheeler could look down on all his boys, as he called them, and he frequently sent down written messages through the Senate pages. Probably two or three times in a day he would call one of the senators out into the corridor for a consultation, and when there were recesses, Wheeler went into the hallways to exchange small talk.

He seemed to know the wets as well as the drys, and to treat them with the same jolly affability. He was a funny sight, a head shorter than most of the senators, his suit a mess and his tie twisted sideways, mingling in the corridors with a crowd of older, dignified men.

Cannon had come back from whatever he had done in Richmond, and he was quite a different act. He was cordial and courtly, as only a Virginian could be, and always perfectly dressed in a black suit. He wasted no time with glad-handing, talking only to the men whom he knew about business he intended to organize. He and Tom Martin, the Majority Leader from his home state of Virginia, always had something to discuss.

Wheeler, as he had said of himself, believed in being there. Wheeler took the exact same seat in the gallery every day, as though it were his office chair. (Senators joked with him that he had the highest seat in the Senate.) Even though talking in the gallery was forbidden, Wheeler spoke to M. K. in a hoarse whisper, explaining matters more or less constantly in his ruined voice. Today he pointed out James Reed, senator from Missouri, who had stood up to offer an amendment.

"Now watch this man," he said. "He's about our worst enemy. The man has got a bitter sense of humor, and he's very intelligent. I like to shake his hand and tell him how much I admire his elocution. It drives him crazy."

They were watching the post office bill because it had a rider prohibiting liquor companies from advertising their goods through the mail. Of the nineteen states that had gone dry, most still allowed plentiful allowances of liquor consumed privately. The bill Cannon had crafted in Virginia, for example, allowed each adult to import one quart of spirits, one gallon of wine, or three gallons of beer each month. Many states permitted even more, and the liquor wholesalers were making money selling directly to customers across state lines through the mail.

The point of the rider was to keep them from advertising these services through the mail and thus openly promoting liquor consumption in states that wanted to limit it. (The states, of course, could control newspaper ads and the like in any way they chose.)

Something about the self-satisfaction on Reed's jowly face made M. K. pay attention. Reed held his head high, and he wheeled his body from side to side as he spoke in a mocking tone. "My fellow senators, honorable sirs, I am pleased to present an amendment that will meet one of the treasured goals of prohibitionists everywhere. I propose to eliminate not merely advertising for alcoholic beverages in dry regions, but all sales, all purchases, all transports of alcoholic beverages within any dry area, whether locality or state. If any place in America has voted itself dry, it will henceforth be truly dry, by federal law—bone dry."

M. K. saw Cannon sit up straight, his eyes sharp and focused. Wheeler still slouched and wore a vacant expression; he did not seem to have caught whatever Cannon had noticed. Cannon moved next to Wheeler, and they held consultation in rapid whispers. Wheeler took out a pad of paper and scribbled rapidly, showed the note to Cannon, and sent it onto the Senate floor through a page.

"It's a joker," Wheeler said hoarsely in M. K.'s ear. "Reed wants to embarrass us. He knows that we don't want bone-dry prohibition imposed where they're not ready for it. If we come out against it, though, the Prohibition Party will scream that we're not pure, and even the WCTU will remonstrate with us."

"What will you do?" M. K. asked.

"We'll bury it," Wheeler said complacently, leaning back. "The timing isn't right for this."

But Wheeler's note did not seem to have any impact. The senators proceeded to vote for the amendment, almost without dissent. Wheeler watched the dull proceedings below him, then leaned over to M. K.

again. "You won't see that coalition at work again," he said. "The drys voted for it because we've got them trained to think that anything against alcohol is good. The wets voted for it because they thought Reed had put us in a tight spot, and they like to tweak our noses."

"Now what are you going to do about it?"

"It has to go to the House. We'll put a stop to it there. Come on over to the office tonight and you can help me draft a letter."

———————

Nichols ate his supper at a restaurant just up First Street from the Capitol. He had a notebook beside him on the counter in which he wrote a journal of the day's events. The personalities and procedures were not terribly different from Olympia's, but the stage seemed larger and the shadows longer. Whereas in Olympia a rambling cattle rancher remained just that, even if he was a senator, here in Washington a paunchy farmer spilling over with regional yokelisms became, as senator, an eminence in the world's most exclusive men's club, a character, almost a type. Even the House, which was full of small, fulminating men just up from the county courthouse, took on some grandeur from the Capitol's marble stairways and columns.

A man took the seat next to M. K.'s and then nudged him familiarly with an elbow. Startled, M. K. looked to see an unfamiliar, tall, bony man with short hair the color of straw. He had almost invisible eyebrows.

"You're with Wheeler, aren't you?" the man asked. "I've seen you. I work for Senator Reynolds from Idaho."

M. K. shook hands. "I don't think I've met . . ."

"Oh, you wouldn't. Reynolds is wet. They're all laughing at you tonight, you know."

M. K. held out his hand and introduced himself. "Butch Crespo," the man answered. He had blue eyes so dark they looked almost black. "Was there terrible weeping and gnashing of teeth today? I don't mean to laugh at your expense, but wasn't that something how Reed made a fool of you? I realize it wasn't you personally, but you know what I mean. Reed is a smart man. I bet Wayne Wheeler was steaming."

"Actually he wasn't mad at all. The amendment has to pass the House, you know."

"And it will pass the House, just like the Senate, unless Wheeler or Cannon or one of your bosses says to dump it. And that would be just a little confusing to the dry army, don't you think? Oh, it's delicious to me. You don't think I'm gloating, do you? Well, I am. I am gloating just a little."

Crespo seemed to imagine that M. K. would enjoy a conversation about the ASL's consternation. He had a very peculiar face, almost albino except for the dark shadow of his eyes.

"I hate to spoil your fun, but I don't think the bill will go anywhere in the House. It's not our policy to support bone-dry policies."

"We know that. Of course we know that. But it's one thing not to sponsor them; it's quite another to put a stop to them. Oh, just think of it! Reverend Cannon explaining to his Methodists and Reverend Barton explaining to his Baptists that yes, they are against liquor, but they can't support a bill that would eliminate it in dry territory. I don't know if they can do it! I'm not sure they can! They may be the greatest hypocrites this side of Hades, but they certainly don't like to advertise that fact."

M. K. was beginning to feel irritated. "I don't know anything about them being hypocrites. I don't believe they are at all."

"Well, what do you call it when men who are reverends make sure that all the money ends up in their bank accounts? You know they're getting rich off this, don't you?"

"No. I'm sure they're not."

"Cannon has real estate across half the state of Virginia, and he's not getting rich. Wheeler and Dinwiddie take up a collection from a different church every single Sunday of their lives, and all that money goes straight from the collection plate into the good cause. Really now."

"I've never seen anything but straight dealings."

Crespo cocked his head. "You don't believe that. You can't believe that."

"Well, I do. What do you know about it?"

"Nichols, I know the world. Men have a motive. And it's not to help their brothers." The very thought seemed so ridiculous to Crespo that he broke into a sputtering laugh.

At that moment the waitress came up and asked Crespo if he wanted to order. Crespo put on his hat and stood up. "No, I just wanted to see what our dry brothers were saying. I'm sure I'll see you again, Nichols."

After he finished eating, M. K. went to the ASL office to meet Wheeler. Crespo's self-assurance made M. K. wonder whether there was any slight possibility that he spoke truly. But how could it be true? M. K. knew the top leaders of the league, practically every one of them. He had stayed in Purley Baker's little brick home. And Wayne Wheeler did not seem to own a suit that had cost him more than ten dollars. If they were greedy, they were showing it in a very strange way.

M. K. did think of Ernest Cherrington and the strange, unfriendly way he had acted when M. K. first traveled to headquarters. What had that meant? He had never been able to believe completely that the man was jealous, as George Conger had said.

When M. K. unlocked the ASL door, Wheeler's rasping voice yelled for him. The lamps were all off, but M. K. could see a dim yellow light coming from Wheeler's office. Of course, all the lamps were off. Nobody in the ASL would think of wasting a penny.

Wheeler immediately shoved a paper across his desk. "I've just begun," he said. "See what you think of it so far."

It was a letter to the dry congressmen, explaining that the post office amendment offered by Senator Reed, a notorious wet, should be voted down. The amendment was a violation of states' rights. "We might think the state laws too weak," Wheeler had written, "but that is a matter to be determined within the state."

M. K. looked up from reading the letter to find Wheeler leaning forward, waiting for his opinion as eagerly as a dog on point. "So you object because of states' rights," M. K. said, "not because bone-dry laws are too far in advance of public opinion."

"You have to talk to some of these southern congressmen," Wheeler said. "They're fervent for prohibition, but they go crazy about states' rights. If we don't show respect for states' rights, we'll never get an amendment to the Constitution."

"Won't people ask the same about a federal amendment?"

"Yes, but a federal amendment requires that the states agree. Their rights are respected."

M. K. helped write the letter, even though he felt confused. Wheeler had a point about the requirements for a constitutional amendment, but still it would be hard to explain why this law, which fully outlawed liquor in dry areas, was more a violation of states' rights than a federal law outlawing liquor everywhere. This did not seem to trouble Wheeler. He signed the letter with a flourish. "We'll get that out first thing in the morning," he said.

When M. K. came back in the morning, however, he found that the letter had not gone out. The office seemed to be off-kilter. The secretaries seemed to be typing extra fast as though to keep their minds occupied. Wheeler, Cannon, and A. J. Barton, a Texas Baptist who was a member of the legislative committee, were in Cannon's office with Ed Dinwiddie. Dinwiddie had been in charge of the Washington, D.C., office for years until Cannon was put over him and the legislative committee given its authority. Wheeler said Dinwiddie acted as if the place belonged to him. They had needed an official order to get him to take his personal locks off some of the office doors.

It was a long hour before Cannon called in a stenographer. Shortly thereafter the meeting broke up, and Wheeler stuck his head in M. K.'s door. He was grinning. "We found out that Dinwiddie was recommending the bill. I guess he thinks that if the Congress wants to be bone dry, we should be for it. I never thought I'd see the day when Congress was running ahead of the ASL." He grinned and buttoned his coat across his belly. "Cannon and I are of another mind, and so is Barton. We're going to send out a letter to the whole Congress, apprising them of our concerns regarding states' right and urging them to vote as their conscience leads them. Which had better be to vote no!"

"So your letter isn't going to go out at all?" M. K. asked.

"No, we decided that we needed to give a united front."

Wheeler disappeared, and M. K. was left to wonder what had happened. He saw the letter when it was printed and thought it was more likely to confuse people than to help them understand the ASL's position.

Two days later Wheeler stuck his head in M. K.'s door again. "You might want to get in on this," he said. "Cass has asked to see us about the Reed amendment. He's in Cannon's office now."

William Cass was chairman of the House post office committee. A small, red-faced man with apple cheeks, he had come all by himself and sat nervously in the only comfortable chair in Cannon's office. He was ill at ease and barely looked at M. K. when they were introduced.

"Well, I'll come to the point," he said after clearing his throat. "We don't know how to handle this Reed bone-dry amendment. I would have thought that you fellows would be delighted to see it pass. But your letter mentions states' rights, and I don't understand what you are saying. You fellows never told us to vote our conscience before." His face grew redder as he spoke, and he seemed to want to stand up and walk around, for he started to his feet several times and then thought better of it.

Cannon answered in a smooth, eloquent way, pointing out that they had never had legislation before them like this: proposed by a dripping wet senator in an attempt to embarrass them, containing a proposal that they were bound to approve for its effect but that they considered potentially dangerous in its constitutional procedure.

To M. K., he sounded quite convincing, but Cass was so quick to respond he almost tripped over the tail end of Cannon's words. "That's all fine, but you know and I know that most of the House don't have strong consciences about this at all. They want to know what to do so they won't get on the wrong side of your people. You've always been straight with us, and I expect you to be now. How do you want us to vote?"

Nobody wanted to answer that, so it stayed hanging in the air. M. K. wondered whether Cass really understood how complicated these issues could be.

Finally Cannon spoke up. "I'm afraid that we have different views within our own league, Mr. Cass. Our letter meant to convey that, so that each member could decide the matter by his own lights. If we had united counsel, we would certainly be straight to give it."

"All right, Reverend Cannon, you tell me personally. If you were a member of the House of Representatives, how would you vote on this bill? Yea or nay?"

Cannon paused and, through some subtle stillness, demonstrated his complete dignity. He looked grave, austere, spartan in his asperity, and he seemed to grow a foot taller. "As a southerner and a Christian?" he asked.

"Yes, of course."

"As a southerner, I have a great concern for the independence of the states. For me that is a great principle. Yet the evil of alcohol is so immense that I would have it take precedence. I regret that the choice is forced on us at this time when we are not quite ready. Yet if I were in your shoes, I would vote yes."

"What about you, Barton?"

"I don't want to prejudice your own view with an opinion that is purely personal . . . ," Barton began in his Texas accent.

Cass cut him off. "I understand that. How would you vote? You. If you were in my shoes."

"This is just for you. I don't want you to tell anybody about it. I would vote in favor." He said it quietly.

They all tried to equivocate, but they all said yes. Cass got up, said thank you, put on his hat, and left without another word.

Dinwiddie got out of his chair, slapped some imaginary dust off his trousers, and said, "I don't know what all the fuss was about if we would all vote for it."

"Personally we would," Cannon said sternly. "But that is not the league policy. You are quite wrong to give advice if you haven't got the league's approval."

Dinwiddie shrugged.

———————————

The amendment passed in the House by 319 to 72. M. K. was present to see the count, which frankly astounded him. He had expected that the divided counsel of the ASL would result in a close vote, not this landslide. The bill itself was a shocking advance in the law, sealing off dry areas from any liquor, making them truly and entirely dry. Up until now, prohibition had aimed more to close down saloons and breweries than to actually dry up the population. Suddenly the law—the federal law—stood against alcohol, not just the alcohol industry.

Wheeler walked back to the office with him, whistling. He had a jaunty way of holding his shoulders back when he was happy, and nobody could miss the fact that he was pleased. "There's nothing to stop national prohibition now," he crowed to the whole office. "All those congressmen who voted for a federal law to override state law, they've got no more reason to vote against our amendment."

Indeed, with more than 80 percent of Congress voting for Reed's amendment, the prohibition amendment seemed to have an open road ahead. It seemed truly possible that their final goal would be realized soon, quite soon. M. K. kept turning over the situation in his mind, trying to see where problems would arise. He could not find them.

Cannon went to see President Wilson. M. K. was amazed to realize that he could do that—call up and get an appointment to see the president. Truly the ASL was powerful now. Wilson had tried to weasel out of any commitment to prohibition, but he understood political facts. Cannon told him that the only way to get a post office appropriation through Congress was to sign this bill. If he did not, the nation's postal service might be closed down.

Wilson signed the bill. The day that he did, M. K. was accompanying Wheeler through one of the Capitol corridors when he saw the flaxen-haired aide who had accosted him over dinner a week before. It was just a glimpse from some distance, but M. K. was sure of the man's identity. The face was like a photographic negative. What was his name? Crespo.

M. K. hustled ahead, dodging through traffic, to catch the man's arm. "I wanted to congratulate you on the Reed amendment becoming law. You told me the wets were laughing at us when it passed the Senate. Are they still laughing?"

Crespo stared, his deep blue eyes like empty holes under his white eyebrows. "Oh," he said coldly, "you feel you've won a great victory."

"Oh, yes," M. K. said. "Didn't you hear the vote? You know, I think it's no longer the Anti-Saloon League that's carrying this forward. Even James Reed gets caught up in it." He could not help it; he laughed at his own humor.

Chapter 11
1917: At War

In April the nation went to war. Within weeks the streets of Washington were filled with soldiers and sailors, skinny kids in ill-fitting uniforms with faces utterly open to a world they hoped would make them heroes. M. K. encountered scores of them every day as he walked from his apartment to the ASL office. They loitered on the streets as though expecting some exciting event, perhaps a mass mobilization of troops or the appearance of a general.

If anyone needed proof of the power of the government, the war gave it. M. K. felt like the luckiest man, plunked down in the center of the world's order, where the laws were made and commands issued. It was an exciting time in the world's most exciting location. He heard people complain that Washington was provincial and boring, but M. K. saw it as a wide, spacious city, a grid full of temples of democracy, a kind of American Athens. He had a very warm view of American government, miraculously unspoiled by his exposure to the tricks and maneuvers of Congress.

That was perhaps because he was on the winning side so often. War made the ASL revamp strategy, and it threw into temporary doubt the timing of prohibition, but none of them in the office doubted at all that their side was growing stronger and would win, that they were working Congress like a toy whistle. M. K. continued to be astonished that the political world had come around to lie down at their feet. Truthfully the only organized opposition came from the distillers and the brewers, who had no argument for their side except that prohibition would cost them money. They complained that the government confiscated their property. As the ASL pointed out, it did not. The government did not touch their property, but insisted that it be invested in another kind of production, one that did not turn men into beasts.

In his daily work M. K. answered mostly to Wayne Wheeler. Cannon was often gone from the office, and Dinwiddie had his own independent way, but Wheeler loved to collaborate and he loved to talk and, most important for M. K., he loved publicity, good or bad. The other leaders were cautious in their public statements, preferring to work behind the scenes, but Wheeler had M. K. collect his press clippings and send out an occasional mimeographed bulletin quoting an assortment of them. "I want them to think I'm bigger than life," he said to M. K. "I want them to know that I'm loved and hated all over the country, so they'll pay me close attention." He grinned his goofy smile. "Most of all I like them to fear me."

It seemed incongruous that a man five and a half feet tall, seeming like just what he was, a small-town Ohio lawyer trained in night school, should be feared in Washington. M. K. saw it for himself, however. No representative, no senator, wanted to have the machinery of the ASL turn against him. No one wanted to stand against the Church in Action, as they called the ASL. Every chance he got, Wheeler let the politicians know that the dry vote answered to his call. He might have overstated his case, but the politicians could not be sure, so they placated him.

M. K. was at the office six days a week, twelve or fourteen hours of the day. He did not mind. The only day he hated was Sunday because he had nothing to do but go to church and walk around the city. He knew almost no one outside the ASL, and the staff had their families. He didn't go to movies anymore.

Although he was a Christian, something had gone out of it. He dutifully joined a Methodist church but found no Roy Overholt, no Fishermen's Club, not even a Mark Matthews. For some reason, going alone to church made him gloomy and antisocial. He would clear out after services with as little human contact as he could manage. Then he would eat alone and try to find something worthwhile to do with the rest of his day.

M. K. began to fill those blank Sundays by traveling with Wheeler, who would preach in various churches around the region. It had always been the ASL's chief mode of raising money: for its agents to hold an annual temperance service in each cooperating church and take pledges. More than twenty years ago Wheeler had started as the lowliest agent in Ohio, riding a bicycle between towns. Now that he held such responsibility with the Washington office, he could have quit the weekly preaching, but he liked the human contact. He thought he set a good example for the league by continuing to preach weekly. It reminded him, he said, of his early days when he had answered the call of Reverend Howard Russell to give up a business career for the cause of righteousness. Wheeler had a young family, but they stayed home in their own church, so he was glad to have M. K. along for company.

They were a good fit, both liking to talk, both liking the adventure of meeting new people and seeing the country. While they rode the train together, Wheeler would talk about the league's strategy—or, it might be more accurate to say, Wheeler's strategy, which he hoped to convince Cannon and Dinwiddie to support.

"While this war is on we've got to stick tight to Capitol Hill," Wheeler told him. "I don't see how Cannon can imagine it's safe to go off at will when conditions here change every day." Cannon had a habit of disappearing into the South on his unending church business.

"The trick," Wheeler said, beginning to philosophize, "is to use the prevailing wind for your cause. But you have to keep your finger in the air because winds shift. Have you ever sailed, Mr. Nichols?"

M. K. admitted he had not.

"Neither have I, but they tell me you can't go directly into the wind. If you choose the right angle, though, you can use the wind to make progress in your own direction. You see now, Nichols, everybody is thinking about the war. People don't want to think about saloons; they want to know how it affects our boys in the war. So how do we approach it? We don't try to tell Congress that alcohol is just as important as the war. They wouldn't listen. No, we tell them that the war effort requires alcohol controls. We point out that we can't afford drunken soldiers, so we need to close saloons near military bases. And here is the way we are going to surely overcome the liquor interests."

Wheeler sat up straight and smiled energetically at the deliciousness of the thought. "We know that food is precious in wartime and sometimes must even be rationed. The government is bound to consider rationing. Yet the production of beer and liquors consumes valuable grain. For the sake of the war effort, we need to assure that all the grain our farmers produce goes toward the war effort. No more grain for booze while our boys are fighting."

Wheeler gave himself the credit for developing this line of attack, but he did that for everything. Whoever had thought of the idea, M. K. recognized it as genius. How could it be justified to use hundreds of thousands of tons of grain to make destructive beverages when food was needed for the war effort?

President Woodrow Wilson called Herbert Hoover back from the American relief effort in Belgium to head a new Food Administration. Hoover was an engineer, and they made certain he read a report by economist Irving Fisher of Yale University. The barley used to make beer, Fisher calculated, could produce eleven million loaves of bread a day.

They had the liquor trade dancing. One day Wheeler had two callers in the office, first a man from the brewers and then one from the distillers. The brewer offered to throw the distillers to the dogs. Do away with spirits, and the brewers association would support the effort in the interest of the war. Only preserve beer, which workers in industry depended on. The distiller came next and was ready to bring on a tax scheme to finance the war effort, a tax that would incidentally benefit whiskey at the expense of beer. Wheeler made sure to escort the brewer out while the distiller was waiting to come in, knowing how suspicious they would be to find each other in the ASL office. He thought that was very funny.

One of the distillers wrote to Congress that soldiers needed spirits because "the man who rushes a rapid-fire gun should be given the relief from terror that alcohol imparts." Wheeler found this delightful and had M. K. distribute the quote in a circular under the heading "Whiskey Manufacturers Do Their Part for War Effort."

Congress considered a food bill that would do away with the manufacture of alcoholic beverages for the duration of the war. It was sure to pass, but several senators, beholden to the brewers, indicated that they would filibuster unless beer was exempted. Reverend Cannon came into the ASL headquarters in June, called the leaders together, and told them that Tom Martin, the Senate Majority Leader, wanted to see them all in his office. "He told me that the president wants us to let up on the food bill," Cannon said.

"He wants *us* to let up," Dinwiddie exploded. "We're not the ones stopping it."

Cannon had a very gray, icy way of talking strategy, which fit his lean and somber build. "I told Martin that it would be very difficult to give up something that we considered particularly necessary for the war effort," he said unflappably. "I think we can make the best of this. It may even turn out to our advantage."

They walked together over to the Capitol. M. K. was invited along, ostensibly to take notes, really so that he could see how they operated. Martin ushered them into his office, and when he had them all seated, he gave a plea for cooperation. He said the president was furious that it was politics as usual in the Senate. He wanted them to drop their demands so that the bill could go through.

"Why doesn't he ask the brewers?" Wheeler said. "They're the ones holding up the bill."

Martin said dryly that perhaps the president had a higher opinion of their patriotism than he had of the brewers'. "Many of them are what the president refers to as hyphenated Americans."

Wheeler stood up from his chair. "I don't care, Tom. It's just not right that a bunch of Germans should dictate the terms of this bill. It's not right. I believe that we can break their filibuster if we hold on. It's for the good of the country."

Martin gave Wheeler a withering look. "The president doesn't want to wait that long," he said. "He wants his bill now."

Wheeler made another little speech, slapping a rolled-up paper on Martin's desk to punctuate his remarks. Cannon finally stopped him, got him to sit down, and calmed him. Then he spoke to Martin.

"We've known each other for a long time, Tom, and you know that we're a very practical bunch. We aren't extremists, and we work with people who don't entirely agree with us. But you can see that this is a difficult request for us. I don't know whether the president understands just how difficult it is to jettison both our principles and our patriotism."

"My goodness, Reverend Cannon, I should think you would consider it patriotic to cooperate with your president and commander in chief during a war."

"Yes," Cannon said. "Yes, that is the only thing that could bend us. But many of our loyal temperance supporters would not understand why we had dropped our principle unless they knew that the president had specifically asked us to do so for patriotic reasons."

There was a moment of silence as Martin chewed over this statement. "Well, Jim," he said, "do you want the president to get down on his knees and beg you?"

"Oh, no. Oh, no. It would be enough if he would write a letter that we could release to the public, asking for our help. If he could appeal to our patriotic motives and say that the reason for his appeal was strictly the matter of urgency, not the policy specifics."

Martin looked at Cannon balefully, then looked over each one in the room in turn. "You want me to tell the president what he should say in his letter."

"That would be helpful. We would not want to be misunderstood."

When they had been ushered out of the office, the ASL leaders kept quiet through the Capitol corridors until they reached the steps and felt out of reach of anyone's ears. "Well, how-de-do!" Wheeler exclaimed. "Do you think Wilson will go along?"

"I think so," Cannon said. "He may be less enthusiastic for our cause than we could wish, but he is very realistic politically."

"He never likes anything that forces him to stand up for anything," said Dinwiddie, who as a Republican had a poor view of Wilson.

"That is why I made it so clear what the letter should say," Cannon said.

M. K. could not make heads or tails out of the discussion. It was obvious the men were thinking along lines he had not grasped. "Why," he asked cautiously, "why do you think it is wonderful for the president to write this letter?"

"Because," Wheeler said jubilantly, "it makes us the patriots. The president himself publicly recognizes that we are the ones willing to make sacrifices for the good of the nation at war. While the brewers and their allies . . ." He laughed. "You remember what I said about using the war to push for our goals?"

"Yes, I remember."

"Right now patriotism is very strong. Wilson is about to declare our side the patriotic side. We can use that, M. K.!"

Within a week Wheeler had assigned M. K. to look into the pro-German sympathies of the brewers. "The wet cause is the German cause, you see?" Wheeler said. "And though we don't say so, anybody who stands with the wets must be standing with the kaiser. You see? We need facts to back that up. Quotes, proof of financial linkages, publications, meetings that we can verify."

M. K. spent much of the steamy summer in various libraries. The tracks were easy to find. It was only a lot of work because there were so many trails to follow. Most of the brewers were from German immigrant families, so recent they even conducted brewers association meetings in the German language. For ten years at least, the brewers had been funding the German-American Alliance, and their fingerprints were all over political corruption cases that had made it into the courts in Texas, New York, and Pennsylvania.

All kinds of German-American leaders had praised the kaiser, had broadcast their sympathy for the German army against the British and French before America got in, and had spoken of the superiority of German culture and their desire to preserve their German identity for a thousand years. Their papers were full of it. Of course, they had mainly kept quiet about the kaiser since April, but why shouldn't these sauerkraut-eating, German-speaking hyphenated Americans still be secretly backing America's enemies?

Wheeler loved all of it. Every time M. K. brought him a new report he read through it while M. K. sat and watched. "I can use all of this," he said enthusiastically. "All that you can produce. Keep going!" Wheeler began to feed pieces of information to sympathetic politicians and interested journalists.

M. K. was too busy to visit the Capitol very often during the summer, but he happened to be in the Senate gallery with Wheeler one day when Warren Harding looked up and gestured for Wheeler to come down.

Harding came from Ohio, so Wheeler knew him quite well. "He drinks and he gambles," Wheeler had told M. K. once. "But he votes our way."

Whereas many of the senators preferred to speak quietly and privately when they had something political to offer, Harding spoke to them quite openly, as though he were selling life insurance. He was a large man with a handsome, noble face and a vigorous handshake. "That bill of yours for the amendment," he said to Wheeler, who had the disadvantage of looking up to Harding as they stood in the corridor. "I think there ought to be a five-year time limit for approval by the states."

"And why is that?" Wheeler snapped. "There's never been a time limit for any other constitutional amendment."

"Well, you see how things are. The states change their minds. Alabama goes dry, then back to wet, then dry again. Even our beloved state of Ohio can't seem to make up its mind. Some people think that your bill could hang out there forever, just waiting for one more state to approve it."

M. K. glanced at Wheeler, trying to see what he would make of this proposal—if it was a proposal. Wheeler's face, however, betrayed nothing but the sappy boosterism of a lodge member.

"Well," said Wheeler, "what would be the harm in that? I suppose we could wait if we had to."

Harding placed a large, meaty hand on Wheeler's shoulder. "Mr. Wheeler, right now I think we could get a few senators to back the amendment if they could say they were just passing authority on to the states. If you gave them five years, it would be practically an up-or-down thing. We could get a few votes for that."

Wheeler said he would give it some thought.

"I'd like to know soon. Senator Sheppard says he is willing, but I need the league's agreement." Harding winked. "Nobody wants to do anything that the league doesn't like."

Wheeler and M. K. left the Capitol immediately, Wheeler talking nonstop in a disconnected way as they walked back to the office. "It's a trap. I know that. They think we'll never get thirty-six states in five years. But what if we walked into the trap? Could we get the votes? We may never be stronger than we are today. If we had those extra votes, we might look to be invincible. Getting it through the House can be difficult right now, but if the Senate passes it quickly, the House may also."

M. K. could not have gotten a word in, even if he had any. The day was gray and heavy, and by the time they reached the Bliss Building they were both sopping with perspiration. In the elevator the closed-in heat seemed to pack the air like cotton. By then, Wheeler had stopped talking, like a faucet turned off. Once out of the elevator he disappeared immediately into his own office, leaving M. K. wandering the small crowded space by the secretaries' desks, wondering what he ought to do. He felt too excited to work on his papers.

Wheeler burst out of his office again. "Come in here, M. K.," he said. "I want to show you something." On a legal sheet of paper, front and back, he had written the names of the forty-eight states. Next to each one he had written a number. "Reckoning on a beginning next year, that's the number of times their legislatures would meet in a five-year period. I think we can do it. I don't see a problem." He looked at M. K. with an expression of absolute bliss. His fists were clenched like a little boy's. "I think we can do it!" he said again.

"Even so, why don't you go back to them and ask for six years?" M. K. said. That was to be his principal contribution to temperance legislation.

———

They agreed on the six-year period, and with Harding's help a vote in the Senate came on August 1, after three days of dull debate. The only surprise came in the extent of the ASL victory, 65–20.

When M. K. was leaving the Senate gallery, clattering down the marble stairs, feeling full of gratitude and good spirits, he caught sight of Senator Reynolds's aide, the flaxen-haired, blue-eyed man who had accosted him at the restaurant counter one evening. He was standing off to the side, by a doorway, looking straight at M. K. without any expression, neither cheer nor depression. He crooked one index finger up and gestured for M. K. to come.

"Would you be willing to talk?" he asked when M. K. came near.

"Sure," M. K. said, though he was not sure.

The man led him through the doorway into a long, unmarked corridor, rather dank and dark. At the end of it was a set of narrow, steep wooden stairs. Under one of the stairs a small table and two wrought-iron chairs had been placed.

"Let's sit here," the man said, gesturing to the chairs. "It's very private. No one will bother us."

"Where are we?" M. K. asked. "What are these stairs for?"

The man shrugged. "The Capitol is full of forgotten passageways."

When they were seated, the man reached out a hand to shake. M. K.

noted how white his skin was, his hand meatless and bony. "Maybe you've forgotten my name," the aide said. "I'm Butch Crespo."

M. K. gave his name. Crespo had his eyes closed down almost to slits, as though he had a headache. Then he opened them quickly. "You know that the wets are celebrating tonight," he said. "They believe they have a victory."

"I didn't know they were so confident."

"Yes," Crespo said. "They are celebrating. And laughing."

"Because they think we have fallen into their trap?"

"Yes."

A wellspring of good cheer made itself felt throughout M. K.'s body. It did not go far, though, because he looked at the waxen face and the white eyebrows, the almost invisible eyelashes, and saw nothing that he could take joy in humiliating. Crespo seemed like a bird that has flown into a window and sits stunned on the sill while it recovers.

"You don't look like you're celebrating," M. K. said.

"I don't think you people are so easily caught," Crespo said. "I imagine that you think you can get thirty-six states in six years. And I imagine that if you think you can, you probably can."

"Then what is there to talk about?"

"I don't know. You seemed decent. I don't think so highly of your bosses," Crespo said. And he gave just a hint of a smile, very quickly, as though to see how M. K. took it. "I wondered what you thought it would be like when the law passes. What do you think will happen?"

"The world will be a better place." As he said it, a memory of Darla came into M. K.'s mind. He rarely thought of her death anymore, but when he did, the pain suffused his body, like a bone bruise accidentally touched.

"You believe that? You think it will be a better place if a fellow can't get a beer to cool his throat?"

M. K. was tempted to tell him about Darla. His sympathy for the man was curdling into dislike. "The world will be a better place if it's hard to get alcohol. Yes. You need to remember that some of those fellows cooling their throats are taking the food out of their children's mouths to do it."

"And you think that one of those fellows is going to stop drinking because of your law. He won't stop because his wife begs him and his kid is hungry, but he will because of a piece of paper that passed the Senate today."

"I don't think that fellow will have a choice. There won't be any beer to drink, no matter how much he wants it."

Crespo shook his head rapidly, as if in disgust. "Some people are just born to trouble. They'll find it no matter what the law says."

"Maybe," M. K. said. "But there are a lot of other people who can stay out of trouble if they're given something of a chance. Those are the ones who are going to be much better off once we pass this law."

They didn't have anything else to talk about, so M. K. went out via the dank corridor and caught up with the jubilation of the ASL troops.

———

Several times during the fall M. K. thought of that strange conversation. What had been the point? Why had Crespo sought him out? The dialogue had ended inconclusively and without even the common grace of friendliness.

M. K. was not even sure why Crespo stayed in his memory. *Perhaps,* he thought, *it is because the man lacked any obvious venal reason for opposing the law.* Exposed as he was to Congress, M. K. was quickly acquiring the habit of thinking that everyone had an angle. But Crespo did not cry about protecting the liquor trade's property or about the government's intrusion into private matters (there was nothing private about

the huge industrial business that prohibition promised to shut down).
He probably was not German with a name like Crespo. Why did he
care, as he apparently did?

All through the fall, the prohibition amendment lay quiet. The ASL
was not ready to bring the vote to the House. League leaders thought
they had the votes, but with all the recesses and absences of the fall
months, they feared the unexpected. And there really was no rush. They
would do well to have everything prepared before the vote.

If you read the newspapers, you would hardly have known that
such a great national reform was in the offing. The war took everyone's attention, and the issue of patriotism and loyalty was all anyone
talked about. In September the FBI raided the International Workers
of the World, the Wobblies. They seized treasonous papers and
arrested leaders, most notably Big Bill Haywood, he of the huge
shoulders and the wounded eye, who had caused fear to shiver
through many communities by his declaration that the IWW had no
morals. Meanwhile the troops arrived in Europe and in November
saw their first blood. The ASL made a campaign over protecting the
boys from the evils of drink and prostitution in France, and that
attracted more attention than the impending end of the liquor trade
in the entire U.S.

But M. K., Wheeler, Cannon, and all the ASL men never took
their eyes off the amendment, not for one second. The vote in the
House came finally on December 18. They had counted and recounted
their votes, so it was no surprise to anyone that the Eighteenth
Amendment passed, 282 to 128. Unlike the original motion, it allowed
a year's grace for the liquor trade to close up, and consequently the ratification period was extended to seven years. M. K. heard that the wets
felt sure that thirty-six states would never ratify in seven years, and even
Wheeler and Cannon estimated that three or four years would be

needed. Such expectations made the passage seem like an interim step, one that merely passed on to the states the ultimate disposition of national prohibition.

After the vote M. K. walked around the Capitol grounds feeling disoriented, slightly stunned by the calm. There was no celebration, and no distress shown by the wets, either. It was almost as though nothing had happened.

Not to Wayne Wheeler, however. He called M. K. into his office that afternoon and handed over a thick sheaf of papers he had been scrawling longhand: press releases and statements that he thought M. K. could rewrite and hand out as quickly as possible. He had already offered interviews to a number of news reporters, and two of them were waiting impatiently in the outer office. "Let them wait," he told M. K., waving his hand. "It's good for them to wait." Three days ago he had told one of the reporters that local-option prohibition was like outlawing adultery in one room of the house. "We're going to clean up the whole house now," he had said with satisfaction.

He held out a paper sack of peanuts to M. K. "Try 'em. They're good and hot," he said. Wheeler often bought fresh peanuts from the vendors on the street, but M. K. had never seen him pop them into his mouth as rapidly as he did today, throwing the shells into a pile on his desk.

"You better get packed," he told M. K. "We're going to travel all over this country, to every state. Thirty-six is a big number, you know. I don't know how long it will take, but we'll get there. Thirty-six states. You should be prepared to travel."

M. K. was not averse to more work, but he had not expected it, either. He had thought that the state organizations would take up the ratification.

Suddenly a grin flooded over Wheeler's face, and he looked as young as a high school junior who had just thrown a firecracker under the football stands. "We've got our hands on real power now," he said. "We've got the power of the law." He was so excited, it was infectious.

"Almost," M. K. said. "First we have to get the amendment ratified by the states."

"Oh, we'll get it. And then we'll teach them to believe in punishment before death. Oh, we will teach them, M. K.!"

Book III
The Strength of Our Hands

Chapter 12

1920: Keeping the Law

Prohibition became law on a bleak January night when the weather in Washington, D.C., was cold and unforthcoming, not blustery or dramatic in any way but unpleasantly frigid. M. K. hardly noticed, for he felt so desperately happy. He thought of Darla. If she could see him now, if she somehow knew of this night, would she be happy? He thought of his children and of families he had met in little churches in Maryland and Pennsylvania and Virginia. All these faces seemed mixed into the moment. This night the achievement for which he had worked more than seven years came true in the majesty of law. M. K. wore his overcoat when he went out but left it unbuttoned to flap open. He nodded to every person he saw on the gray streets. In the ASL office he talked to the secretaries and kidded them and accomplished no work at all.

They all felt it, those who gathered at Washington's First Congregational Church that Thursday night to watch for midnight, when the law began, and to hear William Jennings Bryan preach. All the Washington leaders were there, Wayne Wheeler, Bishop James Cannon (yes, the Methodists had rewarded his hard work by making him a bishop, the most progressive and forward-thinking of all the bishops), and Senator Morris Sheppard and Congressman Andrew Volstead, who had labored over the law that put the amendment into practice through enforcement regulations. They sang hymns and prayed thanksgiving. Bryan, that old, balding champion of progressive causes, stood proudly before them and declared, quoting from the Bible, "They are dead which sought the young child's life."

The phrase rolled over and over in M. K.'s mind as he took the trolley back to his apartment. In the Bible it applied to the enemies of the baby Jesus, but surely Bryan was right to bring it into the present struggle. M. K. thought again of his own children, Linda and David, whom he had seen only once in three years, at Christmas. He had given up so much of life with them. They wrote once a week, but only at their aunt's insistence, he was sure. The letters were so rigid, missing all feeling. Of course, they barely remembered him. But even that seemed acceptable on this wonderful, cold night because today they began a new day. "They are dead which sought the young child's life." At least for this he could be proud. At least in this he would leave David and Linda some reason to be proud of their father.

The next morning at the ASL offices he lingered over the newspapers. Bryan's service got little notice compared to Billy Sunday's huge tabernacle wake in Norfolk, Virginia. The papers said a hearse with twenty pallbearers had borne an effigy of John Barleycorn to a mock funeral where ten thousand mourners heard Sunday offer a memorial. "Good-bye, John!" the evangelist shouted. "You were God's worst enemy!" Sunday told his congregation, "The reign of tears is over. The slums will soon be a memory. We will turn our prisons into factories and our jails into storehouses and corncribs."

M. K. remembered hearing Sunday preach against liquor in Everett, ten years ago. Linda had been there with him, just a solemn little girl. Who would have believed then that liquor would be banned forever from the United States? It had come so quickly, once events began rushing along. They had expected to need years for the states to ratify the amendment. Instead they had competed avidly for the right to vote it in—thirty-six states in just over a year's time.

The saloons and hotels had expected one last binge last night, and the police everywhere had been out in force, but the party hadn't materialized, even in New York. The mood among the drinking crowd, if you believed the papers, was resignation, even a little hopefulness. "Here's to Prohibition," one beer drinker was quoted by the very wet *Washington Star-Times*. "I'm willing to give up my little pleasure if it can help some poor drunk to get off the sauce." A few people might take Prohibition hard, but that was out of touch with the country. Americans knew they could become a better nation. They were willing to try it on for size.

M. K. wondered what he would do with himself. The past few months had been almost pointless, as the travel Wheeler had predicted proved unnecessary. No longer had they needed to prod progress along. Events had outrun them. Wheeler had been working with Congressman Volstead on the enforcement regulations, and the publicity and argument M. K. usually provided for the magazines seemed mostly superfluous.

Wheeler had asked M. K. to stay on because he said their work was not complete until they had established effective enforcement of the law. He thought M. K. could help put a spotlight on regions where enforcement was lax and publicize good efforts elsewhere. M. K. had agreed to continue through the rest of the year, but already he had begun to long for something different. He thought he might want to try his hand at working for some of the new magazines in New York. Besides that, he wondered whether he could reclaim Linda and David and reunite their family.

Five months later M. K. stood near the banks of the Detroit River, next to a rotund man in a suit with a bow tie who was scanning the water with binoculars. The man was Dennis McGuinern, a Prohibition agent whom Wayne Wheeler had recommended. The day was overwhelmingly humid, repeatedly fogging McGuinern's glasses and his binoculars. He dropped the binoculars onto his chest, where they were held by a heavy leather strap, and took out a handkerchief to wipe his glasses. His face was red and moist, and his neck was prickled pink and white.

McGuinern was a pleasant, talkative fellow, and if he seemed a little inept, he was at least humble about it. He was quite fat, but he had explained his portly figure with a smile and a shrug. "Doctor says I've got biscuit poisoning," he said.

"They're still there," McGuinern said lugubriously as he looked at the far shore of the river through his binoculars. He was watching smugglers who had a small boat ready to run the river.

Wheeler had sent M. K. to Michigan to look into law enforcement, for he said that the Volstead Act meant nothing unless it was enforced. "We've got the power of the law now," he had told M. K. the day before he left on this trip. "But we've got to use it. A hammer is no good if you never take it out and hit with it."

McGuinern does not make a very impressive hammer, M. K. thought. He had met M. K. at his hotel and promised to show him what enforcement was all about, but answered vaguely about his background, except when discussing Congressman Mabry. Yeah, he had finished high school, but he mumbled when asked the high school's name. McGuinern was definite that he was a great admirer and friend of Congressman Mabry. That was undoubtedly how he had gotten the job, Mabry being a reliable dry. Prohibition agents were not under the Civil Service, largely because Wheeler felt that it was better to regulate them by the dry political powers rather than by bureaucratic red tape. "We'll make sure they do their job," he said with his broad, country-lawyer grin. "We can keep the pressure on through our friends." Nowadays

Wheeler spent much of his time at the Treasury Department, which had responsibility for enforcement.

"Here comes the patrol," said McGuinern. He pointed down the broad sweep of silvery water toward a large boat, running up the river at a good speed.

M. K. borrowed McGuinern's binoculars and scanned the cruiser. He didn't know anything about boats, but this one seemed impressively swift. A small United States flag flew from the stern, and he could see a uniformed officer scanning with his binoculars. The officer seemed to look directly at M. K., paused a moment, and then swept on.

"Why would he look on this shore?" M. K. asked. "Aren't the smugglers all on the Canada side?"

"You never know what you might find," McGuinern said vaguely.

"Can't he see the boat on the other side?" M. K. swung his glasses along the Canada shore until he found the small open boat, slightly longer and sleeker than a rowboat. Two men were lounging on the dock.

"Well, of course, he can see them. But they're in Canada. He can't do anything about them."

"Then what's the point of cruising up and down the river? They can see him, and he can see them."

"You never know what you might find."

They waited while the sound of the patrol boat faded away. Then they could again hear the lapping of water against the small pier. Somewhere in the branches a bird made a languid, hollow hooting. M. K. and McGuinern sat on a bank of moist leaves behind some sumac bushes, twenty yards behind the pier. M. K. felt his breathing coming in short, hot puffs. He had never seen law enforcement at work, and he was excited.

"Here they come," McGuinern said. "They're untying." He let his binoculars fall against the leather strap around his neck and smiled at

M. K. He seemed a strangely unfit figure. He might have been a drug-store owner.

"What will we do?" M. K. asked.

"Wait until they've unloaded, and then we'll step out of hiding and arrest them. You don't have to do anything except stand up when I stand up. They won't put up any fight."

"You're sure? What if they have guns?"

"They don't have guns."

McGuinern took a revolver out of his pocket. It was a large instrument with a long barrel, which he held gingerly. M. K. got the impression that he had not handled guns, or at least not this gun. McGuinern noticed M. K. looking at the pistol and smiled roguishly. "All ready for some target practice," he said.

Now they could hear the yammer of a boat engine, snarling gradually louder until, just when it seemed nearly on top of them, it cut back and died into a guttural mutter. From the brush they could see nothing beyond the verdant orb surrounding them: tall trees and brush all around, making the river invisible when they hid behind the sumac. The engine seemed for a time to murmur outside their range, causing M. K. to wonder whether the criminals had seen them and turned aside, or whether they had a different destination from this dock. McGuinern claimed that he had been scouting the same boat all week, and that it took the identical route every day. "I saved this peach for you," he had said. "We'll pluck it together."

Suddenly it seemed as though the boat were practically in their laps. M. K. could hear men's voices, giving soft, short commentary and direction. "Right there . . . Got it? . . . All right." The engine cut out and died.

Muffled sounds of unloading came next: grunts when the cases were lifted, a dull thump when they landed on the dock. M. K. wondered where the whiskey went next. Would a car come for it? Should they watch for an ambush from behind? M. K. glanced toward McGuinern, whose face was turned in the direction of the shore. Apparently he could see something through the brush.

McGuinern turned to M. K. and raised his eyebrows, a devilish grin on his face. He seemed quite jolly about the whole affair. Standing up slowly, he held out his pistol at arm's length. "Hands up! Hands up, gentlemen! Is that good whiskey you've got there?"

One of the men on the dock let out an oath. M. K. had forgotten to stand. He crouched in the bushes, looking at the rotund figure of McGuinern brandishing his weapon. McGuinern reminded M. K. of one of the cowboys in the Biograph films.

"Gentlemen, stop right there! Hands up!"

M. K. remembered that he was supposed to stand and did so. He saw two men dressed in jeans and sleeveless shirts. A stack of wooden boxes rested between them on the pier.

The man nearest the boat shouted, "Who are you?"

"Prohibition Bureau. Now put your hands up or I'll get started plugging holes in you."

Without a moment's hesitation the man who had spoken jumped into the boat. An explosion shattered the air, and M. K. threw himself to the ground. He thought they might be attacked from behind until he saw McGuinern pointing his pistol awkwardly toward the dock and so concluded that McGuinern had shot. The boat engine started up. M. K. got to his feet again and saw the boat cast off from the dock and turn in the narrow channel. As it came around, the second man, still on the dock, launched himself toward it. For a moment his distended body was frozen in space, and then it came up just short, smashing into the side of the boat and into the water. The man clutched the boat with one arm thrown over its side.

Another explosion, and M. K. saw a patch of the dock explode. The boat veered wildly from the weight of one man dragging at its side. Then it straightened and escaped through the channel. They could hear the engine racing irregularly but could not see any more because of the screen of brush and trees along the river.

"They got away," M. K. said, taking stock and beginning to feel disappointment.

"The patrol boat might yet catch them," McGuinern said contentedly, looking over his pistol as if it were a strange piece of evidence he had happened to pick up. Then he put it into his pocket. "Let's go see what we got."

They opened up one of the cases—there were five sturdy wooden boxes, unmarked—and found newly minted bottles of Tall Tree Canadian.

"Nice stuff," said McGuinern. "I hate to spoil it. Do you want a bottle to take with you?"

M. K. frowned. "To take with me?"

McGuinern smiled and hitched his pants up. "For research on that article you're writing." He winked.

"No."

"Okay, then. Step back."

McGuinern held out his pistol and began emptying it into the cases. He had five shots left in the gun, which made a hellish noise, mixed with breaking glass. The pungent smell of alcohol filled the air. McGuinern's gun clicked several times before he realized he was empty and lowered it. He was still smiling.

"What did you do that for?" M. K. asked.

McGuinern shrugged and smiled. "It's war against whiskey," he said. "Now wasn't that fun? Would you like to have a shot?"

From Detroit M. K. went down to Westerville, Ohio, feeling nervous. Ernest Cherrington was the dominant voice at the ASL headquarters since Purley Baker had moved to Alabama. M. K. had met Cherrington several times now, but the chill between them remained. As far as M. K. could determine, nobody really liked Cherrington. Last year Baker had castigated him for trying to take over the organization. They had engaged in a major fracas that sent shock waves throughout the leadership. M. K. also knew that Wheeler and Cherrington did not get along. Yet Cherrington had made himself indispensable running the literature division of the organization. He took care of all the money pledges. He was hardworking and well organized and ambitious to run things.

Wheeler had insisted that M. K. meet with Cherrington. He needed to know the man, Wheeler said, though M. K. did not see why.

To M. K.'s surprise, Cherrington met his train and, while walking to the headquarters building, indicated that he had set aside the rest of the day for him. Cherrington was heavy and sober, and no conversationalist. They marched silently and quickly together, Cherrington insisting on carrying M. K.'s suitcase, which was weighed down with papers.

Cherrington made no fanfare at headquarters but took M. K. quickly into the back. M. K. thought that his office had changed not a bit since he had seen it six years ago. The same books were lined up evenly in the same positions on the same bookshelves. Cherrington, however, seemed more cordial—not particularly friendly, but not hostile, either. He acted genuinely curious to know M. K.'s impressions of Prohibition in Detroit. Michigan was an interesting case, the only industrial state bone dry since 1918, when the state law went into effect. For three days M. K. had talked to dozens of people, had participated in a raid, had seen Prohibition agents on the job, and what he learned encouraged him. He could easily see that the law was at work—literally at work—through the agents.

"You hear different opinions," M. K. said, "but the referendum last year was pretty clear. You know about that, of course. The wets wanted to let in beer and wine, and the voters turned them down, almost two to one. Everybody remarks on that. You hear that there's a lot less drunkenness, that children are getting fed and workers are more productive. They don't call in sick on Mondays like they used to. The factory owners are delighted with the law. Mr. Ford does everything he can for enforcement with his workers."

After pondering this for a moment, Cherrington grunted. "The usual story, then. What about enforcement?"

"They had a lot of trouble with booze coming up the highway from Toledo. But when Ohio finally went dry, that stopped a lot of that traffic. Now the big problem is what comes across the river from Canada." He told of his experience with McGuinern, embellishing the story just a little. He had found McGuinern very entertaining. At any rate, the gunfire and the stakeout had impressed him. He intended to write a piece about McGuinern that would emphasize his cool demeanor under fire.

"I'd say we have some dedicated agents," M. K. remarked, "but we will need a lot more. That river has hundreds of places to cross. They wait for the patrol boat to pass and head on over."

"How many agents do you think you'd need to stop it?" Cherrington asked.

"It's hard to say. There are about fifteen or twenty miles of riverfront. Say, one officer every half mile on the shore."

"Day and night."

"Yes, day and night. Right now they're so brazen they cross in the daylight, but you're right I'm sure, they'd do it at night very happily. Another way would be to get three or four more boats, fast ones. But that might be very expensive."

"What about in the city? Any speakeasies? Any problems with secret manufacture?"

"If it's there, it's out of sight. They make some arrests, sure, but the agents gave me the feeling it was under control. The river isn't under control, but I'm sure when they get additional agents or convince the Canadians to patrol their side of the river, that will all change. Overall, I think the Michiganders are happy. The vote says it, doesn't it?"

Cherrington didn't appear particularly happy at these tidings. He kept his head down, staring into some papers on his desk. "Tell me what the churches are doing," he said.

Cherrington's sour, unhappy aspect began to register. He was not unfriendly to M. K., but he seemed to ask one suspicious question after another, as though he was waiting to hear where the work failed. "I don't know that the churches have much to do with it now," M. K. said. "Of course, they're supportive. For the league, pledges are way down."

Cherrington scowled. "That worries me," he said. "I'll tell you why, Mr. Nichols. The Eighteenth Amendment isn't the end of our activities. It's a very important tool, but it's not the end."

"I realize that. Enforcement is critical."

"I don't mean that."

"Then what do you mean?"

"That America must become a dry nation. That temperance must become ingrained in our national character."

"I thought that was what the Eighteenth Amendment was all about."

"It's a very important statement of principle, but that doesn't mean it's in people's hearts. Oh, certainly, it's in the hearts of rural communities, and most Anglo-Saxon communities, but what about the Negro? What about the Pole? What about the Italian? Or the Russian Jew? Those foreigners come from lands where drunkenness is a birthright, where there's no democracy of any kind. A lot of them don't even speak English. And we've got to help them along or the Eighteenth Amendment isn't going to mean anything. They aren't coming into our churches, so the churches need to go out to them."

"You amaze me," M. K. said. He felt suddenly weary of Cherrington. "You're saying that an amendment to the Constitution doesn't mean anything. What were we slaving for all those years? What could be more basic than an amendment to the Constitution? Not once in the history of our nation has an amendment been reversed, and truthfully I don't believe anyone has ever really tried to do it."

Cherrington half rose out of his seat and dropped his weight on his hands as if to press the desktop into the ground. "Yes, an amendment is fundamental. It won't matter, though, if we can't convince more Americans to understand its worth. The churches have got to carry on with their mission to uplift the lives of these people. The law won't do that. You see? It states the principle in the strongest way. Somebody has got to explain it and reason with people who don't understand. Otherwise all the enforcement that the Treasury and the state and the city can muster won't be enough. The border with Canada is six thousand miles long. We can't station an agent every half mile, day and night."

Cherrington's reaction bewildered M. K. What was there to explain about the law? People needed to know only that they had better stay away from booze; the dry way was the American way. The simpler, the better. That was what was wrong with near-beer laws and other so-called moderate substitutes for a tough, clear law. Moderation confused people. They needed simple directions printed in large type.

"Look," M. K. said, "we're not disagreeing, are we? I'm a writer, like you. I want people to understand that Prohibition is good for them too. But the law is the law. It has to be enforced, or it stops being the law."

Cherrington rubbed his head with his hands. "You're right, Mr. Nichols, you're right," he said, though his tone did not sound convinced.

M. K. took the interurban train down to Columbus, got a quick bite in the station, and then caught a train to Chillicothe and thence to Hillsboro. It was a long, slow ride through farm country. M. K. watched the green hills stream past as long as the light stayed, thinking in a melancholy way of his boyhood in terrain much like this. Farmers got on and off at each stop, to his eyes the same men he had never noticed growing up, because they were a permanent feature of the landscape, like the dirt on your boots. Everything appeared the same even though he had been gone ten years and the world had changed completely.

M. K. puzzled over his meeting with Cherrington, particularly the disagreement or difference in emphasis that had never quite opened up as a chasm between them. He could not grasp Cherrington's point of view—had not been able to do so while they talked, veering close to and then away from the chasm, and could not now as he thought it over. It was almost as though Cherrington thought nothing had changed with the Eighteenth Amendment, that they ought to go right on campaigning for the law as if America remained a wet country, as if they were pleading for the Irish and the German and the hyphenated minorities to grant them a temperate country.

Cherrington would admit that the Eighteenth Amendment was a great and unbreakable achievement, but then he would go on about his educational strategy almost as if the amendment were a fragile and temporary thing. It was a strange way of thinking, and M. K. finally gave up trying to grasp it. No wonder Cherrington had few friends in the league.

He reached Hillsboro on the last train, arriving a little past midnight. Hillsboro was far enough south that summer was very present in the wind, sweet and thick like a milk shake made of air. No one had come to meet him, for which he was glad. He did not mind walking to his brother's house, which was only half a mile away, and listening to this wakeful night. A breeze shivered the leaves of the trees overhead, a sound that he heard in the darkness and recognized, though he could see nothing overhead but a dark sky.

He came around the corner to his brother's house and was standing on the front walk, pondering what to do about waking the family and getting inside, when he heard the engine of a car running along some distance away. He noticed only because it was so late and there were no other sounds. He found it hard to imagine any car in Hillsboro; they had been almost nonexistent when he left in '06. Possibly the car would pass by him, and he would see who it was. Thinking as a man does when he returns to the town he grew up in, M. K. considered that it might be someone he knew, some old high school friend.

When he realized the car was going to pass him, he turned toward it, but saw only the yellow headlights as the car ran past. To his surprise, the car slowed and stopped, not twenty yards past him. *Someone did recognize me,* he thought, and he began to walk toward the auto to offer greetings. He could see that it was a new car, a Dodge.

Then the car door opened and someone got out. A woman. "Hey," he said, "it's M. K. Nichols. Who is that?"

"It's me, Daddy."

"Who?"

"It's Linda, Dad."

"Linda? What are you doing out? It's past midnight."

She did not answer for a couple of beats. "We got lost. The car got stuck, and we had to have somebody pull us out."

"We? Who is we?" He had come up to her but stood at a little distance from her shadow.

Linda leaned back into the car and spoke a few words. The other door opened, and an opaque figure unraveled itself. A man came around the car and approached M. K. He must have been more than six feet tall.

"This is Ray," Linda said. Ray did not offer a hand to shake.

"Glad to meet you, Ray. What did you say your last name was?"

"McCloskey. Ray McCloskey."

"Well, thanks for bringing my daughter home. Let's get in, shall we, Linda?"

There was, he thought, a mute exchange between the two of them, and then Linda came toward him. She had a key, and they went inside. M. K. waited while she lit a lamp. He heard the car still gargling outside. What was he waiting for?

The light flared and he got a shock. Linda had cut her hair brutally short, and her face was painted pale white with blistering red lips. Her dress stopped at her knees, and she looked to him like a bad copy of a woman he might see in a picture in a newspaper. The worst thing was that she was not a girl anymore. He saw that instantly before he took in the reason why. She had the stare of an impudent woman.

"Didn't you know I was coming?" he asked.

She said nothing—nothing in her defense, and nothing in the way of a greeting. That had been a lie about the car being stuck, he knew. The same with being lost. M. K. felt a terrible sickness pass through him, a feeling like being struck from behind.

"Do you know where Aunt Arlene wants me?" he asked, lacking the stomach to face the facts.

"Sure," she said. "In Joey's bedroom."

"Show me, " M. K. said. "We can talk in the morning."

They did not talk in the morning because there was no way to do it around the family breakfast, and then she had to go to school. "She's become quite a beauty," Arlene said after she had gone out the door with her books clasped against her chest.

"She will not go to church," his mother said. "She cut off her hair, and nobody knows what she does out at night. Nobody seems to care."

His mother had come to the breakfast table in her nightgown. Her hair had turned completely gray since M. K. last saw her, and she seemed to have lost all the starch in her body. Her shoulders hunched, and her hair hung down limp and thin. Her appearance repelled him. He had rebelled against her strong-mindedness when he was young, but now she did not seem like his mother.

"I care, Mother," M. K. said. He turned to Arlene. "Who is this Ray?"

Arlene lifted her eyebrows as if to say he meant nothing to her. "That he comes from Arliss is all I know about him."

"He does not go to church with her," his mother said. "I do not know that he goes to any church. I ask her about it and she puts me off."

It was time for David to go off to school. He had come running in while they ate, his wet hair askew and in his eyes, and slammed down his eggs like someone in an eating contest at the fair. He was excited to see his father. He talked, telling everything that he was doing, at the same time he kept his fork moving to his mouth, feeding the harvester. As soon as he finished, he ran out of the house, slamming the back door, and then half a minute later ran in again. "I forgot my math," he said. "Where did I put my math?"

Arlene was already on her feet, smiling. She disappeared with him into the living room.

"Where are you going to church?" his mother asked M. K. "You never mention it in your letters."

"That's because I go to a lot of different churches with Mr. Wheeler from the Anti-Saloon League. Every Sunday it's a new church."

"That is no way to live," she said. "Surely Mr. Wheeler has a church."

"He's a Methodist like me, Mother, but you know how the ASL holds special services. That's what we're doing."

"You do not belong to a church at all?"

"Of course, I do. I'm a member at Garland Methodist, but I can't go very often. My Sundays are full."

"That is no way to live. You need to have a church. I would like to know how you can be an example to your children if you do not have a church of your own."

David ran through the kitchen again, out the back door, and down the porch steps. Arlene came in and sat down, smiling. "He's quite a boy," she said. "You should be proud of him. And I'm not saying you shouldn't be proud of Linda too."

"Is she giving you trouble? I need to talk to her."

"I wouldn't say she's giving me trouble. I worry a little that she might give herself trouble. Things are so different today. We didn't dress like that when I was a girl. We didn't go out in a car."

"You didn't have cars," M. K. reminded her.

"No, and there's no telling where they go or what they do."

"How old is this Ray?"

Arlene shrugged. "He's out of school," she said. "All I know is he lives in Arliss. I don't know where he gets his money. Maybe his daddy is rich." Arliss was a crossroads town fifteen miles to the south.

M. K.'s mother sniffed. "I never heard of anybody having money in Arliss."

M. K. thought about this breakfast conversation while he walked down to Samson's store. *Arlene is a good mother to the children,* he thought. *She seems genuinely fond of them both.* Thank God for Arlene. His mother could never have managed it. All her character and strength had dwindled to nothing, leaving a one-note melody: Have you been to church? Have you been to church?

Even though he was grateful to Arlene, when he thought of his children here in Hillsboro, he felt some soreness. M. K. had never gotten along with Samson, and yet Samson was acting the father to them. They should have had their own mother raise them, but instead they had Arlene. Surely they grew up in patterns subtly alien to his own. A vine will shape itself to the trellis that it finds as it pushes upward, and he was absent from their daily lives.

His mother's harping on churchgoing had irritated him, and he could only imagine how she must irritate Linda. It did cross his mind that she had hit on something, though. He also felt despondent when he thought of his life in Washington. Though he had joined Garland Methodist when he first went to Washington, no one there knew him. He doubted that the pastor knew his name. M. K. had many friends through the ASL, but they were scattered hither and yon, and their friendship did not extend beyond the exigencies of the cause. M. K. felt almost that his Christianity had dried up like a gourd, its shape still strong and hard, but without the greenness of life inside.

Yet he did not really like the fervent Christians he knew. None of them seemed really zealous for the dry cause. They were mildly supportive, but their churches and their revivals and their Christian Endeavor seemed always to come first.

The first thing he noticed when he got to Main Street was that Samson had expanded into the building next door. The brick storefront displayed a large vertical sign in the shape of an inverted T, spelling

NICHOLS from top to bottom, and HAULING in smaller letters across. M. K. went in the front door and said hello to the desk clerk.

"Ah, Mr. Nichols, your brother said you were in town. Are you staying long? I see that daughter of yours. She's quite a beauty."

"Thank you," he said. After he had gotten through some pleasantries, M. K. walked around the counter and through a door to the back, where two large trucks were parked with their hoods up. A man's legs in brown coveralls protruded from underneath one. Running up the stairs toward Samson's office, he considered his brother's success. He must be one of the biggest men in town now.

The last time he had seen Samson, there had been a thaw between them. Samson seemed to appreciate M. K.'s willingness to leave his children, whom he liked. M. K. had been careful to send money regularly. His brother, he recognized, measured much of life in dollars.

Samson had his bookkeeper in the office when M. K. knocked, but he wound up that business in a hurry and offered a seat. M. K. noted that his brother had not been in the sun, so his skin was light and his straw-white hair a little darker than he remembered it. His sky blue eyes burned out of a white face. They talked in pleasantries before M. K. asked him about Linda.

Samson stared at him for a moment, deadpan. "Arlene is a little worried about her," he said. "But I don't think it's anything."

"What do you know about this Ray?"

"I know a little."

"What does he do?"

Samson stared again, utterly expressionless, before he said, "He's involved in some business down near Arliss."

He stopped but seemed to have something more that he wanted to say. M. K. waited.

"I hear—I don't know this for a fact—that there's a little illegal business down there. Something about Kentucky distilleries and some phony invoices for alcohol."

"You mean he's running moonshine?" M. K. had involuntarily gripped the arms of his chair as if to lift himself up.

"Well, I don't know that."

"Why have you let her see him?"

"Good grief, M. K., she's almost seventeen years old. She could be married by now."

M. K. took a deep breath and deliberately leaned back in his chair. "But have you talked to her? Do you think she knows what he does?"

"I've told her I don't particularly care for the man. She doesn't listen. You talk to her. Maybe she'll pay attention to you."

M. K. felt extremely upset. He knew he would have no more impact on Linda than Samson did—probably less.

"Why would anybody do such a thing?" he said almost to himself, though he pronounced the words out loud.

"Do what?"

"Sell liquor. It's illegal, it destroys people, and it undermines the law. What kind of man would do such a thing?"

Samson shrugged. "Somebody who wants to make some easy money," he said. "That's not hard to understand."

Chapter 13
1923: Raising a Grown Child

When M.K. finally talked to Linda, she had very little to say for herself. She had somehow absorbed the fact so few ever get, that a woman is not obliged to explain herself. When M. K. said he heard that Ray was involved with illegal activities, she didn't ask who said it. She didn't deny it or confirm it. She simply glared at him with those intent almond eyes, leaving M. K. with his frustration. She seemed unclaimable.

Ray was no match for her, either, it turned out, and in the fall Arlene wrote to say that he had dropped out of the picture. He was not the cause of concern, however. Linda was. The sheen of womanly sophistication grew steadily more electric. She was no longer an imitation of a picture in a magazine; she was an original composition. To see her walk out of Samson's house every morning was to witness a daily miracle, like a plow's furrow staining the earth purple, or New Orleans jazz rising from a Methodist church choir.

Samson, unburdened by fatherhood in her case, admired her and encouraged her, though Arlene told him to quit. She knew that Linda had no sense of direction. She was only experimenting with dangerous equipment. Men bought her clothes. Men in Hillsboro, Ohio, bought her all kinds of things that she wanted, and she learned to order by mail and boss the storekeepers so that she could get whatever suited her style. By the time of her senior year in high school, it was a joke that she should go to the school dances and football games. The boys didn't even try for her. The girls didn't talk to her. She was a year older than most of her classmates, but the gap was much larger than that.

After her graduation in June of 1923, M. K. told her that he wanted to take her back with him to Washington, D.C. He had come to the ceremony determined to persevere in this, though he fully expected her to fight him. They talked in the Nicholses' parlor where a party was on with white sugar cake and punch, and some of the girls in Linda's class were giggling and wondering how they looked all dressed up. Linda wore a lilac chiffon that suited her so perfectly it would barely be remembered because it seemed as natural as the contour of the ground and brought out her nut-brown hair and eyes and her seamless skin.

"Why do you want me in Washington?" she asked him. She was not defiant, but she asked in the way a self-possessed person wants to know your opinion for her own benefit.

"I don't think Hillsboro is a good place for you now," he said. "It's too small. You can get a job in Washington that won't bore you. You'll meet better society."

"Most people say a big city is less suitable for a decent girl," she said archly. "You don't think so?"

It frightened him to realize that she had grown to talk in such a self-assured, mocking way. "It depends on what you choose to do in a big city," he said. "And now you're old enough to take care of yourself, why shouldn't you live with me? I'd like to have you nearby."

"You're looking for a housekeeper," she said.

"Not really. I keep house all right myself."

"You think you can rein me in then. That's what everybody tries to do, except Uncle Sam."

"What does your marvelous uncle Sam try to do?"

"Nothing. He thinks I'm just fine. Ask him, and he'll tell you."

Nevertheless, she went with him. M. K. longed to take David as well, for David was at a delectable age and merely to watch his activity was a pleasure. In June David lived for nothing but baseball. M. K. walked over to the park to watch him play, and he felt the strength of the town. It would be inexplicably harsh to tear him away from his diamond where he lived his every spare moment. Besides, M. K. knew that still he could not properly raise the boy, not while his work continued. He would not be present many evenings, and how Linda would perform as a substitute mother, he did not know.

At one time Linda had looked like her mother's twin, but she appeared less so now because in some indefinable way she seemed healthier, more robust, than had her mother. Linda was full of rude good spirits, whereas Darla had seemed delicate, ghostly at times. At least that was how M. K. remembered her. Perhaps he did not remember truly at all. He could no longer be sure, and in any case it made no difference.

He was happy just to watch Linda as they rode on the train toward Washington, but his pleasure went beyond that. Linda talked to him. She seemed happy and excited to be going to Washington, asking questions about where he lived and what the apartment was near. He remembered that for all her seeming sophistication, she had grown up in a small Ohio town, just as he had. He well remembered the unbeatable wallop of his train trip to Everett just after college, and he talked to her about that time of his life just before he had met her and her mother.

He noticed that her eyes dropped when he spoke of Darla. He asked her what she was thinking. The train was rolling across Pennsylvania over steep defiles.

"I'd never do what she did," Linda said, making her eyes small. "She ruined it for us."

M. K. was alarmed by her sudden change of mood and asked what she meant.

"I mean she killed herself," Linda said. "She drank herself to death. I'll never do that."

"Do you mean to say that you'll never drink? I hope you won't."

"Not that. It's not the drink that killed her. She just killed herself."

"Linda, do you know how she died?" His words came softly. He had never spoken to anyone about this since leaving LA.

"She was run over by a horse. Right?"

"Yes, they were making a movie, and there was an accident. But she didn't show good judgment, and the reason was that she had been drinking. People gave it to her. It's not right to say that she killed herself. She made a bad judgment."

"Didn't you tell her not to?"

"Of course I did." M. K. paused, listening to the regular thump of the train.

"Then why did she do it?"

He wondered whether to this day he knew why. "She drank because it calmed her nerves when she was nervous," he said finally.

"She was nervous a lot then."

"Yes, especially in the movies. I don't think plays affected her so much because she did the same performance over and over. The movies made her nervous."

"Anyway," Linda said, "she threw her life away. She shouldn't have done that."

He thought how everything seems extremely clear when you are nineteen. "Linda, that's why I'm working for the Anti-Saloon League. If your mother hadn't had alcohol, she'd be alive today. I don't think you're right to say she threw her life away. She had help. People were giving the stuff to her."

Linda was quiet, and M. K. wondered whether she thought of Ray or someone else. He had never spoken to her about Ray's business.

The Rays of the world seemed to be on the increase. The papers were full of stories about Prohibition agents chasing fast cars, boats, even airplanes. They said in New York you could buy a drink as easily as you bought a newspaper. Even the U.S. Senate had its own bootlegger, according to what M. K. was told, though he doubted it was true. Sometimes the newspapers could be quite sensationalistic, and no doubt the car chases and gunfights made for good copy.

A lot of M. K.'s work now involved fighting the battle of statistics, showing that Prohibition had cut crime rates, improved health, and so on. The newspapers didn't give a balanced picture. In most of America, Prohibition was as quietly accepted as Monday night. Even in the big cities, social workers said it had done no end of good for the working class. The trouble was, this didn't make as good a story as the shoot-outs. When you remove an evil from society, the action leaves no trace. The absence of the evil allows good to fill in, but the outline of the evil does not even show anymore. People soon forget because they cannot see anything. It was his job to help them see.

M. K. changed the subject. "We haven't talked about what kind of work you want to do. I could probably help you get something in a government office."

Linda shook her head sharply. She knew her own mind about this. "I don't want to be in an office. I need to be out and about. Maybe I can work as a waitress."

She did get a job as a waitress at a place M. K. had never heard of. He went by to look at it, and it seemed respectable enough. So he let it go, with regrets. He knew that he couldn't control a nineteen-year-old, certainly not this one.

With her first month's pay she bought a radio. She did not ask his permission. He found her listening to it when he came home from a short excursion to Baltimore. It was an elegant piece of mahogany furniture about the size of a large icebox, and Linda had placed it directly in front of her favorite chair, as though it were her personal musical device. He made her move it into the corner, and they both sat in their chairs listening until Linda had to go to work.

M. K. had to admit that it was a fascinating experience. He was reminded of the time when he used to go to the movies every day. That was the last time he had felt a story so vividly. He had heard people talk about the radio shows, but he had never dreamed that they could be so captivating.

Linda asked him once how she could see some of her mother's movies. That was the only time he could recall her showing curiosity about Darla, after that one conversation on the train. Unfortunately he was stumped. "There must be prints somewhere, but I wouldn't know where to look. I suppose I could write Biograph. They might have some in New York, stored away somewhere. Even if they did, I don't know how we could see them. We'd have to rent a theater. Why are you interested?"

"I don't really remember what she looked like," Linda said.

So he knew that she sometimes thought of her mother, but they never managed to converse about it. Not only did she avoid the subject, but with her working hours and his they were very seldom together. Sometimes if he came home early, he saw her briefly before she went to the restaurant. The place, known as Oliver's, had music and dancing, and she rarely came home before midnight. On weekends it was later, and then she slept in very late the next day. Sundays he still went with Wheeler to various churches, mostly in Pennsylvania or Maryland. He encouraged Linda to attend church, but she answered him vaguely and seldom got up in time to go. She was like her mother in not volunteering information easily.

To make up for it, the ASL office was a very happy place for him. Dinwiddie had left and taken his quarrelsome ways with him, and Cannon as a bishop had very little time for the work. Wheeler was completely in charge now, and he seized his enlarged responsibilities with gusto. It was true that Cherrington sniped at him from Ohio, that Baker had his doubts and Cannon his criticisms, but they were not on the scene. Wheeler parried them when necessary, but mainly strutted merrily along.

Cherrington's main gripe was that Wheeler had made the ASL all but an arm of the Republican Party. Wheeler's line, when this complaint was voiced to him, was as follows: "I'm concerned to hear that. My goal all along has been to make the Republican Party an arm of the Anti-Saloon League." He pointed out that as a fellow Ohio Republican, he had the good fortune to know President Harding well. He fully intended to take all advantage of that for the good of the country. When a Democratic administration came to power, he hoped that the complaint might reverse itself, that people would think of them as an arm of the democracy.

He adored elections. He loved to plan for them, talk of them, work them, win them. He knew a thousand tricks. Wheeler had whipped the wets so thoroughly in so many elections that the politicians didn't even test his credibility anymore.

Everyone had known that the wets stood to gain in the 1922 congressional elections. It was natural in an off year following an outstanding presidential election. Nonetheless, Wheeler had made plans. He planted questions with reporters to goad the wets into revealing the candidates they intended to support. Then he used the ASL chapters and churches to bombard those candidates with letters asking why they had allied themselves with the notorious wet cause. Most candidates were shy of that kind of publicity. Some of them openly repudiated wet support as a result. In the election, the wets were routed. The ASL could now claim 296 drys in the House. Twenty-five of the thirty-five senators elected were dry. The wets, Wheeler crowed, had "snatched defeat from the jaws of victory," and they had the driest Congress ever. Wheeler didn't mind letting the newspapers know, either. He loved to brag about his prowess.

One of the newspapers began referring to him as the "Dry Boss," and he liked the phrase so much he used it in his releases to the press. He enjoyed the limelight, was happy to slug it out with the wets in public debate, and felt no doubts whatsoever that he could represent the best interests of the Prohibition cause. The newspapers and magazines thought that Wheeler *was* the ASL. Every day he came bustling in and out of the office, cheerfully greeting everyone in sight, like a little dog that sees himself as belonging to the class of the Great Danes. He even became an author, offering articles to the most popular magazines and newspapers in the country, and showing off his publications like a new father. He liked to tell people that no publication had ever rejected one of his works.

The same with his legal contributions. He had Edward Dunford in a back office writing briefs and opinions, which Wheeler presented as his own. Dunford did not resent this, and neither did M. K. when he wrote an article that appeared under Wheeler's name. Both men took Wheeler just as he was. The man did not lack generosity. He simply and heartily trusted that whatever he believed, the ASL believed, and whatever benefited his reputation was for the benefit of the dry cause, and whatever helped the dry cause helped America. He was irrepressible. It was hard to resent such an attitude, though M. K. could understand, too, why not everyone in the organization felt quite happy with Wheeler.

How many people anywhere could say that they lectured the president? In May, Wheeler went to see Harding, announcing it in advance to the whole office. "He's forgetting where he is," Wheeler said. "I've got to go and remind him." According to his own account, he told Harding that he was embarrassing them by drinking in the White House. "You've got to get off the sauce and declare it publicly," Wheeler told the president. "Make a clean breast of it as an example to the country.

"So Harding says to me, 'I'm not well, Wheeler. I don't know if my health can take the shock of quitting whiskey so suddenly.' I told him I doubted that the Republican Party could take the shock if we had to publicly reprove him. He didn't have much to say to that." Wheeler let out a laugh.

Wheeler practically ran the Treasury's Prohibition Unit, which was in charge of enforcement. He handpicked its head, Roy Haynes, whom M. K. knew slightly from his boyhood when Haynes had been mayor of Hillsboro. M. K. was tempted to laugh when his name came up. Heading the Prohibition Unit was an important job, overseeing thousands of agents and millions of dollars. Nobody in Hillsboro had ever regarded Haynes as anything remarkable.

Wheeler seemed to see something in him, however. When he found out the link to M. K.'s boyhood, he was avid to introduce them.

"Oh, he won't remember me," M. K. said. "I was just a kid. He probably knows my brother."

"M. K., he's a politician. He's bound to remember you."

Wheeler dragged him into the Treasury offices to meet the man. At the end of the first long hallway, M. K. saw a poster with the WCTU's white star and slogan: WE ARE AMERICANS. WE HONOR THE

CONSTITUTION. That was the theme all the drys harped on: whether you were personally dry or wet, you could not possibly favor the undermining of the Constitution. M. K. had felt the power of this proposal all along, but it struck him in a new sense now, here in the building where officers were pledged to uphold that Constitution, here in an office of the government. *Really*, he thought, *the matter is settled. A constitutional amendment leaves no more room for debate, let alone deliberate disobedience to the law.* It made him feel a little angry to think that they continued to discuss the merits of Prohibition when it was not only law but constitutional law.

At the Treasury, Wheeler acted exactly the way he did in the ASL office: he greeted everyone (or people greeted him), he talked freely, and he grinned that country-boy grin. When they arrived at the rather solemn and high-toned exterior of Haynes's office, Wheeler joked with the secretaries as though they were old high school girlfriends. Then leading M. K., he walked straight into Haynes's office without an introduction.

Immediately Haynes was on his feet and clasping hands, making a mild joke with Wheeler while he turned a serious and obsequious face toward M. K. Probably because M. K. knew about him and knew his past, he watched Haynes doubtfully. He had known so many men like that in Hillsboro, men who couldn't think but could only dissemble. Haynes reminded M. K. of a man selling suits.

"Mr. Wheeler tells me that you are the league's communications officer," Haynes said. "You must possess extraordinary talent to carry that function while so young. *No* part of my responsibilities is more important to me than bearing glad tidings of Prohibition. And you are critical to that task, Mr. Nichols, absolutely critical."

He turned toward Wheeler, moving his whole body, M. K. noticed, as though he were a novice actor following stage directions. "Mrs.

Wheeler is well, I hope? Please give her my best. I continue to hear only the best news regarding Prohibition, Mr. Wheeler. The newspapers complain about the cost of enforcement, but they refuse to report the entire picture."

He pointed his body at M. K. again. "Mr. Nichols, we spend less than ten million dollars on enforcement, and last year the fines and expropriations amounted to sixty-one million dollars. The truth is, the government is making a profit on enforcement, and our operations are increasing in their effectiveness. Bootlegging! You read in the papers about the criminals who thrive, but you never read that bootlegging is now all but nonexistent in most parts of the country. Eliminated!"

Did the man believe what he said? M. K. had assumed not when he read his glowing reports on enforcement in the newspapers, but why would he put on an act with them?

"Mr. Nichols actually hails from Hillsboro," Wheeler said, perhaps to change the subject. They spent five minutes establishing whom they knew in common. To M. K.'s surprise, Haynes did not remember Samson.

Suddenly Haynes stopped short, in the middle of a sentence, and stared at M. K. "You can help me," he said. "I'll bet you know this fellow. A young fellow. Not from the town but from the area." He walked around his desk and shuffled through a pile of papers. "Here it is. He's seeking a position as an agent. Name of McCloskey. You know him?"

The name floated in M. K.'s memory. Possibly it was a name he had heard from Samson or one of Linda's friends. Then he made the connection, like two wires joined. "What's his first name?" he asked.

"Ray. Ray McCloskey."

He almost laughed. "He wants to be an agent?"

"Yes, he comes highly recommended by your congressman, Representative Lance. You know him, don't you?"

"No, I don't. But I know this Ray a little. My daughter went out with him a few years ago. The word I had was that he was a bootlegger."

It was Haynes's turn to be flabbergasted. "Your daughter dated a bootlegger? You allowed this?"

M. K. started to explain, but it seemed too complex. He admitted that he did not know McCloskey, he had met him only once.

"Even if he was a bootlegger," Wheeler cut in, "that's not necessarily a fatal objection, is it, Roy? He might have some inside understanding of how these criminals work. No, I think the main question is whether we can keep control of him. That's the genius of our system, that the fellow owes his job to the congressman who recommended him, and the congressman owes his political life to us. If we see that enforcement isn't top-notch, we can put on the pressure. We can turn the screws."

When they were walking back to the ASL office, Wheeler asked him what he had thought of Haynes. "A nice enough fellow," M. K. said. "I have to admit that I was surprised when he asked me about making McCloskey an agent. I'm sure they could find better men than that."

"Probably," Wheeler said, "but they don't pay much, you know."

"Don't you think the pay should be better? So they could attract a higher caliber of man?"

"Yes, but I don't see the Congress wanting Prohibition to cost a lot. You know, we've promised them that it will actually be economically beneficial, and they take a narrow view of that."

"I would think that honoring the Constitution would require a higher standard," M. K. said. "I'll tell you frankly, I don't like the idea of Ray McCloskey upholding the law."

"But he's not the crucial man," Wheeler said. "He almost doesn't matter. We can replace him."

"So who is crucial?"

"His congressman," Wheeler said. "We don't rely on finding angels,

M. K. We rely on power. Power they respect. Do you see why I'm determined to keep Cherrington from getting control of the ASL? Ernest Cherrington is a fine man, no doubt, but he thinks we can sit in Ohio and publish pamphlets and somehow control a situation that changes daily. He thinks our principles are what matter. He doesn't understand that the reason we've succeeded, where no other movement for temperance ever succeeded, is not that we are such fine, principled men, but that we know how to pinch politicians until they scream. There was no other way to get the law passed, and there's no other way to get the law observed. If we know how to make that congressman fear us, he'll make Ray McWhoever do his job. We can make him arrest his grandmother, so long as we have the power to make him or break him. And we do, M. K. We have it right here in Washington. Nobody has ever had the power that I do right now."

They walked together under the spreading green summer boughs that almost covered the street, and M. K. thought what an amazingly lucky man he was to be caught up in the middle of this reform. Wheeler called it unprecedented, and he was right. At Oberlin they proudly claimed the abolitionist heritage, but no abolitionist had ever been able to pull strings in Congress or virtually run a department of the federal government.

After a long silence full of satisfied quiet, Wheeler continued, "I will need your help, M. K. The others think we can stand back and issue fine-sounding pronouncements. They don't understand the workings of power."

"Bishop Cannon does," M. K. said. "People down in Virginia say he is the best politician in the state."

"You're right, but he's a Democrat. He will never have any success with these Republicans."

"What about Mr. Baker? He practically ran Ohio at one time."

"Not really. I did most of the running. But, yes, Purley Baker is shrewd. He's an old man, though, and he doesn't have the strength for it anymore. He wants to hold on to his position, but he can no longer do the work. Power requires a lot of hard work, M. K. It's never automatic. Power is always trying to escape to somebody else."

"What about Cherrington?" He already knew what Wheeler thought of Cherrington, but he wanted to hear his response.

"Cherrington!" Wheeler said with a snort.

M. K. was eager to tell Linda about her old friend Ray. He expected that it would make her laugh, and it would do them good to laugh together. Of course, she was not in the apartment when he got home. She had already left for her work.

The apartment felt moist and warm from the late summer sun that fell through its south window. M. K.'s disappointment opened his eyes to see the shabbiness of the upholstery of the living room furniture. He sat here every night, alone, reading the newspapers before he went to bed, and he was always careful to set the papers in a neat stack by the door before drinking a glass of milk and heading for bed, but he had not seen the threads coming loose from the corner of the cushion or the shiny dark surface on the front edge of the arms on the chair. He wondered whether Linda always saw them. Perhaps that was her reason for not wanting to be in the apartment.

Almost every night he fried a hamburger and ate it with coleslaw he made every Saturday. Every other day he bought a loaf of bread, and he kept a hunk of cheese in the icebox with the hamburger. He bought a quart of milk or, sometimes, buttermilk, and he could eat off that steadily. He never had paid much attention to what he ate, though he

enjoyed a good meal if someone made it for him. That was another disappointment. He had hoped that Linda would cook, at least occasionally. He could not remember that she had cooked a meal since joining
him.

M. K. sat on the sofa for fifteen minutes, idly pondering the furniture and his prospects for the evening. He knew he was making too
much of it, but he really had wanted to see Linda's reaction when he told
her about Ray. M. K. decided to go to Oliver's and see her. He had no
idea whether she would be allowed to sit down and talk, but at least he
could get a decent meal, something different from his hamburger.

The restaurant was on J Street, a little too far for a pleasant walk,
and an awkward spot to reach by trolley. M. K. took a taxi, an extrava-
gance he rarely afforded. When he began to tell the driver where Oliver's
was, the man looked at him and shook his head. "You think I'm new in
town?" he asked and set out for the place.

J Street was deserted, but inside the restaurant were a surprising
number of people, mostly men. He did not see Linda, so he let a waiter
seat him.

"You looking for someone?" the waiter asked. He must have seen
him looking around.

"Yes, Linda Nichols. She works here."

"I don't know her. Do you want some tea?" the waiter asked.

"You don't know her? Dark hair, dark eyes, very pretty."

"Yeah, I think I remember her. What about some tea while you
wait?"

"No, no thanks."

"We got a fresh shipment from overseas. Real tea, you know, not this
rank stuff people are selling."

M. K. looked at the waiter. The man was all seriousness. "All right,"
M. K. said, "I'll have some iced tea, please."

When the tall glass of brown liquid came, he did not have to take a sip to recognize it as liquor. M. K. flushed red. He supposed that he would report this, but why had it gone unreported until now? They did not seem to make a secret of it at all.

Linda sat down at his table. She had a crooked little smile on her lips, as though some little joke had occurred to her. "Hello, Daddy," she said. "What a surprise to see you here."

"You know about this?" he said, nodding toward the drink.

She shrugged, still smiling. "What brings you here, Daddy?"

The humor of his situation reached him, and he gave a little snort. "I came to share a little news, something I thought you'd find amusing. You remember your old friend Ray? I heard of him today. He's been proposed as a Prohibition agent in Hillsboro."

She did not laugh as he had thought she would, but gave two little taps on the table with her knuckles, as though she were practicing knocking on a door. "Ray," she said. "Ray McCloskey. I knew he would come to no good."

"More good than you've come to here apparently," M. K. said.

"I don't think that's called for," she said. "There's hardly a restaurant in town that doesn't serve illegal booze. I don't condemn it and I don't condone it. I really don't have a thing to do with it."

"If you're a waitress, you serve it, don't you?"

"Sure, but if you want a glass of water or a soda or a glass of milk, I'll serve that too."

"You realize it's illegal to serve liquor."

She shrugged. "It's illegal to jaywalk. Nobody is going to convict a waitress, Daddy. You couldn't get a jury to touch that. People understand. They know we don't have anything to do with it."

"Why don't you get another job? I'd help you."

"I don't want another job. Look, Daddy, I know this embarrasses you. Since you're here now and you know what goes on, you might as well understand. I don't agree with you about Prohibition. I don't believe a person's morality or immorality is going to be made by laws. It's a question of character and personal morality, not the police force. If people want to come to Oliver's and drink bourbon, that's not a question I feel I need to involve myself with."

"Sure, I've heard that argument," M. K. said, and he leaned across the table toward her, wanting very much for her to understand him. "I don't agree with it, but I've heard it. Nowadays, though, it's different. Prohibition is the law of the land. It's in the Constitution. Nobody can say, it's not my business. You've got to honor the Constitution, or I don't know how you can say you're a good American. The argument over Prohibition was a good argument, but it's over."

That seemed to amuse her. She gave her head a shake and got out of her seat, smiling. She had a pinafore over her dress, a pink piece with white bows attached, the dress of the house apparently. "I have to work," she said. "Are you going to eat? The steaks are good. Daddy, you may consider the argument over, but I don't really think so. Oliver's isn't so unusual, and it's a pretty strong argument. Look, business is good."

While they had been talking, the place had been filling up. There was hardly a table unfilled.

"Don't worry about me," Linda said. "I'm not going to do what my mother did."

Chapter 14
1923: Back to the West

President Harding died suddenly in August, and all Wayne Wheeler's carefully calculated linkages with the administration were broken. Coolidge was a much more abstemious character—which was not saying much since Harding had been a handsome lush—but it was not clear how well the ASL could work with him. Silent Cal, as he was known, did not leave many hooks for people to grab on to.

That was not the only problem. Purley Baker's health was clearly failing, and in his absence the extremely competent Ernest Cherrington filled the gap. If Baker continued his decline and Cherrington became general superintendent, that would be the end of Wheeler's rule in Washington. Cherrington obviously failed to understand the philosophy of personal enforcement. He thought the league should leave politics to the politicians and put its resources into educating Americans about the evils of alcohol. As if, Wheeler said, they needed educating. How did Cherrington think they had passed the Eighteenth Amendment?

It would never do for Wheeler to complain publicly about Cherrington, however. The man was respected in the league, viewed as having great integrity. To keep Cherrington out of power, not for selfish reasons, but for the good of the league, would require planting seeds of doubt in places where he was treated like a saint.

In November Wheeler sent M. K. Nichols to California. Theoretically his job was to gather evidence regarding the success of Prohibition, to write more articles for the general press. He had a deeper motive, however: to rally support for Wheeler and against Cherrington.

On the way to California M. K. stopped in Albuquerque and Phoenix. He was glad to be out of Washington, talking to leathery men in dark coats and no ties and wide-brimmed black hats. The league officers were plainspoken, factual ranchers or store owners or preachers. They had few words and no small talk, but they made him feel at ease by being themselves at ease and accepting with a quiet pleasure his presence, the way a horse or a dog will welcome you by the way it points its head and stands near you.

He gave an insider's report on the progress of Prohibition. He offered insights on the shake-ups since Harding's death, with a deeper emphasis on how crucial it was to maintain the ASL's hold on Washington. In some eastern states, he pointed out, there was no local effort at enforcement at all. In May, New York State had repealed its enforcement laws entirely. Therefore, national enforcement was crucial. Otherwise, as a practical matter Prohibition became no more than local option. "And local option," M. K. said, "is like a law against adultery in all but one room of the house." Even the pastors would smile at that line.

That was indoors in the dim, ugly church halls. When he got out of doors, M. K. found a landscape that stunned him into silence and inadequacy. He had never seen the desert before. Astonishing wide and high spaces beckoned at the end of straight black roads, in three-sided rectangles of blue caught between buildings, in the half-sphere of cloudless infinity bisected by railroad tracks. He found himself shaking off the cobwebs of city living, realizing how large and free the world really is.

He was thus already attuned to the power of landscape when he reached California. M. K. had not forgotten how, after Darla's death, he had despised the bleached aridity, the washed-out colors, the long, staring, lifeless noons of Los Angeles. It came back to memory as his train rattled into the basin and he saw the terrain assume its familiar shape, high snowy mountains standing over the sweep of hills descending. He found, however, that time had carried Darla's funeral far, far behind him, and the landscape had recovered its first meaning. From the moment he stepped out of Union Station, the lightness of untainted air and the spacious, languorous ways of pedestrians made him happy. The character of Los Angeles affected him just as it had when he and Darla first arrived.

He was barely out of the station when a man grabbed his arm, offering star maps. The street was busy, crowded with automobiles, and buildings hung over the pavement denser and darker than he remembered. What was a star map? M. K. did not understand what the fellow meant until he got a peek at streets with Mary Pickford's and Douglas Fairbanks's and Charlie Chaplin's addresses set with stars.

"Oh, no," he said, pulling away. "I don't need that." He laughed to himself as he walked on. He supposed his little apartment would have had its own star when Darla was alive.

On the trolley he watched carefully to see how the city, like an old friend, had changed. A few blocks from the station the crowding dissipated and LA's familiar, low-slung shape returned. More of the roads were paved than before, and he hardly saw any vacant lots even when they got out toward Biola, but the streets were wide, with tall palm trees marching down them. Feathery, tropical foliage fronted the buildings.

The California ASL had offered him no accommodation, so he had written Daddy Horton of the Fishermen's Club, and Horton had set him up in guest rooms at the Bible Institute of Los Angeles. When M. K. had left Los Angeles, Biola's new building had been under construction. M. K. remembered it as large, but he had unconsciously expected that the passage of years would have shrunk it to a manageable size. He got off the trolley to find an impressive block thirteen stories high. Between two substantial towers was the Church of the Open Door, with nine high arches opening to the street and a motto inscribed overhead: "For ever, O Lord, thy word is settled in heaven." The building was graceful and energetic and modern.

A dapper young man in a bow tie greeted him cheerily in the office, but hesitated when M. K. said he had just arrived from Washington. He glanced at the suitcase. "We don't rent out our rooms," he said apologetically. "We're a Bible school, and the rooms are for our students."

"I thought a room had been reserved for me," M. K. said. "Daddy Horton . . ."

At the mention of the name, everything changed. Yes, a room had been reserved, and a student was quickly fetched to take him to it. Leading up the stairs, the student kept turning his head to look at M. K. and ask about Daddy Horton. Other students bounded up and down the stairs, all neatly dressed young men who greeted M. K. politely and looked curiously at him as they passed. "Good morning! Good morning!"

After he had been shown into his room, M. K. heard a soft knock and opened the door to find a trio of trim, friendly boys. One had a pimpled face and a shock of unruly red hair. "I'm Timothy Shallach and these are my friends," he said. He introduced them by name, and they all shook hands. "We're students here. We wanted to let you know that we'd be glad to help you out if you need anything done. Any errands or anything."

"Thank you," M. K. said. "That's very nice of you. I think I am all right for now."

The young man hesitated. He was not quite ready to leave. His companions looked on as though hoping for something too. "We were wondering. Are you a missionary?" he asked.

"No," M. K. said. "I work with the Anti-Saloon League."

"We heard you came from far away. We thought you might have come from China."

"Why China?"

The boy flushed and glanced at his friends, who were smiling. "We all three want to go to China with the gospel. The Lord has called us to go there, so we're always looking for someone who can tell us about it."

M. K. smiled wryly. "I'm afraid I come from the wilderness of Washington, D.C."

"Well, that's all right. I mean, I'm sure what you do is very worthwhile. It's just that sometimes missionaries visit us at Biola, and I'm sure you can imagine, it's very interesting. For those of us who are called to go out . . . we can't wait to talk to the men who have gone ahead of us."

———————

Roy Overholt came to get him in the late afternoon. M. K. might not have recognized him: Roy had spread out into an ill-pressed brown suit, and a porthole had opened at the crown of his sandy hair. Overholt threw a bear hug over M. K., slapping his back and almost shouting how glad he was to see him. Not since a brief visit in Seattle had they been together, and they rarely found time to write.

As they came out into the sharp afternoon sun, they heard music coming from the church—a choir. "Oh, come on, let's hear," Overholt said, grabbing M. K. by the arm and steering him to the door. "If that's the Biola choir, they're the best."

They stood in the back of a darkened auditorium and listened to sixty or so young people practice their gospel music. Though not robed, they appeared tidy and trim in their shirts and ties. The number they sang was unfamiliar, but its sweetness caught M. K. up nonetheless. He stood almost senseless until Overholt tapped him on the shoulder and led him outside.

Overholt had a Ford, which he had parked on the street. "Your church must be generous," M. K. said, "if they buy you a car."

"It's money well spent," Overholt said. "It saves so much time traveling. With the old Lizzie I can get to five or six homes in an evening, and I'm a lot quicker to get to the hospital too. I can get home for supper with the family and go back to work. I would have thought the league would buy you one of these."

"Oh, no, there's no money in the league to buy cars."

They were driving south into a section of Los Angeles that had not even existed ten years before. M. K. kept his eyes on the houses flashing by.

"That surprises me," Overholt said. "The newspapers say your man Wheeler practically runs Washington."

"There's some truth in that, but it doesn't add up to money. We've got our fingers on the power, but no cash comes with it. A lot of the churches have stopped giving, ever since the law passed."

"I have to say that our church has never given to the league," Overholt said. "We're sympathetic, you know, but our priority is to spread the gospel. We pile any money we get into missions. China, especially. What a field for harvest that is."

M. K. relayed his conversation with the Biola students who intended to go to China and wanted to know all that they could. "Yes," Overholt said, "Grace and I have thought of going ourselves. We came this close."

They arrived at the house, a small bungalow apparently identical to every other house on the street. It might have been built last week judging by the brightness of the paint and the nakedness of the garden. Grace Overholt came out with a baby in her arms. It was his first time to meet her. She had an olive face with round, unwrinkled surfaces. She exclaimed over M. K. and gave him her cheek to kiss. She said she had heard all about him. "And you've never remarried?" she said. "Don't they have any nice girls in the East?"

Before he got in the front door, she apologized for burning the spinach, and indeed he could smell something awful. "I can't cook and hold the baby," she said with a smile and a shake of her head. When she had welcomed them in, she handed the child to her husband and went back to the kitchen.

"Grace is a great blessing to me," Overholt said as he settled into his chair, the baby on his knee. "She is a wonderful mother."

There were two children, the baby and a three-year-old who peeked shyly through the doorway and then was lured in by his father to meet M. K. It seemed very beautiful to M. K., seeing how his friend had spread into the world like a fruitful vine. Yet simultaneously M. K. remembered that Overholt had known him when he, M. K., had the beginnings of a family like this.

As though reading his thoughts, Overholt asked about his children. "Did you say Linda is living with you now? That must be terrific after all these years."

"She's grown," M. K. said a little stiffly. "I don't see her as often as I'd like to. She works at night in a restaurant, and I'm gone in the morning before she gets up." In fact, he had not seen her the day he left Washington. He had considered waking her to say good-bye, but their relations had been stiff since he had visited her restaurant.

He told Overholt of his discovery. "I worry about her. You remember how my wife looked? Linda is a carbon copy. Absolutely beautiful. Yet you feel that she's wandering. She is so sure she knows what she wants."

"She needs Christ," Overholt said quickly. "I've given up trying to talk to people about anything but the Savior. You can talk yourself until you're blue. M. K., the marriages here in Los Angeles are in terrible states. People see all the scandal of Hollywood, and I think it eats at them. Men aren't satisfied with the wives of their youth. Mothers desert their families, or they serve bootleg whiskey right in their homes in front of the children. I don't warn them anymore. I just tell them of the Savior."

"Well, Linda doesn't listen," M. K. said. "She doesn't even go to church most Sundays."

"Even so, keep telling her," Overholt said.

"Have you told Mr. Nichols what you're preaching on?" Grace asked. She had come in to call them to dinner.

"I haven't," Overholt said. "M. K. and I have so many things to catch up on we're still about five years short of the present." He turned to M. K. and said that he was preaching through the prophecies of Daniel. "It's amazing material. It might have been written from yesterday's newspaper. I'll tell you frankly that we do not have much time. The strength of Russia, the Great Power of the North, now that it is held by godless Communists, puts all the foundations in place or out of place. Since the British have come in, Palestine is prepared for the time of the Gentiles to come to an end. Already the Jews are beginning to come in from every part of the earth."

M. K. had only the barest grasp of prophecy. He had tended to avoid hearing it explained because he had the impression that it was impenetrable and fanatical. His religion was more practical, he thought, and this idea was reinforced when Overholt went on to explain that prophecy was the reason why evangelism and missions took priority in his church. "It seems that we have about one generation more of free action. Then the days of tribulation will be at hand. We have got to reach every Chinaman and every Bohemian and every man on the face of the globe now, before the Beast begins to exert its power. And God has opened the doors as never before. The world is so much smaller.

"Now, M. K., I know how you feel about alcohol, and if my wife had died of it, I might feel just the same, but won't you agree that when you look at the world as it is and as it soon will be, the problem of drunkenness is more a symptom than a cause? I'm sure if God has called you and other men to that campaign, it is wonderful, but what good would we do if we could take all of their bottles away and not save their souls?"

"I'm in favor of doing both," M. K. said.

"Yes, but sometimes you have to think of what takes precedence. If this world is about to perish, then all the bootleg whiskey will perish with it. All that will survive the Tribulation ahead is the testimony of those who belong to Christ."

"Well, I will say this," Grace Overholt said while she spooned pabulum into the mouth of her toddler. "If they're drunkards, they don't hear the gospel. We go down to the Rescue Mission, and there are always men who can't even talk, they are so inebriated. They are not going to read a tract or follow a gospel lesson."

"I don't know about that," her husband said quickly. "God can reach the sorriest sinner with His message."

"But since Prohibition came in, there is less drinking," she continued, "and I'm sure it makes it easier for the witness to go out."

"You do see that the law has made a difference then?" M. K. asked, glad to grab at that straw.

"Oh, yes, depending on what area. They say in San Francisco, it's the same as ever. When the federal agents arrest somebody there, they smash all the liquor they can find because otherwise the sheriff will probably confiscate the evidence and drink it himself. You know San Francisco is the devil's playground. And in a place like Pasadena, on the other hand, it's probably no different because they've been dry as long as anybody can remember. In Los Angeles, though, most of the ordinary people have dried up."

"Because they can't get liquor anymore? Or because they feel respect for the law?"

Mrs. Overholt seemed momentarily puzzled by the distinction. "I don't really know," she said. "No doubt there is liquor for those who are determined to get it. From what I understand they can't stop it from coming in from Mexico. No, I think most people want to respect the law."

The next morning, a Saturday, M. K. was to appear at a public rally at Bethel Center, a large Baptist church. He was pleased to find the church festooned, as per his written suggestions, with American flags all up and down the curb. The theme of the morning was "Honor the Constitution." M. K. had sent a program from a similar happening in Sandusky, Ohio, at which all the city's pastors had been present.

Herbert Baines, the California superintendent, was a neat, conservative middle-aged man who wore a thin mustache and an impeccable gray suit. He gave M. K. a typed copy of the program and showed him where he would sit. The first ten rows were set aside for ministers, he said, pointing out a string of gold braid running over the pews. "But I have to leave you," he said. "So many details I have to attend to."

On the program M. K.'s name was listed under the title "Glimpses of Washington." A Miss Baines was to sing "The Star-Spangled Banner," and a pastor was to pray. The main address appeared to be from Mr. Baines himself, titled "America's Future." Evidently Baines was well prepared, which gave M. K. a comfortable feeling. Last night he had discovered that Roy Overholt had never heard of the rally; it had made him wonder.

He had come early, so it was no surprise that the church was empty. By the time of the meeting, however, there were only a handful of people present—and most of them apparently were supposed to speak or pray. The meeting finally began fifteen minutes late with only a dozen or so pastors in the front rows, and the rest of the auditorium sparsely occupied. It made for a listless audience. Baines had whispered to M. K. that he should keep his talk to five minutes, and with a crowd so lethargic he felt no temptation to go longer, but he could not help feeling disappointed. When he sat down, he reminded himself that his main purpose was not the rally, but to discuss strategy with Baines.

When Baines got up to speak, it was soon evident why no great crowd had come. M. K. was painfully aware that others were bored, but Baines seemed oblivious. He had a long speech written out, with twelve numbered points, and he completed each one as though he expected his hearers were preparing for an examination. America's future, it seemed, would be dull.

"I have a room set aside for us to talk," Baines whispered to M. K. as they were both shaking hands with well-wishers. This turned out to be a back room at a local restaurant. Baines ordered a steak and M. K. did the same, though with the sinking feeling that he would be paying the bill.

"A well-organized meeting," M. K. said. "It was a shame that we didn't see more people. I wonder whether the word got out enough. My friend Reverend Overholt hadn't heard that we were to gather."

"I must say that the flags didn't do us any good," Baines said grumpily. "I'm surprised that the league has the money for flags, but that's your business." He reached in his pocket and pulled out a paper.

"Here are the expenses. I hope you can pay me now because we're very short on cash."

On California Anti-Saloon League stationery Baines had listed expenses for flag rental, a fee for the church, an honorarium for his daughter, the singer, and travel expenses for himself of fifteen dollars.

"I certainly wasn't expecting to pay expenses," M. K. said. "I assumed that these were local expenses."

"How could it be local when you ordered it? I doubt very much our board would have justified those expensive preparations."

"Mr. Baines, I don't think I ordered anything. I did make a few suggestions based on a pattern I had seen in Sandusky. If you had done otherwise, that would have been perfectly acceptable."

Baines shook his head, as though he had the misfortune of explaining facts of life to an idiot. "Mr. Nichols, I can assure you that there is no extra money for extravagances in the California league. Of course, I have not indicated an honorarium for myself. I thought I would dedicate that to the cause of our organization quite freely. Perhaps you do not understand how tight money is in California for our work. I am fortunate to pay my secretary."

M. K. nodded, while trying furiously to think what to do. "I'm afraid it is the same at the national level. That is one reason for my coming, to talk over our national priorities." He paused. "I'm sorry for the miscommunication. I'm afraid that I don't have any money to pay these expenses, but when I get back to Washington, I can see whether some funds might be made available."

Baines was quite troubled by this response and said he did not see how M. K. could have come all the way to California without any money. What was the point of the visit if he had no money? They couldn't do anything without money.

M. K. apologized profusely, while sticking to his claim that he had no money. He had learned long ago that it cost nothing to say you were sorry, and he had never understood why others found it so difficult to do. He put on all his charm and managed to placate Baines, who must have known that his claims were doubtful.

"Mr. Baines, when the ASL was flourishing financially, we could afford to do a great many things. Nowadays, with the shortage of funds, it is critical that we analyze carefully the most pressing concerns. I have heard it said that in some parts of California there is no real effort at enforcement. Is that so? In San Francisco? I have been in contact with many parts of the nation where that is so. In New York, they don't have a dry law anymore. They repealed it. If we are not careful, we will find ourselves in a situation exactly like what we had before national prohibition—a patchwork of localities, some with prohibition and some without. You know, I heard somebody say that local option laws were like outlawing adultery in just one room of the house."

M. K. tried to explain to Baines why only national enforcement could overcome the ineffectiveness of local administrations, why Washington was the key venue for the ASL to work. He said plenty of admiring words about Wayne Wheeler and his work there. Baines, however, seemed despondent. Every time he could, he swung the conversation back to his lack of funds. Twice he asked plaintively whether M. K. was sure he didn't have the money for those flags. When the bill came for dinner, M. K. knew that he would have to pay, and he did so even though the expense would inevitably come out of his pocket.

On the way back to Washington, M. K. stopped in Colorado, Utah, Wyoming, and Kansas. He thought he made some headway in getting ASL leaders to understand why the work in Washington remained vital for them. Still, it was bone-rattling travel. When he finally made it back to Washington, he felt utterly exhausted and depressed. He hoped a night's sleep would improve his spirits.

All through the trip he had thought of Linda, wondering how she did without him. When he unlocked the door to his dark apartment, a bitter, cloying smell assaulted him. He groped to find a match, then lit a lamp. In the parlor, Linda's torso spread on the sofa. A dark stain ran down the front of the sofa. Twisting herself away from the light, covering her eyes with her hands, she let out a loud groan. "Please don't," she cried. "Please don't."

Chapter 15
1924: A New Superintendent

M. K. was stroking Linda's temple and trying to talk to her when he accidentally scraped something solid with his shoe and heard its glass scrape on the floor. He looked down and saw a rum bottle, which had fallen on its side and was halfway under the sofa's skirt. Until that moment he had thought only that his daughter was sick. Then he felt sick at heart. Of course, his daughter was doing what her mother had done. Of course, she had played with fire and now was burned.

He was very tender, even more patient after he realized that her sickness was of a kind that would mend itself. He soaked a towel and bathed her head, then helped her to her room and got a nightgown from her dresser drawer. Linda was awake now and crying. M. K. told her not to worry. He patted her and offered coffee. "Now you just sleep," he said.

"I feel so awful," she said in a dragging, dying voice.

"Of course you do. But you'll feel better."

"I don't mean my stomach."

She looked terrible, her skin a brown-green and her eyes swollen as if someone had poked them. "I'm so sorry, Daddy," she said. "You're so kind to me."

He tried to leave her so she could change into a nightgown and sleep, but she followed him out the door, weeping. He led her back to the bedroom and put her under the covers in her clothes. With the wet towel he stroked her forehead again and told her to be quiet and sleep. She nestled against him. "I'm sorry, Daddy," she whispered. "I'm sorry."

M. K. could feel the sinking of his flesh in weariness. His skin was sticky and his body heavy from the long train trip, and he would have happily lain down beside Linda on the bed to rest. Oddly he felt happier, more at peace with Linda than he had felt since she was a child. He felt the deepest fondness.

He stroked her head until he thought she was asleep, and then left her. He cleaned up the sofa and wiped the floor, still feeling happy to serve her. Then he peeked in the door at her. She was still, and her breathing came regularly and slowly, like ocean swells.

The next morning M. K. awoke still happy, alarmed and alert because Linda had drunk herself sick, but also musing that she had clung to him. He had not taken time to bathe before falling into bed, so he drew a tub full and soaked in it. He knew he would have to make a firm stand with Linda. He hoped now she was prepared for that. She had seemed so sorry, so sick and helpless.

Coming out of the bath, he found her waiting outside, dressed in her robe and turned sideways in a chair. She did not look well. Her eyes were lined in red folds, and the skin of her face was pale and tight and slick. He said good morning, but she did not answer. She stood up and slid past him into the bathroom.

M. K. dressed and began to make breakfast. When Linda came into the kitchen and sat wordlessly, staring down at the table, he asked her how she felt. She answered that she didn't want to talk about it. She wouldn't eat any of the eggs that he made, so he let it go, understanding that she felt bad and would need time to recover. He went off to the office.

The morning was bright and cold, and he felt revived and cheerful by the time he walked into the ASL and received the warm greetings of the receptionist. Other staff came out of their offices and cubbyholes when they heard conversation. He felt like a homecoming soldier. Wheeler appeared with some papers for the secretary, and he, too, greeted M. K. warmly, grinning and bouncing up and down on his toes. "Come back to my office, M. K.," he said. "We should talk."

"So what do they think of Cherrington out west?" he asked when M. K. had settled into a chair in his office. They had closed the door so as not to be disturbed.

"They respect him," M. K. said soberly. "But really, they're not thinking about him. They're all broke, and they can't seem to interest people in supporting the cause." He added silently to himself, thinking of Herbert Baines, *And some of them are vain and stupid and worry most about who is going to pay for their lunch.*

"What they know about national headquarters," M. K. continued, "is that Cherrington puts out the publications and he's very efficient and helpful when there are money problems."

"Did you talk to them about the importance of Washington and national enforcement?"

"Of course, I did, Mr. Wheeler."

"Didn't that shake them loose from Cherrington's grasp?"

"I don't know as they think of Cherrington's grasp. Maybe I failed to communicate well, but they don't see much difference between our program of personal enforcement and Cherrington's policy of education. Of course, we're all for education."

"But education with a point. The point of obeying the law."

"Well, yes, I said all that, but I don't know whether I could get them to see."

Wheeler scowled. He looked almost silly, being as short as a sixth-grade boy and wearing a frown as though he had been denied dessert. "I don't know whether you get how serious this is, Nichols," he said. He stood up for no apparent purpose. "The Board of Directors meets in

January, and they'll be replacing Baker as general superintendent. If they choose Cherrington, our work is over. The man thinks we should put out booklets and hold rallies and organize the natives in Bongo Bongo to form their own Anti-Saloon League."

When M. K. got home from the office, he found Linda still there. She had not dressed and sat at the kitchen table with her eyes trained on its dark, polished surface.

"Aren't you going to work today?" he asked her.

"I might go later," she said without looking up.

He felt the warning implicit in her tone, that she did not want conversation. Nevertheless, he tried.

"You feeling hung over?" he asked.

"I guess so."

"It's poison. Alcohol is poison. Now you know if you didn't before."

She looked at him as though spraying poison from her eyes. "I don't choose to talk about it."

That got his dander up. "I don't choose to mop up your vomit. Sometimes we have to do what's required, not what we choose."

She didn't say anything; she didn't even look at him.

"You were sorry last night. What happened between then and now?"

"Nothing happened. This is my business, not yours. Whatever problems I have I can deal with myself. I *must* deal with myself."

"Then you can deal with your own vomit, I assume."

"Yes." She looked at him defiantly with her beautiful deep eyes. "I can deal with my own vomit since that seems to be what you reduce me to."

As soon as the new year turned over, they were busy in the office preparing for the biennial Board of Directors meeting. Wheeler fretted a good deal. He complained to M. K. that there were so many men without vision, men who were small in their thoughts. "I don't see how we are going to stop him," Wheeler said. "I really don't. It would be a shame if we had to murder him," and then he laughed in his distinctive barnyard hee-haw.

The church sanctuary where the board met had perhaps never been so jovial. Men slapped backs, vigorously shook hands, renewed acquaintance. They added up to more than a hundred men, with each state having several representatives. Meanwhile the real business was carried on during coffee breaks, in corridors or quiet corners, and even, when privacy was needed, in the raw January cold. Delegates stood close to each other in huddles of two or three and did not look up when their fellow directors passed.

They asked each other about Baker's health and told stories about him, how shrewd and sharp he had been in outwitting wets and building the league. In other conversations, more quietly and cautiously, they discussed Cherrington and Wheeler and Francis Scott McBride, the popular Illinois superintendent.

On the second day M. K. encountered Wheeler coming out of the bathroom. He had his head down and did not even see M. K. until he said hello. Then he took M. K. by the arm and pulled him back into the bathroom, a small stucco room lit by one high window over the stall. He locked the door, then spoke in a whisper. "I don't think we can stop him," he said.

"Cherrington?"

"Yes. You are quite right. Men don't see that one side is for enforcement and the other wants to publish pamphlets. They think it is all the same, and they trust Cherrington."

Then without warning Wheeler let out one of his high-pitched cackles that startled M. K. Wheeler's demeanor changed abruptly as he said, "Oh . . . Oh. That's it. Who is down there with Brother Baker?"

"I'm not sure what you mean," M. K. said.

"Who is down there in Alabama? Isn't there someone who is reliable anywhere nearby?"

M. K. did not see what he was driving at, but he mentioned the names of several men who were strong dry supporters.

"Hurst, then," Wheeler said, striking his palms together. "Go to the office and get hold of him. Use the telephone. Failing that, use the telegraph. Tell him that something urgent has come up and please to call me tonight at the office at ten. I will be there waiting for his call. Go now, M. K. It is very urgent. I think we can save it."

————————

The next day, a Saturday, they were to choose a new superintendent. The floor was opened to nominations, and the first speech had begun when M. K. heard a flurry in the back of the church and loud whispering. A uniformed Western Union messenger came down the aisle and leaned toward Wheeler, then handed him a telegram. Moments later Wheeler bolted to his feet, asking for the floor. It was gladly granted. No one had been listening to the speech anyway since the messenger came in.

Wheeler hurried to the front of the church, obviously excited and unable to control his delight. He held up the scrap of paper and waved it. "This telegram has just reached me. I suppose it came to me because we are in the capital, where I am somewhat notorious." He cackled to himself. "This telegram is signed by Mr. Bruce Hurst, who as you know is a close friend to Mr. Baker, of whom we have been recently speaking. Here are his words:

PRAISE GOD BAKER MUCH BETTER STOP FULL
RECOVERY EXPECTED STOP ENERGY HIGH
HURST

"These are great, glad tidings!" Wheeler said. "The man who has led us to the Eighteenth Amendment will still lead us in its enforcement!"

Another director was on his feet, seeking attention. "I move," he said, "that we choose Purley Baker as our general superintendent for another term of two years. While he lives we cannot discard this faithful servant of the Lord."

The motion was quickly seconded, and if anyone had any doubts about it, he did not voice them. It was passed by acclamation. The meeting went on to end on a cheerful, almost riotous note. As much as anyone, M. K. was buoyed by the good spirits. The crisis had passed, the league would go on unhindered.

———————

Just over a week later Wheeler called M. K. into his office. He sat with his neatly shined shoes up on his desk, holding a sheaf of papers. M. K. recognized them as an article he had written about the Board of Directors meeting. It was meant to go out under Wheeler's name.

"I don't know about this," Wheeler said, tossing the papers down on his desk and sitting up. "It's a beautiful piece of writing. I'd be very proud to publish that. But for how long? I think it might turn out to look foolish."

The piece was titled "Man of Miracles," and it described Purley Baker's years of leadership in the league, culminating with his miraculous recovery during their meeting. M. K. thought that the *Saturday Evening Post* might take it.

"I don't understand," M. K. said.

Wheeler pursed his lips. "The part about Baker's miraculous recovery. Could we take that out? The point is what a great man Baker is. What difference does it make that he recovered?"

"They usually like a news hook to carry the story," M. K. said. "Of course, you're so popular with editors these days they might publish it anyway, but I don't think it would be as strong."

Wheeler scowled. He seized a crumpled paper bag, rattled out some peanuts, and ate them.

"Why would it be foolish?" M. K. ventured to ask. "That telegram was such a wonderful moment in our meeting."

Wheeler stood up, walked to the door and looked out, then closed it before returning to his seat. "If the article came out and Baker died the same week, it wouldn't look like such a miracle, would it?"

It took M. K. a minute to take this in. "Do you think that might happen?" he asked.

"Sure," Wheeler said. "The man is very sick. You know that."

"But the telegram said . . ." Even as he mentioned the telegram, while watching Wheeler's face, M. K. remembered how he had contacted Mr. Hurst and arranged for him to call Wheeler. He stared. "Wasn't it true?" he asked.

Wheeler stared back and then startlingly burst into a loud hee-haw. He straightened his face and said, "We needed a little more time, so I asked Mr. Hurst to give an updated assessment. I assume it was true. I haven't seen Purley Baker in months, so I don't actually know his condition for a fact."

"It sounds like you got him to shade the truth." M. K. could hardly bear to say it.

"There are shades of the truth in everything we say, M. K. You called Purley Baker a miracle man, but you don't actually think he did miracles, like walking on the water, do you? Shades of meaning, shades of truth. What one man takes to be the gospel truth another one considers stretching it a little. All I know is that Purley Baker is alive today unless you know something I don't."

Wheeler raised his eyebrows and smiled as if to say, "All right with you?" Then he picked up the article from his desk and handed it to M. K. "I think you see my concern. Why don't you see whether you can tone down the miracle telegram a little."

M. K. stood up, his ears burning, and started out of the room. Wheeler stopped him. "M. K.," he said, "we have a lot of work to do in the next few months if we are going to hold on to this organization. I need your help."

In February M. K. caught Linda drinking again. He happened to be awake when she came in past midnight—he could not sleep so he was reading—and saw her tipsy, holding on to the doorway for balance. She saw that he saw. "Oh, Linda," was all he could say. He could smell the booze across the room. When he stood to go to her, she misunderstood his intentions and dodged from him, around the door post and into the corridor. He found her there with her back to the wall, white and dizzy, with her hands held delicately at shoulder level, as though searching for handles to support her weight.

"It's all right," he said. "Linda, darling, it's all right."

She let him lead her to bed. When he asked whether she would be sick, she shook her head, but he got a bowl from the kitchen and put it down beside the bed just in case. "Can I get you anything?" he asked her, and when she shook her head again violently, he left her. Half an hour later he looked in the door and found that the lamp had been put out, and that her breathing came regularly in the darkness. He was glad that she had not become sick.

After that he went to bed, but he had a very hard time sleeping. He kept thinking that she was living her mother's life all over again, and he did not see how he could stop her.

She was listening to the radio when he came home from the office the next day. The presence of the radio, a third party between them, was quite welcome. All day he had dreaded the confrontation. He played in the kitchen at making supper, but when he heard that the show had ended, he went into the living room and shut off the radio. She said nothing; neither did she look up at him. He said, "You know I'm worried about you."

"I'm worried about myself," she said quietly, to his relief. He had feared she would be in a fighting mood.

"But what can I do?" he asked. "I don't want to yell at you."

"Please don't."

"I wish you had a different job, where you wouldn't be tempted, but you won't change, will you?"

"Maybe I should," she said. "But I don't think it would matter. I'm just no good, Daddy. I find the stuff, or the stuff finds me. I'm just like my mother."

"Stop it!" he said. "Don't talk that way."

"Don't shout at me."

He had not realized that his voice had risen. Perhaps even the neighbors heard. He wanted to rise and clasp her in his arms and weep. He wanted to crush her to himself. To stay helplessly seated while she sat across the room from him, separated by oceans of age and personality, built up the pressure of frustration in him so that he felt explosive.

"I don't know what to do for you," he said. "Linda, I love you, and I fear for you, but I don't know how to help you."

"You can't help me," she said with a shake of her head. "Nobody can help me."

Chapter 16
1924: Wheeler Rampant

I like playing checkers when the other fellow is blindfolded," Wheeler said with a low grin. He was relaying to M. K. the delicious fact that Ernest Cherrington had met with Purley Baker and Howard Russell on routine ASL business, and then, the very next morning, had read in the newspapers of Baker's resignation.

For the past several months M. K. had watched Wheeler warily. He realized that he had fixed the "miracle" of Baker's recovery, manipulating the Board of Directors to put off the election of a new general superintendent. Was it honest? M. K. knew he could not approve of such dealings.

Yet all his experience in the Anti-Saloon League taught him to trust Wheeler. Here was a man who lived simply, who cared for his family, who outworked anyone else in the organization, whose success with the American government was unparalleled. He was a decent man without vices. M. K. could not bring himself to accuse Wheeler.

Even if M. K. had been inclined to accuse him, his doubts would have been extinguished by the fact that Russell and Baker, the modest and practical men who had created the ASL, backed Wheeler. Or at least, they were determined to keep Cherrington out of power. Think of it: with only weeks to live, Purley Baker still conspired to keep his health a secret from Cherrington.

The Executive Committee had called an emergency meeting of the Board of Directors. They would meet April 9, in Indianapolis, to choose a new general superintendent. A week before the meeting they heard that Baker had died.

It made for a long week, jittery and gloomy. They were entering the unknown, as though on a ship pushing out of bright sunshine into a fog bank. Wheeler was full of excess energy, leaving the office and coming back, running errands that someone else could have done, and always wanting to know whether anyone had called or cabled or written. They did not know who would come to Indianapolis. If all the states were represented as they had been in January, Cherrington would certainly be elected. They hoped, however, that meeting so soon after January, more distant states would lack funds to send delegates.

Bishop Cannon disappointed Wheeler by writing a public letter of support for Cherrington, saying that the league would make a grievous error not to avail itself of his leadership. Cannon then cheered Wheeler up by stating that he would be unable to make the meeting.

M. K. and Wheeler reached Indianapolis on the evening of April 8, checking into the Hayes Hotel. Wheeler barely took the time to put his suitcase down on the bed before going to the lobby to see who was there. M. K. was not invited—he noticed that Wheeler rarely told him of his machinations until they were over—and would not have followed if he could. He moved Wheeler's suitcase over and stretched out on the bed, thinking of what would take place tomorrow. The amazing thing to him was that Cherrington had done nothing for himself. Perhaps he was working deviously.

Fifteen minutes later Wheeler hurried back in. "He's written a letter," he said. "He says what he would do if he were in charge. No more supporting candidates for office. No more political contributions. All our funds would go through the headquarters. No league official could run for public office. Churches would hold the majority of seats on all our boards. Oh, and we should build a radio station in Westerville. If he wins, we can just close the Washington office down. At least you'll have a job."

"How is that?"

"You can write scripts for the radio station." Wheeler cackled. "The man is so very strange. He is sitting down in the lobby right now, making no attempt to talk to anyone. I went to shake his hand. Nobody else was with him."

"You don't think he has a secret plan?" M. K. asked. To him, Cherrington had always seemed devious.

"I don't know. I do know that things are running our way. All the midwestern states are coming, and many of the southern and the western states have sent regrets. I don't have a count yet. I'm hopeful, M. K. I'm hopeful that we can hold on."

Wheeler gave his high, whinnying laugh. "Cherrington can't stand to see that I'm dominating Prohibition. He hates the fact that I choose the Prohibition agents, that congressmen come to me for guidance. Cannon's the same way. He doesn't like to be eclipsed. They talk about the dry cause, but it's the Wheeler cause they worry about."

He was just warming up. When he began talking like this, he would stalk to and fro in the hotel room. "In politics—and the dry cause is politics, through and through—somebody has got to be the boss. Politicians don't care about ideas. They care about votes. Since we can deliver the votes for them—or against them, which is even better—they find our ideas marvelous. If I say to Congressman X, I want Pierre Lafitte's brother-in-law put into a position, he doesn't care two cents about the brother-in-law. He wants to know about the votes. And he had better know that I control those votes, and that the whole organization will do as I say. Cherrington is too refined for that. He won't even go around the room shaking hands and asking people to support him. You watch him tomorrow. I'll bet he acts like there's a skunk in the room."

Wheeler said he needed to go to the bathroom and went down the hall. He came back quickly, still buttoning his pants, because he needed so badly to talk. "I don't know what makes people care for Cherrington. You tell me. You've talked to people. What does Cherrington have that I don't have? What do they say? Tell me. Don't spare my feelings."

"I think," M. K. said from his position stretched out on the bed, "I think some of our people like the fact that he's not political. Just the opposite of you."

"That's just it!" Wheeler snapped his fingers. "There's no power without politics. Without politics, this league is nothing but a Sunday school picnic. Very nice, but nothing to help anybody. M. K., we are doing something!"

"Yes, we are," M. K. said thoughtfully. "You know, my mother was a temperance lady. I grew up on her stories of kneeling in prayer before the saloons."

"Yes, they kneeled in prayer, and the liquor bosses took it for surrender. There's no respect for weakness. They respect only power. We have power. And we'll keep it if we don't let Cherrington throw it away. Churches controlling every board! Imagine the disputes we'd have! We'd stay up all night trying to decide on mode of baptism."

Wheeler stopped pacing and sat down on the edge of the bed. "Let's talk about tomorrow. What we have to do." He already had a plan, most of which he had explained before. Wheeler's name would be put in nomination, along with McBride's. McBride could not be elected and did not want to be elected because he wanted to stay in Washington. But his nomination would split the vote and give them time. "M. K., you will have work to do. First tell people that Cherrington's work with the publications is far too important, and that he seems to have an aversion to the prominence of leadership. You can make it sound very admirable if you like, very principled. He is so valuable, so respected, let's not thrust him into a job that he doesn't really like."

He laughed. "He'll fall right into that because he won't campaign. He'll sit in his corner sucking on a lemon. We'll explain why he acts that way. We'll tell the men that he's pained at the very thought of being thrust into such a position and leaving his beloved publications, which mean so much to the league."

Wheeler got up off the bed and began to pace again. He rubbed his hands in glee. "We should have at least two rounds of voting to see who we can draw off from him."

"How do we do that?"

Wheeler smirked. "They all have something they want. A position, a position for a relative, funds for a pet project. That's what you'll need to find out. It's no different from Congress. You've watched me work in Congress. Only it's not so open here because, well, because we're the Anti-Saloon League. It comes down to the same thing. What do you want? How can I give it to you?"

He could no longer be contained by the hotel room. He went out again to see who was present, and M. K. continued to lie on his back, thinking of what a fascinating life he had found in the Anti-Saloon League.

The next day went as they had planned. Wheeler was nominated, as were McBride and Cherrington. Nobody had a majority on the first ballot.

Just as Wheeler had predicted, Cherrington hardly said a word, but sat with a few of his friends. M. K. circulated, shaking hands. Being a sociable soul, he gabbed with a great many men and found out who was soft for Cherrington. Sometimes he found out what little prize might sway them or how best to approach them. Sometimes he just knew they were wavering. He wrote information on a small pad of paper and left it open where Wheeler would read it—that way they did not have to talk. Then Wheeler or McBride could talk to the waverers. When they had the votes, Wheeler withdrew from the race, very graciously, with a speech about the importance of unity as they continued the vital work of Prohibition. McBride was elected.

On the train ride back to Washington, Wheeler, though he looked pale and limp, never stopped talking. They had not taken sleepers, but sprawled in the coach. M. K. had his coat spread over him and he periodically drifted off to sleep, but Wheeler's continual speech awakened him.

They reached Washington in the early morning hours, and M. K. took a taxi to his apartment. Unlocking the door, he had an uncanny sense that something was wrong. Something in the smell or the temperature—he could not place it. Ordinarily he would have found his way to his bedroom, but now he paused in the living room to light a lamp. As soon as the room was illuminated, his alarm increased, though still he could not place a reason. Finally he recognized it: Linda's radio was missing.

"Linda?" He went to her room and knocked, then entered. Enough gray light came in the window for him to see that the bed was neatly made, with no one sleeping in it. He lit a lamp and saw that the room was tidy, not a thing out of place.

"Linda?" He walked through the rest of the apartment. In the kitchen he found Linda's note on the table:

> Dad,
> I thought it would be easier for us both if I just left. In fact, I'm getting married. It's too complicated to put in a note. Now you won't have to worry about me.
> Love, Linda

M. K. went back to Linda's bedroom. Now he saw clearly that the room was uninhabited. Pictures were gone from the bureau, and the hangers in the closet were empty. She must have dusted and swept before going. He pulled back the cover on the bed and discovered neat, clean sheets. Something about the crisp geometry of the perfectly made bed seemed like an assault. Putting his face full into the bedclothes, he rested on his knees for a moment. What had he done wrong? A panicky thought shot through his mind, that he had lost her as surely as he had lost Darla. Then he calmed himself by remembering one of his mother's slogans, *While there is life there is hope.* Linda was not dead. What had she written? It was too complicated to put in a note. That seemed to imply that she would come back to talk to him.

He felt so tired. He lifted himself just high enough to roll into Linda's bed and go to sleep on top of the covers.

When he awakened, it was afternoon, the room was hot with his perspiration, and his coat was wrapped around him like a straitjacket. He knew immediately where he was and why, and he lay dazed and uncomfortable. Once again he was quite, quite alone.

His thoughts returned to the meeting in Indianapolis, which seemed so long ago. He could not seem to remember the reason they had gathered there, all those serious men, but the texture of the conversations came back as puffed up and empty. He remembered Cherrington, his face polite and grave and sorrowful after McBride was elected. Cherrington had crossed the room to shake McBride's hand, the first time he had left his seat to talk to anyone.

The realization flowed into M. K.'s befuddled mind that he had lied against Cherrington and had actually enjoyed the man's helplessness. Was it really necessary? He could not think clearly enough. He did realize that he did not like it, did not like the feeling of it at all.

Three months later to the day, M. K. was present in New York City for the Democratic Party convention. M. K. shared a fourth-floor walk-up with two other ASL workers. Wheeler had needed a more luxurious setting to meet political figures, so he stayed in the Herald Square Hotel. He got M. K. a press credential so that he could use the type-writers in the basement of the Madison Square Garden where the convention took place. Wheeler had a statement to issue every day, sometimes more than one, and M. K. was to write them up.

Just before the convention Wheeler met with Al Smith. Smith was governor of New York, but he wanted to be president. He was a hand-some and vain man, who could not feel much more than disdain for an official of the Anti-Saloon League who had won his earliest fame rid-ing a bicycle over Ohio farmland. Of course, Wayne Wheeler answered like a mirror. He expected no more than fancy clothes and hair oil from a wet Catholic whose support came largely from those unacquainted with the English language.

They met in the back room of a New York club, paneled with mir-rors. Smith had on his brown derby. His trademark cigar jutted out of his mouth. Wheeler wore a blue suit that appeared to have come from a mail-order catalog and probably had. Both men feigned politeness. They grinned, they flattered each other, and they paraded their affability. Each recognized and enjoyed the other's potency, seeing it as a mutually rein-forcing tribute, that they had come together to talk. Like every man who breathes politics, each looked for information as to the other's intentions and kept in the very background of his mind the possibility that some-how they might astonish the world and work a bargain together.

Only at the end of their conversation did Wheeler turn serious. Lighthearted comments were made about Smith's ambitions, but

Wheeler suddenly stopped the bantering. "Governor," he said slowly, "you will never enter the White House."

He had recognized with absolute clarity the imbalance in their power. Smith was a very popular politician, rising to national prominence, but the ASL could and would deny him the support of southern and western Democrats. Smith could offer nothing to Wheeler, but Wheeler could deny Smith his greatest aspiration. And he would.

Wheeler found M. K. after that meeting and had him write a press release. He loved the idea of power brokers meeting at a club to test each other. He loved having the last word. "Governor, you will never enter the White House." He said it slowly, portentously, and then broke into a cackle. "He won't, either. I wish he'd try. He's an easy target. I hear that he takes half a dozen drinks a day."

Wheeler wanted to include his prophecy in the release, but M. K. talked him out of it. That was probably the first time he had felt sure his own judgment surpassed Wheeler's. Perhaps he was affected by the convention atmosphere: cursing, sweating, bullying, smoking, grabbing, bribing, drinking. At times M. K. did not think he could get through the corridors, they were so filled with shouting, ugly men. It was politics, but he did not like it and he did not think the general public would like it.

The convention deadlocked between McAdoo of Tennessee and Smith of New York. For nine days they argued and voted through 103 separate ballots. Smith had the balcony stuffed with priests and gun-packing toughs. When William Jennings Bryan rose to speak, they tried to shout him down. Bryan, the grand man, the very soul of progressive democracy! There were moments when M. K. thought the crude, dirty machine politicians would win over the convention, would bully their way to a Smith nomination. But Wheeler and Cannon and their allies hung on, and on the 103rd ballot the convention gave up on both McAdoo and Smith, going for John Davis of West Virginia. He was not a grand choice, but he was dry. Besides, as Wheeler said with jubilation, Coolidge would beat Davis even if he had a stroke.

Wheeler dragged M. K. to the basement where he dictated another press release. He didn't care who heard him, either. His smile was so broad it was nearly a grimace, a slash of hilarity across his face. He exulted in victory: Wayne Wheeler had prevented the nomination of a wet candidate. "We have a hold on the politicians," he said. "Don't write that, M. K., but we've got a hold on them and I won't tell you where. They're screaming, some of them, but we ain't going to let go."

M. K. never knew how Bishop Cannon found out about it. M. K. heard about it later from Wheeler, who was mad as a hurricane. Cannon found Wheeler in his room at the Herald Square Hotel. As was the usual way with him, he did not say a kindly word, but went to war.

"I find it difficult to believe that you cannot see how harmful and stupid such a statement would be for all future relations with the Democratic Party," he said. "For you, a well-known Republican, who will surely support the Republican candidate in November, to publicly crow that you controlled the Democratic nomination is unseemly." Cannon always spoke in neatly constructed sentences that ran in and exploded like torpedoes. "You vastly overestimate your own powers in this place, and furthermore, you boast in an egregious manner. It would do untold harm to issue such a statement, and you have no authority to do so. I believe I have the authority to represent the league before the democracy."

Wheeler tried to defy him, but getting past Cannon, when he had his frost face on, was like head-butting a goat. Cannon told him that if he dared to issue the statement or any statement that Cannon had not agreed on, Cannon would publicly disavow him.

"You think McBride won't stand with me?" Wheeler said.

"I know the methods by which you brought Mr. McBride to office. Do not think others are any less cognizant. For the sake of the cause I do not want to expose you, but I tell you I certainly will, and it will not go in Mr. McBride's favor if I do so."

Wheeler had no choice but to back down. He went out and hunted up M. K., apparently because he wanted somebody to listen to him rant. For an hour he paced up and down M. K.'s hotel room, not caring who heard him. M. K. only listened, trying to understand what had gone wrong. After almost two weeks in New York he wanted to get home. Even his empty apartment would seem sweet after two weeks of pure politics.

Book IV

Love Is Not Proud

Chapter 17
1927: Under the Law

"Mr. Wheeler would like to see you." June McKenzie stood quietly in front of M. K. Nichols's desk. She was a middle-aged unmarried woman who had given her life to the league. Quietly, with no ego and no publicity, she had organized the dingy office.

"Is he fussing?" M. K. asked.

"I don't know," McKenzie said. "He doesn't say much to me these days."

When M. K. knocked on Wheeler's door, the response was so low and quiet he barely heard. Rather hesitantly he pushed the door open and found Wheeler with his worn but well-polished shoes up on his desk in a familiar carefree attitude. His face, however, seemed to hang off his skull in folds of skin—soft as wet newspaper. He had lost so much weight that his shirt collar was loose—his tie held it to his throat in folds. He looked like a sparrow in a man's clothes.

"Hello, M. K.," Wheeler said. "I wondered whether you have seen any press reports on that tribute."

"That tribute" referred to an article in the Chicago *Tribune*. It was an odd piece, rather purple in its prose, lauding Wheeler as "the boss who wields the scepter of the supergovernment and directs the propaganda machinery of the league." It was additionally odd that it appeared in a wet newspaper. Wheeler loved it; he clutched it to himself as though it vindicated his entire career. He had written it up with a few comments, mimeographed it, and sent it out to all the ASL offices, with instructions for giving it to their local newspapers. M. K. had done the distribution at Wheeler's instructions, though he felt misgivings.

"No," M. K. said. "I don't think anyone has reprinted it yet."

"Not even the church papers?"

"Not that I know of."

Wheeler took his shoes off the desk. He had heart problems and last year had promised to slow down, but he was always in his office when M. K. arrived and was still at work in the evening when he went home. Sometimes he did not seem able to drag himself in and out of the elevator, but he never stopped working.

"What is behind it?" Wheeler asked. "Are they trying to get rid of me?"

"Mr. Wheeler, there have been people trying to get rid of you as long as I've been around."

"But not within the league. No, I take it back. Always within the league I've had enemies. But supporters too. Where have my supporters gone?"

"They're still there, Mr. Wheeler. Plenty of them."

"Then why don't they get this published?" For an instant anger clouded his face. "Don't they care anymore? What's happening to our league?" He said this last question in a low voice, barely audible, and his head hung down as though he were exhausted by the effort of speaking.

"It's hard, Mr. Wheeler. Everybody is under a lot of pressure. Remember what it was like when you went to Carnegie Hall?"

Wheeler had gone there in the spring to debate Clarence Darrow. The Manhattan audience had jeered him so that he was barely audible over the catcalls. It had been a noble sight, the frail, sick man, barely able to stand, still equably speaking, or trying to speak. In all the years they had worked together, Wheeler had never lost his temper in public. He had always seemed to like the heat of battle, to relish it.

"It's always been hard!" Wheeler's energy level flared up like a match. "When we started out they said we could never succeed. And now we have, and it's not time to quit because some people don't like the law. It's more than the law. It's the Constitution. Anyone who fights against Prohibition is fighting against the Constitution of the United States. They'll never win! No one can assault our American way of life and succeed. The Constitution has never failed!"

"It's true," M. K. said, "and the voters have not stopped believing it, either. You read the newspapers and you think everyone has gone wet, but then you count the votes and find that we have more dry congressmen than we've ever had. How do you figure that?"

"Why, then, won't our people get this into print?" Wheeler thumped the paper again. "We need to answer these wet slanders! And here we have it! A complete vindication of the league!"

"Perhaps," M. K. hinted, "they don't all see it that way. The piece is about you, not so much the league."

That remark seemed to upset Wheeler deeply. "I don't see how you can say that. Are you with them too? When our enemies attack us, they attack me. Who did they call a poisoner and a murderer?"

Earlier in the year the Association Against the Prohibition Amendment (AAPA), an anti-Prohibition organization founded by Pierre Du Pont and other rich industrialists, had published an account of how many hundreds of Americans had died from drinking poison liquor. It had been good propaganda, and the ASL had been obliged to answer it. Wheeler had implied in his comments to the press that anyone who died from drinking contraband liquor could be considered a suicide. He had been mercilessly criticized for that.

"They go after me. I'm the lightning rod for the whole movement. I don't mind. That's what I'm called to do. I just wish the other men understood that if they cut me down, the wets won't quit. They'll go after the rest of you."

"You don't mean that the men in the league would cut you down, do you?"

"Some of them would. Some of them certainly would if they could. But they're more likely to stand back and let the liquor men do it. Did you see them flocking to my support when the Reed committee had me in its grip?" Wheeler had been subpoenaed by a Senate committee charged to investigate campaign finance abuse. The committee, dominated by wets, had gone fishing into all the league affairs, seizing the group's records from Westerville, and leaking some to the press.

"Mr. Wheeler, I think you're overreacting. It's just turned tough out there, that's all. It's tough for everybody. The men in the league have troubles of their own."

"Sure they do. Sure they do." Wheeler's energy seemed to have leaked out of him again.

He *was* the lightning rod, but principally because he made himself so. Wheeler held the completely innocent assumption that whatever he did was for the good of the ASL, and that the good of the league was completely wrapped up in him. He had always prided himself in knowing how to use the press, and in good times he had been very effective at getting publicity. The problems were different now with an adverse climate. Previously they had been on offense. Now they were fighting a defensive battle.

Partly it was the AAPA. The group had copied the very techniques of the ASL, publishing studies and statistics to prove, perversely, that Prohibition was a bad thing. In the days before the Eighteenth Amendment, the ASL had been able to publish facts about how bad matters were, and those facts proved that life would be better without booze. Now, with national Prohibition, the stream flowed in the other direction. If matters were bad, it was *because* of Prohibition, and life would be improved without the regulation. That was the AAPA's approach.

Last year the AAPA had broadcast that one out of every twelve Prohibition agents had been proved corrupt. But so what? As Senator Herrald from Oklahoma said, "One out of twelve of Jesus' disciples went wrong too." Nobody expected that the agents would be angels, especially since they were poorly paid and new to their jobs.

The truth was, life was better without booze, but it was not perfect. That was partly because Prohibition was not 100 percent and never could be. In the ASL the leaders believed that as enforcement improved so would conditions under Prohibition, but ironically the very people complaining about the problems were undermining enforcement. The poison liquor was a case in point—as though it was Prohibition that poisoned people instead of the bootleggers who provided the stuff.

The wets had the initiative, without a doubt. They had forced Coolidge to drop Roy Haynes, Wheeler's handpicked man, as the Prohibition commissioner. That had hit Wheeler terribly hard.

Wheeler picked up the mimeographed copy of the tribute to reread. He had a strange, fierce look in his eye. "M. K., this is a magnificent piece. I believe that if people read this piece, they will understand what an achievement we have made. Not one newspaper has reprinted it? That's not an accident, M. K., that's a plan. Somebody is working to keep it quiet. Somebody in our league."

He paused, panting slightly, his eyes glassy. "I can't do anything about it. I need to go up to Michigan and rest. You know what the doctors have said. I want to fight it, but I can't. You're still a young man, though. Everybody likes you. I want you to get to the bottom of it."

M. K. listened with a sense of helplessness. He did not believe there was any "bottom" to what had happened.

Wheeler had his head so low he seemed to be studying a paper on his desk, except that the space at which he stared was blank. "Cherrington," he said. "I'm sure it's Cherrington. With Russell. He must have gotten Russell. What about McBride? Not McBride."

Then Wheeler lifted his dull blue eyes to look at M. K. "Go on up there. You'll find out."

When Wayne Wheeler instructed him to go to the ASL headquarters, a happy thought occurred to M. K.: he would be able to stop over in Hillsboro and see David. The ASL travel budget was as tight as a ten-year-old suit, so he had been stuck in Washington and had not seen David in more than a year.

M. K. went to Westerville, therefore, and found no conspiracy. Certainly there were plenty of darkly competing theories about how the ASL should adapt to adversity. Headquarters was tense. After two days M. K. found it a relief to go south to Hillsboro where people did not think so much.

David seemed charged up to see his father. He was fifteen, a handsome, dark-haired boy who presently was collecting biological specimens with a thoroughness quite beyond M. K. David showed him his notebook in which he tried to note and describe the entire collection of living creatures in their neighborhood. He had nearly filled the booklet.

They sat in the parlor, huddling over the notes. M. K.'s mother sat with them, reading her large black Bible. The day was a Sunday, and it obviously fretted her to overhear David talking about his interests in biology. M. K. did not require an explanation of his mother's reaction.

He knew instinctively that she would consider theirs an unholy subject for a Sabbath, having to do with outdoor exertion and the use of biological science, with all the atheistic connotations of Darwin. Sometimes she would interrupt them with a verse from Scripture, making some devotional comment, as though to lure them on to better subjects. Other times she would frown at them fiercely, thinking apparently that she would frighten them into holiness.

David did not seem aware of what his grandmother was doing, but it irritated M. K. sufficiently that he finally suggested to David that they go out on a walk where David could show some of the living things he had observed and collected.

They were on their way out the door when his mother called his name.

"Do not stand there letting in flies," she said. "Close the door and come in."

When he did so, she said he had better tell David to go on. She had something important to discuss with him.

"Can't it wait, Mother?"

"No, it cannot." His mother never used a contraction. She considered them common.

"You may remember," she said, "that some years ago I begged you to talk to your brother, Samson. You do remember? I asked you to talk to him about the Savior."

He acknowledged that he did remember. He had not quite understood that request or the urgency behind it. It had come during one of his brief visits, and he had done nothing about it.

"I did not tell you then the reason. Now I must tell you. Samson is a bootlegger."

The word fell on him like a five-hundred-pound anvil. At first he did not think she could possibly know what the word meant. He asked her how she knew, and she said that a lady at the WCTU had called on her to tell her.

"And how did she know?"

"She understood it from her husband."

He did not know whether to credit his mother. That Samson should be so involved was simply unbelievable, and yet, at the same time, it did not seem impossible.

"But this is just hearsay, Mother. You shouldn't believe such a thing about Samson unless you have evidence."

She frowned at him. "I spoke to Arlene. She knew all about it."

Simply amazed, he sat looking at his mother.

"I cannot talk to him. I am his mother. Arlene says that he will not listen to her. I brought him into the world. But you, as his brother, are his lone, last hope."

If she had told him that Samson printed up twenty-dollar bills in the basement, he would have been less surprised. They had been raised to believe that the drink was evil, pure evil. That his brother could do such a thing. He supposed it must be true. If Arlene said it was so, then it surely was.

His mother wanted to go on and on. He promised that he would take action, and he escaped the house. David was waiting for him on the porch. M. K.'s first reaction was protective: How could he keep this from his son?

"I'm sorry for that," he said. "Grandma wanted to tell me about some personal concerns."

"It's all right," David said. "I know how she talks." He had his notebook out and was drawing some kind of grass he had plucked from the garden, little shiny green bayonets thick with seeds. David led his father through the garden, pointing out plants and insects that he seemed to think interesting. M. K.'s mind was elsewhere—and even at his most attentive, he would have felt little interest in these small living things. What he did feel was helpless love for his son as he watched his face and observed his moving limbs and listened to the timbre of his voice, thinking how precious he was, and how beautiful, and how he had missed his life.

M. K. felt himself more and more agitated at his brother as the news sank into his soul. So much of M. K.'s life had been ruined by alcohol. He had lost his wife, and in a way he had lost his children. Here he was forty years old with no money saved and no house or family to call his own. Samson was rich and had his own children around him. Why should he be so greedy, so venal, so evil as to sell alcohol and endanger his own children and David? Was this also why Linda had been lured into drink? Had she known, too, what Samson was doing? Of course she would have known. She probably knew before anyone else. Now it all made sense, how Samson had known about that Ray character and his slimy business.

Anger grew into a rage. His son's words glanced off as if they were the conversation of a foreigner, hard and angular sounds hitting his ears like sticks or pieces of brick. M. K. heard, but he could not understand.

If Samson had been there just then, M. K. might have physically attacked him. He could not hurt Samson, who was bigger and stronger than he. Samson would throw him aside and laugh at him. Sometimes, though, you want violence so much you will try any foolishness, only because frustration has reached a fever peak and broken out.

M. K. suddenly broke in on something that David was saying and announced that he had to go. David looked at him questioningly. Why? his face asked, and M. K. could see that he wanted to continue showing his plants and talking about this lovely subject of living things. Why did his father have to go? M. K. could not explain.

Leaving David quickly, M. K. walked toward Main Street. Samson would be in his office. He had lost all respect for the Sabbath and worked every day of the week. It was a lovely green summer day, still and warm but dry, almost autumnlike. M. K. could distinctly hear his own footfalls on the brick sidewalk. It was only a few blocks to his brother's office— down two streets, turn left, and then he was at the large vertical sign, NICHOLS. He intended to go in, but as he approached the sign, his heart began to hammer and his armpits were damp with sweat. At the doorway he could not make himself turn in. He kept on going down the street.

What Samson did was not a matter for two brothers to quarrel over. It was a concern of the law. If he attacked his brother, that would do nothing. There were brotherly matters certainly. He would have to take David away immediately. That would not address the sin, however. It was a matter of law. If he thought of the whole problem of alcohol, all over America, he could see clearly that the answer did not lie in brothers assaulting brothers, but in the clean, efficient operation of the enforcement mechanisms.

He kept on walking, two more blocks to city hall. The police were in the back. You climbed a narrow set of brick stairs and walked along a kind of concrete porch with a half-inch pipe for a railing, and then you went inside. One skinny uniformed officer with a black shadow over his chin looked at M. K. when he came in.

"I want to report a crime," M. K. said.

"All right," the officer said, but didn't move a finger.

"I have information about a bootlegging operation going on here in town."

The officer raised his eyebrows.

"Samson Nichols," M. K. said. "He runs the Nichols hauling operation."

The officer broke into a smile that looked as if it might crack his bony jaw. He had the kind of jawbone that shows all up and down the side of the face, like a metal frame.

"What's so funny?" M. K. asked.

"Mister, you don't live here, do you? Everybody knows Samson."

M. K. hesitated for a moment, confused. "So what? I don't see what's so funny about that," he said.

"There's nothing funny about it. You say Samson is running hooch? How do you know?"

M. K. hesitated again before saying, "His mother told me."

The policeman leaned back in his chair, stretched his legs, and smiled at the floor. "What did his mother tell you exactly?"

"Just that he was bootlegging. That his own wife had admitted it to her."

"Do you have any proof?"

M. K. felt that he was being treated like a fool. "That's your job, to get proof. I'm reporting a crime. You're the police. You enforce the law."

The man stretched lazily. "Mister, that's a nice theory, but we have a lot of problems in a town like this. A lot of rough characters to catch violating the law without putting down traps for one of our outstanding men. You get some proof, and we'll go from there."

M. K. was incredulous. "You aren't going to do anything?"

The officer just looked at him.

"Look," M. K. said. "I'm his brother. I grew up in this town. I don't like the whole business. I wouldn't bring it in if I didn't know for a fact it was true."

He was cut off. "That's very nice . . . you're his brother. If you're his brother, I'm sure you want to report him to the police." When M. K. tried to speak, the officer put up his hand to stop him. "Mister, don't waste any of my time here. I'm not going to bother Mr. Nichols because somebody I don't know says bad things against him."

On the sidewalk outside M. K. stood for several minutes, feeling that his face burned red. He *had* sounded like a fool. Why, though, had the man shown so little interest? Was it because he didn't believe Samson capable of such a thing?

It was more likely because of the same malaise that afflicted Prohibition everywhere. The tide of sentiment had turned against them. Maybe that officer had been bribed, but whether he had been or not might make no difference if he considered smuggling booze an innocent adventure. Surely if Samson were murdering children and hiding their bodies, he would show some interest! And essentially that was what Samson did if he sold liquor. Good liquor or bad liquor, it was all poison. But people wanted to believe otherwise now. They wanted to think that liquor was just a party.

M. K. walked back up the street. Nobody was to be seen. Everybody was at home on Sunday, except Samson. If the law wasn't enforced, what else could he do? Once again he reached the large vertical sign and was about to turn in. He was not so agitated this time. He thought this was the approach he should take: he should talk to his brother. However, almost as though a leash tugged him along, he continued walking down the sidewalk. From shame he pretended to look in the windows of the shops, even though the street was deserted and no one watched him.

If the local police weren't interested, what about the federal agents? It came on him that this was why Wayne Wheeler cared so much for the Prohibition Bureau. If the local authorities would not enforce, if bribery or laxity had made them lose respect for the Constitution, then the federal government must exert federal power. Otherwise it would all be anarchy.

The nearest federal agent was in Chillicothe, a considerable train ride. He did not suppose that anybody would be in the Prohibition Bureau on a Sunday. Yet he did not see how he could wait until tomorrow, knowing what he knew. How could he eat a meal in his brother's house, feeling as he did?

He walked by the train station, a little cream-colored wooden band-box, to find out when the train to Chillicothe would run. The station was just big enough to keep a dozen people out of the cold and wet, but today it was empty and stuffy inside. The ticket window was deserted, though a Sunday paper strewn on a little side table suggested that an agent might be nearby. M. K. looked behind the station house and found him sitting on a stool, smoking a cigar. He said there was a train leaving at half past six. That was in two more hours.

Possibly M. K. might take that train and stay the night in Chillicothe. But should he take David with him now? The boy could not stay any longer in Samson's house. He supposed he must take him to Washington.

Yet M. K. dreaded the scene. It could not be done quickly, he supposed—they must gather all David's things—and by the time he was ready to go, Samson would probably come home and demand an explanation. Then he would have to confront his brother, the very thing he was unable to do at Samson's workplace. He would do it, instead, with the whole family watching.

When he got back to the house, he had still not decided what he should do. The place was peaceful, full of sabbath rest, the huge elm on the corner throwing a lake of deep green shade over the front yard. He saw that Arlene was rocking on the porch. She had not yet seen him. He would have to decide what to do. The thought crossed his mind that possibly the whole concern was imaginary. Conceivably his mother had dreamed his brother's involvement.

Arlene spied him and stood up suddenly. "M. K.!" she cried and came down the steps quickly. His first thought was that she had learned what his mother had said. Perhaps she would clear the air. Perhaps it was not true.

"Don't you work for that Wayne Wheeler?" were her first, rushed words. "Mrs. Parton heard something on the radio, that his wife had been killed."

M. K. had heard from Wayne Wheeler just once since he left for recuperation. Wheeler had sent a clipping from the Oberlin newspaper, reporting on his speech to the new graduates. The clipping had been stapled to a note, scrawled in Wheeler's hand but unsigned: "They still love me here."

It was perfectly natural that Wheeler would go to Oberlin for healing. He had worked his way through college there, taking any odd job to pay his bills. When Howard Russell first went recruiting for the new ASL, he had found Wheeler working as a student janitor. Russell loved to tell how they had knelt in prayer on the spot in Peters Hall, committing Wheeler's calling to the Lord. For Wheeler, a poor farm boy, Oberlin was the highest pinnacle of both learning and piety—the first place he had ever been where you could speak of making the world a better place and not get laughed at. Wheeler's strong, rasping voice became soft and almost whimsical when he spoke of Oberlin.

Wheeler had proceeded from Oberlin to Little Point Sable, Michigan, where he had a summer home. M. K. had fully expected to receive a constant flow of memos, telegrams, and letters from there. Instead, nothing had come. M. K. got a note from the Michigan superintendent, who had stopped by to see Wheeler. "Wheeler says to tell you that he is too busy rebuilding his corpuscles to write."

Wheeler had been in Michigan several weeks when his wife caught on fire. She was cooking dinner when the gas stove threw a spray of fuel on her, soaking her apron and making her a human torch. She staggered out of the kitchen into the living room where her father, Robert Candy, was reading. Candy fell over with a heart attack. Wayne Wheeler heard his wife's screams and rushed in. Wrapping a rug around her, he beat out the flames, flapping his arms against her like a great pelican. Then he lay by her exhausted. She had scorched skin over her hands, her arms, and her torso, black and pink.

The Wheeler home sat on a track paralleling the Lake Michigan shore, almost untouched forest, far from any town. They had only a few neighbors in the quiet woodland, and it took time to find a doctor. It probably would have made no difference. Mrs. Wheeler gave up breathing later that day.

They carried the two to Columbus, Ohio, the Candy home. Under the circumstances M. K. felt no choice but to attend the funeral. He felt deep fondness for Wheeler. Besides, he knew what it was to lose a wife in an accident. He remembered very well his own fury, the pointless blaming he had done, the disgust he had felt even for the geography of Los Angeles, after Darla's death.

Roy Overholt, he remembered, had been the most helpful of all his friends, but he could not quite recall why. It had been a great surprise, he remembered, that such an active man, built large but often seeming even larger, someone who could be downright aggressive when he had an idea in his head, managed to offer just the right kind of comfort: sympathetic without being cloying, quiet without being uncomfortably silent. He could recall watching Overholt's large hands at the funeral where Overholt sat by his side. M. K. had not heard a word of the service, not to remember, but those hands seemed to be real, as real as that awful casket holding that unthinkable body.

Stretching out his own hands to look at them, M. K. had to laugh: his were of an ordinary size, weak and uncalloused.

He arrived in Columbus by rail and did not know how to find the Candy home, so he went by streetcar directly to the Methodist church where the service would take place. For a short time he could not find anybody. The cavernous, cool old tabernacle, with its sloping floor and heavy wood beams, its panels of colored light radiating through the darkness from great height, was empty and so was the corridor that led from it to a locked door. He had to circle the building, wiping the perspiration from his neck with a handkerchief, before he found the pastor's study.

He hoped someone could tell him where the Candy home was located. Instead he found Wayne Wheeler himself deep in conversation with the pastor. There was no secretary. M. K. blundered directly in on them and then tried to back out, apologizing. Wheeler, however, urged him to come in and sit, and he insisted so much that it would have been embarrassing to refuse.

They were discussing funeral plans. The pastor, a square-shaped man with short, graying hair and a bristling mustache, had a paper on which he recorded Wheeler's desires. While M. K. listened, they discussed the choices of music, who would accompany what soloists, the choir's musical numbers, the scriptures to be read, the readers of scripture, the prayers, the Lord's Prayer. (Sung or said congregationally? Wheeler changed his mind twice before settling on having it sung, and then the two men discussed the varying voice qualities of possible soloists.)

"Now Mrs. Brewer has a very nice voice," the pastor said. "She sang the Lord's Prayer at Mr. Packard's funeral just last month. Very nice."

Wheeler's face looked dreadful to M. K.—sunken eyes, a nose that looked like a beak, skin so pale and fragile it seemed to be made from waxed paper.

"I don't think Mr. Candy favored Mrs. Brewer," Wheeler said in a low monotone. "Doesn't she tend to get rather breathy when she goes to the high notes?"

"Well, yes. There's Mr. Parker. He has a fine voice, but very deep. He usually pitches it down two notes."

"I don't think I know him," Wheeler said. "You say he has a fine voice?"

The pastor seemed reluctant to recommend the man. He sighed. "Yes, but having to change the key."

"What's the trouble with that? I'm no musician, Reverend Smalley."

"Oh, there's no trouble. Some think that music should be sung in the key it was written." He sighed again, as though to indicate the trouble created by changing a key.

They eventually settled on Mr. Parker. Then they moved on to the graveside service, which had nearly as much detail, and then to the procession to the grave, the order of cars, the route for the pallbearers. Finally they began to discuss the reception at the Candy home. That was when M. K. broke in.

"I don't think Mr. Wheeler need involve himself to this extent," he said. "He may need to rest. Others can settle these details."

"I am all right, M. K.," Wheeler said. "She was my dear wife. I want above all else to do this for her." After a pause he went back to the discussion of the schedule of food to be brought to the Candys. He wanted to know how many hams the pastor thought would be necessary, and together they drew up a list of the women who would work in the kitchen.

There was something admirable and yet alarming about this. It seemed almost hypnotically mechanical, like shelling peas while the earth beneath buckled and roared. M. K. could only sit and watch until they had completed their plans and then reviewed the details painstakingly.

M. K. found himself angry at the pastor. What kind of man, how insensitive to pain, would want a wounded man to care about such trivia when the foundations of his life had broken apart? That was the way in which M. K. tried to interpret the scene, but indisputably he saw that Wheeler must want it just the way it was. At any point he could have stopped and said that he would leave the details to others, but indefatigably he bore on.

When they completed the arrangements and stood up, shaking

hands, Wheeler asked M. K. if he had any business with the pastor. When M. K. said no, he said, "Then why don't you come home with me?"

Outside the door to the church, having reentered the hot, orange sunlight of a late summer afternoon, Wheeler took M. K. by the wrist. "I want you to know," he said solemnly, "that this tragedy will have no impact on my commitment. I give you my word that I will only redouble my devotion to the cause in which I am enlisted. Nothing will shake me."

He looked M. K. full in the face for a moment before dropping his hand and moving down the steps, going slowly with the right foot and then the left on each step, like an old man who has suffered a stroke. At the bottom step he looked up at M. K. again. "You don't have a car, do you? No, of course not. Well, I think we can walk. It is not more than a mile." M. K. suggested that he go back into the pastor's study and see about calling a taxi, but Wheeler remained firm. They walked slowly, almost wordlessly, to the Candys' simple cottage. Once, on the way, Wheeler stopped and took M. K. by the wrist again, repeating his promise almost word for word.

In the Candy house a dozen or more visitors stood when Wheeler entered. The curtains were drawn and the room was dim. Candles were burning. Two simple caskets took up the center of the room, both closed. Wheeler explained that his wife had been badly burned, and they felt it would be simpler to have neither body displayed.

He took a seat, which evidently had been left vacant for him. A cousin brought a chair from the dining room for M. K. They were informed that Mrs. Candy had retired to her bedroom. Wheeler seemed only partially aware of these arrangements. He stared at the various guests, each in turn, and then solemnly told them what he had told M. K.: that he would only increase his devotion to the cause that had captured his life. When various friends expressed their sympathy or expressed concern for Mrs. Candy, he barely seemed to understand.

More visitors arrived. When they entered the room, they silently walked near to the two dominating boxes, sometimes placing a hand on the edge of one or the other, sometimes seeming to bow in prayer, sometimes letting a sigh escape their lips. Then they came over to Wheeler and solemnly greeted him.

It seemed to be understood that M. K. would stay with Wheeler, a sort of chaperone. Women visitors disappeared into the kitchen with their towel-wrapped packets of food, while the men sat with their hands on their knees and tried to find something to say. At six o'clock they all sat down for supper. Far more food had been provided than an army could eat: ham, green beans, mashed potatoes, biscuits, rolls, Jell-O salad, all kinds of pickles and preserves. Some of the mourners joined them in the meal, but most who came during the meal were met by a bustling young woman, a wide-hipped, black-haired niece of Wheeler's, who sat them in the living room to wait.

There was no missing their curiosity about how the accident had happened, but Wheeler seemed not to notice it. He sat with unnatural stillness, his hands crossed in his lap, and promised each one his devotion to the cause. Sometimes he did it more than once to the same person, as though he were a windup device that could not help his mechanical repetition.

In the evening some of the Anti-Saloon League officials began to trickle in. The Executive Committee was meeting in Winona Lake, Indiana, and so was the World League Against Alcoholism, one of Cherrington's educational enterprises. Both groups had sent sizable delegations for the funeral, but only a few came over to the house. They were state superintendents and district superintendents from the midwestern states, some of whom had worked with Wheeler from the time he first earned his fame going door to door on a bicycle. One by one they came in, clasped

Wheeler's hands together in theirs, looked him in the face and spoke their sympathy, placing hands on his shoulders, his wrists, his arms. Some of their voices cracked, or they were even unable to make a sound because they were thinking of their own wives whom they could so easily lose.

To each one Wheeler made the same pledge of his loyalty to the cause and then sat down, summoning his guest to sit in a chair next to him. He started to discuss the league's factions, its difficulties, its strategy. M. K. watched as each ASL leader in turn registered surprise, discomfort, and sometimes alarm at being asked to discuss the league's problems. Wheeler did not seem to notice their reaction. He acted like a man whose insides had been shot away but who keeps on walking.

When it was too late for visitors, Wheeler still sat in his chair as though expecting to receive more. M. K. sat across from him, exhausted. The women had gone away, into the kitchen or to their own homes or upstairs to bed.

"There may still be time," Wheeler said, nodding his head. "When we get back to Washington, I will see the president again. We cannot accept this loss."

The mention of loss made M. K. think Wheeler was referring to his wife's death.

"Haynes has been a perfect comrade-in-arms," Wheeler continued. "Always optimistic. Willing to cooperate. We cannot find another man the like."

M. K. understood that Wheeler was referring to the dismissal of Roy Haynes as the Treasury Department's Prohibition commissioner. Wheeler had fought for Haynes, though even ASL leaders complained of his incompetence. Haynes's principal strategy regarding every problem was to announce that Prohibition was an outstanding success, with ever-increasing efficiency in enforcement. In the face of constant newspaper reports of bootlegging, he would tell the press that the Coast

Guard had eliminated all but the last vestiges of rum-running from the seas. When Prohibition agents were busting up huge stills in cities up and down the East Coast, Haynes announced to the nation that home manufacture was not a significant problem under the administration of the Volstead Act.

"You need not think of such things," M. K. told Wheeler. "You have suffered a far greater loss."

"The league must not abandon the policy of personal enforcement. We have the laws, but men make them reality. The task is too critical to entrust to men we don't know. It must be our laws enforced by people who depend on us for their positions."

"For now," M. K. said, "you can let others in the league attend to that. For the good of the league, you must rest and recover fully. We will need you again."

"The loss of my darling wife will not cause me to lose one ounce of my devotion," Wheeler said. "If I must burn out for the cause, I will do it. I will not rust out, but burn out."

M. K. felt the conversation like heavy waves beating on a shore, signaling a hurricane far to sea. Wheeler seemed far away, with only his repetitious pieties pretending to life in this room.

"Why should you do either?" M. K. said. "If you can rest, you'll be as good as new."

Wheeler didn't seem to hear him. "I want you to help me," he said and patted the seat next to him for M. K. to come and sit close by. "So many friends have written. Hundreds, I would say, and I'm sure there will be more. I want a letter to send them." Wheeler's rusty voice seemed to wane as he spoke; he did not so much finish his sentences as run out.

"All right," M. K. said. "I'll gladly help you."

Wheeler stood up and walked haltingly, like an old man, across the

room. He fumbled behind an upholstered chair and brought out a familiar scarred leather briefcase. Opening it slowly, he pulled out a handful
of envelopes. "You see? They have written me. So many, deeply worried.
I want to tell one and all that this tragic loss can never interfere with my
work on behalf of the dry cause. Reassurance. Reassurance." Once again
his voice trailed off.

"They know you will never leave the cause," M. K. remonstrated.
"Surely no one could doubt you."

Wheeler looked up, staring blankly, as though he had been inter-
rupted in his thoughts. "Of course they don't doubt me." His voice
seemed stronger for the moment, rasping like a saw. "They worry for the
cause. If I fall, what can happen?"

He walked across the room again, sat down next to M. K., and pulled
out another fistful of letters. He set it on the floor, then slowly pulled out
another packet. None of them had been opened. The envelopes, in all
their different sizes, were addressed to Mr. Wayne Wheeler. "I want a letter to answer these. I should write each one, but I can't. Not yet. The work
must always be before personal considerations. No, I can't write, but you
can send a mimeographed letter with my very words. Will you do that?"

"Of course," M. K. said.

"You won't make up anything? Just my words?"

"No," M. K. said. "I'll show you the letter before I put it out."

"Oh, no," Wheeler said in a voice suddenly weak with weariness. He
lowered his head almost to his knees, as though he were faint. "Oh, no,
I won't be available for that. Must be careful of my strength."

The funeral was a curiously impersonal event. Many men in dark
suits crowded the pews, shoulder to shoulder, memorializing a woman

whom they probably would not have recognized. M. K. had barely exchanged ten words with Mrs. Wheeler, for she was a quiet woman content to raise her children and support her husband. As for people in Columbus, they had lost her when she had moved away to Washington many years before, beyond the public eye of her neighbors and even, to a large extent, her family. Her fame was her husband. She shared the funeral with her father, who was well loved and remembered in the town, but his memory, too, got lost because the twin deaths were so grim and sensational that they overwhelmed the ordinary sympathy and love that a funeral can show.

M. K. sat directly behind Wayne Wheeler in the second row of the sanctuary. He was placed there as a support in case Wheeler should faint or suffer a heart attack, he supposed, and he spent the entire service watching the thinning hair on the back of Wheeler's head and listening to the service Wheeler had planned so carefully. He stayed near Wheeler at the graveside and again at the house where more came to offer sympathy and provide food. Several times he suggested to Wheeler that he go upstairs and rest, for the man's skin looked like a thinly stretched balloon, and his voice fell so low he was barely audible even when mourners stood with an ear cocked toward his lips.

Wheeler simply shook him off. He continued standing for new visitors, greeting them, and reassuring them that he would not be deterred from the work God had called him to do in the league. Many of the guests, M. K. suspected, could not understand what Wheeler was saying, but they caressed his hand and pursed their lips and sighed heavily.

By suppertime they had stopped arriving, and once again M. K. sat silently with Wheeler. The afternoon torpor had almost overwhelmed M. K. His face hurt, he was so tired of putting sympathy on it. He wondered whether he could go back to Hillsboro tomorrow.

"I want to go to Winona Lake," Wheeler said suddenly and heaved a sigh as though he was glad to have come out with it.

M. K. explained to him that he needed to rest, that he had no business in Winona Lake.

"Isn't Cherrington there?" Wheeler asked, and he gave a sly smile, as though that proved everything. "The league is facing a crisis. I must go and speak."

Chapter 18
1927: The Empty City

Despite the best efforts of everybody in the ASL, Wayne Wheeler stood to speak at Winona Lake. Word of his presence had spread through the conference grounds, and a vast crowd filled the Billy Sunday auditorium, a wide, open-sided structure built for summer revival meetings.

M. K. felt that there was something distasteful in the interest, and he cringed from it. Such a throng would certainly not have come to hear Wheeler previously, but under the circumstances of violent death, they would crowd in to see the man who had just buried his wife. Some must be the very people who criticized Wheeler for his political tactics. Nevertheless, when Wheeler was introduced to speak, the audience began softly to applaud, which was not usual in that religious setting. The applause gradually grew until the whole auditorium was filled up with the wave-crashing blur of sound.

M. K. sat in the front row, watching Wheeler as though he were a delicate china cup. He could remember Wheeler's jaunty smile and the way he would cock his head when he talked, but what he saw at the podium now was a shrunken figure, a pygmy whose clothes hung off him, topped with a death's-head. He could barely see Wheeler's eyes, for they seemed buried in the depths of dark bowls. Wheeler's voice rasped out weakly and diffidently. He had a speech written out, but he had read no more than half a page before he had to stop from exhaustion. He coughed, apologized, and said he would just mention one or two main points. Then shuffling through the papers, he read a few selected sentences, as dully as though he were reading from an encyclopedia.

"I'm afraid I'll have to refer you to the printed speech," he said. "We've made enough for everybody." Probably no one beyond the front few rows understood him, his voice was so low. Slowly he waved his hand to the crowd and tried to grin, though showing his teeth made his face more gruesome. He shuffled off the stage. M. K. helped bring out the piles of mimeographed papers, which he had been making late into last night. They passed them down the long rows in complete and stunned silence.

Then while the meeting continued, M. K. accompanied Wheeler to the train. He was going back to Little Point Sable, where his wife and father-in-law had died, but he denied that he was dreading the prospect. "They are gone," he said. "I plan to lie in the sun and forget everything. Before you know it I'll be back in my chair in Washington." He paused to take a deep breath and coughed. "The Dry Boss," he said and started a smile that never quite crossed his face. Wheeler liked the phrase, which some antagonistic newspaper reporter had stuck on him.

M. K. would take a later train, traveling in the opposite direction back to Hillsboro. While he waited he met Howard Russell, who was going to Columbus by the same train. They boarded together.

Russell was a sweet-looking older man with liver spots on his hands and a slightly uncertain stutter in his words. Though twenty years older than Wheeler, his eyes were bright and his smile was cheerful. It had been years since he held any administrative role for the ASL, but various leaders trusted and confided in him because his heart and his soul were so sound.

"I'm praying for Brother Wheeler," Russell said when they first sat down. "That his health will recover. He has taken some terrible blows."

"On top of years spent overworking his body," M. K. said.

"Well," Russell said gently and with a smile. "I understand that you sometimes do the same."

"Not like Wheeler."

"No, perhaps not. He will be in my thoughts and prayers." Russell smiled beatifically. "Mr. Nichols, I hope you remember to pray for this great cause we are engaged in. We depend upon the Lord almighty, and we forget that at our peril."

M. K. said nothing. He had acquired a slight aversion to the pious talk that sometimes went with the dry cause, especially when they visited the churches. It seemed unnecessary to make a point of their religion.

"You see," Russell said gently, "when we lose the divine grace on our work, it becomes dreariness and labor. Not only is it law for others, but it becomes law for us, which brings death to the soul. What man does without God, no matter how much good he intends, turns out to be for death. We are creatures incapable of creating life. Life belongs to God and to Him alone.

"Not that I think Mr. Wheeler has fallen into that trap, not at all. No, don't mistake me. I am sure that Mr. Wheeler is a praying man. I remember too well the first time that I talked to him." Russell smiled as he warmed to the memory. "He was a student janitor and his business was cleaning the dormitory. You went to Oberlin, didn't you? I thought so. Well, Mr. Nichols, we talked it over, that Mr. Wheeler could work hard for the Lord in the dry cause with a lot more uncertainty as to pay than he would have cleaning a dormitory, but with a great deal more assurance that he would reap eternal rewards. And then we knelt together, at his simple bed, to pray. That day was consummated with prayer. I know Mr. Wheeler is a man of prayer. I know that he started that way, and I trust he will press on in the same way. This is a grand cause, isn't it?"

The last question startled M. K. He quickly said that it was.

However, he was not quite willing to let the pious talk go completely unchallenged. The last two days, with the great amount of religious oratory he had heard, had made him somewhat irritable. "I'm sure you're right about Wheeler praying," he said. "He's also a man of work. He works long hours, and he's never content with a poor job. That is the Lord's will, too, isn't it?"

Russell had closed his small, wrinkled eyes, and he seemed to have turned his thoughts elsewhere. "Oh, yes, indeed. We work as unto the Lord."

Only after Russell had left him in Columbus did M. K. begin to recognize how really annoying he had found the conversation. Though he disavowed it, Russell seemed to imply that Wheeler's physical breakdown was a spiritual failing. He had failed to pray, so the work had become a burden. In principle M. K. believed that the cause depended on God, but it had been a long time since he had prayed for God to change the votes in Congress.

M. K. sat slouched in his seat, physically weary and aching to sleep, yet well aware that it would be many hours before he could rest. He would stop for the night in Chillicothe, he had decided, and see the federal agents in the morning. Making that plan had reminded him of all the troubles he faced with Samson.

Night had fallen, and there was only a faint gray throb of light over the horizon to the west. The train lights reflected in his window and obscured the stars. Only occasionally did he see a light in a window at a farmhouse by the tracks.

So, have I prayed for Samson? He put the question to himself because it seemed germane. Russell had said that the law without grace brought only death. Who would it kill? Samson showed no danger signs. Perhaps he, M. K., was the one dying, according to the way Russell thought.

He thought of Linda. It had occurred to M. K. that perhaps David might go and live with her rather than stay with him. She was married now and had a house with room for somebody extra. Her husband was a schoolteacher. M. K. would never have dreamed Linda would marry a schoolteacher—that seemed too mundane for her. On the other hand, she still drank. He knew that because he had asked her.

In Chillicothe he got off and wandered up and down dark streets until he found a flophouse. Mercifully he slept until nine o'clock in the morning. He put on his suit, the same one he had worn every day since setting out for the funeral. Today, thankfully, he would have fresh clothes. M. K. ate a leisurely breakfast in a cafe, sucking down eggs and flapjacks while he read the Chillicothe paper. He was surprised to find no mention of Wheeler and his appearance in Winona Lake. Events that seemed epochal, swallowing all attention, had vanished without a trace. He wondered just what local people knew about the accident in Michigan, if anything.

The morning was misty and warm, the sun a yellow disk trying to bore its way through low clouds. The weather might clear and turn hot, or it might turn to a sweaty drizzle. M. K. found the federal office in a storefront, plastered with WANTED posters on the front windows, and displaying a large poster of the Volstead regulations on a wall inside. There were five government desks, partitioned by low dividers, and an electric fan swiveling across the space, blowing air around. Two of the agents were talking in low tones across their divider, and another had his feet on his desk and was inspecting his fingernails. None of them showed an immediate interest in M. K., who stood undecided just inside the door. After several glances between them, the agent with his feet on his desk stood up and asked M. K. what he wanted.

"I've got a tip," M. K. said. "A bootlegger out in Hillsboro."

The agent glanced behind him at the other two agents, who had stopped their conversation. "Is Hillsboro in our territory?" he asked them. "I think that is Cincinnati."

"No, it is your territory," M. K. said firmly. "I came because it is in your territory."

"Oh, that's right," the agent said. "How could I forget? Let me get a piece of paper. No, why don't you come to my desk and we'll get the information down." He led the way, saying as he went, "Chances are good, we already know about it. We've got Hillsboro well covered."

"I don't think you have this covered," M. K. said when he took a chair by the agent's desk. "He's a prominent citizen, Samson Nichols. He runs a hauling company, and I guess some of the hauling must be bootleg whiskey."

The agent had stopped writing. He looked at the other agents, who had continued their listening. "You fellows know anything about it?" he asked. "A Samson Nichols?"

One of the agents laughed, though it was unclear what he was laughing at. "No," the other said. "Maybe Fred knows. He's out, mister, tracking down some criminals." He glanced at his partner, who laughed again.

"Well, let me write it all down, and we'll look into it." He made a point of spelling Samson's name correctly, but he didn't show any curiosity about what M. K. might know or why he suspected a crime. He asked for Samson's address and the name of his hauling business, and said they would be investigating.

"Don't you want to know who I am?" M. K. asked.

"Oh, sure, that's a good idea." The man wrote down M. K.'s particulars but did not comment on his last name being the same as Samson's. He stood up, shook hands, and said not to hesitate to bring any more information to them.

"Is that all you want to know?" M. K. asked.

"Sure, what more could there be? We've got to investigate. It might take quite a while. You're welcome to check back if you get curious."

When M. K. left the office, he heard low laughter behind him while the door was closing.

———

All the way to Hillsboro he pondered what he should do. He even took Russell's advice and prayed about it, although the prayer did not seem to bring any illumination. By now the feelings of the funeral and the ASL executive meeting had washed out of his thoughts. He had to pick up where he had left off and take action. One fact seemed obvious: David could no longer stay in the house of a bootlegger.

He was relieved when, on walking in the front door, he found David reading in the living room. Relieved, because M. K. did not want to talk to Arlene or Samson any more than necessary. They would have to know, of course, but M. K. would be happy to put that off as long as possible.

"David," M. K. said after he had said hello. "You are going to move with me to Washington. You'll go to school there. I need to go as soon as we can. Today, I mean. This afternoon if we can. So go upstairs and pack all your things. Get everything you want to take with you. We won't be coming back."

David stared for a moment. "To Washington?" he said. "I'll go to school there?"

"You'll get a better education. The school will be more advanced, I'm sure. Washington is a big city compared to Hillsboro."

"Is that why I'm going there?"

"No. That's not the main reason. I've just decided that it's time.

You're old enough to live with me and take care of yourself when I'm not around." David seemed to accept that. Perhaps later on he would ask more questions.

M. K. washed and put on fresh clothes, and when he came back downstairs, he found Samson. He was standing in the living room with his hands in his back pockets, a towering hunk of muscle with broad shoulders and a grizzled dome. He had been waiting. His demeanor spelled impatience. He was alone. "What's going on?" he demanded.

"I just got back from the funeral," M. K. said.

"I got a call this morning on the trunk line from Chillicothe. They said somebody had reported me for bootlegging."

That was the last thing M. K. had expected to hear. He understood the implication, that Samson had been tipped off. "Who called you?" he asked.

"None of your business who called." Samson cracked a mean smile. "You little dummy. You must think I'm as thick as a mule. You think I don't have that covered?" He looked sharply at M. K.

Samson laughed. "Do you think they're going to arrest me and lose a regular paycheck? I'm not so stupid as you think I am. I wouldn't take chances. That's smart, which is more than I can say for your boys who send out agents that don't get paid enough to buy groceries and expect them to be as virtuous as you are. Or more virtuous, I guess. I understand you Anti-Saloon League boys get plenty of money out of those campaign funds."

"You can believe that if you want to badly enough," M. K. said. "If it makes you feel better about yourself."

"I feel fine. Very fine. I mind my own business."

"The Constitution of the United States is everyone's business, I believe."

"Don't bring me that. What it says in the law books isn't what is real in this country. All those laws do is put dumb, fat guys in uniform to collect from businessmen like me. They encourage the real lawless types to try to cut in on us. It was a lot cleaner before these phony laws. M. K., you probably hate to think about it, but you have wasted your life on this thing. It's a pure waste."

His brother's scorn had since childhood been able to flatten him. He was not going to give Samson the satisfaction of overwhelming him. Nor would he allow his son to live in this house another day.

"I wonder that you know so much about what is real," M. K. said. "I was under the impression Hillsboro was a pretty small place."

"Yeah, well at least I know what goes on here. And if it goes on here, you can guess what goes on in Cincinnati, brother dear. I doubt you know what goes on outside a church service. There's a whole world of people who work for a living and don't have time to mind other people's business."

M. K. realized that David had reentered the room and was watching them. His son had heard the argument, at least part of it.

"Are you ready, David?"

David nodded.

"Ready for what?" Samson demanded.

"I'm taking him to Washington."

"Like fun you are. Why do you want to do that?"

"You may feel justified in what you do, Samson. But I don't want David to grow up in it."

This seemed to penetrate Samson as nothing else had. "It hasn't hurt him yet, has it? He's been here since he was barely talking."

"And you've been defying the law that long, I suppose."

"I don't think it's hurt him. Has it, David?"

David did not answer. His face was sharply attentive, like that of a wild animal stopped on the edge of a clearing. Looking at him, M. K. felt full of ardor. How could he have let this boy be raised so far away from him and in this house? Evidently he had known about his uncle all along.

"It hasn't hurt him," M. K. said. "And it's not going to."

When they arrived in Washington, D.C., they were preoccupied with the chore of moving David into Linda's old room and finding him a school for the fall term. David did not seem to miss a beat. He wanted to see the monuments and the museums, and was especially fascinated by the Smithsonian, the red castle on the Mall with its glass cases full of arcane knowledge. M. K. took him to the Capitol and introduced him to a few of the dry leaders, and that, too, he treated with eager interest.

David brought such life into the apartment that M. K. was struck by the contrast with how empty and dusty it had been. He had barely lived in the place. He had never gotten pictures on the wall, and he made do with blinds and no curtains. Now he was challenged to think how to make it a home without the influence of a woman. Vaguely he knew that the challenge would grow when Congress came back to work. He would be preoccupied, working late hours, and then how would it be for David?

In the back of M. K.'s memory was the year in Seattle when he had tried to care for David and Linda and had made a miserable failure of it. An experience like that sticks with you.

On the first Monday, he went back to the ASL office, where the staff crowded into his office, anxious to hear firsthand about the funeral. When he had told them everything, they still wanted to linger, as though they had nothing worthwhile to do. M. K. acted cheerful and tried to urge them to carry on, but he didn't manage it wholeheartedly. Wheeler had dominated everything so thoroughly that they did not know how to act in his absence.

Their uncertainty increased when, on Tuesday, they heard that Wheeler took sick and was rushed to the Battle Creek Sanatorium. M. K. managed at great expense to reach one of Wheeler's grown sons by telephone. He said that his father was resting peacefully and seemed to be out of danger. The voice, sounding thin and mechanical as it traveled a thousand miles of wire, failed to convey a sense of confidence. Out of danger? No one had spoken of danger before.

On Sunday M. K. took David to his church—a strange and lonely experience, so seldom had he himself been there. He would need to attend with David from this time forward, but he did not look forward to it. After the service they went by train into Maryland to see David's sister. Linda—her name was Mowatt now—and her husband, Guy, met the train and walked them to their home, a row house in a poor Baltimore neighborhood near the harbor. Most of their neighbors were Portuguese. Guy taught French in the Baltimore schools, and he wore a beret. M. K. saw a bottle of wine on their kitchen counter. They made no attempt even to hide it. At least they did not try to serve it at dinner.

During the meal, Linda frequently lifted her eyes to stare at David. She said nothing when she did so, letting her husband carry the conversation, but M. K. saw the feeling in her eyes. This he admitted to himself: he was jealous that this stepdaughter did not look at him with the same feeling that she did her brother.

M. K. reminded himself that she and David had grown up together and had more history than he had with either of them. But seeing Linda made him heartsick. He itched to know how she truly was. He wanted to know whether she still drank and how much and when. Though she maintained a pleasant demeanor, Linda gave M. K. the sense that he was a distant acquaintance.

The visit left M. K. thinking of his brother's harsh charge that he had wasted his life. He did feel rootless. Perhaps it was a symptom of summer when the work did not drive forward. He needed the work, perhaps as much as the work needed him.

On Tuesday morning M. K. stopped at the corner newsstand to buy a paper. The headline took the whole front page: "Dry Boss Dead."

There on the corner he stood reading. It seemed so peculiar to receive this news as journalism when it belonged to the realm of the most personal. He felt that he might be learning about the death of a Russian premier, not the little man he knew so well. According to the paper, Wheeler had been sitting up in a chair when, without warning, his heart failed. The doctor described his death as instantaneous. The story included numerous tributes from politicians as well as from league officials in Westerville.

M. K. was surprised and a little chagrined that no reporter had come to him. The reporters knew him; they often talked to him about league news. Yet when it came to this momentous event, they had not thought of him at all.

Then when he realized what an egocentric reaction that was, M. K. was ashamed and wondered why such thoughts even crossed his mind. Surely it was a result of this strange melding of public and private lives.

When he reached the office, he found the other half dozen staff sitting or standing in the front reception, talking in low tones. They sprawled on the cheap green sofa or leaned against the wall. None of them had heard anything more than what they had read in the newspapers. "We'll just have to keep on going," one of the staffers kept saying, punctuating the others' mundane reminders that you never know when death may call, and that Mr. Wheeler had not been in good health, and that it was hard to believe that he, of all people, was dead. They were all frightened, but no one could admit it.

"I suppose," June McKenzie said, "that we must go on with our work." They all murmured assent, but nobody got up or moved. Finally M. K., who had been leaning with his back against a wall, stood up straight, stretched a little, and walked quietly back to his office. He shut the door and sat in his desk chair, staring.

What an amazing thing death is. That a man with so much drive could be stilled and permanently removed from the scene—that he could become, in an instant, an object. M. K. tried to picture Wheeler, with his leering grin and his ears sticking out from his head. He had been very fond of him. Perhaps he had even loved the man. Wheeler had believed in M. K. and, more important, had believed in the cause, wrapping M. K. in its purposes. It was a heady thing to be in on changing America for the good. It had served for M. K.'s redemption. When he had been lost and weary, the cause had given him life and hope. Wheeler had believed in himself so fully, so ecstatically, that it would have been impossible to work with him and not think of him as the living embodiment of the dry cause. M. K. had needed something to believe in, and Wheeler had given it to him in flesh and blood.

The cause goes on, M. K. reminded himself. *Wheeler would have been the first to say so.*

Failure seemed to dog their efforts these days. The wets could make their statistics ring true and their stories sound heroic, while M. K.'s efforts to counter them seemed repetitious and strained. Somehow the dry cause had come to stand for the very opposite of what it really was. It had been stained with a reputation of thinking negatively about humankind, of being cramped and pessimistic. In reality it represented the best, most soaring hopes for the redemption of the earth and its people. If they could eliminate this ancient scourge from the lives of new Americans, what would not be possible? If Americans could be made into a truly sober people? If, at the very least, they could create a government standing against the commercial exploitation of poison, the licensed sponsoring of rooms where poor men paid for the privilege of destroying themselves?

Because he dealt with news reporters and magazine editors, M. K. felt the current against the cause. Yet it was still hard to believe that it could become so distorted and their ideals presented as narrowness.

Perhaps, he thought, *Wheeler's death will reverse this. Perhaps his selfless death will capture Americans' consciences, and they will understand that they crucified him, who wanted only to help them, and that they crucified themselves in so doing.* For a moment M. K. caught at this spark, and his spirits rose, but soon they sank again. As much as he loved Wheeler, he knew that he could never be made into a martyr for the cause. He was too much disliked, and he had savored that dislike like a man tasting dessert. No one could turn the Dry Boss into Saint Wayne.

M. K. stood up and went to the door of his office. He had his hand on the doorknob before he changed his mind and sat down again. He was a sociable man. He liked many people, and people liked him. Only with a very few, though, had he committed himself to love and to give his life. He had loved Darla with all his heart, and she was dead. Linda treated him as if he had leprosy, and she would surely die like her mother if she kept on the path she was following. David was still pure, enthusiastic, hopeful, unspoiled, but how long would that last?

M. K. suddenly caught a vision, vivid as real life, of Wheeler at his last speech in Winona Lake. The face was an unearthly pale yellow color, the voice almost too low to comprehend.

Trying to shake himself free of this miserable reverie, M. K. thought of his job. He took out a clean sheet of paper. Today editors would take almost anything on Wheeler, on his life and his ideals. For a few days they would be happy to sentimentalize him. Possibly M. K. could write a personal reflection on the man he had admired so much. He tried to think how to start such a piece and got through a sentence or two before he began to imagine Samson reading the piece and was too upset to go on.

His brother was a hard-boiled egg, disinterested in ideals. He would consider all these thoughts poppycock. Samson cared only for the bottom line.

Then M. K. wondered whether he was any different. Hadn't he, just moments ago, fussed that the reporters had not called him about Wheeler's death?

He had lost his sincere first love. He had lost his friends. Roy Overholt, where was he now? They had not communicated since M. K. had seen him in LA.

M. K. felt a numb certainty that Overholt would tell him he had lost his love for the Lord. M. K. had no defense for that. Certainly it was true. That was a bygone era of his life, when he had been young, when Darla had been alive and full of hope and need. In those days he had been glad to pray, happy to talk about the friendship of Jesus. He still believed those things, but the ease and happiness were long gone.

Even in Seattle he had gone to church gladly, and he had prayed over little David and Linda. Nowadays, did he ever? They were grown, but why should that matter? When did he ever pray? M. K. felt his own accusations against himself sorely, and they added to the heavy weight that was trying him.

He stood up again. *This is ridiculous. I have work to do. I ought to get on with it or else quit. No good is accomplished through all this introspection.*

Yet the load of his regrets weighed on him. They pressed him down so he felt torpid. His hands weighed fifty pounds each—he could not lift them. He sat down again. *This is awful,* he thought.

He lowered his head onto the desk, pressing his forehead onto the cool wooden surface. Everything in his life seemed to be disintigrating. "Help me." He articulated the words in a low, rattling moan. They came out of his mouth unintended, but he recognized in a split second afterward that the words brought a faint brilliancy with them. He said them again. "Help me." It came to him that this was a prayer, real and heartfelt.

Chapter 19
1927: Reeducation

In November M. K. and his son, David, had to move back to Westerville, Ohio, where the Anti-Saloon League had its national headquarters. It seemed to M. K. like the last nail in Wayne Wheeler's coffin—or the last nail in his hands, as M. K. sometimes thought. Cherrington had won at last, and the league was scaling back its Washington operation. The group was not going to pursue personal enforcement any longer, but would keep a more distant, impersonal view of Prohibition from a thousand miles away.

Bishop James Cannon explained it to M. K. The bishop had aged severely. He still stood straight and thin, with an ascetic sourness around his lips, but he had a slight shuffle to his walk now, and his hair had gone completely gray, the undistinguished dull color of a rat. Cannon had not given in an inch to age, however. Just this year he had taken harrowing trips to the Congo and Brazil, visiting Methodist missionaries. Now, with Wheeler gone, he held a predominant role in the league.

"You're wanted in Westerville immediately. As soon as you can get there, Cherrington wants you to start." He must have seen M. K. wince, for he immediately emphasized with great firmness that Cherrington would be in charge. "You will find, I believe, that Mr. Cherrington knows how to use you to the greatest effect. Our emphasis will be education more than politics. Under Mr. Wheeler, this office became very expert at its influence on Capitol Hill, but unfortunately we lost much of our influence in the highways and byways of America."

M. K. felt bitter over the change in policy, with its implied disrespect for Wheeler's—and his own—work. Apart from that, he did not mind leaving Washington. The ASL office was exhausted. When he went to Capitol Hill, dry politicians seemed surprised to find that he continued to exist now that Wheeler did not.

"Are we to quit politics entirely?" M. K. asked. He was prepared to argue the point. The ASL's program was not moral reform but legal Prohibition—an abolishment of the liquor trade. That had been done by law, and laws were made through politics.

Cannon looked at him coldly. "No, of course not." He looked away, out the window. After a few moments of contemplation he turned back to M. K. "Many of my political friends say that the Democrats are very likely to nominate Governor Smith for president. As a Democrat—you know I am a Virginia Democrat—I would consider that a great disaster for my party. The latest *Nation* reports that Al Smith drinks between four and eight cocktails a day. He is wet through and through. I hope we will not elect a Tammany politician to take an oath to uphold the Constitution of the United States and then proceed to flout it in the Executive Mansion."

For this little speech Cannon's temperature seemed to rise. He stopped and glared at M. K. "Certainly we cannot quit politics. I will do all that I can to see that Al Smith never sets foot in the White House. However, we will proceed by raising dry principles to greater public awareness. Our league will be faithful to those principles, not to party or person."

From one side of their mouths they said they wanted to back away from politics. Then they talked about Al Smith as though he were the devil himself. How much more personal and political could it get? M. K.

figured that one way or another, they would get back to Wheeler's politics because it always came down to that: Who are you for? Who are you against? What have you got to trade?

But that was none of his business. He didn't set policy. He was going to work for the ASL, and he might as well do it in Ohio as in Washington.

———

By the last week of November M. K. had purchased a tiny two-story bungalow on a street shrouded by tall, naked, black-barked elms and had launched David at Westerville High School. He borrowed the down payment from Cherrington because he had no other way to make it, but nevertheless, for a week he avoided Cherrington. That was the most aggravating aspect of the move. He would work for a man whom he had never liked, who had persistently undone his work with Wayne Wheeler, who seemed small-minded. He would work for a man who knew he had betrayed him, and yet would loan him money.

Cherrington acted friendly—friendly for him, that is, who was not naturally affable. M. K. supposed it was a triumphal cheer. Cherrington had finally gained control over the organization, although M. K. thought it might be a Pyrrhic victory. The first thing he noticed at headquarters was a quiet, sluggish dullness, the still, dry hush of a place that is sleepwalking. It said something about his mood that he took this in coldly, as though it had nothing to do with him.

"What do you want to do?" Cherrington asked him when they sat down to talk. He still had a dark, thuggish appearance, looking older than his forty-plus years. His face had grown heavier, and he looked as if he needed a shave.

"I thought you would tell me that."

Cherrington gave an infinitesimal shrug. "I know you are a good writer. I don't know what you like to write." He paused, then added, "The work we do here is different from what you did for Mr. Wheeler."

"I know that," M. K. said. "So tell me what you want me to do, and I'll do it. I can do anything."

Cherrington nodded soberly, as though to himself. "I know that I can give you almost any assignment and you'll do it well. That's fine, but we need something more imaginative. The league has lost respect in the minds of many people. Politicians can run against us now, can accuse us of terrible things, and people believe them."

"Congress is more dry than it's ever been," M. K. countered.

Cherrington nodded again. He did not want to argue; he stubbornly wanted to communicate his point. "It's true," he said. "We have continued to succeed politically. It can't last, though, if we lose the argument in the streets. And I don't mean on Main Street of towns like Westerville. I mean on Broadway. I mean in New York or in Chicago or even in Richmond. Correct me if I'm wrong, but in some of those places I believe Prohibition is treated like a joke."

"But those big cities are a small part of America," M. K. answered. "And the people laughing aren't native-born Americans. They're foreigners, along with some crooked politicians and some wise-guy newspaper editors. That's not the real America."

"It will become the real America," Cherrington said. He said it and then shut his mouth, letting his prophecy hang in the air.

"All right," M. K. said. "If that's the kind of country we're in, why don't we just quit?"

"Because we can change their minds," Cherrington said, and he leaned forward. "That's why education must be our policy. That's why we must stay close to the churches because the churches can reach into a thousand streets and tenements and factories to convince a new gen-

eration of Americans. The country is changing, and we need to help it
to change."

"All right. Let's do it then. I'm just here to help. That's what I did
for Mr. Wheeler, and I'll do the same here in Westerville. Just tell me
what to do, and I'll do it."

"I think we need something better than that," Cherrington said.

M. K. was getting mad. "What could I do better than that? I just
told you I'll do anything you tell me to do."

For the first time M. K. saw a slight smile cross Cherrington's lips.
He sat back and crossed his arms over his chest. "I'll tell you something
about myself," he said. "I'll tell you, but I don't want anybody else to hear
this. Do you understand? You know I worked for the newspapers, just
like you did. And I thought I was a pretty good writer. You know how a
newspaper reporter or an editor can think he is a pretty good writer?"

M. K. acknowledged that he did, and Cherrington smiled an ugly
smile through his dark jowls. "Of course you do, because you are a pretty
good writer and you take pride in it. Just like I did. And I'll tell you
something else. I'm a good, hard worker and I can get things done, but
I don't take much pride in that. You understand?"

Cherrington was warming to his monologue. He leaned back in his
chair and tipped his chin up. "Of course, you understand because you're
a writer. If you're a writer, nothing matters but writing. So now I'll tell
you something else you'll understand. I didn't like you when you joined
the league. You noticed that, I'm sure. I didn't like you because I was a
pretty good writer and I recognized that you were probably better. You
had written for the moving pictures, and I'd read a few things you wrote
in Seattle." Cherrington stopped suddenly and looked hard at M. K.
"You understand what I'm telling you?"

"I'm not sure I do."

Cherrington sighed, smiled, and wagged his head a little, as though amused at something. "We need some creativity," Cherrington said. "We need some new approaches. That's why I asked the directors to have you come here. You are the best writer we have, I think. I can give you assignments for the *American Issue,* but those may be too restrictive. I'd like to know what you like to do. Think it over if you want."

"I don't need to think," M. K. said. "I like to tell stories. I like to write about people and the stuff that happens. I might like to write about Wayne Wheeler, who was a great man."

Cherrington made a face. "I don't know about that. But you can convince me if you're as good as I think you are. Keep in mind what I've said, and we'll talk about it. And you can write about whatever you want."

"Even Wayne Wheeler?"

"Sure. Come on, I want you to see the operation. It's changed since the last time I toured you around here."

The publishing operation had slowed down. Large sections of the plant were quiet, stacked with boxes of outdated publications. M. K. was alarmed to see the difference. He had not realized the full impact of the shortage of funds.

He could not get over feeling distant from the ASL—a natural feeling, he supposed, born of his disappointments—but his detachment made it difficult for him to work. He could see their situation with chilly accuracy, and knew this was the wrong place for someone wanting to convert new Americans to the dry cause. Cherrington might be right about education, but he was in the wrong location. In Westerville the raw, urgent dreams of immigrants seemed incomprehensible. And no doubt Westerville was incomprehensible for those new Americans.

M. K. let this concern cross his mind and then discarded it, however. Somebody else would have to worry about that, somebody named Cherrington. M. K. felt that he was taking deep breaths, clearing out the old air and trying to begin again.

If he looked at the ASL coldly, he did not see the town of Westerville that way. It was a quiet, conservative town, and the college lent a sense of eternity, for there were always freshmen, year after year experiencing the newness of the world outside their families. As he walked around the streets, M. K. thought that he could start over here.

He had decided, after Wheeler died, to revive his faith. Westerville gave him a hopeful feeling that he could, for its peace seemed to flow from some deep subterranean source, some spiritual reservoir. He now attended church regularly, twice on Sundays and every Wednesday night, and he thought it did him some good. It was a hearty, serious Methodist church with an active Christian Endeavor for David. The pastor came to call—so glad to have another leader from the ASL in the congregation—and M. K. joined. He even began to tithe his income, which affected him sorely.

More than going to services, what could a widower like him do in a small town? He got occasional dinner invitations after church on Sunday, but he had no other social possibilities. Courting widows did not interest him. He worked long and hard, as he always had. In a way he was glad to be alone.

His life could not be the same, however, with David in his care. In Washington, M. K. had gone from his apartment to work and back again like a man who carries his lantern with him in a dark house. Whenever he left a place, his office or his apartment, it went dark and lifeless until he returned. Now, life carried on in the house when he was gone, and that made his doings far more complicated.

David was in and out of the snow and the rain, left his things everywhere, and had constant piles of dirty clothes that grew in the corner of his room. Also David complained about the food. He did not like canned stew, which struck M. K. as absurd until he talked to the grocer and had it confirmed that, yes, some of the young people did not like the cans. M. K. tried to cook other meals, such as Kraft macaroni and cheese, and pork chops with fried potatoes, and bacon and eggs, but then the dishes and the dirty pans faced him. David was supposed to clean up, but he was always going somewhere. *He* had no trouble making friends in a new place.

When Mr. Echols, the Sunday school superintendent who also ran the pharmacy, said that he wished to share a concern about David, M. K. found it hard to believe. Echols had come around to his office to talk.

"What on earth is the matter?" M. K. asked.

"When a boy has no mother, he may not understand that a gentleman must be gentle with the girls. David has been rude with one of his classmates in Sunday school, and when the teacher reproved him, he sassed her."

"David? Are you sure?"

Mr. Echols raised his eyebrows. He was a large, fleshy man with reddish blond hair that looked as though too much bleach had been applied to its coloring. "Of course I am sure. I have talked to David, but I felt that I had better come to you. When a boy has no mother, he is sometimes treated more gently than he ought to be, out of pity."

M. K. did not appreciate the harping on David's motherlessness, but he spoke to David about Mr. Echols's visit nonetheless. David had his jaw clenched before Mr. Echols's name had finished coming out of M. K.'s mouth. "It's that girl's fault," he said. "Not me. She thinks she's queen of the world."

"What girl?"

"Marie Clare, her name is. She's a little cripple and thinks we should all bow down to her. None of us can stand her. Even the girls hate her."

It seemed to be petty stuff. As far as M. K. could understand, a younger girl in David's Sunday school demanded that everyone move out of her way because she walked with braces.

"Why don't you just ignore her?" M. K. asked. "Or do what she wants? It can't hurt you."

"Why should I do that? She doesn't own the world."

"What's wrong with her anyway?"

"How should I know? She has big, ugly braces on her legs. Mike says she's paralyzed."

"But she can walk."

"Sure. She clanks around just fine."

It was hard to understand why this squabble deserved the attention of the Sunday school superintendent. M. K. also could not understand why David would not back off.

That Sunday he saw for himself when he went to meet David at the conclusion of the Sunday school hour. The hallway was crowded with children, and one small, dark-headed girl on crutches swung her way quickly through the swarm. She had her mouth set tight, her chin down, and she nearly ran over a towheaded little boy a head shorter than she.

M. K. reached out and grabbed her arm. "Slow down," he said. "You'll hurt somebody."

"Get your mitts off me," she said and wrenched free. Before he could say anything more she had swung ahead, down the hallway.

David had a cockeyed grin on his face. He had seen the spat. "Congratulations, Dad. I guess Mr. Echols will be coming to tell me about your bad habits."

M. K. did not get the joke until David explained. "You just met Marie Clare."

"She's certainly a handful. Doesn't anybody control her?"

"I try," said a woman at his elbow. She was small-boned, dark-haired with thick eyebrows sheltering her chocolate eyes and a thin, white face. "I'm Marie's mother," she said. "Eva McCallum." She stuck out a bony hand to shake. When M. K. looked at her, he saw the resemblance to Marie. She was short and frail, but she looked at him directly.

"I'm glad to meet you," M. K. said and introduced himself and David. He reached out to hold David's arm to keep him from escaping. "I don't know whether you've heard, but my son, David, had some problems with your daughter."

"She's a handful," Eva said.

"What makes her think that she can run over people?" David asked. "Why does she think that she gets special rights?"

"Probably because she has special problems," Eva said. "I'm not excusing her, but three years ago she could walk as well as you and I can."

Eva wore a heavy red dress, neat but faded and worn at the sleeve endings. Her dead-serious expression seemed forlorn, almost wistful, but she talked with a matter-of-fact forcefulness.

"What happened to her?" David asked.

"She got polio. It's a disease."

"Will she get over it?"

"I guess not. She's got to make do with what she has."

"Why does she have to take it out on the rest of us?" David asked. He was usually easygoing, but Marie seemed to have touched something. "She's so mean."

Eva showed no sign of resenting David's question. "I know," she said. Her eyes remained serious and businesslike. "She didn't used to be that way. Right now she's a handful. She can't stand what's happened to her."

Eva turned and was gone before either of them could say any more. M. K. watched her walk away, head down, her small shoulders turned inward.

Howard Echols, the Sunday school superintendent, came up, and M. K. told him that he had talked to Marie's mother. "Plus I got a sample of that Marie. From what I saw, she's more the problem than David is."

Echols was wearing a red bow tie, a neat pinstripe suit, and a red silk handkerchief. He waggled his pale head back and forth to show his ambivalence. "But David is older, and he's not crippled. They're not equals."

"I don't want to be equal with her," David said.

"You have to remember how she's suffering," Echols said. "And they are quite poor."

"What does the father do?" M. K. asked.

"There isn't any father. They say he was killed in a factory accident."

"Recently?"

"Oh, no. The mother has lived in Westerville for six or seven years. She takes in laundry, cleans houses, that sort of thing. Marie is really very bright, I'm told. So try to be gentle with her, David, as you know Jesus would."

During the service, M. K. located the mother and daughter, seated across the aisle from them. He liked to see that Eva rested a hand on her daughter's neck, and Marie did not shrug it off. They were interesting to look at, like two blackbirds with bright eyes and shiny feathers.

After the service M. K. worked his way over to them as they filed out in the center aisle. "Mr. Echols told me that you do housework," he said to Eva. "I wonder whether you would come and work for me."

"Possibly," she said, her eyes looking straight up into his.

"Do you cook?" he asked. "David and I need meals. I'm a little bit helpless in the kitchen. And cleaning, laundry, those kinds of things."

"Sure," she said. "I cook. But I'd have to bring Marie along. I can't leave her alone after school."

M. K. almost asked her why not, but then he thought better of it. "All right," he said. "At least we could give it a try."

Chapter 20
1928: The Anti-Smith Democrats

Still a quarter mile from the fairgrounds in Jackson, Tennessee, M. K. could see that they would have a good crowd. On their right, a row of Negro houses hugged the ground, colorless shacks set on piles, with sagging porches seating whole families, children to grandparents, watching their car pass. On their left a big pasture had quit greening but hung in October gray, not quite prepared to die but shabby and faded. Even this far away from the meeting place cars had pulled into the field: Fords mostly, a Dodge truck, and a Nash. White people in white shirts and ties (the men) plus a few neat women in ankle-length dresses picked their way carefully out of the field, watching their step while also trying to twist their scrubbed necks to see the big car and who might be in it.

They crossed the railroad grade into a neighborhood of white people's houses, four-room cottages and dogtrot cabins. Cars were parked all along the edge of the road here, two wheels on the sparse grass that revealed red earth between its stalks, the other two wheels on the edge of the sandy dirt road. Pedestrians walked down the middle of the road, reluctantly spreading apart to let the car go through. Most of the men had left their coats behind because of the heat, and they carried straw hats or the occasional bowler in their hands, fanning themselves.

The bandstand stood on top of a slight rise. Masses of white shirts and colorful dresses filled the park. Gray military blankets and faded quilts were spread on the grass. Somebody recognized them and waved them ahead to the right, up a grassy track, until they reached the end of a line of parked cars and could go no farther.

M. K. sat in the front with the driver, a young Baptist preacher who sweated profusely under his heavy black coat and wide-brimmed black hat. His eyes were grinning. "Looks like Mr. Smith better watch out," he said. "Half the county has come out."

Bishop Cannon, chief dignitary of the occasion, sat in the back with another senior Methodist pastor. "Everywhere it's the same," Cannon said. "They don't like Smith. Let's get out."

"The solid South is solid no more," Cannon's backseat companion said.

"On the contrary," Cannon said acerbically. "The South is proving itself more emphatically solid than ever. We are solidly against whatever would deviate from the security and piety of our way of life. When certain leaders prove themselves willing to betray the traditions of the party, the solid South will remind them that our party depends on principle."

They made their way through the throng toward the bandstand. Many people recognized the two pastors and called out greetings. Halfway up, a half dozen black-suited men met them, and they all shook hands, serious as deacons at a funeral, and yet with some underlying gaiety, an enthusiastic energy. From the platform a string band played, and before the stage, people were crowded in to hear them. M. K. and Cannon and their entourage filed up the stage stairs, and each shook hands with the musicians, who never stopped the song but lifted a hand for a quick shake, then continued. The dignitaries took seats in a line of folding wooden chairs set up across the back of the stage. A few minutes later the band quit, and the proceedings began.

M. K. estimated better than a thousand people had come out. He had limited experience in politics but recognized this as a strong turnout even for a Saturday afternoon three weeks from the election. It did not necessarily mean, of course, that all these people would vote with them, but it probably meant they at least were thinking of it. To separate a southern white man from his Democratic candidate took a hard, cold chisel.

They heard several speakers before Cannon. The quality was poor because most of the officeholders in Jackson had stayed away. Cannon said he had yet to meet a Democratic leader in the South genuinely enthusiastic about Al Smith, but they were afraid of what party disloyalty might mean to them. Personally they had nothing to gain from opposing Al Smith, and everything to lose, politically speaking.

The first man to speak was a county judge who ran unopposed and had his nose buried into his speech so deeply that people in the back kept shouting at him to speak up. Then came the sheriff, a rotund man who was obviously hugely popular, for the audience began hooting at him before he even reached the podium. He was a poor speaker, however, and before he had talked for five minutes, somebody yelled out, "Sit down, Shell, and let the bishop talk." The crowd laughed, and even Shell smiled and stuck his tongue out of the corner of his mouth.

The effect was to make Cannon seem like a better speaker than he really was. Cannon wore black and stood straight and tall, lean as a rake, with the poker-playing face of a schoolmaster who would just as soon fail you as look at you. M. K. had heard him give the same speech twenty times now. Cannon was incisive, intelligent, and argumentative, but try as he might, he had no hint of how to grab a man's lapels and pull him into the emotionality of the cause. He appealed to reason, which was only half a man—and not the dominant half in elections.

Even so the people listened closely, and they would surely remember what they had heard and ponder it. After his preliminary greetings and thanks, Cannon went right into his reason for coming.

"I have been accused," he said, "of intolerance. To be specific, I have been accused of intolerance toward Governor Al Smith because he is a Roman Catholic. I would suppose that the same complaint might be made of many of you, who have come here today with honest questions regarding the Democratic candidate for president."

He looked the crowd over with his proud, cold stare. "I utterly repudiate such a charge. I resent it to the core of my being. If Senator Walsh from Montana were running for president, I would support him even though he is a Roman Catholic. Why? Because he supports the Constitution. He has no corruption from Tammany Hall trailing behind him like the slime from a slug. The charge of religious prejudice is nonsensical. I do not need religious reasons for opposing Governor Smith, and I am utterly unwilling that I or our southern people shall be branded as bigoted and intolerant fanatics in order to whip us into line to vote for Smith."

He stopped to ponder his angry eloquence and seemed slightly startled when the crowd let off a ragged cheer.

"I will say more," he went on. "I resent that the charge of bigotry should come from those whose own faith has demonstrated more than its share of bigotry over the centuries and does so today." Cannon then listed a number of Catholic teachings that he said were intolerant and undemocratic. "The Roman Catholic hierarchy is opposed to freedom of speech, freedom of the press, freedom of conscience, freedom of education, a free church in a free state, and the salvation of anyone outside its own church. The leaders condemn Freemasonry, oppose Bible societies, fight the YMCA, and oppose the separation of church and state. They do not recognize marriage performed by a Methodist or any other Protestant minister. They do not send their children to the public schools to learn alongside others of different faiths. And they call me intolerant!"

That brought a larger, more confident cheer. The crowd might not have followed all that Cannon said, but they seemed to feel that it was on the right side.

"What need do I have for religious intolerance if I want to oppose Al Smith? Is it not enough that he is thoroughly wet? That he drinks, according to a reliable and sympathetic authority from the *Nation* magazine, as many as eight cocktails a day? Is it not enough that he is the leader of corrupt Tammany Hall? Ladies and gentlemen, I have had many occasions over the past years to visit New York, where Governor Smith's most favorable constituency lies. I have studied the people of New York. I have seen that in Harlem dance halls, a white woman may dance in the arms of a black man. I have seen thousands of illiterate immigrants just off the boat from the belly of Europe, Russian Jews, Sicilians, Yugoslavs, Romanians, people so unlike the strong, hardworking folk who have built this country. In the New York classrooms all this refuse of Europe mingles with Negroes and Cubans, along with the native white children whose God-fearing parents are the salt of this land.

"Illegal liquor flows freely in New York. Drunkenness is unhindered by Governor Smith and his policemen. The people on the sidewalks of New York are not like you in this gathering today, but these are the people whom Al Smith champions. Is this our future? I hope not and I pray not. I hope for a better America. My forefathers hoped and worked and died for an America better than the corrupt, drunken, repressive Europe that they came from."

Bishop Cannon allowed that many, himself included, had never in their lives voted for a Republican. It would be difficult to do, especially feeling that you were deserting the party that you had trusted all your life.

But, Cannon said, he did not advocate deserting the party. He wanted them to vote for all the Democratic candidates save one. He hoped that Tennessee would be represented by 100 percent Democratic representatives, senators, state and county officials. But he would tell them frankly that to vote for Al Smith would be to betray the party they had trusted. They had not supported a wet Tammany party all their lives, but a party that was decent and hardworking, that believed in order and harmony, that protected the southern way of life. Evidently some leaders within the party did not value those same principles. They must remind those leaders what the party stood for: decency, not licentiousness and corruption. It stood for sobriety and the enforcement of the law, not drunkenness and the liquor trade.

M. K. thought that the same speech in another speaker's mouth might have excited the crowd into genuine, roaring enthusiasm. Instead, when Cannon sat down, they applauded and then, after the closing prayer, slowly dispersed. Cannon's speeches always sounded more uproarious when they were quoted in the press the next day.

They stayed that night at the Perimeter Hotel, a plain brick building downtown, populated mainly by drummers. Bishop Cannon came down to the dining room but hardly ate a bite. The strain of the day showed on his face, though he was not giving in, not in the least, to exhaustion.

He seemed to be surviving on willpower alone, sitting up straight as a stick with his face deathly. His wife, Lura, was terribly ill and staying at Murphy's Hotel in Richmond because the bishop had no home of his own anymore, he traveled so. Though he rarely mentioned Mrs. Cannon, M. K. assumed he must feel the pull of her spirit.

M. K. and Cannon had been on the road together for weeks, with Cannon speaking every night and often two or three times during the day as well. M. K. was officially his press secretary, but also functioned as his man of all work. The pace was relentless, and Cannon's spirit was as dry as a rye cracker, but M. K. enjoyed it nonetheless. He had never been in the South before. He was surprised by the country's wide, soft beauty and its well-mannered, friendly people.

Besides, the tour was exciting. For the past several years the dry cause had seemed to languish, and now suddenly, thanks to Al Smith, they had the drive to agitate and call vast crowds together. M. K. had never witnessed such enthusiasm, not even in Seattle in the early days. Money poured in.

Cannon said little about Hoover in the public meetings—it would have been unseemly to actually support him, as distinct from opposing Smith—but in private he spoke well of the man, saying that he was an intelligent and disciplined individual who would take a sensible, serious approach to law enforcement. And so they felt the hope that if Hoover could win, if Smith and his wet constituents could be defeated, then Prohibition would gain a new life.

The dining room at the Perimeter was not an elegant place—the wainscoting was scarred and beaten into multiple shades of brown, the chairs were mismatched—but it nonetheless offered a gloomy intimacy. On a Saturday night the drummers who could be home were, and the remaining few ate quietly and went out. Cannon had been told the Perimeter was a local rarity, a hotel that was genuinely dry.

The timber man arrived on schedule, just as they finished eating. He was a hulking, awkward-looking lunk in a cheap brown suit, a Republican who had moved into the South from Illinois and wanted to further the party of Lincoln. One of Cannon's North Carolina friends had sent him; he shook hands all around, and then Cannon took him off to the lobby to sit together over coffee. Cannon had found a corner where the bar had once been, invisible to passersby. He was happy to get Republican money but would be glad not to be seen too publicly.

That left the Baptist preacher for M. K. to talk to. He said he had no family except the church. "I'm praying for a wife, but the Lord hasn't given me that yet," he said with no trace of humor in his eyes. He had large, dark eyes with long eyelashes, which dominated a face that seemed naturally sad. His gestures were nervous—he constantly drummed his fingers on the table, just as he had done on the steering wheel when he drove—but he had settled into conversation with M. K. as though planning to spend the night. He wanted to know what it was like for M. K. to be on the road and how he had been chosen to do it.

"It's not so much that you *get* to do it," M. K. said. "Nobody likes the travel, I don't think."

"Well, I would," said the preacher, whose name was Harlow Jones. "I love to go places. Today when I got behind the wheel of Reverend Staples's Plymouth, I thought, *Why not drive forever?* My goodness, we could go to Michigan or Montana in a car like that."

"That's because you don't have any family," M. K. said. In the ASL he rarely met someone as young as Jones.

His remark got Jones thinking about the wife he was praying for, and his face grew sad again. He was cheerful so long as he thought about cars. "You have a wife at home?" he asked gloomily.

"No," M. K. said. "My wife is dead. But I have a child. Two children actually, though one is grown and married. My son is in high school."

"So where is he now?"

"He's in Westerville, where I live."

"Did you just leave him?"

"Oh, no. I've got a house sitter to come in."

He had been forced to make arrangements at the last minute. Eva McCallum, who had been cleaning and cooking for him, had agreed to live at his house, bringing Marie with her. And that was M. K.'s concern: he wondered whether David and Marie could get along together. He also wondered whether Eva, who was so slight, could handle David if he got into one of his moods. David was usually a very agreeable character, but when he thought he was right, he could be very headstrong.

Somehow, though, Eva had given him confidence she could manage. She had a way of looking right at you when you talked.

Jones said, "If I had a kid, I wouldn't leave him with a house sitter. A kid needs his own flesh and blood. My daddy married a woman after my mother died, and that was a worse tragedy than losing Mama."

"Why so?"

"She didn't treat us fair. She favored her own kids. She made no bones about it, except when she talked to my daddy. I resented it. I resented it strongly. Still do."

"I don't think this lady would do that," M. K. said. Eva struck him as a generous person, who rarely thought of herself. He had a hard time getting her to take money for the food she bought. From where had Marie collected her greedy, pushy personality? M. K. did not know about the father. He had not died in a factory accident—Eva had settled that rumor when he brought it up. But she was mum about where he had gone. Evidently he had deserted, but M. K. knew nothing about that. Eva was not one to tell her own troubles.

Thinking about his stepmother had plunged Jones deep into depression. He put his nervous hands together and leaned forward over the table, as though in prayer. "What's the bishop doing with that big fellow?" he asked.

"I think he's asking for money," M. K. said.

Jones lifted his eyebrows. "Doesn't he get a pretty good salary for being a bishop? I thought the Methodists took good care of their people like that."

"It's not for himself. It's for putting on this campaign against Smith."

"Oh. I thought the Anti-Saloon League paid for it."

"The league doesn't have any money except what people give it. We've been terribly short on money ever since Prohibition passed. People thought that the battle was over, I guess. Just in the last year we've started getting people to give again in large amounts. There's a millionaire up in Detroit, Sebastian Kresge, who's promised to give us money to fund an education department."

"Is that the Kresge stores man?"

"That's him. He's a good Christian man, I'm told, and we hope his generosity will get some of those other millionaires to give likewise. In a way, Al Smith is a good thing for us. He's alarmed people. They realize that Prohibition could be lost."

Jones had started tapping his fingers on the table again. "Well, I've got to go."

"Got a sermon to prepare for tomorrow morning?"

He tipped his head sideways. "I've already got a text. I always have something to say if I've got a text to preach from. No, but I need some sleep. Preaching takes a lot out of you, you know."

He pushed his chair back and stuck out his hand. They were the last ones in the dingy, discouraged dining room. "I don't think we'll lose Prohibition," he said, "if people come out like they did today."

"That's what I think too. This election is going to show what the people really think about Prohibition. We've never had a clear-cut choice for the whole nation. Al Smith against Herbert Hoover. I think that's a strong enough contrast to knock the wheels off party politics."

In the hotel room, Cannon was already preparing for bed. The tall, straight cranelike man wore red silk pajamas, as he brushed his teeth. "How did it go?" M. K. asked. In answer Cannon pointed to his bed where a stack of money an inch thick lay, tied tightly with loops of string.

Few things are more cheering than stacks of money, and it buoyed their spirits until the very week of the election. And so did the crowds of voters, who only increased as the election day came on.

Yet on some of their train trips the bishop simply stared, not even looking out the window. M. K. judged that he must require a supreme effort simply to keep his head level, he was so exhausted. When he felt well enough to do anything, he had his notebook out, preparing addresses or writing detailed screeds for the newspapers.

As a companion, he was miserable—no small talk, no humor. Duty ruled him. Watching him and living with him, M. K. developed a crooked kind of admiration. A surface so hard and so polished could not help but repel most people. The man was sour. How could he leave his wife in a hotel, deathly sick? Yet Cannon made M. K. ashamed of his own weakness, his inconstancy. He felt like a jellyfish next to the bishop.

They parted in Richmond on the Saturday before the election. M. K. stopped over Sunday in Baltimore in order to see Linda. The visit proved upsetting. Her husband, Guy, still wearing his beret, declared that he would vote for Smith and that Prohibition had to be modified. M. K. thought how odd it was that after resisting any authority from her father, Linda had married such an opinionated, peremptory individual. Linda herself picked no fight about Prohibition but criticized M. K. for leaving David with a woman he barely knew.

"You deserted him, do you realize?" she said. "First you took him away from the only home he has ever known, and then you left him with a woman who is probably on the mental level of an idiot."

"Why do you say that? You don't know anything about her." The complaint grieved him partly because he feared it might contain a grain of truth. Eva sometimes did act and look as if she might be simple.

"You said it yourself! You said that she was uneducated."

"That's not the same as saying she's a half-wit."

"Has she written you since you've been gone? Does she even know how to write?"

"How could she write? I never knew where I would be from one week to the next. You didn't write, either, but nobody calls you an idiot." He wondered why Linda attacked him on this score. What motivated her to this sudden concern for her brother?

"Well, doesn't she have an idiot child?"

"No. Not at all. Her daughter has polio. She's actually very bright, I'm told."

Linda shook her head. "I can't bear what you're doing to David."

"Do you want to raise him? We could try that, you know."

"No," her husband said. "We couldn't."

The conversation made M. K. all the more anxious to get home, to end the silence and uncertainty he had felt ever since leaving five weeks before. He reached Westerville on Monday night, glad to feel the chilly, misty air of autumn. Nearly all the leaves had dropped while he was gone. A few dead bonfires left traces of black ash in the street, but he smelled none of their bitter smoke, only the dank mold of sagging vegetation, the fall death.

A lamp had been lit and hung outside his front door—a single clear, yellow flame that set each blade of grass, each dry, jagged leaf, into silhouette. M. K. would have run up the walk if he had not carried his suitcase. He was burning to see David.

He found all three together in the kitchen. At the sink Eva had her hands in soapy water. Strings of wet, dark hair had crawled toward her eyes. David and Marie sat across from each other at the table.

"You're all here!" M. K. said.

"Sure," Marie Clare said. "Where else could we go? I wanted to go dancing, but David said no gimps were allowed."

"I never did," David said.

"Marie," Eva said. "Why do you say such things?"

"I like it when David squeals." She did not smile, so it was difficult to say what she really meant. She had a pugnacious set to her jaw.

Eva wiped her hands on her apron, brushed her hair from her eyes, and smiled. "She doesn't mean it," she said. "They've gotten along."

"Have not," Marie protested.

They chatted for a few minutes about his trip, and then Eva said they would go home. "Marie, get your things."

"You don't have to do that. It's dark," M. K. said.

"No, we're all packed up and ready to go. We thought you might come tonight."

"That's why the lantern?" M. K. said. He had not written of his arrival, so the lamp over the front steps had surprised him.

He made David help carry their things, which were wrapped in a large cloth bundle and tied with rope. M. K. supposed they owned no suitcase. Why would they? Eva and Marie lived just six blocks away in what they called a cottage but looked more like a shack, built behind the Presbyterian manse. They all walked together, Marie skipping ahead on her crutches faster than any of them, and David lagging behind with the bale of clothing.

"So the children really got along?" M. K. asked Eva as they walked.

"You know, at that age they have a lot of energy," she said. "The way puppies will nip at each other? I don't count that too seriously."

She paused to think before going on. "David is a good boy. He's so blessed with strength he doesn't realize other people's weaknesses. Marie, that's all she thinks about. Her weaknesses, that is. I would say, given that, they got along. They kept each other busy."

"Really? I thought they would avoid each other."

"Oh, no. They were together, doing homework. Marie listened to the radio. I must say she really loved that."

He had bought a radio with the thought that it would entertain David while he was at work. It turned out that David was not much interested—he was too active to sit still for a radio program.

"And what did David do when she listened?"

Eva chuckled. "He would tell her to turn it off."

"And what did she do?"

"She would make it louder."

Marie heard what they said and turned on her crutches. "I wish we had a radio," she said. "How could you ever be bored? Mother, can we get a radio?"

"After we get a car," Eva said. "And a house in Florida."

Marie made a defiant noise and went on ahead.

"You could come over tomorrow," M. K. said. "I plan to listen to the election results."

"Thank you," she said. "That's very kind."

"David. Was it awful?" he asked when they had left Eva and Marie and were walking back.

"Awful? No, Dad. I like her. She's a great cook."

"What about Marie? Mrs. McCallum said you got along."

"We didn't at first. But Mrs. McCallum talked to me. She explained that you can't get Marie to do anything if you yell at her. But if you act nice, she isn't such a bad girl."

"Your sister sends her love. I was there yesterday. She thought I did a terrible thing deserting you."

David said nothing, which made M. K. suddenly shy, wondering whether David did indeed feel that he had been deserted. When this fear seized him, his pride in his work disappeared like water thrown on the ground.

Then David spoke. "I didn't like it at first, Dad. But I like Mrs. McCallum. She taught me a lot."

David seemed very moody the next evening. He would not even eat the canned stew that M. K. heated up, choosing instead to wolf down half a loaf of bread with butter spread thick on each slice and a sprinkling of white sugar. For M. K., it seemed wonderful to eat in his own kitchen after so many meals in hotels, plus he was tired from his day at the ASL office, telling so many people about the anti-Smith Democrats. He did not appreciate a grumpy son and told him so.

The atmosphere improved when the McCallums arrived. Eva had baked an apple pie, which they cut apart and ate in the living room while listening to the election news. Marie immediately pounced on a spot on the floor directly in front of the radio, controlling the dials and periodically fiddling with them for better reception. David squawked at her and told her to leave the radio alone. Her response was to huddle closer and turn her back against them, fiddling all the more.

"Why do you do that?" David shouted. "Leave the thing be!" She gave him no response, and he got out of his chair and started toward her.

"David!" M. K. said.

"Why does she have to act like that?"

Eva had also risen, and she went to Marie and stooped over her, putting one small bare arm around Marie's shoulder. She said something inaudible to Marie, and then managed to steer her to her feet, across the small room, and into the chair Eva had sat on. The two of them cuddled up in the chair, and Marie buried her face in her mother.

David went over to the radio and adjusted the sound until they could hear the Columbus station clearly. They dug their pie out of the bowls with spoons, listening to the early results from East Coast states. Eva had gotten out some socks she was darning, and she hummed tunelessly. Later on David got up and brought a jigsaw puzzle out of his room. He spread it on the floor and they all worked on it, even Marie.

The news continued, not only presidential results but state and county and city as well. "It's like watching the results at the county courthouse," M. K. remarked, "except that they come from everywhere." The amount of information, coming all at once, was stunning. And to think that it came here into his living room.

There were surprises and disappointments at different points, a state here or a state there, but slowly the overall portrait became obvious. Herbert Hoover had won a stunning victory. Al Smith was completely repudiated. The solid South had broken; five southern states, including Virginia and Tennessee, had gone to the Republicans. Drys would command the largest majority ever in both House and Senate.

The results made M. K. feel giddy. Ordinarily he liked to have David in bed by 10:00 P.M. for a school day, but he said nothing as the hour grew later. This was a historic night, and the atmosphere was so snug, so comfortable that he let David bring out another puzzle at 10:15. Finally past eleven Eva announced that they had better go. Only as he helped her on with her coat did he realize how little she had shared in his emotions.

"Did it go well?" she asked.

"Did what go well?"

"The election. I'm sorry, but I don't know anything about politics."

M. K. was momentarily stunned as he felt the whole evening slide into a different shape from what he had perceived it to have. "It went very well," he said. "It could hardly go better."

"Somebody told me, the grocer I think, it was almost a referendum on Prohibition."

"Yes. Yes, it was, and the people want Prohibition, Eva. Hoover has won the most smashing victory in history, and nobody in either party will have any doubt at all about law enforcement. Smith wanted to change the law, you see."

"Oh, I heard that."

"But Smith got demolished. Hoover wants to enforce the law. That's what we're going to do. We're going to keep on. Eva, America will never go back to the way it used to be."

He felt his chest fill up with exaltation as he said this, but then he realized again that Eva might not understand. "Did you not even vote?" he asked.

"Oh, sure, I voted, but I always go straight Republican."

"Why do you do that?"

"I told you, I don't understand politics, M. K. My mother was a Republican, and I know it is the party that set the slaves free. So . . ." Smiling, she held her hands out, as though to show him that they were empty.

Chapter 21
1929: The Crash

The first months of the new year were very happy. Hoover's victory gave them energy for the battle, and Ernest Cherrington's educational plans provided direction. The education department was finally launched—the election had delayed its implementation—and with Kresge's half-million-dollar pledge, they finally had enough money to combat the efforts of the AAPA. They looked for capable young men to compile the results of scientific research on the effects of alcohol, work with government agencies and even foreign scientific establishments to gain the best information available, and then pass it on to the press. They were developing curricula for the public schools and for Sunday schools. They were providing background information to reporters. Finally the government was allocating funds—modest, still—to communicate the civic necessity for sobriety.

Cherrington became almost chummy in the midst of all this new activity. Sometimes when M. K. looked at his heavy face, he felt a twinge of resentment, remembering Wayne Wheeler. But it is hard to hold a grudge against a happy man, and Cherrington was happy in exactly the same way that M. K. was happy: the work grounded him in hope. Both men had comparable capacities for hard work, and both tended to rebound toward optimism. Cherrington's beefy, thuggish face was a misprint; he often looked miserable but was more truly upbeat.

Cherrington believed that the progress of history was certainly on their side. "Think of the impact of the automobile alone," he liked to say. "A drunken man can plow a field with a horse. He can walk from the saloon to his home. But behind the wheel of a car he is a menace! And soon everybody will drive a car. Everybody! Even poor people! My goodness, I foresee the day when women will have their own cars to go to buy groceries! Now you tell me how that fits with the saloon. How can we afford to let drunkards drive automobiles? It's ridiculous!"

He would go off on other subjects. Buying on credit, for example, which the modern economy depended on. The system demanded a sober income earner who could be depended on to provide. Or assembly line manufacturing, in which literally hundreds of men might have their work impeded by one careless or inebriated worker who caused an accident and stopped the line. "The wets love to talk about personal freedom, but there is no personal freedom in the modern world. Every person depends on a chain of others. Every individual can endanger countless others. In the olden days a farmer could get drunk and claim it was nobody's business but his own, but that's sheer nonsense today."

They had only to lay out the facts, and resistance must gradually die. It all made too much sense. Meanwhile the government was doing its part to stiffen enforcement. Washington's Senator Wesley Jones put forward a law that increased the penalties for liquor violations. Instead of a slap on the hand, violators would get a maximum of five years in prison or a fine of ten thousand dollars. Naturally the wets reacted violently to the Jones "Five and Ten law," calling it cruel. But President Hoover declared that he intended to enforce the law, even if they had to double the number of federal prisons to keep in all the bootleggers and gangsters.

They were glad to hear such firm talk—imagine if Al Smith were in the White House!—but they were sure that the long-range effect would be exactly opposite. They would need fewer prisons because the more the law was enforced, the more it would be observed, and the more observed, the more obvious its benefits would become. You might never reform the drinkers, but the children of drinkers, growing up in a new, modern world, would see life differently.

M. K. was so busy with the work that he rarely got home in time for supper. As a result, Eva McCallum and her daughter, Marie, became more and more a part of their home, almost, as M. K. sometimes kidded, honorary Nicholses. Eva came every afternoon to cook supper and meet David when he came home from school; she also did laundry and housecleaning for them. Often when M. K. got back from the office, he found David sitting at the kitchen table ostensibly doing homework but, it appeared, making more conversation. He obviously liked the woman.

David's relationship with Eva surprised M. K. because she struck him as exquisitely ordinary, someone whom he would have expected a young man to find completely lacking in relevance. She was by no means a woman of the world. She wore clothes that his own mother would have found familiar, including, sometimes, a genuine old-fashioned black bonnet with satin tape. At first M. K. thought this lack of fashion came from poverty—that Eva dressed as she did because she had no money for better clothes. Eventually, though, he came to the conclusion that she might dress just the same regardless.

Eva had grown up on a farm, and while many farm kids are drawn to the city life as though by a magnet, she seemed only slightly aware that the world was a bigger place. She had not attended much school, a fact that showed itself when she left him a written note or when she asked questions about politics. What she knew, she knew well. She handled home chores with efficiency and authority. But when there was talk of any subject beyond the boundaries of Westerville, she acted as if she were listening in on a conversation about life in Tibet. Her face grew passive and distracted.

M. K. would never have thought much about Eva left to himself, but David's obvious attraction nettled him a little. M. K. had lived his life on the borderline between farm and city, piety and sophistication, and he realized that it was a matter of need for him to be on the far side of the river from his Hillsboro upbringing. When it came to David, he took pride in the boy's intelligence and curiosity and all that they might open for him. He wanted David to be good, but he also wanted him to streak through the world like a flaming star. Anything hinting that David might settle for less, might happily exist like M. K.'s own father, locked into the narrowness and lifelessness of teaching school to dullards, or anything like that, troubled M. K.'s peace.

He could not make out what David liked in her. Eva was not much of a talker. Most of the time she was willing to sit peaceably while he ate, listening to him if he felt like talking, but saying little. When she was alone, she would sing to herself in a breathy soprano—M. K. would hear her repeat fragments of a song while she ironed or washed. Occasionally she would talk to him about David, always with a point—something she had observed that she thought he should know. Regarding children, she suffered no lack of confidence. She repeatedly returned to the same theme, that David was very strong and prone to run over people. She wanted him to become gentle.

It was unusual, though, for her to speak of something outside her own personal orbit. She did that on February 15, the day after Al Capone shot seven gangsters from Bugs Moran's gang. The newspapers and the radio news were screaming the St. Valentine's Day Massacre, but it had not made much impact on M. K. He passed it through his mind, considering an article—he could write it, or he could suggest the idea to others—that might be called "The Legacy of Personal

Freedom." He didn't go anywhere with it, though. It seemed too garish, too inflammatory.

"M. K., what does it mean?" Eva asked. She looked genuinely troubled. "Seven men. And somebody said most of them were young men. It makes you wonder whether it's worth it."

"Whether what is worth it?" He was eating mashed potatoes and gravy with a pork chop that had been reheated and was now tough as a board. She had saved his supper for him because he came home late, and now she sat with him while he ate.

"All these laws. Mrs. Ramis says they have killed hundreds in Chicago. This is just the first time they've killed seven at once. She says it is like a war."

M. K. glanced at Eva's face. Did she actually care about these gangsters? She had her hands clenched together on the table, and her slender face was luminous, tender. She had her lips pressed tight.

"It is war," M. K. said. "It's war between criminals. Let them kill each other off if they want to oblige us that way."

Eva looked startled, as though he had suggested something dreadful. "Mrs. Ramis says there have been *hundreds*. I never heard of such a thing. Don't you think there is something wrong?"

"Of course. What's wrong is that criminals know no restraint. They have no fear of the Lord. They don't care what the law is. They are more than bootleggers. They're murderers. This is just a proof of how bad they are. I don't waste a lot of pity on them."

She sat very still, not quite looking at him from her sober brown eyes. "I want to have pity on everyone," she said, not accusing him, just stating her feeling.

He did not know how to answer that, so he concentrated on his supper. He finished his potatoes while Eva watched patiently. That was her usual quiet way.

"Eva," he said, "the law has pity on everyone. It's for the good of everyone. If we took away the law, the murderers would still be murderers, and the thieves would still be thieves. And in addition we would have children who went without food because the money was spent on liquor. You know what drinking does."

"Yes, I know. We still have drinking, though, even with the law."

He was aggrieved. "Eva, we do indeed have drinking, though not as much as we used to have. We will always have lawbreakers. That's a given. What isn't given is the future. What kind of country do you want Marie to live in? It's a new world already with industry and commerce like our parents never dreamed of. I don't believe we can afford alcoholic poison. And I certainly don't want David to grow up with the evils I've seen, let alone worse ones."

His comment seemed to give her pause. "Do you think David might still have his mother?" she asked.

"Yes, I'm sure of it. Darla didn't want to drink. If the booze hadn't been available, if people hadn't been guzzling all around her . . ." He trailed off not because he was emotionally affected himself, but because Eva so obviously was.

"I feel for David," she said. "And for you."

"He's doing all right," M. K. said. "He's lucky to have you to talk to."

"He has a father," Eva said. "He can thank God for that."

Eva's sympathy struck M. K. She really was a very caring person, genuinely focused on others. No wonder David liked her company so well.

"What about Marie's father?" he asked, feeling that she had opened that kind of intimacy.

She answered directly. "He left when Marie was barely a baby, so she can't remember him. Somehow she knows she is missing him, though."

"What do you mean by that?"

Eva worked her mouth a few times before she responded. "I think of it like a jigsaw puzzle with all the edge pieces missing. She has a lot to put together, but she doesn't know the overall shape."

"Was it alcohol?"

He saw that she was confused for a moment. Then she understood. "Oh, no. He didn't drink. He had tuberculosis."

Now it was his turn for bewilderment. "He *died*?"

"Yes." She stared at him, not understanding his surprise.

"You said he left."

"Yes. I meant, by dying. They put him in a sanatorium. We could visit only on Sundays. And it was far. So, yes, he left. It felt like he left."

"I'm surprised you never told me about this."

"Oh, well, I don't like to go around telling my troubles." She gave a slight upward motion of her shoulders, as though to shrug, but he thought she was pleased by his interest. *I should ask more about her past,* he thought. *She seems to like it.*

It was just then, at that very moment of his enjoyment, that his conscience sliced into him like a knife so sharp you cannot tell at once whether it has drawn blood. How egotistical he had been. Not for two seconds had he thought about Eva or even shown curiosity. Not until this moment. Even now he was proud of himself for giving a little half-hearted attention. He had thought of her like a servant class, and what had given him the right to think that way?

He looked at her, as though for the first time. She had a small mouth with pushed-out lips that gave her a cheerful look. She sat very happily, very patiently, unaware of his thoughts. Eva had not tried to tell him that she, too, knew about life and suffering. Eva had not tried to tell him anything, but she had taken care of David and made him a home. M. K. had thought he was hiring a servant, but now the largeness of Eva's generosity struck him. She had never acted menial. She was humble and yet always clear. He thought of the image she had used for Marie's father: like the pieces on the edge of the jigsaw puzzle.

In two minutes his views on her flipped over. Eva had been nothing in his eyes, and suddenly she seemed a subject for his curiosity and admiration. The thought crossed his mind that, by Christian standards, she was much greater than he.

———

Bishop Cannon's wife, Lura, had died three weeks after the November election. M. K. had written a note of condolence and had in turn received a short, handwritten acknowledgment. It seemed odd to have no relations after being constantly together for six weeks, but then Cannon had a national profile that kept him far above the commonplace work in Westerville. He had been lauded and awarded among the faithful, recognized by the *Christian Herald* as "the American citizen who made the most significant contribution to religious progress in 1928." By June he was involved again in Virginia politics, up to his neck in the Democratic primaries for the governor's race.

In late June, news came out in the *New York Evening World* that Cannon was mixed up with a fraudulent stockbroker named Harry Goldhurst. Goldhurst's firm, Kable & Co., was bankrupt, and Goldhurst was charged with illegal stock manipulations. Such things happened in New York every day, but the newspaper pointed out with glee that it was not every day that a Methodist bishop was involved.

Cherrington was due to leave for a meeting when they heard the report. "You had better see what we need to do," he said to M. K. "Put out a statement that I can sign."

Cannon had already made a statement to the press, to the effect that his private business operations had no place in the public press, that he had been neither charged nor implicated in illegal activities, and that the timing, just before the Virginia primaries, suggested political motives. Such attacks, he said, "deserve the contempt of all decent men and women."

To M. K., that seemed exactly right. His thoughts were untroubled until he talked to David that evening. The night was so warm and delicious that M. K. had joined David sitting on kitchen chairs they had carried out into the yard. It was a rare June when the light lingered until very late, a warm reddish purple glow in the sky allowing them just to see the outlines of bushes in the yard.

"Didn't you work with that Bishop Cannon?" David asked. "I thought you liked him." He had heard the news on the radio. "It almost seems that everybody is crooked," David went on when M. K. said yes, he did like Cannon. "He's a bishop. He's supposed to be good."

"I think he is good, David. A man like that has enemies, a lot of them. You should judge the truth accordingly."

"He hasn't denied playing the stock market, has he? The news said that he refused to deny it. And Goldhurst named him in court as a good customer."

"That's not illegal."

"Maybe not, but, Dad, it means he was trying to make money that he hadn't earned. That's what you do when you play the stock market. How can that be right? It's gambling."

"A lot of men do it," M. K. said. He saw a firefly and thought of changing the subject by drawing David's attention to it. David was very serious about the matter, surprisingly so for a boy who rarely seemed to think about moral or religious matters.

"You wouldn't do it, would you, Dad?"

M. K. laughed briefly. "I've never had enough money to think about it."

"But you wouldn't."

"No," M. K. said. "I was raised to consider it gambling, as you say."

"Then how could Bishop Cannon?"

"I still don't know that he did, David. But if he did, I'm sure he had his reasons. I know him too well to think that he would ever do something against his conscience. We'll have to wait and see what comes out of this. Maybe someday you'll have a chance to ask him for yourself."

That seemed to satisfy David. At least, he dropped the question. It left M. K. uneasy, however. He remembered the sermons he had heard all his life. Nobody had ever mentioned stock trading as anything but sin. It was among the evils of the immoral city. His answers had perhaps satisfied David, but literally thousands of Methodist ministers, not to mention Baptists and Presbyterians and Church of Christers, would find such answers very doubtful.

———

The story of Cannon and the stock market did not go away. Cannon had enemies working behind the scenes, men such as Carter Glass who had long histories with him in Virginia and frankly hated him. No doubt they were feeding the newspapers a very slanted version of events. It was hypocritical certainly. The reporters and editors and politicians didn't really believe there was anything wrong in playing the stock market. They knew that the ordinary rural believers did, however, and furthermore (due to the newspapers' own constructions) that many people were prepared to think the worst of the bishop. Cannon's unflinching career had been effective in many respects, but if he was to be tried in the newspapers (if not in the courts, since nobody brought any charges of wrongdoing) his unyielding history would feed a longing for vengeance.

That was how M. K. analyzed it at any rate. And if that was an accurate analysis, what could he do to sway opinion toward the ASL's side?

He could not change Cannon's character to make him easy or affable. He could not make the newspapers less hypocritical. He could expose the hypocrisy, but he didn't want to get into a slanging match with reporters. A couple of times that summer he held long conversations with Cherrington about the problem, but most of the time he was left on his own to devise a public relations strategy. Cherrington was too busy trying to get money for his educational department—money that was proving hard to find.

The current had evidently swung away from them again. That was hard to believe, coming so soon after the smashing victory in the elections, but how could you avoid it? Nobody wanted to give Cannon any benefit of the doubt. In July the papers published an old accusation that Cannon had hoarded flour during the Great War. No one in the press seemed to question why an accusation fifteen years old had suddenly surfaced—they dug in with gusto.

In August, Cannon put out his defense—almost book-length—titled *Unspotted from the World.* M. K. read it carefully, hoping to glean crucial information. As usual, Cannon was articulate and convincing, but why did he have to write so voluminously? Even M. K. found it hard to finish. The detail was suffocating. Nobody would read it. Nobody would reprint it. And the truth was already lost in the charges and countercharges because people knew what they wanted to believe. Wets wanted to believe anything awful about Cannon, and drys knew all they needed to know when they learned that Cannon had played the stock market. As the influential church magazine the *Christian Century* put it, Cannon had engaged in legitimate business practice. But "are the ethics of business the ethics of Jesus? Are they even the ethics of the best men?" the magazine asked.

Indeed, as more detail emerged, it was obvious Cannon had speculated. He had traded large amounts, sometimes holding stocks for only days, buying and selling strictly in the hope of making a large profit.

In the fall Cannon went to Brazil as part of his episcopal duties, and that did not help. Nobody could answer the accusations on his behalf, and they only multiplied in his absence. Then, incredibly, H. L. Mencken, of all people, came to Cannon's defense, writing repeatedly of his admiration for the bishop. To ASL supporters, it was a commendation from the devil.

The stock market, which had soared to a record high in September, began to fall. M. K. had never understood stocks. Cherrington, visiting industrialists and businessmen seeking large donations, told him of the anxiety of those men. Cherrington caught their gloom and carried it home with him. He often seemed despondent, but this was a genuine discouragement that M. K. could not lift. They could not do the education work without money. "Kresge . . . I don't know. He wants to know who else is pledging. He's putting me off."

On Tuesday, October 29, Cherrington knocked softly on M. K.'s office door. He stood in the doorway with his meaty shoulders sagging, his back bent. M. K. tried to think who might have died. McBride? No, that would not cause such grief. Cannon? The same.

"I just talked to Mr. Firestone," Cherrington said, throwing his deep eyes around the room, looking anywhere but at M. K. "He says Wall Street has gone mad. He hung up while we were talking."

"Mad?" M. K. said. "What do you mean?"

"I don't really know. I thought perhaps," Cherrington said, "that we could go to your house and listen to the radio. Perhaps there will be some news."

That seemed an extraordinary reaction. M. K. looked carefully at Cherrington and concluded that he was really worried. "All right," he said and closed the office door behind him. They walked over quietly, Cherrington lost in his worries, and M. K. in his uncertainty. A few times M. K. tried to get information, simply to relieve the silence, but conversation sputtered and went out rather quickly. All Cherrington seemed to know was that Wall Street was mad.

At the house they surprised Eva. She had a rag tied around her hair and rubber gloves on her hands. "Do you want some lunch?" she asked. That was the only reason she could conceive of for his coming home during the day. He never had before.

They found some news on the radio. M. K. did not understand the import when they spoke of billions of dollars lost. "What do they mean lost?" he asked Cherrington. "Lost to whom?"

Prominent men had leaped from windows of their Wall Street businesses, not just a few men, either. It was a godless society with a rootless urban sophistication that could not absorb financial losses. What could make a man kill himself? What could possibly justify it? Didn't the men still have a roof over their heads? Weren't their children well fed? How could you kill yourself while wearing a good, clean suit, as those men apparently did?

After they had listened in mute fascination for about an hour, Eva came in with her bucket and stood listening with them. "What does it mean?" she asked. "I don't understand what it means at all."

M. K. had no idea how to answer. What could it mean that some pieces of paper, owned by a few rich men, were suddenly devalued? Everything about it was theoretical, and he did not know the theory. Nobody he knew, except Cannon, had ever owned stock. No doubt Cannon could explain it to him.

He glanced at Cherrington. "Can you explain it, Ernest?"

Cherrington shook his head. "I know that the rich men say it matters to them, but I don't understand how."

Chapter 22
1932: Eva McCallum

In January of 1932 the Bank of Westerville failed. The scene on State Street was so dead quiet that the lines of waiting people did not register in David Nichols's eyes until he was almost past them. He stopped and realized he must have walked past a hundred people on the far side of the street. The line ran far up along the sidewalk, keeping politely close to the shops so as not to block foot traffic.

The day was a freak thaw, the temperature up to fifty degrees, and David was sporting around town with his jacket fully open. To the best of his memory, he had never seen a line in Westerville before, not even at the movie theater. He knew immediately what it was about, however. Every newspaper these days told of bank closures near and far. Why else would people wait in line before a bank door? And yet he could hardly believe his eyes. The day was so fair, the sky blue with threads of mares' tails blowing high above. The brick storefronts were so familiar, and the people stood so patiently, not pushing as he had seen people do on the newsreels. It did not look like a picture of heartbreak or ruin.

He walked along the line, trying to find someone he recognized. Nobody met his eyes. They seemed ashamed to be there, and perhaps they were. How could anybody leave his money in a bank? David thought he knew half the town, but he found no familiar faces. Finally he addressed a woman who was brave enough to meet his eyes—who looked hostilely at him, in fact, as though daring him to humiliate her any further.

"What are you all waiting for?" David asked.

She was muffled in a large, heavy coat and had her hair wrapped in a thick woolen scarf. She seemed not to know the warmth of the day. "They've closed the bank," she said.

"I can see that. But why are you waiting?"

She stared at him. "Mister, if you had all your money in there, you'd wait too." Then she looked away, as though he had reminded her of her shame.

David walked over to the ASL offices to find his father. He could remember as a young boy going into the offices and finding people careening back and forth, but nowadays it was as quiet and dreary as a museum. You could smell the dust and the mildewed newspapers. The older woman who watched the door said hello to him, and he exchanged pleasantries. Then he walked back through the quiet hall to his father's door.

"They've closed the bank," he said.

"Our bank?" M. K. asked.

"Is it our bank?" David asked.

M. K. smiled. "We've never had money to speak of in it. So I guess it's not ours."

"I was surprised how many people were lined up. Over a hundred, I think. And I didn't recognize a single one of them."

"I wonder how they knew?" M. K. said. "Well, I suppose this proves Westerville is no different from any other town." He paused and felt the rough edge of panic rising from the upper part of his chest. "I don't know what is going to happen."

"Somebody has got to stop it," David said with a sudden youthful outburst. "People can stand only so much."

M. K. stared at him wearily. "Who are they going to stop?" he asked.

"I don't know. The banks. The stores. Whoever has something."

"Don't talk like a Red."

"Dad, I just know that people have a limit. And we need a Moses to lead us out of this. I don't think it's President Hoover, either."

"Herbert Hoover is the smartest president we've ever had. He's trying."

"He won't be president for long."

"Maybe not." M. K. stood up slowly from his desk. "Let's go tell Mr. Cherrington what you saw."

Cherrington was working at his desk in virtual darkness. He said he had been frugal all his life, and it was a habit. Just as always, his office was painfully neat. When he heard that the bank was closed, he made no reaction. Then he slowly lifted one hand and slammed it down on the desk. M. K. had never seen him make so dramatic a gesture.

"We didn't have any money tied up, did we?" M. K. asked.

"We've got no money to tie up," Cherrington said. "We owe them."

"I don't suppose they'll be collecting," M. K. said.

"No," Cherrington agreed. "They won't be collecting."

For a full minute they stood silently in the darkened room. Something was dreadfully wrong, more so than M. K. had imagined.

Finally David asked the question. "Then what's bothering you, Mr. Cherrington? If it doesn't affect us."

"It does, though," Cherrington said slowly. "For years we've been using the bank's credit. Hand to mouth, you know. That's why we owe them. Now there will be no more."

"Can't we just live on what we've got?" M. K. asked.

A second time Cherrington raised his hand, but rather than slam it down, he turned it over in a gesture of supplication. "We haven't got anything, Mr. Nichols. Nothing. And nobody wants to give us anything."

After a while there seemed no reason to stay on at the office, so M. K. went home with David. They passed by the bank where the same patient file of people waited, though for what or for how long, it was impossible to say. M. K. looked at them from the end of the street but did not go nearer. "I see them," he said. "I don't need to see their eyes."

Since Christmas a year ago, the churches in town had provided a noon meal, usually soup and bread. Most of the blight of poverty was invisible in a small town like Westerville, but since the meal began, you could see each day a line of people around the back of the Presbyterian church hall where they offered the meal. M. K. avoided going by. He did not like to see what otherwise he did not need to think of. No more did he now want to see the faces of people who had lost their savings in the bank.

By the time they arrived home, the last yellow light of the day lay weakly on the front of their house. "I wonder where Eva is?" M. K. asked as they got in the door. "Come on, let's sit down and talk a little."

The house was cold, so M. K. kept his coat on. He had learned to live in a cold house these past few years. In the kitchen he and David sat across from each other in the dark in unconscious imitation of Cherrington. After his initial reaction to the news, Cherrington had just sat in his seat, saying nothing, moving nothing. The effect had been frightening.

"I want you to go back to Oberlin," M. K. said to David, who was due to return from the Christmas holidays in a few days. "But I don't know whether I can help you with tuition this year. I will if I can. You better get another job if possible. Or you could go ask your uncle Sam for help. He has money. I don't know if he's willing to share it."

"Uncle Sam would. But I don't want to ask."

"There's nothing wrong with asking."

David shrugged his shoulders and then stood up. "I'm sick of school," he said. "I wish I could be out doing something."

"Like what?"

"I don't know. Something. I think I'm going to go read. Do you want me to stoke up the furnace?"

"Sure."

Half an hour later Eva came in to make supper. She was surprised to find M. K. sitting in the kitchen. "Why don't you turn the light on?" she asked.

"I'm not doing anything," he said, "just thinking. I don't need light for that."

"You heard about the bank," she said and sat down next to him.

"Yes," he said, "and Eva, I might as well tell you. Mr. Cherrington says that he can't be sure of paying me."

"He never could, from what I understood." The salary had been much delayed several times.

"True, but this is worse. We've used the bank's credit to print things, to buy paper and ink. I think he's going to let all the printers go tomorrow morning."

"People all over this town are in sorrow tonight," she said.

David had slipped back in, and he stood in the doorway listening. "But there are a lot of people," David said, "who don't feel it at all. In fact, they gain from it. They can cut people's wages until they're starving because they know there aren't any other jobs. They can pick up farms and houses at bargain prices. Whenever people are losing, you can count on it: somebody else is gaining."

"That's what I don't understand about the stock market," M. K. said. "Where did the money go? People lost everything. Did somebody else gain it?"

"Somebody's gaining," David said. "The rich people can sit in their castles. I don't see why the Republicans do nothing."

"It's easy to complain," M. K. said. "What do you want them to do?" These political comments bothered him deeply, coming from his own son. Hoover was mocked and derided everywhere now; hobo shantytowns near the railroad tracks were universally known as "Hoovervilles." The president had not caused banks to close. He was the most intelligent leader the nation had ever known, and if he could not help this depression, who could?

"Anything is better than sitting still and letting the whole country starve," David said. "Pass some laws. Make it illegal to throw people out of work. Illegal to steal their homes and their farms at sale prices. Make it illegal to pay slave wages just because so many people need work. If those big farmers aren't using the land they've got, make them give it up to the poor people who can get some good out of it."

"I never thought I'd send a son to Oberlin and get back a Red," M. K. said. "You sound like those Wobblies I used to see at the docks in Los Angeles. Take the rich man's yacht and let the poor man use it to catch fish. Let the workers organize their own factories. That's what they used to say."

"That doesn't sound so bad to me," David said. "It's easy to call names."

They had been having this argument all through the holidays. At another time in his life M. K. might not have minded. He had always found the exchange of ideas unthreatening because he had no great ideological commitments. Now, though, he was edgy and prone to argue.

He still had the barest hope that somehow Prohibition would survive. As long as the law remained, it was possible to hope for a change of heart. Perhaps Americans would recognize that they wanted the law and needed it. Yet much anger and hurt and turbulence were present in America today, and people burned for change, any change. This being an election year they would change politicians—that was sure. Even if they had no idea what any other president might do that Hoover did not, they would vote for change. That meant they would go Democratic, and the Democrats would surely get rid of Prohibition because they believed bitterly that the drys stood against them. Prohibition had not caused the depression, and neither had the Republicans, but there was no helping it.

At any rate, anybody could take the temperature of the nation and know that people were sick of Prohibition. They were sick of reading about gangsters and sick of speakeasies, sick of complaining, sick of being told what to do. They were sick to death of the ASL, thanks to the way the press had treated them.

Of course, they had brought it on themselves. Bishop Cannon, in particular. The stock trading had been the beginning, then he had been investigated for campaign finance abuse, then he was accused of adultery with a younger woman—now his wife—who had been his traveling secretary even before his wife died. Oh, none of it had been proved, and Cannon swore it was all trumped up by his enemies, but there were just enough facts, just enough grounds for suspicion, to make a lot of people quite sure that he was just what they needed him to be: a nightmare moralist, wagging his finger at others while carrying on in secret himself.

"David," Eva asked, "if you were in charge of Westerville, just our town, if you were the mayor and could do anything you wanted, what would it be?" She did not fight with David, as M. K. was prone to do.

"All right," he said. "For a start, I'd make the bank open up and give those people their money. That's wrong. The banks can't take people's money and lock their doors. We ought to stop that and make them explain where that money is."

"They'd have to give back all the money people put in," Eva said. "And what if they ran out of money? Is that possible? Can banks run out of money?"

M. K. did not understand banking, but he knew that banks loaned their deposits to farmers and businessmen, even to the ASL. And he thought David knew it too.

"Yes, sure they can. That's where Hoover comes in," David said. "The government can print more money and give it to the banks."

"The government can do that?" Eva asked. "Just print money?"

"Sure. Who do you think makes the money? And then I'd make a law that nobody can fire anybody."

"Like the league?" M. K. asked. "You heard Cherrington. He has to let all the printers go because we don't have paper to print on. Nor do we have money to pay them. Would the government print money for us too?"

"At least they should do something," David said angrily. "What's your plan?"

M. K. shrugged.

The light had faded to nothing. Eva's face shone faintly, with deep shadows pocketing her eyes and the cleft under her mouth. M. K. watched her closely, filling in the dark spaces with the glittering dark eyes he knew from memory.

"It doesn't do to blame anybody," Eva said. "It's like a tornado blew over us, tossing everything around and leaving a wreck. This is how I felt when Marie's father left. You feel helpless and mad."

David said, "This isn't a storm. A storm is when nature assaults you. Nobody can blame nature for this. It's a matter for humans to solve."

"I just hope that when all is done, we still remember how to be friends with each other," Eva said. "That's the only way I know to get through hard times."

"Well, fine, friends, but I think we need to go back to the drawing board. This system doesn't work anymore. It was fine in the time of Jefferson, but now it's broken, and we need to junk it and start over."

Uncharacteristically, M. K. stepped out of the conversation. His son's impulses upset him, but he realized that he did not know what should be done. Never had he imagined such a condition of paralysis as now afflicted him. He had read somewhere of a spider that paralyzes a beetle and then lays her eggs in its living flesh so that the eggs hatch and meals are provided from the lifeblood of the living, paralyzed creature. He felt like that beetle.

He supposed that other people all across the country felt the same or worse. So many had lost farms and houses and jobs. So many were feeding their children on scraps, and the winter was just beginning. He had lost nothing really—except that he had lost everything for which he had worked twenty years. He and Cherrington were now like beggars living in a ruined castle, rattling on in endless conversation about the day when the kingdom would be restored. He knew nothing anymore. He knew only—what he had not really known during most of the years of his work at the ASL—that he had loved the dry cause. It had made his life seem real. And it was lost. He was lost. He did not know what the future might hold.

M. K. watched Eva patiently talk it out with David, though she knew no economics and had barely been to school. She listened to David and even drew him out, but she kept returning to the human relations involved. What did he think the bankers in Westerville should do? She never got lost in the towering abstractions that David tossed out. What was it she had that M. K. did not? She was extremely simple and humble. As far as he could tell, she did not even think of herself, not at all. Yet she was also confident. She knew what she knew.

Gradually it came over him, as he watched her and listened, that he loved her. He had not known it, but it had been true for some time. It seemed powerful and consoling. He loved her.

Eva in no way fit his idea of love. Her face was pleasant and warm, but she was small and scrawny of body and possessed no inkling of style. It jolted M. K. to think that he could love someone who reminded him of a raccoon, quick and lithe yet shapeless, like a bag with limbs. Something else attracted him, apart from anything visible. It was her manner and her mind that flowed from her body. M. K. thought of a curve in a quiet, warm stream shining under moonlight; so was her spirit.

He left them talking and went out for a walk. A cold wind had come up from the north, and it was obvious the thaw had ended. The ponds would freeze tonight. Something ominous comes with a night wind, blowing the bare branches so they click and clack together. So, he loved Eva. He would certainly not say anything of it to her. God knew she had seen enough trouble in her life without his adding to it. What could he give besides poverty, failure, and gloom? He could not even be sure to pay her anymore for her housework.

David went back to college, hoping to find enough work to squeeze through, so the house stood empty all day until Eva came in the afternoon to stoke the furnace and cook a meal. M. K. got paid some of the time, when people sent in pledges to the ASL, and both Eva and her daughter, Marie, earned some money doing odd jobs, laundry and baby-sitting and mending. By the summer, when David came home from school, they had abandoned any pretense of employer-employee.

You could say they pooled their money, but it wasn't even that developed a scheme. They worked out their finances a meal at a time. Whoever had any money bought something with it. Mostly they pooled their conversation. Together they sat at the dinner table in the only warm room in the house for much of the year, and they talked over the world until late when Eva and Marie would return to their small, cold house. How they managed without any heat at all, M. K. did not know. Fortunately it was not a cold winter. More than once he invited them to move into the house, but Eva would not have it. She did not consider it proper, and she acted as though she did not think he was serious.

Rarely did they speak of events in Westerville, which were generally depressing, or of events in the wider world, which were more so. More often they talked of where they wished to travel, what careers Marie and David might follow, and how the automobile and the radio were changing the world. In March the Lindbergh baby was kidnapped, and they discussed the case avidly for months. They knew all the names of the Lindbergh servants just from listening to the radio. They still had the radio. They also read out loud, taking turns with the book. They read all of *Pickwick Papers* and sometimes laughed until they had tears in their eyes.

At the league office it was different. Nobody would talk; people only worked. Their unspoken conspiracy was to work so hard, they dug themselves out of their hole. But they did not want to talk about the hole. It was better not to think too much about the hole.

Cherrington still put out appeals for funds, and he would write a letter to anybody with money if there seemed to be the remotest chance the person would give. More of his time, though, was devoted to the coming election. He sent out stacks of letters to ASL agents and sympathizers all around the country, appealing for information as to convention delegates, especially whether they leaned dry or wet, and what arguments or loyalties they might be susceptible to. It was the tried-and-true ASL strategy, working behind the scenes to sway delegates and work factions.

He had an elaborate filing system for keeping track, and he could at a moment brandish fistfuls of information about the possibilities of, say, Nebraska Democrats. M. K. made sure he never said a word questioning who would use this information and how. He thought privately that Cherrington might as well collect information about the mating habits of kangaroos.

M. K. continued to write every day. They lacked money to print their own materials, but that was not essential. All along they had relied on the popular press to carry their arguments, and so M. K. typed and sent off piece after piece to newspapers and magazines. Inevitably somebody would publish whatever he wrote, even if only a small church paper hungry for copy written in complete sentences. He didn't find it hard to get published (though the biggest and best outlets were much more resistant), but he found it more and more difficult to muster the will to write.

He had all the old arguments at his disposal and all the familiar appeals, but he could not afford to think about what he was doing very much or the sounds of the words would all start echoing against each other to make a holy cacophony that obliterated sense. It was so laborious to write when you thought no one could believe you. He felt he was babbling on paper, repeating familiar sounds. He endeavored simply to write: to produce so many pages a day, so many articles a week, to send them off to editors without reflecting on what good they might do. What else could he do but work?

Sometimes he wondered whether it would be better for them to talk at the office. Usually he thought of it at the end of a wearying day, having watched the clock creep its way to five o'clock. (He no longer worked late—he was worn out just by the regular hours.) Possibly if he and Cherrington and McBride and Russell could sit and talk, they might find a way ahead, a change of plan to salvage all their years of work. By the morning, however, when he returned to work, he had lost the courage. What if they were to talk about their position and discover, as they surely all suspected, that it was hopeless? *Far better,* he thought, *just to work and not to talk. Even,* he sometimes added, *not to think about what would happen to them.*

In June, John D. Rockefeller Jr. released a public statement favoring repeal of the Eighteenth Amendment. He had been one of the staunchest supporters of Prohibition; his defection seemed to sweep away a last island of safety. On the same day Eva told M. K. that her landlord had told her she would have to get out. She was six months behind in rent.

M. K. was so numb from bad news that he barely reacted. "What will you do?" he asked. "Where will you go? You can still come here if you want."

"I've got a sister in St. Louis," Eva said. "She'll take us in until we can find another start."

"How will you get there?"

"I'm not sure."

"You can't just hitch a ride."

"No."

"I wish I had a car."

"Well, you don't," Eva said brusquely with a force that made it more than a mere mention of fact. It was about the hardest thing he had ever heard her say, and it shocked him awake. They were at the kitchen table, and dinner was cooking on the stove, but Marie had not yet come. Marie had to rehearse for her graduation ceremony, so she would be late.

Eva had pulled her hair behind her ears, and it hung straight down, making her face seem longer and bonier to M. K.'s eyes. She studied her hands folded in front of her.

"You can't possibly leave me," he said. Even as he said it, he felt how devastating it would be—like the end of the world with the last wall crashing down.

She lifted her eyes to glance at him. Then she stretched out her right hand across the table and sneaked her fingers into his hand. He did not think that she had ever touched him before. "I don't want to go," she said. "But I have to have a place to live."

M. K. pulled on the hand. At first he pulled gently, a mere tug, and then he lifted half out of his seat and pulled her across to him to kiss her on the lips. The act was unpremeditated, but so full of passion and tenderness he began to tremble. She returned his kiss. For a moment they broke apart and studied each other's face, then kissed again, leaning toward each other over the table in a back-wrenching posture.

"You can't possibly leave me," M. K. said. "Let's marry each other."

"Do you mean it?" she asked.

"Of course I mean it," he said. "It's the only practical thing to do."

He repented the next day. His courage had come from her predicament, that she needed a place to stay and he could offer that. In the morning, though, he saw the idea for what it was, a desperate and futile gesture. He had nothing to offer Eva, no future, nothing but failure. She undoubtedly would be better off with her sister.

He woke with his futility on his mind—it had crept in through his dreams, he supposed—and looked around at the clean but threadbare house. Just sticks and shingles it was. Almost any man could offer as much, and it did not even belong to him. If he failed to pay the mortgage, he could soon be out on the street, like so many others.

When he got home a little early and found Eva in her familiar apron, smiling, he was frightened half to death to think of what he must say. Quickly, before she could reach him, before he might lose his courage to face the truth, he blurted out his firm conclusions. "Eva, I have been thinking all day. I was wrong last night. I spoke without realizing what I was saying. I don't see how I can offer marriage."

She stood frozen for a moment, a hard, dazed look on her features, and then she broke out crying. He had not expected that. He had fully expected that she might be relieved, though perhaps confused. Not, however, heartbroken.

"It's all right," she said when he tried to comfort her. "You are right. I am not good enough for you."

"It's not that at all," he said. He tried to take her hand away from her eyes, but she resisted. "Just the opposite. Eva, you don't know what a wreck I am. I have nothing to offer. A house, which I don't own. You only see me here. You don't see me in the office. There's nothing there but skeletons and dust."

She drew away and gave him an even harder look, a stare that was exaggerated by the red that rimmed her eyes. "Sit down," she ordered him.

He grabbed a chair and did so without daring to take his eyes off her. He had never seen her angry. He would have thought it impossible.

Then she gave him a smile, which appeared from nowhere and seemed at that confused moment like a morning glory opening itself to the first streak of golden dawn. She sat down and took his two hands in hers. The smile had turned into a kind of Cheshire cat grin. "You aren't going to give me that kind of difficulty, are you?" she asked. "Please don't. Have I given you any reason to think that I do not know my own mind?"

He stared at her until she said that she expected an answer. "No," he said.

"And can you think that there is anyone on the face of the earth who has seen you as much or heard your mind as often as I have over the past years? Anyone?"

"No," he said.

"Then please. Don't annoy me. Marie is quite enough trouble, thank you. You're probably right. You don't have a thing to give. I know that. I don't want anything you have to offer. I would like to marry you if you are willing to have me."

———

The ceremony took place just two weeks later on a Tuesday afternoon. To M. K.'s surprise, most of the church came out and seemed genuinely delighted at their marriage. Cherrington stood up with him, and the pastor's wife witnessed for Eva. No relatives came, except David and Marie. M. K. had written his mother and Linda with the news, and Eva her sister in St. Louis, urging them not to trouble themselves to come because it would be an almost private ceremony. They had not, in fact, issued invitations, and they were surprised when so many appeared. The gifts were as you might suppose. Very few were store-bought, and there had been no time for elaborate quilts or handwork, but a few simple hand pieces had been made, and there were glass dishes and gimcracks that must have come out of families' own private stores of possessions.

They simply walked from the church to the house, along with Cherrington, the pastor and his wife, David, and Marie. Eva had cooked a goose she had gotten in exchange for milking some goats while a farm wife was sick. They sat around the kitchen table as of old, except for the three extra guests. The difference was that, instead of walking Eva partway home, when the night was over M. K. walked upstairs with her to the bedroom they would share.

Less than a week before, at the Republican convention, Herbert Hoover had accepted his renomination while stating plainly his intention of undoing Prohibition if he should be reelected. Cherrington's careful assemblage of political data now certainly meant nothing since both parties were pledged to undo the law. Unless they witnessed an unprecedented political cataclysm, Prohibition was over. M. K. found himself thinking of it as he and Eva prepared for bed. It was odd. He was thinking of the wedding, of his new wife. He was full of wonderment and doubt about how it would be to sleep with Eva after twenty years without a woman. Yet Prohibition infiltrated everything. Its failure—and his failure with it—he could not even now banish from his mind.

"It's odd," M. K. said as he sat on the edge of the bed. "I should be frightened about the future, but I'm not."

"You're not frightened of me, are you?"

"No." He laughed. "You're just a little thing."

Eva sat down beside him. "'The Lord is the strength of my life,'" she quoted. "'Of whom shall I be afraid?'"

"That's true," he said, "but it doesn't always seem to work. Not for me."

"But you said you should be frightened. Frightened of what?"

"You know. Of the unknown. Everything I've worked for is blown to pieces. We're starting out with nothing."

She played with his hand. "Then you have nothing more to lose," she said.

"Wrong," he said and took her into his arms, holding her very tightly with his eyes closed.

Chapter 23

1932: Recovering Dreams

On the afternoon of election day M. K. and Eva drove through Amarillo, looking for a place to stay in the square brick hotels near the train station. After the blinding blue of the Texas sky and miles of wasted, gray land, the city seemed happily familiar—buildings and sidewalks and human density. Amarillo almost looked like Chillicothe, at least more like Chillicothe than the Texas landscape looked like Ohio's green hills. That was good because M. K. felt he needed something familiar.

He was used to a different mode of travel, whereby a train carried you from one point in a city center to another. Then you could move freely within the limited range that your feet (and taxis and trolleys) would go. You were tethered, as it were, to a center—the downtown, the train station. You got on a train that took you to another center.

Driving, however, you had no frame of reference, no central place. At any crossing of roads you could turn in any direction and keep going—never, necessarily, to come back that way. Your center moved with you. You were, in fact, your own center. Driving out of Westerville had given M. K. a thrill of liberation that almost scared him, but after a thousand miles, he found it chafed him with a vague anxiety. So much seemed to depend on every fork in the road.

They drove up one street and back another, past the train station and around the block, but M. K. did not like the looks of anything he saw. The hotels seemed dark and inhuman, either too expensive or too cheap. Perhaps it was the view from the car, which went by too quickly to let him see into the lobbies. He got only an impression, and he didn't particularly want to take time to park. Being in a car made you think you had no time because while you stopped and parked you might have driven somewhere half a mile off easily. You could do so much in so little time it made you hurry.

Finally M. K. said to Eva, "Let's just keep going. Maybe we'll see something on the way." On the western edge of town, just as the buildings cleared out and he began to worry that they would have to turn back, he saw an auto park and felt right away that it would meet their needs. Everything was visible at a roadside glance. Twelve tidy frame units, painted blue and white, were set around a graveled semicircle with a scraggly gray lawn in the middle. A swing set and two picnic tables occupied the lawn, and the weather was warm enough that a family had taken over both tables for a picnic supper. Behind the left-hand set of units, adjoining the highway, stood a small yellow house with a hand-painted sign saying OFFICE.

They parked and went up to the porch to meet the proprietor, who sat listening to his radio. His name was Grant, and he was a friendly, round-headed fellow who said he had built the units himself, seeing that the highway got busier every day. "I like to sit and watch the people pass, and one day I thought that some of those people might very well stop if I gave them a reason." When Grant talked, he never stopped moving, shuffling his feet, swinging his arms, jingling change in his pocket.

"How much do you want for a night?" M. K. asked.

Grant looked him up and down before answering. "It's three dollars," he said. "Pay in advance."

He showed them a cabin, not that there was much to show. The walls were board and bat, painted a pale green, the floor covered in a patterned linoleum carpet. Eva pulled back the sheets on a corner of the bed to see if there were bedbugs. She nodded at M. K. to let him know it was all right. Grant made a point of showing how to flush the toilet. "Every one of these cabins has its own," he said. "Sometimes I get folks who haven't used one.

"You folks eaten your supper yet?" he asked. "There's a cafe just back down the highway toward town, about half a mile. Pretty good eats, and if you ask for an iced tea with their special mint, you'll get something that will really quench you, if you understand my meaning. And if you want, you can come up to the house and listen to the election on the radio. Of course, I don't know your political persuasion, so I'd ask you not to bring any guns or knives." He laughed at his own joke and jiggled some coins in his pocket.

"All right," M. K. said. "Thank you. We might do that. I've got some things to get out of the car, so I'll walk with you." Grant would have stood around to talk all evening.

The trunk to the DeSoto was loaded with possessions, as was the backseat as high as the back window. M. K. got their suitcase off the top of the heap, waved to Grant, and went back into the cabin. Eva was leaning over the sink, rubbing water into her face. She looked up and smiled, then pulled the towel off the rack and dried herself with little pats. M. K. sat on the bed and watched her, trying to absorb the peace she usually brought him.

"What do you want to do about supper?" he asked. "Want to get some of that tea with their special mint?"

She gave a faint smile, respecting the pain in his raillery. "We can make do with sandwiches," she said. "I'd rather eat at those tables if you don't think it's too cold."

"It's getting dark," he said.

"I don't care. I'd rather be outside."

A chill had cut in on the evening. M. K. remembered LA, which had the same surprising tendency—a warm day could turn cool by dusk and chilly by the evening. They put on their coats and sat opposite each other, serenaded by the shrill cries of the children playing some sort of tag or hide-and-seek in the gloom. Eva got a loaf of bread and a hunk of bologna out of a paper bag, along with a jar of mayonnaise. She had a long knife, which she handed to M. K. "Here," she said. "Cut some slices of bread and I'll make sandwiches."

They had bought the food at a grocery store earlier in the day. The bread was wrapped in colored waxed paper, with BRAGGS printed in large red letters. "Look at this," M. K. said as he sliced it. "It's so soft I can hardly cut it." He put his face close to the loaf and breathed in the feathery aroma. "The crust is so thin you don't notice it. You can't make bread like this, can you? It has to be store-bought. I wonder how they do it."

He sliced the bologna, and Eva assembled sandwiches, neatly slathering mayonnaise on both sides right to the crusty margin. She folded her hands and said a grace for them, and then they ate. The darkness had descended so far that M. K. could barely make out Eva's face.

"It tastes good," he said. "I was hungry."

Eva got up to take their tin cups into the room, to fill them with water from the sink. When she returned, she asked, "When do you think we'll get to California?"

He calculated in his head. "Three days to California if everything goes right. But it's a big state. It will take another day to get to Bakersfield."

"And tell me again about this friend of yours? You're sure he'll want us?"

"Roy Overholt. His wife's name is Grace. And they have children, but I can't remember their names. When I first went to Los Angeles, Roy was the one who took me to church and led me to Christ. We started going to Bible school together. Now he's a pastor in Bakersfield, which is a little farming town in the middle of the state. I haven't seen Roy in years, but he invited us to come." M. K. paused for a moment, thinking. He realized that it must seem strange to Eva or anybody else that they should travel two thousand miles to see someone he had not visited or written in years. It must seem desperate. For some reason he felt drawn to Roy. He had written to him about his search for direction, and Roy had suggested they come west.

"We don't have much choice now, do we?" he said.

"We could have stayed in Ohio."

M. K. shook his head. "We could, I guess, but I really want to be out of there. I want to go somewhere that nobody knows me." By September he had felt that his work was a pantomime. Whatever he wrote seemed ludicrously ill-informed, as though he were writing to an audience in some other century. Everybody knew that Prohibition was dead. Had the news missed him? The breweries were openly preparing to start up business again. Besides, there was no money for the ASL, and Cherrington had stopped even apologizing for missing paychecks. He roamed in the office like a ghost. Even when they were the only two in the office, Cherrington would pass by M. K.'s open door and not say a word.

Eva took his hand in her small fingers. "You don't need to feel that way," she said. "Nobody blames you."

"I suppose not," he said. It was not blame so much as exposure. He could not stand to think that people looked at him and knew him for this failure.

They had exchanged the house for the DeSoto. It seemed a funny bargain: the rooted physical presence of a domicile in exchange for a moving, temporal tool. When he had made up his mind to go, however, he wanted to leave quickly. A family with six kids had lost their farm to the bank and moved into town, needing a place to stay. They had the car from more prosperous—perhaps foolish—days and did not need it now. Monetarily, it worked out about the same if you counted how much M. K. owed the bank. You always had to pay the bank's mortgage, even if some other bank had folded with all your money. Some people had tried to pay their mortgage with checks drawn on the defunct bank, but that got no sympathy.

So they had traded, even up, with the furniture (such as it was) thrown in, except for the radio. That they had loaded into the car with all their other things and taken to Hillsboro. They planned to leave it for David when he finished college. In the meantime Samson's family and his mother could enjoy it.

The visit had sealed his desire to be gone from Ohio. His brother had seen the car loaded up with possessions and thought he came to move in. Then, assured that they were heading west, Samson assumed that M. K. came to ask for money. Without even checking his idea, Samson told M. K. that he wasn't going to give him anything. "You made your bed and now you've got to lie down in it," he said.

"I'm not asking for help," M. K. said.

Samson didn't hear. "I'm not going to use my money to bail out somebody who called me a criminal."

"Samson, what did you think you were? You knew the law."

"The law," he said contemptuously. "I don't need lectures from you about the law."

M. K. would have expected some softening, now that their differences were moot, with Samson so clearly the victor. "I want you to know I've got plenty of jack," Samson said. "Everything I've got I paid cash for. I got my money out of the banks a long time before the crash too. I could help you out and not even notice it, but I'm not going to do that."

"I haven't asked you for help," M. K. said. "It didn't even occur to me."

When he told his mother good-bye, she did not seem to take in the significance of the event. Of course, she was very old now, over seventy years, and had lost all her sturdiness of body and character. Her hair had turned silver-white, and she had lost weight until she seemed as negligible as a bit of dandelion fluff, drifting in the wind. She made very little reaction when he told her of his plans. She acted as though Samson and his family were all that existed for her.

She had said good-bye to him many times, and perhaps it seemed no different to her that he would be in California instead of the northern part of Ohio. She did not even ask about David and Linda. And she barely seemed to notice Eva, whom she had never seen before.

———————

Thinking of this as he sat solemnly chewing his sandwich, in the dusk of a Texas night outside a motor hotel, M. K. felt as rootless as he had ever been. He remembered feeling something this way when he was a young man going west, but now, twenty years later, he had no sense of excitement or pleasure in it. "I wonder if I'll ever see them again," he said.

"See who?" Eva asked.

"My brother's family. They aren't dying to see me, that's for sure."

"Oh, you'll see them, M. K. There's a lot of life to live. David and Marie will probably stay in Ohio, and we'll want to visit. Naturally you'll go to see your brother. You have to see your brother."

"I'll never see my mother again. Not that it seems likely to trouble her."

Eva gave his hand a squeeze. "You're very melancholy tonight."

"I remember getting out of college," he told her. "I'd never been past the Mississippi before I took the train west. I was so glad to be gone. I had all kinds of dreams about the way I would lead my life in a new place. Where it was, I didn't care, so long as it wasn't like Ohio. I was sure I could make my mark. And now, I'm glad to be gone from Ohio again, very glad, but I don't have much confidence I'll make any kind of mark. I just want to get away. I'd be happy to disappear."

"You're very dramatic," Eva said. She was a practical woman, a good tether to his highs and lows. "Why don't we go up to see Mr. Grant and listen to his radio?"

They could just as easily have sat on the steps to listen because they could hear the radio clearly from there. Grant had it squawking as loud as it could go. He opened the screen door when they knocked and shouted at them to come in. All around the little cluttered parlor sat a variety of persons: two men in suits and bow ties, their hats balanced on their knees, the mother and father of the family the Nicholses had seen picnicking when they arrived, a teenage boy whose teeth stuck out from his upper lip, a broad-built, dark-skinned man, possibly an Indian to judge by looks, and a couple of sunburned young men in boots with cowboy hats neatly centered under their chairs. You could not hear anything except the radio, but nevertheless Grant tried to introduce them all, and M. K. understood enough of what he said to gather that these were a collection of neighbors and customers. Grant apparently lived alone. At least, no woman asserted herself as his wife, and when Eva went through the kitchen on her way to the bathroom, she found a room ankle-deep in papers and empty jars and tools. She did not know any women who kept their kitchen that way.

Early totals were already coming in from the eastern states, and soon the great Midwest began to pour its votes into the airwaves. They got a fog of results from all over, and it was hard to make sense of it. But as the evening went on, there was no missing that Roosevelt was sweeping the field. He had the solid South back in the Democratic column, and he captured almost every other state as well. Each time his lead in a state grew, Grant jigged in a little circle. Others smiled. One of the cowboys pulled a flask out of his pocket and had a pull. He offered it to Grant, who also took a swig and then offered it around the room. "Just a little of our fine tea," he said to M. K. with a cat's smile. "You want any?"

"No, thanks," M. K. said, trying to match the smile. He wished that he had not come, but he did not like to show his disappointment in public.

The radio roared over them, and Grant, who had not brought any chair for himself, stood leaning against the cold stove and swinging his arms. He seemed very happy. He had a party whistle in his pocket, which he brought out to blow every time the radio gave any update on the voting. When presidential totals showed Roosevelt ahead of Hoover, he would look around the room with a blissful, conspiratorial smile and blow his whistle. The little paper tongue uncoiled itself and a thin, papery tooting was heard.

Finally M. K. touched Eva's elbow. "I think we know what we came to know," he said in her ear. "Do you mind if we go?"

The porch was lit with a single bare bulb, blazing its staring light into the yard, but by the cabins the only light visible was the one over a sign by the highway, GRANT'S CABINS. The rest of the semicircle was dark, and they had to carefully navigate their way to their front door. After fumbling with the key, M. K. got them inside, switched on the light, and then stretched out on the bed. Eva went into the bathroom.

"I was remembering the night when Hoover beat Smith," he said. "We felt so sure that the country had spoken its mind on Prohibition."

"I guess people have changed their minds," Eva said.

"And how," M. K. said. "I find it hard to believe that an ordinary fellow like Mr. Grant, who has worked hard and built this little place, should want to encourage America to go back to drunkenness. He acted as if we were celebrating his birthday tonight. They all did."

"I wasn't sure that everybody had the same mind," Eva said. "You were smiling, after all. They probably thought you were happy too."

"Whatever the people in that room were thinking, the people in the voting booths made their minds pretty clear."

"Yes," she said. "I think we knew that before, didn't we?"

"What, that people wanted a change? Sure. But I guess I wasn't prepared for it, all the same. It's so emphatic. I feel like somebody kicked me in the head. The most educated man we've ever had in the White House, and he's thrown out. It hit me tonight, to see the little celebrations. They don't want it. They just don't want it."

"These are the hardest times anybody has seen, Marion, and people want change for all kinds of reasons that have nothing to do with Prohibition."

"I guess that's so," M. K. said. "They feel about Hoover the way people feel about the dentist—he's the fellow that whenever I see him my teeth hurt. They'd rather not see him anymore if they don't have to." He laughed softly to himself and rolled over onto his side.

Eva had put on her nightgown, a soft, faded red flannel garment that dusted the floor. She came to sit beside him on the bed, so small she barely dented the mattress, as light as a cat. M. K. was glad to feel her near, to hear her sane voice. The finality of the election kept striking him. He would begin to think of how the ASL might take its next step and then suddenly remember the parlor scene he had just left, the celebration that might grow a little more vivid without him. It was all over. The law that he had spent twenty years working for, the law that had promised so much good and had done so much good, was history.

It still had an ephemeral existence while it stayed on the books, but within months the beer would begin to flow. And more men would come home drunk, having spent the rent money, to terrorize their children and beat their wives. More families would live in poverty, more children would go hungry or cold, and more drunks would be beaten up or robbed. The criminal element would feel bolder because the stimulant numbed the conscience, and even very good people, weak people, would catch their hands in machinery or fall under horses or run their automobiles into trees because they were inebriated.

"At least we can say we tried," M. K. said. "We tried to do good. We spent years of our lives for the sake of our fellowman. They may not appreciate it, but we tried."

He could not, however, draw much satisfaction from this thought. He and Eva had no money to speak of, they had no home, they were traveling through this desolate country where a breakdown or an accident could ruin them—and these troubles seemed insignificant beside the deep wound of his failure, the failure of his attempt to do good.

"It never really worked, did it?" he asked Eva with sudden force. "The first few years it made a difference, but pretty soon the bootleggers got busy and then there was no way you could say that Prohibition was working. I should know. I tried every which way to make the case. A lot of people didn't want it to work, and they sapped the strength in the law, even though it was so obvious that the stuff was poison and that whatever little pleasure it brought was paid for in death and poverty and criminal behavior. Eva, why did so many people never see that?"

She took a long time to answer. The questions were almost rhetorical, and he was not sure he even expected an answer.

"People are difficult," Eva said. "They don't always make sense."

"I don't see what you mean, that people are difficult."

They were both lying on their backs now, close enough to talk in a low voice. "Marion," she said, "it's not anything complicated I'm trying to say. You can get only so far with rules. People will fight them, and sometimes they will do themselves harm no matter how hard you try to stop them. In fact, sometimes the harder you try, the more they fight against you. If you aren't careful, you become a dictator, and they hate you. You know that, don't you?"

"I guess," he said.

"I remember your telling me about your wife," she said. "Darla. Didn't you try to stop her from drinking?"

"Sure, I tried. I did everything I could think of."

"And none of it worked. The same thing with your daughter, I think. You couldn't watch her every hour of the day. When she got old enough, she was going to go her own way."

"And she did. Even though I loved her and pleaded with her."

"Yes," Eva said softly, almost in a sigh. "Believe me, I'm very glad that Marie hasn't taken to drink. I couldn't control her."

"Yet," M. K. said. "She hasn't taken to drink yet." Marie had decided to stay in Westerville to go to the college there.

"That's true. I expect the girls now may grow up to drink just like the men. She has always been a challenge, especially after the polio. She craved love, and yet she made it so much more difficult for herself. People are difficult. People right in our homes are difficult, M. K."

"You're not saying that it's hopeless. We should just throw our hands in the air and not try?"

"What I'm saying is that you have to be wise, to know when to use a rule and when not, and what kind of rule, because rules should be a tool of love. You love your children and you want the best for them, and sometimes rules are the best way to bring that love to bear. But it's tricky, very tricky, and you have to judge the situation carefully. 'Provoke not your children to wrath,' the Bible says."

M. K. had been caught up in memories of Darla. He did not often think of her anymore. Her face, which once had been so substantial to his imagination, had faded so much that when he looked at his few old photos, she seemed to be a stranger he had met or a distant cousin yanked into a picture at a family gathering. Now, though, thinking of his own fevered attempts to keep liquor out of Darla's reach, feelings of that time welled up inside him, feelings of hope, desperate love, frustration and anger, wild uncertainty.

"I did love her very much," he said.

"Who?"

"Darla. It was her death that drew me into the ASL. I guess I was fooled twice."

"What do you mean by that?"

"First I tried to stop her from drinking, and failed. Then I tried to stop the whole country from drinking, and failed."

Eva reached a hand out from under the covers and found M. K.'s. She gave a tight squeeze, hard enough to hurt. "It's not such a terrible thing to have tried," she said. "It's not a disgrace."

"What else could I have done?"

"I don't know," Eva said. "I don't know if the law was a mistake from the beginning. I don't know if it got in the way of things. Maybe it created a spirit of rebellion."

"Wheeler always emphasized enforcement. I think he loved it, in fact. He used to talk about showing them the meaning of punishment before death. Maybe that was a mistake. Cherrington thought it was. He wanted to put our stress on education."

"Sometimes," Eva said, "it is very hard to figure how you can help people if they don't want to be helped."

———————————

The cabin's flimsy walls let all the cold in, and when M. K. awoke in the first dim morning light, he huddled under the covers and pressed Eva's small, bony body against him. That he did not want to face the day he knew from his first moment of consciousness, but only after five minutes of drowsy reflection could he remember why. He struggled up out of the covers. Splashing water in his face from the sink, he felt his toes burning on the cold linoleum rug.

In the yard outside he heard Grant's radio, even though the first rays of the sun had not yet come over the horizon. M. K. stood still to listen. He could not quite make out the announcer's voice, so he moved across the gravel semicircle, closer to the yellow house. He knew the results, but still he was curious. Grant must have seen him through his kitchen window. He came out on the porch, waving, and bellowed in a high tenor, "Democrats all the way! Roosevelt swept him! They say it's a record."

M. K. nodded. Pretty soon he went back inside and began packing their things. It took only a few minutes for Eva to get dressed and washed, and then he threw the suitcase into the back of the DeSoto, started up the engine, and they crunched out of the gravel driveway. He was glad to get under way. The prairie, if that was what you called it, caught the first pale rays of sun on its wasted surface, throwing long shadows ahead of them that gave the illusion that they were driving into darkness.

"Funny," M. K. said to Eva. "Yesterday I had a feeling of rootlessness, driving like this, and it bothered me. I had some hankering for a familiar way to travel. Today, though, I'm glad to be going, going, going. I want to put miles behind me."

They crossed over the New Mexico border at midmorning, and the farther they went in that desert country, the better he felt. A glinting sun warmed him on the left side of the car, growing almost hot, so he rolled down the window and let the wind blow their hair. *I can see for a hundred miles,* he thought, *without one sign of a green or living thing.* Occasionally a fast car would shoot past them with a throaty grumble; occasionally they would pass a farmer's truck or a smoke-belching car packed with possessions and children, making a more desperate move west than theirs. The country was vast and there was nothing in it.

They reached Bluewater that afternoon, stopping at another tourist camp. The adjoining units, built in one long block, had walls so thin that they heard their neighbor's footsteps. In back of the long building, under some battered cottonwood trees, travelers had been allowed to camp. They had put up tents and tarps in the dust, and built fires for cooking. M. K. went out to stare at the blue mountains that shadowed the valley. A man at one of the fires called out and offered him coffee. "Don't burn yourself," he said when M. K. came over and took up a cup that had been fashioned from a tin can with its lip cut off short and rounded over.

The man was a string bean, wearing an unbuttoned shirt, his hair so short you could see the nicks and scars in his scalp. "You going to California?" he asked M. K. "Hope there's some work there for a man."

"How do you like this country?" M. K. asked.

"I don't see how a man could make a living off it. I hope this isn't like California."

"Oh, it's not. You've never seen such farms as you'll see in California."

"So you've been there?" the man asked hopefully. He was hungry for any news.

"I lived there a long, long time ago. I've been in Ohio." M. K. took a sip of coffee. "What did you think of the election?" he asked.

"What election was that?" the man asked with an apologetic smile. "We've been on the road and can't keep track of the news." After M. K.

told him, the man said he was glad to hear that Roosevelt had won. "Maybe the Democrats will try something different. Whatever the Republicans have been doing doesn't work."

M. K. asked what he thought of Prohibition. "You think they'll change the law?" the man asked. He shrugged when M. K. said yes and then thought for a time before answering. "I guess it hasn't done any good, so they might as well. You want some more coffee?" He poured some for himself. "I just hope I can get some work in California. What about you? Have you got anything lined up?"

They stood around the campfire talking desultorily about work and travel. After a while they ran out of things to say and stood looking off at the long shadows stretching across the valley, the mountains deepening from blue to black.

———————————

They got to Bakersfield two days later, winding down out of the desert mountains into hazy, flat farmland spotted with tracts of pumping oil wells, like giant, slow grasshoppers. Bakersfield seemed to be a tough town, with no women in sight but plenty of young, muscled, dirty workingmen on the downtown streets who stared silently before answering their questions. Nobody seemed to know where Reverend Overholt lived, and M. K. and Eva were tired and cranky by the time they located a blue house shaded by tan and silver sycamores. The few shrubs appeared to have been battered into defeat. Two boys of ten or twelve threw a football on the front lawn.

When M. K. got out of the car and said hello, one of the boys quickly tucked the football under his arm and went inside. The other boy, who had deep, dark hair and matching eyes, stared at them silently even when M. K. asked his name. M. K. heard the door open and saw a woman scuttle out, hurry down the porch steps, and jog toward him with outstretched arms. "Is it Marion?" she cried in a low voice. "Oh, my heart, my heart! Let me hug you! You precious thing!"

He did not remember Grace as such a flamboyant personality. She was dressed as though for Sunday, with a purple dress in a sheer fabric and a netted hat with artificial grapes. She soon had her arms around Eva, calling her precious and darling. "Oh, you must be tired and hungry. Don't worry, I'll get you so much food to eat. Oh, I love to cook for hungry travelers. Seth, you go get your father. Tell him that the Nicholses have arrived. He'll be so excited. He's been wanting to see you."

Short, broad-shouldered, with a mop of curly black hair under her purple hat, she ushered them into the house while keeping a blizzard of conversation pelting them. Inside she scooped a toddler up in her arms. The boy who had gone inside with the football stared at them. Grace sent him off to get lemonade and then sat down, put her hands under her chin, and said, "Now, please, tell me all about your trip. Roy has told me about you a hundred times, and I have been on pins and needles for you to get here. He always talks about you, really! We are going to have such a good time! I hope you can stay for months! Do you think you can? But first, tell me about your trip."

Before they could begin talking, however, Roy Overholt arrived and wrapped M. K. in a hug. M. K. had forgotten Roy's height. The hair had gone from the top of his head, which seemed to make him taller, and he had filled out to the solid, unmaneuverable bulk of middle age. "I'm so glad to meet you, Eva," he said as he shook her hand. "I knew you had to be something to capture the heart of that old man." He reached out and gave Grace's hand a squeeze. "Grace took quite a sacrifice when she married me." He smiled.

"Oh, don't listen to him. I was lucky to get such a man." She shooed his silly comment away with a wave of her hand.

Living among midwesterners, M. K. had forgotten the direct, undesigning way of the West. He had always liked it, though, and after he got over the shock of Grace Overholt's overpowering greeting, he saw that Eva was happy too.

After dinner on that first night Roy began to ask M. K. about his plans, particularly what kind of work he wanted to do. They sat in the living room, with Roy swinging the toddler in his arms, while the women washed the dishes. M. K. said that he felt his guts had been scraped out by Prohibition, and he did not know what he could muster the will to do. It was the first time he had admitted his feelings to anyone besides Eva. He would not have done it except that it was such a relief to arrive to warmth and care. Right from the moment he had written to Roy, he had felt a mysterious attraction to the man. That was strange, after all these years.

Roy wasn't especially sympathetic, however. He was a vigorous man and quite direct. "I'll tell you frankly, M. K., I don't have much use for the Anti-Saloon League. I won't let them have my pulpit because all they do is talk politics and divert people's attention from the Lord's work. They claim to be the church in action, but they want to keep control of the offerings and the pledges. Frankly I don't think they are interested in the church's business. I think they have always had their own plans, and they just use the churches for them."

"But good plans," M. K. said. It was painful to hear the criticism, even though that phase of his life was over. "The league gets all the churches working in the same direction. In politics you have to have a common goal. It doesn't work to have a hundred churches pursuing a hundred plans."

"You're assuming that we are supposed to be involved in politics. I don't think so. Politics is the kingdom of this world, which the Lord is coming back to judge. Woe to us if we are entangled in worldliness! That's what I mean when I say that you drys don't seem interested in the church's business, even though you claim to be the church in action."

"And what is the church's business, Roy? Aren't we supposed to do good and love our brother as ourselves?"

"The church's business is the same as it has been since Jesus Christ sent out His disciples. We are fishers of men. This world is under judgment, and we can tell people how to avoid the judgment through the precious blood of Jesus. You don't see Jesus telling Pontius Pilate to make a law against wine, do you? You don't see Peter campaigning for votes in the Sanhedrin. God forbid!"

It had never occurred to M. K. that there was any other way for a Christian to act than to try to influence society for good. "But this is a Christian country," he said. "This isn't the Roman Empire."

"Is it a Christian country truly? Maybe it once was. Nowadays you see decadence everywhere, and shameful deeds are done in public. M. K., as I've been studying the Bible I've realized that the only Christian country will be the one Jesus returns to as the King. And He is coming. I believe He is coming in this generation. Are you aware of what is happening in Israel right now while we are speaking?"

Roy began to tell about Jews who had gone back to Jerusalem to reestablish their nation. He got out a Bible and came across the room to sit next to M. K., putting his large, flat index finger under one passage after another where the return of Israel was predicted as part of the end times. "That's one sign," he said, sitting back. "The Jews return. Then you consider Rome. Do you know what Mussolini is trying to do? He is reestablishing the Roman Empire. That's exactly what the Bible predicts for the last days." He showed M. K. verses in Revelation where the whore of Babylon rules over the great city with ten hills. "That's Rome, M. K.

Rome is the city with ten hills. Now where, M. K., do you go to find the great deceiver, the ruler who sits on a throne pretending to represent Christ? In Rome, correct? Doesn't the pope live in Rome? And now Mussolini is reestablishing the Roman Empire, the cruelest and most powerful civilization in the history of the earth.

"And another sign. We have a godless rule in Russia, the first truly and proudly atheistic nation in history. If you get out a map and draw a line straight north from Jerusalem, do you know what you find? Moscow. And the Bible predicts a great scourge and persecution coming from a country to the north, known as Gog and Magog. I tell you, all the pieces are falling together. This is the time. Now read what Jesus said about it."

Roy flipped rapidly through his Bible and put his large, firm finger under a verse. "Read it," he ordered.

"'For as in the days that were before the flood,'" M. K. read, "'they were eating and drinking, marrying and giving in marriage, until the day that Noah entered into the ark, and knew not until the flood came, and took them all away; so shall also the coming of the Son of man be.'"

"'Eating and drinking,'" Roy said. "I don't see any sign of Prohibition, do you? Now read this." He moved his finger down on the page.

"'Therefore be ye also ready: for in such an hour as ye think not the Son of man cometh.'"

"Yes," Roy said. "'Be ye also ready.'"

Four days later Eva came into the bedroom—the two boys had moved into the dining room so she and M. K. could have their room—where M. K. had set up a study area for himself. He had borrowed Roy's books and pamphlets and had spent hours studying the Bible, trying to unravel the complicated themes of prophecy. He found it irresistibly interesting. At the moment, he was not reading but was working on a piece of paper. Eva could see that he had drawn letters and lines between letters.

"What are you doing?" she asked.

"I'm trying something," he said. "I don't know whether it works, but it's interesting. I wrote out *MUSSOLINI*, and I'm trying to see whether I can find some kind of number in it using Roman numerals. Look."

Eva bent down to the bed where he had put the piece of paper and was studying it from his knees. "You see the *I* and the *N*? Suppose I take the first line from the *N* and detach it, letting it lie across the *I*? Then I get *LXVI*, right? And that is the number 66 in Roman numerals. In Revelation, the mark of the beast is 666. So I'm trying to see whether somehow that number is encoded in Mussolini's name. Six hundred would be a *D* and a *C*. Maybe the top part of an *S* could be read as a *C*, and the *O* could be read as a *D*, but they would be in the wrong order. I can't quite figure it out. It's intriguing, though, don't you think? You know, the Antichrist will reestablish the Roman Empire, and that is exactly what Mussolini is doing."

"Are you sure you want to go into all this?" Eva asked thoughtfully. She had watched him warily as he studied—had asked a few questions but had mostly kept her distance.

"Absolutely," M. K. said. "I'm finding it very interesting, and I think it's helping me to understand what we did wrong in the Anti-Saloon League."

"What was that?"

"We were trying to make the world good. And the Bible teaches just the opposite. That the world is in rebellion against God, and that the evil will grow stronger and darker until there is a cosmic collision. And then when Jesus comes back to reign, *He* will make the world good. But it will be a new world, purged of all evil.

"That's why Roy has an altar call at every service, he told me. Methodists used to do that, too, I think, but nowadays it's considered old-fashioned. Roy says it's the one thing the church has to offer: the blood of Jesus to cleanse us from sin and make us ready to meet Jesus when He comes. And the Word of God, of course, which reveals all this. Roy is convinced that Jesus must be coming soon."

Eva sat down on the bed, a sober expression on her face. "Unless He's coming this afternoon, we've got to figure out a job," she said. "We can't carry on with the Overholts' hospitality forever."

"No," M. K. said softly. "I know that. They've been awfully nice, don't you think? My own brother wouldn't take us in, but they're willing to give us the clothes off their backs. And they don't have too much, do they? Do you like Grace?"

Eva smiled an inward smile, as though she was thinking of a joke. "I do. I need a break every so often. She's like rich food. But she's very kind. And funny too."

Eva stretched out a hand to hold M. K.'s arm. "I feel like you've been holed up in a cave. Why do you have to study in here?"

He thought for a moment. "It's hard to explain. It's so intense, what I've been learning." He had delved into books he hardly knew were in the Bible, such as Ezekiel. Just to help himself he had drawn charts connecting the verses in Daniel and Revelation and Matthew. He had been reading the Bible his whole life, but until now he had had only a vague idea that prophecies existed relating to today, let alone that they came in such a rich vein. One of the books Roy had given him had an enormous chart of all the biblical prophecies—a chart so large that it unfolded from the back of the book into a poster covered with two-headed beasts and Babylonian statues. Every verse he had studied fit neatly onto that chart.

"I won't stay in the cave, Eva. Don't worry. I'll come out. I just want to understand this first. I want to have it clear in my own head. Then I think I'll know what to do."

"What to do?" Eva said with slight consternation. "What do you mean by that?"

"I don't know exactly," M. K. said sheepishly. "I feel as though it's going to become clear to me if I study this. It reminds me of how I first got involved with the ASL. I think I've told you. I went through a dark period, a dream, a nightmare, and then suddenly I emerged into the light and I knew I had to fight against liquor. Roy thinks it was a mistake, but his opinion doesn't really bother me. I feel it was something I had to do. I think you told me, it's no disgrace to try your best to fix something, even if you fail. Didn't you say something like that? When we were in Texas and we heard about the election?"

"Something like that," she said.

"It's funny, but this feels the same way. I feel that I'm in a nightmare, the kind that isn't really scary, but where you know something is wrong, and you're waiting, waiting, waiting for a change. I have this feeling, Eva, I can't really explain it, and I wouldn't want to tell anybody, even Roy and Grace. I have this feeling that you and I are going to play a very important part in these events. That's why I want to understand them as well as I can, so that I'll recognize what is going on."

"All right," she said. "But in the meantime . . ."

"In the meantime," M. K. said, "I've got to make a living. I will, Eva. If hard work can do anything, don't you worry, I'm going to make a living. Roy thinks there may be something for me to do in publishing Christian literature."

She looked at him fondly, and he returned the regard. They had been married for less than a year, and yet they lived together like an old married couple, comfortable and well worn. Marriage had brought few surprises, since for years they had all but shared a house, and all but raised children together. Nevertheless, M. K. found himself continually surprised when he looked at his wife. For so long he had judged by externals: her plain, long face, lack of pretension, weak education. *Glory takes many disguises,* he thought.

"It's a new beginning," Eva said.

For Further Reading

Behr, Edward. Prohibition: *Thirteen Years That Changed America.* New York: Arcade Publishing, 1996.

Blocker, Jack S., Jr. *American Temperance Movements: Cycles of Reform.* Boston: Twayne Publishers, 1989.

——. *Retreat from Reform: The Prohibition Movement in the United States, 1890–1913.* Westport, CT: Greenwood Press, 1976.

Clark, Norman H. *Deliver Us from Evil: An Interpretation of American Prohibition.* New York: W. W. Norton, 1976.

——. *The Dry Years: Prohibition and Social Change in Washington.* Seattle: University of Washington Press, 1988.

Engelmann, Larry. *Intemperance, the Lost War Against Liquor.* New York: Free Press, 1979.

Hohner, Robert A. *Prohibition and Politics: The Life of Bishop James Cannon, Jr.* Columbia, SC: The University of South Carolina Press, 1999.

Kerr, K. Austin. *Organized for Prohibition: A New History of the Anti-Saloon League.* New Haven: Yale University Press, 1985.

Kobler, John. *Ardent Spirits: The Rise and Fall of Prohibition.* New York: Da Capo Press, 1973.

Odegard, Peter H. *Pressure Politics: The Story of the Anti-Saloon League.* New York: Columbia University Press, 1928, reissued 1966, Octagon Books.

Pegram, Thomas R. *Battling Demon Rum: The Struggle for a Dry America, 1800–1933.* Chicago: Ivan R. Dee, 1998.

Steuart, Justin. *Wayne Wheeler, Dry Boss: An Uncensored Biography of Wayne B. Wheeler.* Fleming H. Revell, 1928, reissued Westport, CT: Greenwood Press, 1970.

About the Author

Tim Stafford is Senior Writer for *Christianity Today* magazine. He has written many books, including *Knowing the Face of God; That's Not What I Meant; Love, Sex, and the Whole Person;* and *A Thorn in the Heart,* a novel. *The Law of Love* is the third book in a four-part series that began with *The Stamp of Glory* followed by *Sisters.* Stafford has served on the editorial staff of *Campus Life* magazine and helped found *Step* magazine in Nairobi, Kenya, and Accra, Ghana.

Stafford lives in Santa Rosa, California, with his wife and three children. He enjoys backpacking, running, and baseball.